PRAISE FOR *BESIDE MYSELF*

'An extraordinary kaleidoscope, a dazzling journey across culture, gender and time.' Krissy Kneen

'Sasha Marianna Salzmann thoughtfully and cleverly addresses the themes of memory, identity and migration, asking if language, nationality or gender are important for our self-definition.' *World Literature Today*

'Full of nooks and crannies and reflections, the novel succeeds nonetheless in unfurling its breathtaking story of a family and a century like a shimmering kaleidoscope.' *Frankfurter Allgemeine Zeitung*

'An incredible mark-maker of contemporary storytelling.' *Süddeutsche Zeitung*

'The expectations for the first novel by Sasha Marianna Salzmann are high...[*Beside Myself*] surpasses them.' *Frankfurter Rundschau*

'Salzmann narrates brilliantly, poetically... An intoxicating reading experience.' *Missy Magazine*

'Salzmann's sentences flow across the page, her style is lavish and immediate.' *Literaturspiegel*

'It is above all the intensity, the vivid language and the compassionate eye cast on generations, and the story itself, that make [*Beside Myself*] such a thrilling novel.' *Der Tagesspiegel*

'An artistically composed coming-of-age novel.' *Der Freitag*

'A book that stays with you.' *Stern*

'This is writing by someone who has something to say.' *Die Welt*

SASHA MARIANNA SALZMANN is a playwright, essayist, curator and writer in residence of the Maxim Gorki Theater in Berlin. She is the co-founder of the culture magazine *freitext* and was the artistic director of STUDIO Я. Her work has been translated, shown and awarded in more than twenty countries. *Beside Myself* is her first novel, and was shortlisted for the 2017 German Book Prize.
sashamariannasalzmann.com

IMOGEN TAYLOR is based in Berlin. She is the translator of Sascha Arango, Dirk Kurbjuweit and Melanie Raabe, among others.

BESIDE MYSELF
SASHA MARIANNA SALZMANN

Translated from the German by Imogen Taylor

TEXT PUBLISHING MELBOURNE AUSTRALIA

textpublishing.com.au
textpublishing.co.uk

The Text Publishing Company
Swann House, 22 William Street, Melbourne, Victoria 3000, Australia

The Text Publishing Company (UK) Ltd
130 Wood Street, London EC2V 6DL, United Kingdom

Originally published as *Ausser sich* in 2017 by Suhrkamp Verlag Berlin
First published in English in 2019 by The Text Publishing Company

The quotation on page 156 is from *2666* by Roberto Bolaño, Farrar, Straus & Giroux, 2008, translated by Natasha Wimmer. The quotations in the 'Aglaja' chapter are from *Warum das Kind in der Polenta kocht* by Aglaja Veteranyi, DVA, 1999, as translated by Imogen Taylor.

Book design by Jessica Horrocks
Cover image by Tara Moore / Getty
Typeset by J&M Typesetting

Printed and bound in Australia by Griffin Press, an accredited ISO/NZS 1401:2004 Environmental Management System printer

ISBN: 9781911231257 (paperback)
ISBN: 9781925626933 (ebook)

A catalogue record for this book is available from the National Library of Australia

Time passes and passes. It passes backward and it passes forward and it carries you along, and no one in the whole wide world knows more about time than this: it is carrying you through an element you do not understand into an element you will not remember. Yet, *something* remembers—it can even be said that something avenges: the trap of our century, and the subject now before us.

James Baldwin, *No Name in the Street*

CHARACTERS

Anton

Alissa/Ali—sister, brother, me

Valentina/Valya—mother, mum and everything

Konstantin/Kostya—father, kind of

Daniil/Danya—father, grandfather

Emma/Emmochka—grandmother, sometimes mother

Shura/Sasha/Alexander—great-grandfather, grandfather, father,
    Red Army hero

Etya/Etina/Etinka—mother, grandmother, great-grandmother,
    superhero

Kato/Katarina/Katyusha—dancer, multiple rocket launcher

Aglaja—mermaid

Cemal/Cemo/Cemal Bey—the uncle

Elyas—the friend

And all the other parents and parents' parents in Odessa,
    Chernivtsi, Moscow, Istanbul and Berlin

Ingeborg Bachmann writes:

> 'But I had to think long and hard about
> the time because I find it almost impossible
> to say "today", although it's a word we say
> every day...'

The time, then, is a today, from a hundred years ago
until now.

ONE

'GOING HOME'

I don't know where we're going. All the others know, but I don't. I'm clutching a jam jar that's been thrust on me, clasping it to my chest as if it were my last doll, and watching them chase each other round the flat. Dad's hands are shiny with sweat; they look like unwashed dishes—huge slabs swinging past my head. If I got caught between them, that would be it—splat, squashed head.

My brother's growing out of his bag like a stalk, standing with both legs in the bag, unpacking things. Mum tells him off and he puts them back. While Mum's in the kitchen, he takes out the pirate ship in its big cardboard box and pushes it under his bed. Mum comes into the hall where I'm standing and bends down to me, her forehead hanging over me like a bell, like the sky. I take one hand off the jam-jar doll and run a finger over her face. The sky is greasy. Mum knocks down my hand and thrusts more jars on me; I hold them tight. There are such a lot, I can't see past them. She puts a bag down on my feet and says: 'I want you to eat properly on the journey; you can be in charge of the provisions.' I've no idea what provisions are, but I'm glad they're something sweet, not chicken in tinfoil.

We go downstairs; it takes us a while. We live on the top floor, where the rooms are all beams and sloping ceilings. On the ground floor is an undertaker's; it always stinks down there—not of corpses, but of something I don't know and can't get used to. The jars clink in the bag as I drag it down the stairs behind me. Dad's about to take it off me when a neighbour opens his door.

'Going home?'

'Going to see Mum and Dad. Been a while.'

'First time back?'

Dad nods.

'You never forget the first time.'

Dad answers the neighbour's questions as if he were telling him a bedtime story, stressing every word and making his voice go up at the end. My brother's gone on ahead. I pull the bag carefully past Dad and try to catch up with him. It stinks and it's cold. Downstairs, behind the undertaker's display window, are people. I'm scared of the faces sitting there behind the glass, in the office; I'm scared they might be green and dead, so I never look until I'm out on the street. I scan the ground for my brother's feet. Dad comes out of the house and pulls me along. I don't look up until I think Mum will be waving goodbye—and she is; her hand hangs out of the window for a moment, then the window flies shut and Dad begins to sing.

Pora, pora poraduemsya na svoyom veku. It is time, it is time to rejoice in this time.

TIMELESS

The tiles in the toilets at Atatürk Airport were cool on Ali's left temple. The blur in front of her eyes refused to come into focus: in the gap between the cubicle wall and the floor, heels smudged to lumps of coal, leaving black scrawls in the air as they scraped past. Ali heard a babble of voices but no words. Echoey announcements. She tasted chicken. She hadn't had any on the plane—hadn't eaten chicken for years—but there was a putrid fowl stuck in her throat. She'd been here before like this—lain on the floor with a dead bird in her throat and shoelaces creeping towards her like insects. But when?

Her eyes were dry from the flight; her eyelids rasped when she opened and shut them. *Chronic lack of tear fluid*, the doctors had told her, a while ago now. 'And what should I do—use eye drops?'—'Just blink when it hurts or itches. Keep blinking; the fluid will come automatically.' But it was no good. She breathed slowly, listening. Outside, stiletto heels and bouncy rubber soles set the rhythm. Everyone was in a rush—desperate to get out of the terminal, out of the non-air. They were being met off the plane after their long flights—just a quick dash to the toilet, a dab of powder on the rings under their eyes, a tongue over their lips, a comb through their hair, and they could go and leap into the arms of the people waiting for them—like plunging into warm water.

Ali had no idea whether anyone was waiting for her; she hoped so, but didn't know. She lay on the floor, beating her eyelashes the way a fly beats its wings. She longed for a cigarette to smoke away the taste of flabby boiled fat on her palate, and the craving pulled her up by the scruff of her neck and out of the toilet cubicle. Careful not to look in the mirror, she steadied herself against the basin and held her lips under the jet of water. A woman gave her a nudge and signalled to her that it wasn't safe to drink. She held out a plastic bottle to Ali who pressed the narrow bottleneck to her lips and drank noiselessly. The woman took back the empty bottle and ran a hand through Ali's curls as if to tidy them. Then she ran her thumb over the thin skin under Ali's eyes and over her pointy chin, grasping her chin for a moment between finger and thumb. Ali smiled; the woman smiled too. They walked slowly out into the lobby, Ali following the woman and a crowd of others who seemed to know the way. She walked alongside the moving walkway where people were jostling one another, followed the echo of the marble floor and got in line for passport control. She began to grow impatient and tried to push the queue forward, but it was stuck and she could only look left and right. Her head was spinning. All the world was in the queue: miniskirts, burqas, moustaches of every style and colour, sunglasses in every size, silicone lips in every shape, kids in buggies, kids on backs and on shoulders and between feet. On all sides the crowd pressed in on Ali, so dense she couldn't fall. A little girl pushed against the plexiglas wall at the barrier and a pane of glass fell out with a bang. The girl screamed. Her mother forced her way through the crowd and gave her a fierce shake.

Ali was sure she tasted chicken in her throat again. She rummaged for her passport.

The passport officer stared for a long time at what Ali supposed must be her photo. He looked up at her, then back at her passport, over and over, as if every time he could look a little deeper. He was a young man, younger than Ali, but he already had the shoulders of an old man, sunken and rigid, and his hollow chest didn't fill his pale blue shirt. Sitting there in his cubicle, he seemed miles from the airport, miles from his country, as though he were looking through the Earth's mantle and back again into Ali's face. She found herself wiping her chin; she hadn't thrown up—or had she? She was suddenly uncertain. Was there something on her chin? It felt as if puked-up chicken were hanging out of her throat. Mustering all her energy, she pulled up the corners of her mouth, and her left eyebrow shot up with them.

The boy on the other side of the glass looked at her, climbed down off his chair, got out of the cubicle and went round the back. Ali propped herself up on the narrow counter in front of the glass, watching him through dry, scratched eyes. He showed her passport to a colleague, tapping one of the pages with a finger and shaking his head. When he came back, he said something she didn't understand, but she knew what was bothering him: he wasn't sure it was her. She didn't look anything like her passport photo; she'd had her hair cut, and in other ways too her face had changed. Everyone said so; even her own mother didn't recognise her in photos. But what did that tell you? The other passport officer joined his colleague and asked Ali the standard questions. Ali lied, so as not to confuse the men any further, saying she was visiting a good friend—the usual.

'How long are you staying?'

'Dunno.'

'You can't stay more than three months.'

'I know.'

'First time here?'

'Is there something wrong with my passport?'

'The woman on the photo looks quite like you.'

'That's because she is me.'

'Yes, but there's another possibility.'

'What?'

'That this is a fake passport and that you—'

'That I what?'

'We have trouble in this country with Russian imports. I'm talking about women. Imported women. Women trafficked from Russia.'

Ali opened her mouth to say something like: 'But I'm from Berlin!' or: 'Do I look like a trafficked woman?' Instead she burst out laughing. She tried to fight back the laughter but it shot out of her and flew at the pane of glass between her and the two passport officers, who looked at her in disgust. Ali pressed her fingers to her mouth and her bag fell to her feet. She looked down and then up again. She looked about her and saw the entire queue—all the miniskirts and sunglasses and moustaches—turn and whisper. The passport officers waited for Ali to readjust her blushing head and put it back on her shoulders. Her eyes were wet with tears of laughter, and she looked into the men's confused faces and tried not to start grinning again.

'Is there any way I can prove I'm not a Russian whore?' she asked.

The two passport officers looked at her as one man. They looked right through her. Then one of them raised his hand and brought his stamp down on the counter three times without taking his eyes off her. There was a buzz. Ali grabbed her bag and pushed open the glass door.

•

Uncle Cemal stood at the front of the crowd of waiting people who hung over the barrier like the fronds of a palm tree. You could tell from the faces of the men around him that he'd elbowed them out of the way to get there, and now, seeing Ali come through the arrivals gate, he threw his arms in the air and landed a hook to the chin of a small man whose moustache took up half his face. The man swayed but couldn't fall in the throng. Cemal gave the shouting moustache a glance of annoyance and turned to look at Ali again with a big smile, pointing left to tell her which exit to take out of the terminal; he'd wait for her there.

Cemal, or Cemo, or Cemal Bey was Elyas's uncle, and because Ali had kind of grown up with Elyas (you could even say they'd grown together), Cemal was *her* uncle too, even if this was the first time she'd set eyes on him. Elyas had never talked about his uncle, but when Ali told him she was going to Istanbul, he pressed a phone number into her hand and said Cemal would pick her up at the airport. And here he was. He hugged her as if he'd been hugging her all his life. Then he took her suitcase and they went outside and rolled cigarettes. Ali didn't tell Cemal why she'd been so late coming out of arrivals; she didn't say she'd locked herself in the toilet with her head on the tiles, or that her circulation hadn't been able to keep pace with the outside world—you don't say that kind of thing when you've only just met someone. You share cigarettes like old friends and from then on that's what you are.

After one drag on the roll-your-own, Ali collapsed again. Cemal carried her to a taxi and then up to his flat. She came to on his sofa in a blue-tiled room with nothing but a mute, flickering television on the wall and a heavy desk at a window dark with ivy; it seemed to be growing into the room. She felt as if she'd been asleep for years. Cemal was sitting in front of the television, smoking, his hands braced against his thighs, his silhouette curvaceous, his chin moving as if he were talking with his mouth shut. The ash from his cigarette fell on the floor next to his shoe. His face was bigger than his head and spread in all directions: his nose stuck out a long way, his eyes bulged, his long thick eyelashes curled up towards his forehead. Ali looked at him and decided she'd never go anywhere else again.

Cemal got up, fetched steaming çay from the kitchen, handed her a pot-bellied glass and pointed at the desk. 'The keys to your flat are over there. You don't have to, though. You can stay here if you'd rather.'

The next day Cemal showed her the flat and she fell in love with it, especially with the little roof that she could jump onto from the terrace—and then stand looking out across the Golden Horn to Kasımpaşa. She fell in love with the crooked rooms and the steep road outside that you could slide down standing up.

More than anything, though, Ali fell in love with the empty evenings, when she and Uncle Cemal would sit in his flat trying to outsmoke one another. They smoked until you could hear the rasp in their throats, until their eyes drooped, until they were falling off their chairs—and all the time, they talked. Ali steered her walks towards those evenings, roaming about near Cemal's house until she was tired, then knocking cautiously at his door and collapsing on the sofa. She got used to falling asleep on that sofa over books of photos and Cemal's endless stories, then waking in the middle of the night, hunting for her shoes in the hall with tired red eyes and waiting for Cemal to take them out of her hands.

'Where are you going? You weren't thinking of walking home, were you? It's far too late.'

'Yes, I was. I can still walk.'

'Of course you can still walk, but the others are faster. You don't want to walk to Tarlabaşı at this time of night.'

They'd sit down again and smoke and talk about nothing, just to hear the sound of each other's voices.

Since coming to Istanbul, Ali had often heard how dangerous Tarlabaşı was for a young woman—or, indeed, anyone: 'All those Roma and Kurds and transvestites—there are bad people around, you know.'

'Yes, I know, there are bad people around. But not in Tarlabaşı.'

'Sleep here, kuşum. I'll fetch you a blanket.'

And on the whole Ali stayed; even the red spots on her wrists and under her chin couldn't stop her.

Some people looked for old Istanbul in the mosques or on the steamers that plied the water between Europe and Asia; they bought themselves plastic souvenirs at the bazaars to take home to San Francisco or Moscow or Riyadh and display in their glass-fronted cabinets alongside their chunks of the Berlin Wall. Ali found *her* Istanbul on Uncle Cemal's rust-brown sofa whose upholstery was ridden with bed bugs that began to suck her blood at about four in the morning and went on until about five. She woke at eight with itchy red spots spreading over her lower arms and face, and when she asked Cemal, he blamed the water. 'Those old pipes—I must do something about them. The water runs brown, I know.' There were no bed bugs in his flat—impossible.

She sprayed her entire flat in Aynalı Çeşme with some noxious substance from the chemist's, then sat on her balcony and smoked, hoping she wouldn't finish the Veteranyi book she was reading until all the bugs were dead. When she was sure not a single one had survived the attack and she wouldn't be getting any more red spots, she went back to Uncle Cemal's, slept on his sofa again and returned to Aynalı Çeşme with a new load of little creatures in her hair and clothes.

Today Ali didn't care about anything. She buried herself in the sofa cushions, trying to dig herself as deep as she could, urging the bed bugs to suck every last drop of blood out of her body until there was nothing left of her. She wanted them to eat her up and carry her all over town, little bit by little bit. That way she could stay here on the sofa, not having to do anything or go anywhere, and eventually disappear between the cushions like a crumbly biscuit. Ali's eyes were wide open and so dry that they ached. Now and then she blinked to flush away the film of dust, but it was no good; the dust came back—falling from the ceiling, seeping out of the air conditioning, swirling out of her mouth in little puffs of cloud.

Anton wasn't going to get in touch. He probably wasn't even in the city. People were predicting imminent disaster in Turkey. Yılmaz Güney was long dead—and Uncle Cemal pranced about his desk and told her the story he always told her, the one about the public prosecutor who'd insulted Yılmaz Güney's wife and been shot in the eye for it by Güney. He, Cemal, had been there when it happened. No, he hadn't, but he'd represented Güney in court, back in the days when he was a famous lawyer. He'd represented Öcalan too—no, he'd hoped he would, but it hadn't come to anything and now Öcalan had gone quiet—not a word for six months, although he'd been such a vociferous prophet of the resistance. Maybe he'd died in prison, and then you could expect civil war here at any moment—well, really it had already begun, but it would come to the cities, and then it would spread all over the world, but Cemal wasn't going to give up, not even if the whole world was at war. All this he told Ali, or rather himself, as he dusted furiously; it seemed to be about more than a bit of grime. Ali hardly listened, watching him move frenziedly about the flat like a child's top, spinning on the tiles and knocking against the table legs. Cemal's womanly body made her laugh. If he hadn't been going so fast, she'd have liked to put her arms around him, but she couldn't, so she let him talk. He talked endlessly about himself—ever-changing versions of his biography.

He'd been born seventy or seventy-two years ago in Istanbul's Zeytinburnu, an area that was built on sand and would slip down between the tectonic plates at the next earthquake—his ninety-year-old mother still lived there. Cemal had been the second-youngest of eight brothers and sisters; they'd all lived in one room under a corrugated iron roof, all slept side by side on the floor, all washed in the same bathwater. He'd had second go in the water, then the next oldest child and so on—their father had washed last of all, in a grey-brown soup. Cemal never saw where his mother washed.

Cemal was the first in the family to study, the first to come home in a suit and be teased about it by his brothers and sisters. He represented important people in court and was often locked up himself, though it wasn't clear when or under what circumstances; the stories varied. But they all ended the same way, with Cemal turning up at his mother's after eight months in prison, finding her at the kitchen table in a veil (a woman who'd gone fifty years without a headscarf) and getting into such an argument with her about his life that he never went to visit her again. She didn't meet either his first or his second wife—sometimes there was even mention of a third. Whether two or three, the end was always the same: they loved him, but he had to work.

Sometimes Cemal would begin to speak about his father, but he never got further than opening his broad cracked lips, taking a dry breath, running his tongue over the insides of his cheeks and moistening the corners of his mouth. That was as much as he could manage, and Ali didn't probe.

In recent years it had become increasingly rare for Cemal to leave the flat that was also his office and hammam and goodness knows what else. Why should he? Little Orhan from the shop downstairs brought him milk and cigarettes and meat, and the ivy at his window kept out the sun. Safe at home, Cemel could continue to believe in things; he didn't have to know that his office was now surrounded by cafes hung with English-only signs and advertising free wi-fi—or that even Oğuz the greengrocer had moved away, his friend of forty-two years' standing, who used to sell peaches as big as boxing gloves in the narrow doorway between Cemal's and the butcher's shop. Cemal didn't know why Oğuz hadn't been in touch for so long; he didn't know that he now stood on Taksim Square selling brightly coloured bird whistles to tourists. Nor did Cemal know that the Zurich Hotel had opened in the building next door and that the street was thronged with tourists buying samovars at Madame Coco's on the corner—or that the shop downstairs where little Orhan helped his aged father wasn't doing too well and would probably be the next to go, leaving another shopfront that would soon be plastered with wi-fi symbols. Why would Cemal bother going out into that world as long as he had his old sofa and black-and-white floor tiles and turquoise-tiled walls?

Cemal needed things he could believe in. He believed in the People's Democratic Party, in Marx, and in young women who came laughing and crying to his flat once a month to ask for money. He believed in love and he believed that Ali would find Anton in a city of almost fifteen million inhabitants, without a sign from him, without even knowing whether he'd actually ever been there—because, of course, the fact that the postcard had been posted in Istanbul didn't mean a thing.

Cemal had been to police stations with Ali to hang up missing-persons posters of Anton. On one such occasion he'd run into an old friend he used to look out for in the schoolyard when this man was a little boy a few classes below him and a few heads shorter. During the hours of kissing and hugging and tea-drinking that followed this encounter, Cemal had kept pointing at Ali with the flat of his hand: 'Like her, he looks like her!' His schoolmate looked her up and down—looked at the short brown curls she never combed, their matted ends sticking up in a kind of triangle, at the thin, bluish skin shimmering under her round eyes, at her dangling arms. He hugged Cemal again, kissed him on both cheeks and said it was hopeless, unless Fate or God decided it was to be. Then the two of them sighed and lit cigarettes. Ali lit up too without knowing what they were talking about, and Cemal tried to tell her that somehow or other it would all come right in the end.

It was because of all that Cemal believed in—and because he'd picked her up from the floor of Atatürk Airport like a small child—that Ali knew she'd never leave him. The thought formed in her mind as Cemal stumbled nervously and clumsily about the room, as if trying to impose order on the three pieces of furniture it contained.

Ali thought Cemal was jittery because his rakı supplies were low, or because of the disaster that was about to strike Turkey and was very much on his mind. 'Something's about to happen in this country,' he'd say. 'Nothing good.' But then you could always say that. Next he'd change his tune, claiming that however bad people might be, it was always worth talking to them; they were bound to disappoint you, but wasn't that all the more reason to fight for them? Cemal was forever contradicting himself in his paeans to a better world—a world that would one day come, even if everything was going down the toilet just now. Cemal believed that people came back to you because they loved you.

Recently a woman of Ali's age had started leading him a dance. He insisted that she was serious about him—it was just that right now she needed money, time, rest, a change of scene, a change of pace. 'She's only young, you know.' Nothing Ali said could convince Cemal that though this young woman's treatment of him went by many different names, love wasn't one of them; Ali couldn't shake his belief in something she didn't even have words for. It was a mystery to her how Cemal could believe in any of it, but she was touched to see the old man blossom in his heartache, touched to catch him squinting surreptitiously at the green phone on his desk (an old one with a cord because Cemal was fond of all things old-fashioned; he thought it made an elderly balding man attractive), touched to see his heart race when the phone rang, and break when it wasn't her, his girl, the reason he couldn't sleep at night. It never was. But he was happy waiting all the same. It made him jittery. A good reason to be jittery, thought Ali—maybe the best.

In the photograph that Cemal showed Ali almost every evening until she asked him to stop, the red-headed floozy hanging from Cemal's shoulder had almost no nose, only a thin line with small dark nostrils and freckles all over, as if a strawberry had exploded in front of her face. Her crooked mouth smiled into the camera, shapeless and endless. Cemal, his hand around her waist, his chest swollen, looked grave. The woman's red hair, static in the heat, stuck out every which way, most of it in Cemal's face. Ali could understand that Cemal longed to plunge into that hair and said so—at which he changed the subject and talked about the elections in this country on the brink of civil war, and then about the lack of rakı in the house.

Today he was jittery in a different way. Maybe it was the delayed time change, thought Ali, the suspension of time between the elections, which meant that you could rely on neither the moon nor the planets to tell you if it was night or day. For now, it was the president who decided what time it was. Maybe Cemal sensed that time was out of joint and that no amount of chewing tobacco could protect him. Maybe he sensed that nothing would ever come right again—not with Turkey and not with the redhead either. Cemal spat as if a gnat had flown into his mouth. Then the brief knowledge that he was beaten flashed across his face and spread like a blush—and when it had gone, he began to talk in a loud voice, pushing his chair back and forth from one wall to the other and grumbling at Ali:

'You're scared, kuşum. Scared to believe in goodness. Where will that leave you? How are you going to live?'

'Good question.'

Although the thirty-year-old slut was probably spending a dirty weekend with another man in Antalya and the elections were going to turn out exactly as everyone feared, Cemal was quivering with fighting spirit.

'After the attack in Ankara, we'll all be stronger—'

That attack in Ankara. Ali saw the images of explosions repeating themselves; she saw the *Breaking News* ticker on the screen of her laptop, her phone flashing. She saw herself ringing her friends, talking to her mother who'd called to tell her to come home immediately. 'Are you counting on staying there? What are your plans?' Her mother had tried to keep the panic out of her voice. 'I'm in Istanbul, Mum, not Ankara,' Ali said. 'I'll find him, then I'll come back.'

And when the attacks reached Istanbul, she felt the explosion all the way in Tarlabaşı and didn't go to the phone until the names of all the victims had been announced. She held her breath until she knew that Anton's name wasn't among them. Then she clenched her teeth, realising that secretly she'd been hoping to hear his name. That way she'd have found him. Then, at least, her search would have been over. When her jaw relaxed and she could open her mouth again, Ali rang her mother, who made no effort to control herself this time, and nor did Ali.

The third time Cemal bumped into the sofa Ali was lying on, as he dashed around the flat, she called after him: 'Why are you so restless? Come and sit next to me and we'll look at the pictures of Ara.'

He refused. Ali sat up.

'Your jewel. Tell me about your jewel.'

'My jewel?'

'The girl you're so in love with.'

'Leave me, kuşum.'

Ali was about to leap to her feet and kiss Cemal's temples to calm him, when a beige suit appeared in the doorway carrying a bottle of rakı.

'Mustafa! Thank God! We've been waiting for you all evening.'

Ali screwed up her eyes. The visitor's suntanned face gave a fat grin and Uncle Cemal beamed.

Mustafa Bey greeted her effusively and told her in dizzyingly fast German that he'd heard a lot about her.

'What have you heard? There's nothing to hear,' Ali replied, wondering whether to find some pretext—the bed bugs, the advanced hour, the dust in her eyes—for leaving immediately, but Cemal was beaming and she knew she couldn't go now—not when he was putting out the little white meze dishes on the newspapers that covered the table. His voice cracked.

'White cheese, olives—hang on, I've got green ones too—no, I haven't—sit down, I'll get water and ice—I said, sit down—here's an ashtray—would you like pickled tomatoes too, or is that too sour?'

Ali pushed her feet into her sandals and watched Cemal's face soften, bristle by bristle, growing more yielding and childlike with every word. She suddenly knew what he must have looked like as a young man—how proud and silly and gangling he must have been before he put on weight. She imagined him reaching for his airgun down by the water at Karaköy and shooting at the brightly coloured balloons trembling on the surface of the water—that depressing tourist attraction where young men showed their girlfriends what they'd learnt in their two years' military service, apart from competitive masturbation. Cemal had promised to teach Ali to shoot. 'First we'll practise aiming at the balloons, then we'll take it from there,' he'd said, laughing, and Ali couldn't help laughing too. She'd have liked to throw her arms round his neck and bury her forehead in his shoulder, but she didn't.

Now she knitted her brow and had a good look at the man in the beige suit. He'd sat down at the table, still clutching the bottle of rakı, and was exchanging pleasantries with Cemal: *I'm very well, thank you, how are you, that's good, that's what I like to hear, and how are you, I'm well too, thank you, that's good, that's what I like to hear, thank you.*

Cemal put three rakı glasses down on the newspaper and pulled Ali off the sofa. She stared at the earthenware ashtray that once, long ago, had contained yoghurt from the Islands, and was now covered in a film of damp ash. She didn't want to look up. They drank to this and that, including 'the life of Demirtaş' and Ali's health. The small dish of olives stood on the chest of a singer who was opining on the war in the neighbouring country. Ali saw the words *refugees...and live here... In our...hungry and...off my blood.*

She silently filled in the gaps in her head, wishing she could return to the days when she hadn't understood a word of Turkish. Or German for that matter. She wondered whether it wouldn't be easier to be sitting stupid and monoglot in Russia, singing love songs to the president. 'Of course she'll go with you—won't you, Ali?' The words tore her away from the jukebox in her head which was playing the pop songs she'd be singing if she were in Russia. She glanced up.

Mustafa Bey had big tobacco-coloured teeth and, looking at him in the dim light and through the filter of her second rakı, she thought to herself that she had yet to meet a man in Aynalı Çeşme who didn't wear one of those suits. They looked as if they'd been born in them— as if they'd slept and drunk and fucked and fought in them—gone up into the mountains in them to take up arms.

'Where am I going?'

Ali pictured Mustafa, sitting on a low stool, his chin resting on his knee, a tesbih in his hand. He'd drink only half his çay, then he'd stand up, wind the tesbih a few times around his fingers and get in his car, feeling under the seat to make sure the boys next door hadn't nabbed his gun to impress the girls. Then he'd drive off, the wind ruffling the few hairs on his bald head.

'Why don't you come too, Uncle Cemal?'

'What would I do there? You have fun, you young folk. It's not my thing.'

Ali looked at Mustafa and wondered whether Uncle Cemal could possibly be talking about him when he said 'young folk'—and why he was sending her out of his flat into the unknown with a person with such big teeth. But then she saw Cemal's broad smile and she nodded.

It felt good to sit in a car and be driven through the city. That was something Ali never had to be talked into. She dropped onto the passenger seat, gathered herself into a knot, with only her head peeping out, pressed herself up against the window and things were all right.

Elyas had often taken her for a drive—when she'd gone days without leaving her room again, digging her shoulderblades into the mattress on the floor and scanning the ceiling in silence. He'd throw his car keys onto her belly, as if to say: *Get out and get in the car*, and she'd claw her way up the door, crank down the window—that's the kind of car Elyas had, the kind with a window crank and a tape player, and what else could you do with a car like that, it was asking to be driven—and when the window was as wide as it would go, she'd poke her head out and smoke. The cigarette smoke was sucked back into the car, past her ears to Elyas who'd be changing tapes and talking to himself. She'd begin to grow calmer; eventually she'd smile, and when she started to talk, Elyas knew they could head for home, stopping off at a petrol station to round off the evening with a paper cup of espresso that stained their lips like squid ink, and a dirty end-of-the-night truck driver's joke—though Mustafa Bey didn't know any.

Ali had no idea how Mustafa or Cemal knew that a drive was the best medicine for this matted head of curls on its squished child's body. She didn't think Elyas rang his uncle regularly to enquire about her. She couldn't imagine him telling Cemal in the confiding tones of a doctor: 'If she does such-and-such a thing, you just have to sit her in the car. Wind down the window and let her climb halfway out and smoke—she'll soon come round.'

But now she came to think of it, why not? Why didn't he ring? Why wasn't he here? Where was Elyas when you needed him?

Mustafa and Cemal had said something about a theatre—that's where they were heading. A dance theatre, very unusual—Mustafa had been before and recommended it highly, but she hadn't been listening; she'd been staring at the newspaper that was sodden with rakı and whey, trying to project herself into the photos.

When they drove past Sultanahmet, the car was lit up for a moment; floodlights shone in at the windows, bright as the moon. Then it suddenly went dark again, and the road vibrated. Now and then the yellow light of the streetlamps broke the grey of their profiles.

'What have you seen of Turkey apart from Istanbul?' asked Mustafa after a brief silence. 'Anything at all?'

Ali said nothing. She pressed her forehead and the tip of her nose against the window, leaving greasy marks on the glass.

'I could show you round the west coast. I was a tour guide for years. German and English tourists. All the sites—Pergamum, Troy. I could show you Olympus, if you like.'

'I thought that was in Greece,' Ali breathed onto the window.

'Greece was here.'

'I see.'

'Do you like that kind of thing?'

'What kind of thing?'

'Olympus. Travelling. Shall we go travelling together? We could hire a car and drive up from Antalya.'

21

Ali peeled her face off the glass and turned to look at him. What was left of Mustafa's grey curls looked like her own. Is that how she'd look at fifty? Maybe it was. If she carried on smoking and started wearing suits, she might look something like that in twenty years. She'd give lifts to young women and offer to take them to Olympus—could do worse.

'I'm not here on holiday.' She scanned the inside of the car, hoping to find a tape player—something to silence Mustafa.

'Cemal told me why you're here, but I meant if you wanted something to take your mind off things. I'm sure it would do you good. It's important not to tense up; if you tense up, you won't find anyone, and since you're here, you might as well see some more of the country—or don't you want to see anything?'

Ali smiled. 'I'd like to see Kurdistan. Do you know your way around Kurdistan?'

Mustafa looked at her. He had very tired eyes and very tired skin that hung down from his cheekbones in tear-shaped bags, as if his skin were dripping off his face in slow motion. His big round pupils sucked you in. They rested expressionlessly on Ali.

The rest of the drive passed in silence.

When they got out of the car, Ali found herself surrounded by ads in Cyrillic letters. Neon signs in Russian promised discount furs and best quality pretty much everything. Dimly lit faceless window mannequins shimmered in snakeskin, arms extended, fingers splayed. Ali stopped outside a bridal-wear shop. The mannequins in white dresses had bridal veils covering their faces, and their heads were turned back over their shoulders.

It was too dark to work out what kind of theatre they were entering—or whether it was a theatre at all. There were no signs on the outside, not that there was anything unusual in that; you often didn't know what bar or club or office you were going to end up in when you set off up the spiral staircases in the old alleyways of Beyoğlu. Ali had strayed here a few times, drifting among strangers in the hope of finding Anton—in the hope of finding anything at all. People kept a few centimetres' distance; men talked about their jobs and the beauty of Almanya. They wanted to marry her and some were more direct and said they wanted to sleep with her, but they were afraid of her eyes—they said something about the evil eye—that she looked evil. Pure superstition, of course, but it helped keep unwanted arms off her shoulders.

A young man in a suit was sitting in the doorway, playing a game on his phone; it sounded as if he were smashing glass bottles. He glanced up and mumbled good evening, then went back to his phone. They climbed the stairs, Mustafa leading the way. Past the second floor, greenish neon morphed into a warm red flashing light and bass lines pulsed through the banisters like electricity. The walls were peeling and covered in graffiti; another young man in a suit stood outside the door. He looked at the two of them. Mustafa said they were on the guest list. The bouncer said he knew nothing about a guest list and Mustafa replied that he knew the owner—the bouncer should fetch Hafif. Ali lit a cigarette and leant up against the graffiti. On the opposite wall someone had written *Ich bin Ulrike Meinhof* and some words she didn't understand. She was stretching out an arm to point at them, when the door above her opened. 'Gel,' said Mustafa. It was the first time he'd spoken to her in Turkish. He sounded annoyed.

The room looked like the set of the seventies films Cemal sometimes had on in the background. There was a large stage and a polished parquet floor with a few rows of plastic chairs. The entire ceiling was mirrored and hung with kaleidoscopic chandeliers resembling plucked parrots. Faces flashed red; Bülent Ersoy purred out of the speakers; the mirrors reflected the silver shards of disco balls. The few customers hovering undecidedly between the bar and the chairs were wearing suits; the waiters wore tails and white masks that came down to their nostrils. Ali tilted her head to one side and watched them come and go. She looked down at her jeans and jumper, and at Mustafa in his crumpled jacket. Then she went back to watching the waiters.

Next she made for the bar. Mustafa followed her, calling out to her, something like: 'What will you have to drink?' But the question came too late; Ali had already ordered a vodka and tonic, and answered Mustafa by asking if he wanted the same. He nodded, fishing for his wallet, but again he was too late; Ali had paid and begun to suck on her straw before Mustafa had found his money. He propped himself up at the bar and asked if she knew who Bülent Ersoy was. Ali didn't reply and Mustafa launched into a lecture about gender reassignment surgery, the military coup in the eighties and Bülent Ersoy's exile in Germany. She turned away from him and left the bar to saunter across the room. Near the back, she found somewhere to sit where she had a view of the stage—a bulbous, red velvet sofa with a metal rod on top of the plateau that formed the back rest. She laid back and looked up at the bilious green plastic crystals of the chandelier overhead, and at her eyes between them, shattered and rearranged in the mirror. Then she saw her face again. A body just like hers, slender and rangy and dressed in the same black jumper and jeans and white trainers, placed a vodka and tonic on the sticky parquet, sat down on her right and leant back. Their shoulders touched, but nothing else; their heads lay resting on the sofa back, looking up into the mirrors overhead. They had the same curls—corkscrews that stuck up at their temples and hung down at their earlobes, scraping little cracks in the ceiling.

Ali looked into Anton's face beside her and smiled, and Anton smiled back, an exact mirror image. She moved her little finger towards him along the sofa cushions in the hope of finding his finger, but didn't take her eyes off him, keeping him pinned to the ceiling with her gaze.

Then something flickered on Anton's face and a crystal came adrift from the chandelier fitting, contorting his face and hers in the mirror and falling straight into the glass of vodka and tonic in Ali's hand. She jumped, stared at the green stone in the clear liquid, swirled the drink in her glass, took a sip and laid her head back on the sofa. No Anton in the mirror, no little finger next to hers on the cushions; she looked at the room reflected on the ceiling, without blinking.

The show began, or something like a show; you couldn't have called it a play. The master of ceremonies wore a gold dress and a white mask that completely covered his face. The dress reminded Ali of her first dress from the west, which her mother, at risk of her life, had bought under the counter for an entire month's wages. It was gold all over with puffed sleeves and Ali would rather have died than wear it; she wailed and screamed and even bit, but there was nothing for it: her mother wanted photos—why else had she put herself to the trouble? There was no peace until Anton climbed into the dress without being asked, even raising his arms and wiggling his hips as if he were dancing. Ali had a clear memory of that photo: her teary self in leggings and a vest—and Anton in the gold dress.

A drag queen greeted the audience and announced the program in a speech stuffed full of jokes and allusions that Ali didn't understand. She wasn't even sure that anyone in the audience was listening; whatever people had come for, the chink of glasses betrayed tension, anticipation. On either side of the stage, swathes of heavy, dark material fell from the ceiling, and two women in black underwear began to snake their way up them. The air in the room seemed to thicken to tar and a short, round woman in a velvet dress pranced across the parquet and sang 'Sex Bomb' two octaves too low. Ali sat up, blew into her straw and raised her eyebrows, puckering her forehead. Her mother had always counted the wrinkles, plucking at them in front of Ali's aunts: 'One, two, three, four—don't do that, Alissa. Don't pull faces

25

like that. You're young now, but you know how you'll look when you're thirty-five?'

'No, how?'

'Like Uncle Seryosha.' Ali would push her mother's hand out of her face and to avoid an awkward silence her aunts would twist the knife a little deeper: 'If you'd stop running about like a dyke, you might actually make something of yourself.'

A waiter wearing a mask that covered the left-hand side of his face bent down to Ali and breathed in her ear, asking if he could bring her anything to drink. He came so close, she felt she ought to say, *Yes, I'll go to the toilet with you*, but instead she said: 'Votka, lütfen.' The drink came immediately and she paid. The room had filled up; the air felt sharply damp. Ali couldn't see Mustafa and hoped he'd left in a huff or was at least getting drunk with the hungry-eyed men at the bar. She wondered whether Uncle Cemal would shoot his friend in the right eye, if he knew where he'd taken Ali, the way Yılmaz Güney had shot the public prosecutor.

As Nena's 'Neunundneunzig Luftballons' started up, a horde of scantily clad bodies in gold hotpants and black afro wigs threw themselves into the crowd and danced between the rows of chairs towards Ali. She suddenly realised that the thing behind her back that she'd taken for a pointless piece of metal, the remains of a flawed construction like those pipes on the fronts of the houses in Tarlabaşı that led nowhere, or that had once led somewhere but were now no more than a memento, an embellishment, something for the ivy to grow up and the tourists to admire as beautiful or, worse still, authentic—that this construction was a pole-dancing pole and very much still in use. One of the dancers came and stood right in front of her, evidently about to climb onto the plateau that Ali had taken for a backrest. Gold-clad hipbones stared Ali challengingly in the eyes. She didn't move, but stared back, sucking on her straw, and the girl climbed over her. Setting her right foot on Ali's knee and her left foot on the arm of the sofa, she pulled herself up and thrust herself against the metal pole. Spotlights stung Ali's eyes. The audience had turned round; everyone wanted to see what the agile young woman would get up to with the pole. Ali had no choice but to press herself into the upholstery and look up. The dancer threw out her legs; they flew past Ali's ears like white toothpicks, and the black synthetic wig tousled her curls. Ali chewed slowly on her straw.

She waited until the straw had nothing more to yield and the toothpick legs had disappeared—until the light had mellowed, turning dim and milky, and she could be sure that no one was watching. Then she heaved herself up off the sofa. The audience had split into little groups of hoping, laughing, waiting people. She found the toilet. She was sure the cubicle would be occupied by some couple with their noses glued to the cistern, who would no doubt stay and amuse themselves when they were done—but it was free and clean and strangely sterile, with a bright white fluorescent tube over her static hair and red eyes. She didn't blink. She washed her hands and face slowly, then held her lips under the jet of cold chloriney water and checked in the mirror again. Anton looked back crossly. A woman came in. She seemed to have been laughing or crying a great deal; her make-up was smudged and she began to redo her face. Ali watched her dab colour on her skin and paint lines around her eyes and mouth. Her lipstick was black. When she was finished, she turned her head. Ali asked if she could borrow the lipstick, took it and wrote *Anton woz ere* on the white tiles. The woman started to shout, something like: 'You've ruined my lipstick, do you know what that cost?' Ali took a step towards her, grabbed the back of her neck, pulled her face close, kissed her on her newly drawn mouth and walked past her.

Just find the door and get out; you don't need to be here, she told herself—then Aglaja came on stage.

She was wearing an accordion, or the accordion was wearing her; the heavy instrument took up the entire top half of her body and she played it as if she were ripping open the bones of her fishlike torso. A round head with short red hair stuck out at the top, and below, two legs in fishnet tights melted together into long, low black shoes, as if into a mermaid's tail. Her arms, clasping the monster of an instrument, were clad to the elbows in black fish-scale gloves. She threw back her head as if someone had slapped her in the face, her red-painted lips swallowing the entire ceiling, her tongue poking out like a sticking-up finger. Her voice rose, trembling, from her throat to the crystals on the ceiling and into Ali's guts. The fierce vibrato made Ali stop and stand still. Then she saw Aglaja's face. Ali's eyes widened, tears shot up, she began to blink. Then she looked again.

The crystals over Aglaja's head swung to and fro; her long cloth-covered fingers slowly pressed the accordion buttons. Ali could have sworn she could smell the woman all the way across the room. She smelt of freesia and bergamot, of pineapple, oranges, cedar wood and vanilla. Ali opened her mouth and imagined the red hair growing into it. She imagined walking on stage and taking this woman away, somewhere, anywhere. She imagined everyone else leaving the room immediately—imagined that there had never been anyone there but the two of them.

The accordion player received a smattering of applause and left the stage. Ali sat down at the bar and waited. She craned her neck for a glimpse of the mermaid, but only saw Mustafa sidling towards her and quickly looked around for an excuse not to talk to him. A shaven-headed woman in gold hot pants, her synthetic afro tucked under her arm, was suddenly standing in front of her. She couldn't tell whether or not it was the pole dancer who'd stripped above her head just a moment ago.

The woman had opened her lips to say something, but now she looked down at Ali's hand resting on the P&S packet. Could she have one of her German cigarettes?

She said her name was Kato, Katarina, Katyusha, like in the song 'Vykhodila na bereg Katyusha'—'Katyusha Went Down to the Riverbank'.

'Do you know it?'

Of course Ali knew the song. There wasn't a child whose mother tongue was Russian who didn't. Ali knew that, Katarina knew that, and now Katarina came and stood between Ali's legs (balanced precariously on the bar stool and doing their best not to shake) and quietly sung a few lines of the song in her ear. Of course, it wasn't really about a woman who went down to a riverbank where 'rastsvetali yabloni i grushi'—'the apple and pear trees were in blossom'; it was about a multiple rocket launcher that was developed during the Great Patriotic War of '41 to '45, and affectionately dubbed 'Katyusha' in Russian. It's true that the rest of the song was about powerful emotions—but not the ones thought by some to be the Russian soul howling for love.

Katarina sucked on her cigarette. Ali heard a harsh indrawn breath and a soft smacking sound as Katarina filled her mouth with smoke and released the cigarette from between her lips. Ali's ears went red, especially the right one, at Katarina's cheek. She gave a sudden laugh, drew back her head and stared into the face of this woman—a face as open as if someone had flung up a window. The far-apart eyes looked as if they might tumble down the broad cheekbones, so that Ali was tempted to catch them with her own. She followed the lines of Katarina's eyes and cheekbones down to her mouth and saw her jaw tense. They spoke Russian; that sped things up. Katyusha the rocket launcher kissed Ali before she'd even ordered a second drink. Ali tasted thick oily lumps of paint, and then little else.

Katyusha studied Ali's face, running the fingertips of her left

29

hand over her eyebrows. Ali looked down and saw a thin gold ring on the fourth finger of Katyusha's right hand.

'To frighten off the men,' she said, 'make sure they leave me alone.'

'And do they?'

'Course not.' She stubbed out her cigarette on the bar without taking her eyes off Ali. 'But who cares? Everything that could happen to me already has.'

'I hope not, Katyusha.'

They'd stopped counting the vodkas. Out of the corner of her eye, Ali saw Mustafa approach and then recede again, like a pendulum. The ceiling seemed to be sinking lower and lower too; the crystals jangled overhead.

'Can I ask you something? That accordion player, does she—'

Ali felt dizzy. Katarina took her by the arm and pulled her off the stool; they staggered out onto the stairs where Katarina left Ali and vanished into the changing room. Ali leant against the Ulrike Meinhof graffiti and smoked; she managed to start a conversation with the bouncer. When he decided it was time to put his hand on her thigh, Katarina appeared in jeans and a T-shirt and led her down the stairs. Ali didn't know how, but she found the way home, Katarina squeezing her arm. They kept ducking into doorways to suck each other's faces out of their heads, pressing their pelvises against each other and stopping when they heard footsteps—then Ali pulled Katarina on down the steep streets, stumbling over grey cats, fumbling for the key—it took her forever, but at last they were in and she threw Katarina on the bed—or Katarina threw her—and time stood still.

The moon hung over Süleymaniye Mosque, shining on the slender body stretched out on the bed beside her, pale toes sticking out over the end of the mattress, shaven head pressed against the wooden frame. Like a marble-coloured line she lay there on the sheet—like an elongated question mark. Her breasts rose and fell; her face was turned away.

Katarina's nipples gleamed in the moonlight. Ali was tempted to touch them with her forehead, but resisted for fear of waking the body, of making it move, making it wriggle out of its question-mark position and begin to talk. Her phone had slipped under the bed when Katarina pushed her onto the mattress—or had it been the other way round? The rest of the night was a series of flashing images in Ali's memory. She put her feet down on the cold lino and pulled the curtain aside. It was night.

Katarina was cooing softly, her mouth half open, her eyes moving beneath the lids—Ali couldn't see them, but she was sure that was what they were doing. The muezzin was saying his morning prayer. Ali's eyes were throbbing; the moon confused her. She let go of the curtain, knelt down, laid her forehead on the floor and groped for her phone among the dust balls under the bed. As far as the vodka in her brain would allow, she tried to remember what Katyusha (now breathing softly on the mattress above her) had said to her—who she was, what stories she'd told. But she recalled only a few Russian proverbs that Katyusha had let fall somewhere between the fourth shot and the seventh.

Lying on the floor under the bed with her head among the dust balls, Ali didn't know what she'd lost of the words and images of the previous night—the previous few nights, the previous weeks. She got to her feet, banging her head on the edge of the bed, and stared helplessly at her phone. The display had got a crack in it the night before; she stared at the time and had trouble making sense of it. In her jeans pocket she found a half-empty packet of P&S. Amazing that it still worked—slap a packet of German cigarettes on the table and people will come and talk to you—like Katarina, this question mark on her bed—probably, Ali guessed, an au pair girl from Ukraine, or a politics student from Romania—they all spoke Russian.

Ali lit a Player's and stared at Katarina's body. It looked like pure oxygen—oxygen and a bit of moon—and she wondered what she was really called—Anna, Elvira, Zemfira, Petka—could be anything; Ali found no name to fit her face. She looked out of the window again. The muezzins interrupted one another unrhythmically.

The muezzin to the left of her balcony had a cold; he whined today rather than sang, and the other always came in a little after him, relishing his superiority. Ali imagined an Elvis lookalike adjusting glittery silver sunglasses, smiling to reveal two rows of white teeth and perhaps a single gold incisor, then tapping his mike before launching into the morning prayer. He sang well. He knew he was the best for miles around. God is great. And prayer better than sleep.

At the smell of the cigarette, Katarina screwed up her pale face and opened her eyes, squinting slightly. Her cheeks were puffed out, her lips puckered into a chrysanthemum, and she blinked several times before she understood where she was—or that she didn't know where she was. She curled into a half moon, her head cocked to one side. Ali handed her a cigarette.

'What's the time?' she asked, sitting up.

'The clock says five. Can't be right, can it? Look out of the window—the moon's shining as if it were the middle of the night, but the muezzin's singing the morning prayer. Everything's mixed up.'

'Yes.'

'They've done away with time.'

'Have you slept?'

Ali had slept. She could even remember her dream, which was happening to her more and more since she'd come to Turkey. In this particular dream she'd been dancing with Uncle Cemal in a crowd so dense that their bodies had moved to the music of a seventies film as if by themselves. They'd stood locked in an embrace and the crowd had rocked them to and fro. Then Cemal had caught sight of someone, and staring over the sea of heads, he'd fixed his gaze on a shock of red hair at the back of the room, and letting go of Ali's hips, he'd gone off and left her—pushed past the other couples and left her standing there, swaying to and fro on her own. For a few seconds, Ali had continued to hold her arms where Cemal's shoulders had been a moment before, her head bent forward as if it were resting on his chest. Then she'd melted to a puddle in the crowd.

'No, I don't like sleeping.'

'I do,' said Katarina with a yawn. 'I love sleep. I wish I could sleep all my life.'

'Oh, Katyusha.'

Katarina wrapped her arms around her knees and suddenly looked serious and almost mean; she cut the room with her eyes and said in a voice that was perhaps more her own than the one she'd used earlier to vie with Ali in Russian vulgarities—a voice deeper than the one that had whimpered and shrieked as she'd come in Ali's mouth: 'I have to tell you something.'

It flashed into Ali's mind that she was in the exact situation of which her mother had always warned.

'I'm not Katyusha.'

'No, I didn't think you were,' said Ali with a nervous laugh, hoping that was it. If it was only the name, that was okay, but she was afraid of more revelations—contagious diseases or feigned financial difficulties.

'I'm Kato.'

'Okay,' said Ali, thinking that she desperately needed other words beside this 'okay'. She didn't even know what exactly was okay.

'I'm not a she.'

33

'Aha.'

'I'm a he.'

'Yes.'

'Do you understand?'

'Do you need money?'

'What? Why would I need money?'

Ali couldn't work it out—had she forgotten her Russian, or was she still drunk, or had she just not understood? Kato got up, reached for the packet of cigarettes and left the room. Ali stayed sitting on the floor and looked out of the window. The lights of the city tugged at her eyelids. The windows of the gecekondular cut through the froth of colours, and a chain of lights around a rooftop car park drew a white line across a little piece of black in a sky that was otherwise made up of yellow, orange, red and violet oblongs, some of them flickering with synthetic television light. Above the nearest row of houses, three minarets, loamy grey by day, rose up, illuminated yellow, bristling with loudspeakers like tiny thorns, too small for such thick stems.

Kato came back with the glowing cigarette and sat down on the edge of the bed, planting his legs square on the floor.

'Funny, the moon always lies on its back here. It never stands up like the crescent on their flag; it lies there like a segment of orange—look at it.'

Kato didn't look at the moon, but down at Ali who turned her head to him.

'Do you want breakfast?'

He stubbed out his cigarette on the window frame, pulled up his legs, crawled under the covers and mumbled through the sheet: 'It's night time. Let's sleep.'

The blood ticked in Ali's throat. She looked up at where Kato's body must be, though she couldn't see it, and climbed onto the bed in search of him.

She squeezed her eyes shut and waited until it was light enough to get up. Red curls and a tongue sticking out at a mirrored ceiling kept popping up on the back of her eyelids; she opened her mouth and snapped at them. A sudden taste of salt made her open her eyes. Kato's lips had worked their way up from her neck and pressed themselves on hers. Ali started up, spun round and jumped out of bed. The lino was so cold it burnt her feet. Kato turned onto his belly and said something into the pillow. Ali slid into her slippers and locked herself in the bathroom. The boiler gave off a whistling sound; lukewarm water trickled over her shivering limbs. She looked down at herself and examined the hairs on her arms; they were pale as pale, long and soft, almost invisible. Then she squatted to inspect her calves—furry white cat's hind legs. Shampooing her head, she thought about what Kato had told her in the night—that she was a he. Kato was a he. Her scalp itched; she scratched her temple with the inside of her lower arm. Shampoo ran down her face and back, and she stuck out her tongue, opening her mouth wide, trying to flush the vodka out of her head. Just as the scent of the accordionist was rising to her nose again, the smell of freesia and bergamot, pineapple, oranges, cedar wood and vanilla, the boiler stopped whistling and the lights went out. The water promptly ran cold and all at once Ali was awake. She jumped out of the bath, wrapped a towel around her and staggered out into the arms of Kato who was standing in the hall looking about him in bemusement.

'Power cut. Often happens when I have a shower.'

With the towel tucked under her armpits, she went down to the cellar. On the stairs she met her next-door neighbour and said good morning, the shampoo still in her eyes, the blood throbbing at her temples. He avoided looking at her. She wasn't sure if he'd heard them yesterday, but judging by his face he had, and now here she was, walking around the communal areas half naked. She flicked the flat black switch in the fuse box and ran back upstairs. Kato was standing in the kitchen, his shorn head illuminated by the light from the fridge.

'I wanted to make breakfast, but there's only a lump of old butter.'

'And a bottle of tonic water.'

'And a bottle of tonic water.'

'Come on, let's go out.'

The streets were empty, as empty as in the summer, as empty as in the holiday season, when people fled the hot city—but it was November and the light wasn't in sync with the clock or the muezzins. It was strangely still, the air tense. The crumbling facades looked like a frozen stage set; there were still chairs in the deserted bars on the ground floor; a lot of houses were in ruins, but not all. It was as if a wrecking ball had struck once and then moved on. Some flats were still lived in; the curtains were closed, but they couldn't cover the gaping walls spewing cables. Two cats crawled out of a burnt-out car, a single tangle of fur. At the greengrocer's, balloons hung on a post next to boxes of brown bananas, and there was a flag bearing the symbol of the People's Democratic Party: a tree, its trunk two purple hands, its green leaves interspersed with stars—*Vote, Vote, Vote*—the whole neighbourhood was full of it.

There was a smell of detergent and paint. When they turned off at the Armenian church, Ali stopped in front of old red graffiti of a woman with birds coming out of her head. She stepped closer to examine it, but Kato pulled her on. In the half dark, boys were kicking a leather ball against the church doors; it bounced off and Kato stopped it and kicked it back. The boys' teasing voices echoed down the streets after them; Ali and Kato heard them all the way to the park, where they sat down on the damp grass.

The fountains were dry, the motorway made a loop over their heads; that too was deserted. Ali stretched out on her back, her stomach rumbling. Kato talked and his voice sounded tinny, like the echoing voices of the boys.

He told Ali about the hormones he was taking; soon he'd be covered in black hair. You couldn't tell from his shorn head what colour his hair was, and his arms and legs were still smooth—but his square eyebrows were drawn on with a black kohl pencil. Ali imagined the line of his eyebrows extending to his chin and tried to picture him with a beard, drawing a frame around his broad, open face. The face reminded her of someone, but she couldn't think who.

Kato said he'd soon lose his job—because of the beard, and because of the hairy legs—they didn't look so good in gold hot pants, so someone else would have to wear them and he'd go back to Ukraine and show himself to his parents—his father in particular. *Look, Dad, this is me now.* He told her about his alcoholic father. Ali hardly listened; her mind wandered and she asked herself why all fathers had to be alcoholics—couldn't they be chess players or compulsive yerba mate drinkers and, whatever else they did, couldn't they keep quiet? Couldn't they just keep quiet and never talk? Kato's mother, it seemed, was a heroine—a heroine of labour, of the kind envisaged by Lenin—and there were two little brothers and sisters as well. He didn't send them money; he never sent anyone anything, but he sometimes thought of them and wondered if they were thinking of him. Kato talked and talked, and the sky above their heads turned as white as dishwater.

I've missed Russian, Ali thought. But missing wasn't something you could think. She didn't know exactly what she missed, and if she began to think about it she'd only make room for a sense of missing, so why bother? Her mother had once said something about thoughts being parasites, but she couldn't remember the exact words.

Kato had gone quiet and was looking at Ali. She realised he'd asked her something. He leant over her and repeated the question.

'A ty?'

And you?

There was no expectation in his face. He wasn't going to kiss her; it was a serious question; he really wanted to know. *And you?* Ali looked past him and thought: *Tarlabaşı is going to be pulled down. Everything's going to be pulled down. I'll never find Anton.*

A street vendor pushed his barrow past them, behind the glass a gleaming layer of greasy rice, big mother-of-pearl-coloured chickpeas, then more rice and on top, a brown layer of boiled chicken.

'Pilav! Tavuklu pilav!' he cried. 'Want some, girls?'

Kato looked away. Ali shook her head. She stared at the oily layer of chicken meat and tasted bile.

'Fresh chicken. Pilaf is comfort food, sisters!' The vendor stood over them, fists on hips, little head nodding down to them on its thin neck.

The chicken stared at them. Ali tried to withstand its gaze.

THIRTY-SIX HOURS

The pieces of meat slid down her throat like liquid. The dead bird lay naked and half demolished on the small table between them, in the fourth carriage of the Moscow–Berlin train. She and Anton had window seats. Their hands sticky with chicken fat and potatoes and tomatoes, they pushed each other and drew letters on the window-pane, while their parents swayed on twelve suitcases and even more boxes. Inside the boxes and cases were bedclothes and Adidas track-suits in plastic wrappers, maybe to sell, you never knew—there were gold-plated watches too. But mainly there were bedclothes and socks and pants and books. 'Why are you taking so many books with you?' their father's father had asked, shaking his head. 'Are you out of your minds? You can't sell *them* over there.' Mother and Father sat in the carriage, their lips pressed together and their knees pressed together, watching the children gnawing their chicken drumsticks with big grins on their little faces. They hadn't been told they were leaving for good, and all that stuff about children knowing everything without being told is a load of nonsense; all children know is how to play, so they played and horsed around and paid no attention to their parents who were shitting themselves. This made them scream at each other all the time—but so what, the children didn't notice; their parents were always screaming at each other and the kids weren't to know that if they were always screaming at each other it was because they were always shitting themselves. Mother's father sat in the next compartment pretending not to hear and smoking out of the window; now and then he looked in on Valya and Kostya and Ali and Anton to ask if Valya had Analgin for him, and Valya dug around in her handbag for the foil packet that crackled and popped open, spitting rust-brown pellets onto the waiting hand which made the twins stare because it was so big and yellow with such dark blue lines. Valya pressed a plastic beaker of water into her father's other hand and he disappeared again. The smell of nicotine lingered.

His wife, Mother's mother, hadn't come with them; she had to wait a bit, had to sell the flat they'd never live in again, say goodbye to her friends, prepare her own parents' move—because they were coming too, Mother's mother's mother and the father to match; everyone had to be packed up, no one left behind—you weren't asked if you wanted to go. Ali and Anton hadn't been asked, nor had their parents' parents' parents. Some were taken straight away and others had to be fetched later—that's just the way it was. Mother's mother would follow in the aeroplane with a suitcase full of money from the sale of the flat, and these five here were going on ahead with suitcases full of things you couldn't sell over there.

The rocking of the train was comforting, deep breathing lulling them to sleep, and the hot tea that the guard brought them was comforting too: 'Here you are, my darlings,' she said. 'Nice hot tea with lemon and sugar. Wouldn't want you feeling cold.' Mother stuck a hand in her bra and pulled out a note. 'Thank you, thank you, my sweethearts'—and the guard vanished again. Ali peered after her and just glimpsed a man in a white undershirt, his hips as broad as the corridor, trot along behind and disappear into a compartment with her.

If it hadn't been for customs, the journey would only have taken thirty-six hours. Customs was when the train shuddered in the night and the bed frames were bashed so hard that the thick chains fixing them to the walls rattled like bars being shaken. You had to get up and pretend you'd been asleep. You had to put your hand to your heart, into your bra where the two hundred dollars were waiting for the customs officer, an unshaven man with bloodshot eyes who stared so hard at Valya that she was glad to have her husband in the compartment with her, even if he was cowering nervously in the corner. She knew what would have happened if he hadn't been there. And she knew what would have happened if she hadn't had those two hundred dollars next to her skin for just this situation: they'd have been turfed out onto the platform in the freezing cold, along with all the others, the have-nots or the know-nots—it was all the same in sub-zero temperatures. She looked out at them through the steamed-up glass, then at old Bloodshot in front of her, then at her children, two pairs of eyes peeping out from under a blanket on the bed above the window. Bloodshot spat something through his teeth, but she wasn't listening; she knew her papers were in order. She stared out at the platform again, counting the people gathered there: three, four, five, seven... more and more of them, families with children and even babies, young men, a lone woman—and as if a conductor had raised his baton, they all made the same gesture at the same time: they all reached into their jacket pockets and pulled out cigarettes, and watery smoke rose above their heads. Then the compartment door fell shut, the grown-ups fell back into their beds and the twins clawed each other's shoulderblades and held each other tight to make sure they didn't fall off the bunk with all the rocking—or that if they did, they'd fall together.

When the Chepanov family got off the train the next morning, the world pretended to stay still, but beneath Ali's little body the rocking continued. The chicken fat trembled in her throat, climbed back out of her stomach and into her mouth. Maybe the food had gone off in the warm carriage—Anton grinned, right as rain, but the chicken was determined to get out of Ali and onto the shoes of the man helping Father with the suitcases. Uncle Leonid, who'd come to collect the emigrants (or immigrants, depending how you looked at things) and take them home to his place and then on to the authorities—the wonderful Uncle Leonid stood before them and spread out his arms, and Ali puked all over his shoes, puked up the whole half chicken she'd eaten, and then fell over.

'Alissa? What's the matter? Alissa!'

Alissa lay in the vomit next to Uncle Leonid's black trainers and saw his shoelaces crawling towards her. Outside her head, time passed more quickly; things moved at lightning speed—shoes snapping about them like snakes; otters and giant insects pouncing at her. She gave a scream and felt as if she'd shrunk and been put in a picture she'd once seen on the wall at McDonald's—all jungle and bright colours and scary; she didn't know if she was lying on the ground or had fallen down a hole.

'Say sorry,' she heard, the words echoing down from the sky.

Her father picked her up from the ground, held her in front of Uncle Leonid's face and said: 'Say sorry.'

'You don't know where to put your feet, do you?' Mother asked, dabbing at Alissa's puke-soaked little T-shirt. 'Do you know, Leo, we were thirty-six hours on the train—'

'Longer!' Father interrupted.

'Longer. And the ground still feels wobbly. My knees are shaking too. Are yours?'

'Mine? No.'

'Nor are mine,' said Anton. Ali shot a glance at him, but he dodged it. Father jiggled Ali from side to side in front of Leonid and told her again to say sorry.

'Come on. What are you waiting for?'

'Izvinite.' Ali burst into tears.

'No, say it properly.' Father gave her a shake. Mother said: 'Leave her.'

'Izvinite,' Ali squeaked through her tears.

Uncle Leonid wiped the bile off his trainers with a handkerchief, a paper handkerchief from a plastic packet—Ali had never seen such a thing before; she only knew cloth hankies in trouser pockets with snot on the corners. Leonid mumbled something like: 'Not to worry,' and looking into Ali's teary face, he gave a laugh and said: 'Do you know how to say sorry in German?'

Ali shook her head, everyone shook their heads, the whole family shook one big head; none of them knew any German except for Mother's father, who'd gone for a smoke—Valya and Kostya's language lessons were yet to come. They might, at a pinch, have managed *eins, zwei, drei* and maybe *Hände hoch*, but you couldn't go around saying that; it was nothing to joke about.

'*Entschuldigung*,' said Uncle Leonid, saying the German word slowly and clearly. '*Izvinite* in German is *Entschuldigung*.'

'Aha.'

'That's the word. You say it. Say it in German. *Izvinite* in German.'

Ali stared. Everyone stared.

'Say it. Say it in German. *Entschuldigung. Izvinite* in German. Go on.'

43

Ali smelt vomit and wrinkled her nose.

Mother helped, shaping the word *E-ntschu-ldi-gung* with her lips: 'Go on, my little one, say it. *E—*'

Father rocked Ali gently to and fro, whispering the word into her curls, her first German word. 'Come on, say it, don't be awkward, what's the matter with you? Just say the word—*E-ntschu-ldi-gung*. *Izvinite* in German.'

Ali felt like crying again, but instead she looked from Mother to Anton to the uncle with the paper hankies, said: '*Izvinite* in German,' and buried her face in Father's neck.

There was a pause, glances were exchanged, everyone was so relieved to have arrived, one way or another, all the suitcases intact, the bags too, and the children—ach, what was a little bit of sick? *We're here!*—and the grown-ups burst out laughing, laughed till their throats were sore—*Izvinite in German!*—and the child's face red and confused. They laughed and laughed, and Ali looked at Anton running to and fro between the grown-ups and tugging at their clothes, as clueless as she was, but aware that something seemed to need laughing at. So he laughed. And Ali threw up again.

And the grown-ups laughed on and on without stopping—laughed at the shy gurgle from their child's throat that sounded almost like a hiccup, like a sigh.

Valentina and Konstantin—what names! Why would you give someone a name like that, unless you were trying to hide the fact that they were Jewish and ought really to be called Esther or Shmuel or something? Certainly in the Soviet Union in the sixties you didn't give your children names like that unless you hated them—or hated yourself.

In the case of Valentina, known as Valya, there was at least some reason to give the girl an ugly, honest-to-God socialist name, because the day on which her mother catapulted her into the world, almost losing her life, was also the day on which the first woman in the world was launched into space. Valentina Tereshkova broke through the Earth's atmosphere at five miles a second and flew to the stars—and Valentina Pinkenzon tore through the tissue between her mother's vulva and anus, and landed in the hands of a thoroughly masked doctor who gave orders through the green paper over his mouth that her mother undergo immediate surgery.

Konstantin's parents had no such excuse. Konstantin was called Konstantin, Kostya for short, Kissa affectionately, end of discussion. But excuse or no, these two Russified people were brought together, as if love were something you could order—and, indeed, something that was best ordered, if you didn't want to be beaten black and blue, like Valya in her first marriage.

Valya had made her first mistake when she was young—too young to think, though not too young to marry. Where, you might ask, were her parents, when their daughter decided to marry a goy, their black-haired daughter, so much more beautiful than the astronaut Valentina Tereshkova—and with Pinkenzon as a surname, she might just as well have been called Esther Rahel to begin with (what use was 'Valentina' with a surname like that?), but her parents hadn't been very careful, not when it came to naming her and not when it came to the bridegroom either. They were staring at the mountains of Kislovodsk, where they'd gone for a rest cure, when little Valya decided that a school-leaving certificate wasn't complete without a husband. It wasn't the boy's big moustache that appealed to her (she didn't like moustaches) or his persuasive skills as a trumpeter, though that made him such a favourite with the others—a favourite of the girls at any rate, and the envy of the boys: 'What's he showing off for like that? Does he think he's Armstrong or something?' No, jazz wasn't Valya's thing at all; it got on her nerves. What appealed to Valya was the prospect

45

of finally being able to leave home, and in that respect she resembled many girls—or even all.

So she watched a few Soviet films about love, to find out how it went—what kind of looks you had to give, maybe even how you kissed, though there wasn't a lot of that in the films—usually not until the end, when the couple pressed their lips together, the man gripping the woman's shoulders and crushing her to his face while the woman looked surprised and desperate. It bore little resemblance to what really happened when you kissed, or to all that followed. It was only later that Valya realised the significance of that fat tongue in her mouth.

When her parents were out, she rehearsed looks and gestures. Good pupil that she was, she would sit cross-legged on the floral carpet and take notes, inches from the television. She liked school and loved reading; Tolstoy and Akhmatova were carefully hidden between her exercise books. But she found nothing in her reading telling her what to do when a man gripped your shoulders—not, at least, in the books on the Pinkenzons' shelves.

It helped that Valya was unusual looking—you could say unusually pretty, but more important, she looked different from the other girls, with their long straight hair. Her hair was thick and curly and cropped short; ever since she was little, her mother had made sure that her daughter had a proper socialist haircut, more or less the same as the boys. Then there was her straight nose and her firm mouth, and some would say that her hips, too, deserve a mention—at any rate, the moustachioed trumpeter thought it worth his while to watch Valya's black curls crawl across the white sheet and out of bed every morning.

Neither of them asked their parents; ignoring all words of wisdom they shut themselves in the bedroom and soon it was clear that the maid was a maid no longer and must get married. The wedding dress was made by the groom's mother out of a tulip-patterned tulle she'd bought too much of for the living-room curtains. The headdress was made by the bride herself out of papier mâché; she fashioned a kind of pudding basin and covered it in white silk, and though the white of this wedding bonnet didn't quite match the white of her dress, Valya looked as stunning as a photo model and crackled like a pavlova at every step.

The marriage lasted nearly a year. After seven months and a few days, the nineteen-year-old Valya had bruises on her face when she got in her grandmother's car to drive with her to the family dacha. Etina, known to those who loved her as Etinka, grabbed her grand-daughter by the chin; the girl looked neither distressed nor sad—nor even surprised and desperate. Far from it; she smiled because she was pleased to see her darling grandmother whom she missed more than all her other relations. Valya beamed at Etinka, almost forgetting that her grandmother's very dark worried eyes could read a bit more in her face than her delight at the prospect of the days on the Volga and the homemade jam. She'd tried to conceal the bruises with make-up, but she was surrounded by doctors; everyone in the family would know exactly what was shimmering under her pale skin—there was no point trying to hide it. Etinka's eyes grew darker still and she ran her rough fingertips over the blue marks on Valya's face.

'You're getting a divorce,' was all she said before starting the engine.

Valya caught her breath. Perhaps it was shock at the sudden roar as the car revved up, its tyres spinning—an old Lada, what could you expect? Or perhaps it was because Etinka had sounded so firm—but then everything that came from Etinka's mouth sounded firm; she hated unnecessary words (above all, she hated garrulous males). Etinka firmly believed that the less you said, the cleverer it made you look, and so when she did say something, it almost always turned out to be right—in this case, that Valya would get a divorce. Valya found the whole thing embarrassing more than anything. She didn't want her family to see her covered in bruises—but what she really didn't want was to have to move back in with them. Still holding her breath, she realised that Etinka wasn't going to probe.

She'd have liked to talk, to tell her grandmother that the trumpeter with the ridiculous name—and only now did she realise quite how ridiculous it was, so much so that she didn't ever want to have to say it again: Ivan, that was his name, like the Russian fairy-tale hero, the folk hero, the idiot—she'd have liked to tell her grandmother that Ivan had watched films too, to find out how to be a man. The kind of man *he* wanted to be. Then he'd learnt a bit more from watching and listening to his father and uncles, and two things had become clear to this very young man—he was twenty at the time. First of all, a man drinks. A man drinks before he speaks and after he's spoken. In between, he might shed a tear or two—but only if he's drinking. If he cries without drinking, he's either a poofter or a yid—and that brought Ivan to point number two. Because, you see, it hadn't escaped his attention that the black curls that Valya tossed over her white sheets, and the surname that she'd kept rather than take his, were possibly the reason she was to blame for everything that had ever happened to him. In his vodka-drenched brain, this insight led him to such well thought-through conclusions as: 'You Jewish bitch, go and rot in that Israel of yours; you won't destroy me—'

But yelling such gems of wisdom was soon not enough to satisfy Ivan or make up for all that he'd been through, and the terrified Valya had never heard such things as now left his mouth—well, she had; she'd grown up with all kinds of playground rhymes about yids—but not like this, not so close, the breath hot on her cheek.

Dva evreya tretii zhid po verevochke bezhit. Verevochka lopnet i zhida prikhlopnet. There'd been plenty of that kind of thing, but the vehemence with which Ivan the Trumpeter shouted down Valya's neck as she pored over the *History of Medicine* left her speechless. She was studying to be a medic; Akhmatova would just have to wait. She'd been wrong on several counts anyway, Valya now decided—either Valya had missed something, or else Akhmatova had lied.

Valya had missed something.

There was no shouting in Valya's family. That was unusual for families, but Valya couldn't know that. Her parents loved one another; if her father made her mother breakfast, it was because he wanted to, not because he had to. Valya's father had changed her nappies when she was a baby and taken her to school when she was a little girl; her mother had gone for massages while he coached Valya for university, and no harsh words were spoken—or not that Valya could remember. She didn't know that people hit each other. She knew that wars were waged and that the woman next door often screamed after midnight, but all that seemed a long way away to young Valya and nothing to do with her own life—until, that is, Ivan started to behave like a real Russian.

Esli b'et—znachit lyubit: an old Russian proverb. *If he hits you, he loves you.* Valya would remember the adage when she saw her husband staggering towards her; she sometimes muttered the words to herself.

Neither in the films she'd watched nor in the books she read was there anything telling you what to do if you were beaten, other than put up with it. Another Russian proverb that sometimes came to Valya was: *If you can't stop the rape, relax and try to enjoy it.* Plenty of women were, apparently, in the same boat; it was normal and Valya was part of the club, one of the loved ones. Maybe she really did mean so much to Ivan that he had to shout in despair; maybe he really was trying to make sense of the world. Valya, at any rate, tried to relax; she didn't think of the future, didn't ask herself if the rest of her life was going to be like this. She was too young for that; she couldn't even begin to think about things like the rest of her life. She didn't think at all; she swotted for her medical studies, feeling grown-up and important because she had a secret, and a weight settled on her face— the weight of adulthood, she told herself, and it was true; adulthood had lodged itself in the skin under Valya's eyes. But before it could gnaw and distort Valya's face like that of her namesake Tereshkova, Etinka had ordered her to leave that pig of a man—and if he dared lay hands on Valya again, she'd call in a butcher to settle the matter. All that and more Etinka would say later, outside the court building, where the couple had a hearing, but now, in the car with the spinning tyres, she said nothing, and her firmness filled the small blue Lada, leaving no room for contradiction. Valya thought Etinka didn't probe because she was afraid her granddaughter would start to cry and say things like: 'but I do love him' or: 'he's not really like that', but Etinka had images of her own to distract her. She felt a sudden pain in her jaw and in her right cheekbone, and forced as much air into her gullet as the stuffy Lada would yield. She mustn't say anything now, mustn't ask Valya any questions.

Etinka felt tears in her eyes. Even she hadn't expected that.

With Etinka's help—Valya's parents had gone somewhere for another rest cure—the girl was swiftly divorced. It wasn't to be, was it? Some called it fate, and the kid with the even shorter hair that she now cut herself, the flared jeans, roll-neck jumper and a suitcase so small you'd think there was nothing in it but a gramophone, moved back into the walk-through room at her parents' where her father had his study. Her parents didn't say a lot; they asked how she was getting on at university, praised her good marks and told her she could do even better, and Valya lay down on the spring mattress that made her feel fifteen again, put a book over her face—*The Woes of Wit* by Griboyedov, who had died a far too early, far too stupid death in Tehran ('Just think how much more he could have written,' Etinka would say)—and didn't stir until her parents left their plotting at the kitchen table to come and tell her that in Moscow! Moscow! Moscow! dream city of all the Soviet Republic—no, what were they saying, of all the world—in Moscow, there was a distant cousin who wasn't yet spoken for and, more important, he was Jewish. He'd never hit her or call her a Jewish bitch.

That's what they thought. They were wrong.

What Valya's parents didn't seem to realise was that despite the distant kinship between the families (Konstantin's father's cousin's brother was the cousin of a brother, et cetera, et cetera), Kostya came from a very different background from his future wife, the future mother of his children, the woman with whom he would one day decide to leave the country when tanks rolled through Red Square in the early nineties. (The name of the square has nothing to do with the colour of blood, but came about because 'red' and 'beautiful' are one and the same word in Russian.) Valya's parents gave little thought to such matters; they wanted to see their daughter provided for, and who could have guessed that the day would come when tanks would roll through Beautiful Square and the family would apply for American visas and end up in Germany, with Uncle Leonid and his puke-covered shoes.

Kostya's parents came from a village—not a shtetl, there was no such thing so near to Moscow, but a good Soviet village, where men had beards down to their waists, and women wore floral headscarves and floral housecoats; where you tossed a vodka down your throat every morning before setting off for work, and where all work was manual work and all hands were strong, men and women's alike. Only Kostya's father's hands weren't strong, though there was no skimping on butter in the porridge in his family. They didn't grow strong either, not like Kostya's mother's hands, which could do the work of two, and no bad thing because it's what they'd end up doing. Both his parents had the kind of surname that got you beaten up in a good Soviet village—at any rate, they both had to do a fair amount of running, and it brought them together, all that running did, not that Kostya's father was ever much good at that either.

'Look at the dirty Jew! Runs like a poofter!'

Kostya's father was short and gangly and ran as if he had stones in his shoes, his toes turned in, like a small limping animal about to stumble and fall. Neither the butter in his porridge nor the fat in his soup could make a difference to the way he ran, and he sure as hell couldn't put up a fight, so before long he was the butt of the whole village—especially the boys, when they were done poking out cats' eyes. That changed when Kostya's father did a stint in the military; he learnt a few tricks there and was soon defending himself by pouring canfuls of hot oil in the others' faces.

Kostya's mother was a sturdy young woman who'd never really been a child. She was only six when she began to take care of her drink-ravaged mother and her five brothers and sisters, and ever since she could stand, she'd known how to bath babies, make soup, extract splinters and bury relatives. It was a mystery why she agreed to marry Kostya's father; she'd always been keen on the idea of security so you'd have thought she'd have chosen a proper Russian peasant, taken a proper Russian surname and forgotten all about the Torah in the cupboard—that way her children, at least, would have had a chance of a decent life. But she decided differently—or perhaps she had no choice; after all, the only dowry she had to offer was that Torah in the cupboard and a large family full of diabetes and dementia. There was never any butter in *their* porridge—nor, indeed, was there always porridge; Kostya's mother made up her mind all by herself to grow strong in spite of everything and get away fast—away from her family, away from the quietly crumbling house, away to Moscow, where she knew no one and would never again have to wipe the arses of semi-putrefied corpses. Realising that she wouldn't manage alone, or with a Russian peasant who had no reason to leave his birthplace, she married the only other yid in the village.

Kostya's parents decided to move to Moscow even before the wedding. The city was only thirty miles away—more or less on the doorstep by Russian standards. Later, Kostya would ask them about the village where they'd grown up—couldn't they go and have a look at it together; it was so close. But they always said no and Kostya didn't persist; he realised that the subject pained his parents, and he loved them.

His father became a tailor. Shaky and clumsy though the rest of his body was, he was deft and precise with his hands, and had soon worked his way up—maybe the business instinct he had developed as a survival strategy in the military also played a part—and before long he was sewing suits for *important* men, as he liked to stress, maybe even men in the Kremlin. Although he never learnt to read or write, he made it to department manager and would walk up and down the corridors, rattling his abacus like a tambourine and sending the wooden beads clacking as he calculated his employees' deficits out loud to them. Kostya's mother stayed at home after the boy's birth, making him soup with butter and spooning up a fair amount of it herself. Kostya was a thin baby, as thin as his father, which wouldn't do at all; you couldn't go bringing invalids into the world. *I can see your ribs, it's a disgrace. Are you trying to tell me I'm a bad cook?* Kostya's mother was a very purposeful woman and made sure that her son put on fat from an early age.

Kostya loved his food and he loved toy guns. He also loved music. When Uncle Vasya dropped in on the young family in their tiny cardboard-walled flat on the fourth floor of a thirteen-storey block on the edge of the woods, he would heave his accordion onto his shoulders, and Kostya's ears would waggle, his mouth would water. There, in the district of Chertanovo, on the outskirts of Moscow, Uncle Vasya sang as if they were still in the country, out in those wide open spaces where songs are belted across the fields and come echoing back like a breath of wind—he sang as if nobody cared about the noise, as if there were no one downstairs to bang on the ceiling with a broom handle and shout: 'You fucking your mothers up there or something?'

And afterwards, when Uncle Vasya set down his accordion to drink and eat and discuss things with Kostya's father—the sorry state of the world, mainly, and wages that weren't even enough for tobacco and decent booze—*you can go blind drinking the rotgut here*—and the thighs of the cashier in the shop across the road, and the awful, overpowering, bittersweet stench of the dump behind the flats—*stinks all the way up to the fourth floor—don't open the window; you're better rotting in your own filth*—when, that is, the men were being men and no one was looking, Kostya would crawl behind Uncle Vasya's accordion, stick his skinny arms through the broad leather straps, and press his little pot belly against the instrument. He couldn't lift it, so he lay behind it, hidden from view, running his fingers over the shiny black buttons that felt like marbles. After a while, the family noticed that the boy was always nestling up to the accordion, so Uncle Vasya took him on his lap, heaved up the monster of an instrument, placed his fleshy fingers on Kostya's little ones and pressed his nephew's fingers down on the keys.

What Kostya's parents didn't know was that two things were going on when this happened, things they couldn't know about because they didn't exist in their world. The first was that Kostya began to feel the stirrings of a passion for music. Another eight years, and the sixteen-year-old Kostya would declare his intention to become a musician—a pianist and accordionist: 'Mum and Dad, this is what I want to be. I'll go to the military and I'll learn a trade, but I'm going to be a musician and perform all over the country.' His mother's laughter was so loud that it echoed in Kostya's ears until his premature end.

The second thing was that something else stirred when Uncle Vasya took Kostya on his lap; the man was not entirely selfless. Nor was he ashamed to do what he did in front of the child's parents; they couldn't know what Kostya felt moving under his tailbone; such a thought would never have occurred to them. As Uncle Vasya pushed the weight of the accordion down on Kostya's lap, he made gentle circling movements with his hips and rubbed his trousers against the boy's bony little bum. Squeezing both accordion and Kostya tight, he breathed heavily, his mouth open, and the acrid smell confused Kostya because he knew it wasn't alcohol, a smell he knew well; it was sour and eggy. Still, he continued to climb onto Uncle Vasya's lap to push down the keys and feel the puff of cold air on his cheeks when the heavy accordion was pressed shut. Neither the acrid smell nor his uncle's soft groans could stop Kostya's resolve to spend his life with the instrument. But Kostya was now familiar with a feeling he'd never shake, a sulphurous-smelling feeling that would often return. It tasted sour on his tongue and he blamed everyone and everything for it—socialism, politicians, the state, his parents, his wife, and all those other bastards-may-they-rot-in-hell. The feeling of abuse.

Kostya and Valya were brought together, as people said then—and still say today, although these days matchmaking is made to sound more like wedding planning than arranged marriage. Back then in the real-life socialism of the eighties—not bad years, Valya's parents would say, in retrospect—back then, it was no big deal, a simple matter of survival, perhaps, coupled with the feeling that it was a good idea to cover up the disgrace of a daughter who was getting a divorce though she wasn't yet twenty—*and who knows if she'll ever find anyone now, with her looks.* Not that she was ugly, but she was quite—you know, what was the word—unusual.

Kostya's parents didn't care who he married, just as long as he stopped whoring around with the goy next door—*waiting for him to knock her up, she is.* You could bet the girl had her eye on the gold watches and growing pile of Adidas tracksuits in the cupboard; it was even possible she knew about the jewellery that had been bought under the counter—but never worn, of course. *Wear it? What? Strut around in the yard in it, in front of all the other grannies?* One thing was clear, though: that blond nympho wanted to get her claws into their only son, and as if that wasn't bad enough, he'd set his mind on becoming a musician; swift action was called for. Just as Kostya's parents had no idea what was going on in Uncle Vasya's crotch under their son's tailbone, they had no idea about many other things that had no place in their world, such as the notion that making music was different from eating onions and getting drunk and holding tearful conversations about your sorrows until you fell into each other's arms in a brotherly (and not remotely gay) embrace—or that there was such a thing as love, and that Kostya and the supposedly dowry-mad goy might actually be in love with each other. That, Kostya realised, was something else he wasn't going to get into their heads. Ever since his mother had fallen off her chair laughing at him when he'd mentioned his plans of a career in music, he'd known he was better off keeping his mouth shut. It didn't stop him from being in love.

The girl was called Oksana and had hair down to where her wings would have sprouted, if she'd had any. Kostya once tried to tell her this, as a compliment, but she didn't understand until he was brave enough to put his hand on her wing stubs. *Feel that? That's where they'd grow.* It was a wonder to him that Oksana deigned to look at him. He had red hair; his face, neck and shoulders were strewn with freckles, and although he'd inherited his dad's gangly build, he was already getting a belly—so determined had his mother been to stamp out his father's legacy. He had a slight stutter, though less and less; it was only when he looked into Oksana's face that he had to stop talking for a moment and wait for the consonants to sort themselves out. But there was one thing he wasn't, and that was shy.

He walked straight up to her in the rhombus-shaped yard between the tower blocks where she was sitting with a few girlfriends, drawing in the dirt with her finger.

'Privet,' he said. 'Kak dela?'

Hi, how are you? And they all stared—Oksana least of all, but that was before western television, let alone the internet, had taught young people how to approach and reject one another, how to take the piss and then show an interest—the whole gamut of tricks for making a good impression and not selling yourself short. Long before any of that, Kostya walked up to Oksana and said: 'Hi, how are you?' and when eventually she looked at him, she knew that even the flicker of attention he gave her in that moment was precious and not to be scorned. So she smiled and from then on they were a couple—to the outrage of Kostya's parents, who saw those Adidas tracksuits disappearing before their very eyes, sold at Chertanovskaya metro station for a ticket to Leningrad at a fraction of their value.

But it wasn't only Kostya's parents; Oksana's parents, too, considered the relationship a total mistake, an absolute disaster. That yid must not be allowed to have their girl, most beautiful and best of daughters, the jewel here on this pile of shit, here on this edge-of-town estate—*I mean, just look how stunning she is, skin like on TV.* With that skin and hair of hers, she could work her way to the centre of town. With her perfect profile, she had chances of a good match. She might end up in a city-centre apartment; she might marry a man who'd take her on business trips with him—but she didn't want to get involved with a red-headed village yid and his meshchanin parents (a good Russian word that translates as something like 'filthy petty bourgeois with bad breath'). In short, both sets of parents were against the match, and since the children were still living at home—that was free human life under socialism; it was not uncommon to live at home until well into your thirties—since they were still at home, it was their parents who got to decide what constituted free. If Oksana were to get pregnant, she'd just have to have an abortion—that tried and tested contraceptive. But before it could come to that, Kostya's parents called the relatives in Volgograd—or perhaps the relatives called them—either way, providence intervened: here were two families—distantly related, Jewish, as they put it, *through and through*, and desperate to see their children out of harm's way. So it was that Valya came to Moscow.

When Kostya met Valya, he knew he'd end up proposing. In spite of his expectations—or hopes—of never managing to like the girl from the distant town on the Volga, as long as he had this warm Oksanary feeling in his belly, he did notice that she was extraordinarily pretty in a way quite unlike Oksana, and, what's more, that she looked familiar, she looked like someone he'd seen before. It was this sense of familiarity that gripped him, more even than her big earth-coloured eyes, as round as her curls. Does such a sense of familiarity strike out of the blue, or is it something you feel because your parents spent the first twenty years of your life telling you you're best sticking to your own kind if you want to be let alone—*been through quite enough as it is; time we were left in peace.* Who knows. The fact is that something about Valya made her look like someone in Kostya's family. Not his mother or father, and not Uncle Vasya either, who wasn't actually related—it's even possible that the person this frizzy-haired girl resembled was known to Kostya only from photographs. But what can you do about feelings? If they're there, they're there. Kostya and Valya started going out and on the fourth night they slept together.

Jumping into bed with someone was nothing unusual. Despite

the lack of rooms for performing the act, there were frequent opportunities: a friend would be flat-sitting for people who were barbecuing at their dacha, or one or other set of parents would be away—and for the truly tough (which excluded Valya and Kostya) there were always park benches at night. The first time Valya and Kostya slept together was at Misha's place. Misha was Kostya's cousin, had a beard like Trotsky even back then, and spent every spare moment drawing caricatures because he wanted to become a famous Russian cartoonist—an ambition he would eventually fulfil, with broadcasts on state television and seven children by enthusiastic female fans who all came and demanded alimony. He would, despite his considerable success, eventually have to abandon his dream in order to provide for his numerous progeny by taking a sensible job like all sensible people—but that wasn't until later; at this point he was still in the process of becoming a cartoonist, and lent Kostya and Valya his flat so that they could conceive twins.

The second wedding was less spectacular than Valya's first, but the preparations were more exciting, for the simple reason that there *were* preparations. Kostya's parents took Valya to Beriozka, the department store, to let her choose a dress—a risky undertaking, because everyone knew that you couldn't simply buy things in the Univermag Beriozka; you had to pay in vouchers that stood for money that didn't exist in the Soviet Union. Being caught with green banknotes in Russia meant jail, but Valya's in-laws didn't have actual dollars; they had little slips of paper to represent them.

Kostya's mother dragged Valya behind her, up and down the rows of gorgeous dresses, Valya's heart beating so loud, she hardly heard Kostya's father comment on the cloth and guess the prices as they passed. She was bundled into a changing room where she stripped to her underwear and looked in the mirror. She'd put on weight around the hips, and her thighs seemed to be growing softer. Her waist was still flat and high, but the twins were pressing themselves out of her flat belly, her breasts swelled upwards and she already had backache. Her hair curled from the roots and the curls bobbed up and down like a doll's hair when she raised or lowered her head. She looked at her swollen feet; thick veins were bulging out of her reddened skin. She'd have to wear flat shoes.

She started when her mother-in-law burst into the changing room as if they were in a great rush, and began to pull a dress on over Valya's head, two more hanging ready on her arm. She didn't wait for Valya's opinion, but pulled off and put on, tugged at fastenings, popped press-studs, held up hems, grabbed Valya's bum, turned her neck this way and that, examined her breasts, apparently never satisfied. Valya was too nervous to hear what she was muttering—and would, in any case, have been happy to accept anything. So Kostya's mother decided on a dress, while Valya stood there with her arms sticking out, a smile fixed on her face from the adrenaline coursing through her body. When she peeped out of the changing room and saw her father-in-law putting vouchers on the counter with a meaningful look at the cashier—and when she saw the cashier nod slowly in response and pile the white mountain of cloth into a big bag, rather than call the militiamen, Valya had to bite her lower lip to stop herself from screaming.

This shopping trip remained one of the most exciting moments of Valya's life, certainly more exciting than the wedding itself, where she couldn't drink and was, in spite of her flat shoes, afraid to dance with that life—those two lives—in her belly. Before the wedding she'd had to spend a couple of months in hospital because her body had threatened to reject the babies—two long months munching sweets from the girl in the next bed, another medicine student, only this one was brought daily supplies by her parents. Valya's parents were in Volgograd and had a lot of work on—that's what they told her over the phone. Etinka dropped in twice; she brought flowers and sat on the edge of the bed and told Valya about the dead children in the tuberculosis clinic that she ran. For the first time, Valya noticed how old her grandmother was.

When she was let out of hospital, she was warned not to move too much or overexert herself; there was still a risk of premature birth. And so Valya spent her wedding sitting quietly at table, watching her husband kick his legs out in front of him, the sleeves of his blue shirt rolled up to his elbows, the sweat pouring off him.

And as he hadn't spoken to her since saying yes in the registry office, and no one else was paying her any attention either, because they were all too busy partying, she spoke to herself, recalling all the nice things Kostya had repeated to her:

'You're the most beautiful thing I've ever seen.'

'I'll lip-read your every desire.'

'When I close my eyes, I see you lying in a big bathtub surrounded by precious stones and silk and gold watches, and I'm going to get you everything, absolutely everything you want.'

So Valya moved into Kostya's khrushchevka, one of those master-pieces of Soviet architecture, those tower blocks named after Nikita Sergeyevich Khruschchev, the man who'd taken off his black leather shoe in the crammed United Nations General Assembly Hall and whacked the rubber sole against the mahogany table top, crying: 'My vam pokazhem kuz'kinu mat'!'

The UN interpreters had no idea what the man was on about and translated the words literally: Nikita Sergeyevich was going to show them Kuzkin's mother. It doesn't bear thinking about what would have happened back then in 1960, if the translators had relayed the true message of the Soviet leader to the United Nations over their microphones: 'We're going to clobber the lot of you!' It was the speaker of these great words who'd given his name to the block where Kostya had grown up, the block his children would be born into. Their flat had two rooms: Kostya's parents had kept the living room; the newly-weds were given the bedroom. Kostya's mother inspected Valya and decided she had promising hips. She thought it all right that her daughter-in-law was studying medicine. Doctors didn't earn anything, of course, but it was good to have one in the house—though that didn't mean she should think herself better than the rest of them, or leave her books all over the kitchen table.

Books were about all that Valya had brought to Moscow. Kostya's family had harboured vague hopes that, coming from an educated family, all of them doctors, she'd arrive laden with fine and service-able things: good cloth, perhaps, a gold watch, family jewellery—and that at the very least she'd wear something more sensible than all this hippie stuff. But the bride turned up in flared jeans and a leather jacket, bringing almost nothing but books. This was highly suspicious, so while Valya was out at university, Kostya's mother went through those books, shaking them to see if she hadn't hidden any claret-coloured banknotes—or any other colour of banknotes—between the pages or in the dust covers. She found nothing, but Valya remained suspicious to her in-laws.

'Where have you been?'

'At university.'

'Do you know what time it is?'

'We had a chemistry study group.'

'Don't treat me like an idiot.'

'I'm going to bed.'

'You've been to the theatre, I can smell it.'

'You can't smell the theatre.'

'Ah, so you have!'

Valya's body swelled, demanding double quantities of everything: buck-wheat, butter, white bread with sugar, chocolate—lots of chocolate and biscuits, and luckily her mother-in-law didn't scrimp on the cream in her gateaux. But there was no fruit on the market and Valya's parents didn't think it healthy for her to eat nothing but wheat and yeast products.

'Then send me something. Father-in-law refuses to shop on the black market. He says the fruit there comes straight from the morgue—that they store it alongside the corpses.'

Her parents promised to send her something, but when Valya asked when they'd come and see her, they were hazy. Soon—they couldn't say exactly.

A week later, Valya went to Paveletsky Station and waited on the platform for the blue train from Volgograd to arrive. It had been travelling across the steppe for days and Valya envied it. She watched the clouds of smoke rise to the top of the high station dome and felt a sudden yearning to read Conan Doyle and the other books of her childhood. It all seemed so far away now and she had nothing with her but a newspaper, and couldn't read that because she needed it to sit on and stop her bum from freezing on the cold bench. She stared into the big eyes of the engine, then at the legs leaping out of the carriages—everything blue and beige. No one stopped for a second; everyone was running somewhere. Elena Vladimirovna, the guard on the Volgograd–Moscow line and an old and valued family acquaintance, got out and came towards Valya, pulling a familiar-looking cardboard box behind her on a length of sturdy red tape.

'Your parents are crazy. I think there are watermelons in here.'

'Thank you. How are your children?'

'Ach, they'd like to see me in my grave.' Elena Vladimirovna lit a cigarette, offering one to Valya, who shook her head.

'How many months pregnant are you?'

'Seven.'

'And how were you thinking of schlepping the watermelons home?'

'I'll ask someone.'

'Daughter, daughter, take care of yourself.'

Valya took hold of the red tape and pulled the parcel along behind her like a dead dog. When she reached the metro station, she rang Kostya and asked him to come and pick her up. Kostya's speech was slurred, but he came.

It was months before Valya found out that Kostya drank. He didn't drink like a Russian Orthodox, nor did he drink like a yid; he was more like a little boy who's been told he can't join in a game until he's licked every last drop of mucky water out of a puddle. He hated it and couldn't stand the taste, but he knew he had no choice, so he drank clumsily and nervously, his puny body struggling to cope with the alcohol in his veins, always staggering between two extremes: sleep and rage.

At first he directed all his rage at his father. He had ample reason; it was already quite enough that he lived under the same roof as this man who ran a knife over the plastic tablecloth, tracing the red and blue flowers with the blade and sending spittle flying through his stubble as he hissed: 'You'll do as I say.' This father, this small, clumsy village creature who could barely set one foot in front of the other and had spent half his life being the butt of anyone stronger than him, had only just managed to walk tall, and already his son had outgrown him and got what few hugs his wife distributed—and goodness knows, she wasn't generous with them—leaving him compelled to exert his authority with cutlery from the kitchen drawer. He thought it was entirely thanks to him that the family survived—nothing to do with his wife who worked in a factory, did the cooking, kept house and then got into bed with him every night to make him feel like a man. And seeing as how his only son Konstantin didn't understand the first thing about life—he still wanted to be a musician, got thrown out a few weeks into every apprenticeship after flying into a rage or falling asleep, and had to be bought out of the military after God knows what happened to him because he couldn't look after himself—*look at him, he's only half a man, he let them skewer him with a broom handle*—he had a lot to teach the boy, and the way his father saw it, the only way to get Kostya to listen was with a knife in his hand.

Konstantin wasn't afraid of the blade in his father's hand; he thought it almost funny. It would have been easy to knock it out of his bony hand, if the worst came to the worst, which it never did—or only once, when they were talking about leaving for good, emigratsia, emigration. What did frighten Kostya was what his father was doing to his mother. He didn't know exactly what it was, but he saw the deepening lines on her face, the drooping corners of her mouth etched into her skin, the red threads in her bulging eyes, and he preferred not to give the matter too much thought. His mother had once been a beautiful woman, he was sure of that, but you wouldn't have known it to look at her furrowed skin and the tattered housecoat she was forever mending. She had at least ten new dresses hanging in the wardrobe, still in their wrappings, but why touch them as long as she could use this one? Kostya was at home a lot because he was always losing his work, so he saw all this—and had plenty of time to give himself over to his emotions.

Valya came home to find Adidas tracksuits in rustling plastic wrappers flying through the air and crashing into the rug on the wall. Valya came home to find Kostya hanging halfway out of the window, stripped to the waist, thrusting his curly red chest hair towards Chertanavo, and yelling that life had a meaning: 'Yes! It does, it does, it does!' Valya came home to find Kostya lying huddled in front of the sofa, giggling like a child and going on about how much he'd missed her and how she must never leave him. Valya came home to find Kostya saying the whole world was burning—by which he meant he had heartburn. He reeked so strongly of homemade schnapps that she couldn't bear to sit next to him; just the smell was enough to leave you with a headache for days.

It was in this atmosphere that the twins grew under Valya's heart, and Valya guessed that it wouldn't be long before she too—and not just the state of the world—would be blamed for Konstantin's heartburn.

The first person to hit her, though, was her mother-in-law. Valya got back from university later than usual. She was in a good mood; a fellow student had spent hours discussing Solzhenitsyn with her, then told her, looking deep into her eyes, that her belly suited her very well indeed. She threw back her hair that now came all the way to her shoulders, and put her head round the kitchen door with a smile. Her mother-in-law, who was stirring something on the stove, looked her up and down, threw the ladle in the sink, walked up to her and slapped her round the face. Valya let out a short, dull sound. She felt no pain, though her mother-in-law was very strong. She felt nothing at all.

She stared into the wan face of this woman who had once, for nine months, carried in her belly what was now Valya's husband, and presumably suffered a whole string of miscarriages and abortions and rapes before and afterwards—did you even call it 'rape' in those days? It was a face like a hollow wall, behind which, deep down below the plaster and fungus and mould, someone was said to have lived once. Valya looked and looked, trying to find some sign of life. Tears welled in her eyes. She rubbed her cheek and asked: 'Why?'

'Because you're a whore, always whoring around with other whores. You can see that a mile off. You reek of expensive perfume. Where did you get the money? Where do you hide it, you little slut? Where have you been? Do you think I don't have eyes in my head? Do you think I don't know what you're up to? God curse the day I gave my only son to you, you whore. Do you think you're better than the rest of us just because you study? Do you think you're better than the rest of us just because your cretin of a mother is a doctor, along with all the other bastards in your clan? Do you think you can destroy my only son? Look at him. Look at the state he's in. Look where you've driven him—'

It is idle to speculate whether this outburst from Kostya's adoring mother was triggered by the loss of yet another apprenticeship that day, or because tension inevitably mounts when girls like Valya—their jeans flared, their curls all over the place, their bags full of books rather than silkworms—come and live with people who not long ago were being chased around the village like animals for half a loaf of bread. It was the first blow Valya had been dealt since her divorce from Ivan, and it was quite different, maybe because it came from a woman—and a mother at that. Valya didn't say a thing, she didn't cry. She went in the bedroom, sat down at her desk under the window and unpacked her books.

Kostya didn't want to hit his wife. He didn't want to hit anyone. He was a peaceable man who only wanted to make music. With money that he'd saved and begged, he bought himself a small piano for the room where he and Valya slept. His parents were horrified, but though they berated him, they were powerless to stop the piano from coming up the stairs, carried by three of Kostya's friends. His mother even poured the boys a few shots and had one herself, which was unusual for her. She laid a heavy hand on one of the friend's shoulders.

'Tell me, what am I to do with my boy?'

'What can you do? It's too late to do anything.'

'But you'll keep an eye on him, eh?'

'Yes, of course.'

'If I sold the piano, would you come and take it away?'

Kostya enrolled at music school and really did seem to possess talent, even if he didn't learn any Schumann or Schubert or Rameau. He played only what he wanted to play, which was Russian pop music, cabaret songs and hits—music everyone could join in and have a laugh over. That's what he liked. He liked it when his friends met up and were happy together. He liked entertaining them. He loved their exuberance, the sound and cadence of their voices, their different intervals and keys. Secretly, he also loved Schumann, but he knew he'd never be able to play him well enough to whip up any enthusiasm in his friends, so he didn't even bother trying. Whenever he experimented with the foreign Romantics, his nostrils flared, his eyes grew moist, he sweated heavily, even by his standards—it wasn't worth the effort. He did, it's true, have a feeling that this mysterious world of music had the power to carry him off to spheres where he might see the universe or God—preferably the universe and the stars and a meteorite trail or two—but all those things remained shut off to him, because he didn't dare take risks, awed by the world of classical music, where there was no room, he thought, for people like him.

He didn't know why he hit Valya the first time. He didn't hit her directly—hadn't intended to, anyway. The blow wasn't meant for her; she'd got in the way—got between him and his father. She'd come in the kitchen to ask for a bit of peace, a bit of quiet, or maybe just to fetch a slice of watermelon from her parents' parcel, when Kostya raised his arm and hit her for the first time. Something hard bounced off his hand and when he saw that it was Valya's head, and not his father's bald pate, he hit again, because he felt a sudden tingling in his throat muscles; hitting Valya seemed to give him greater satisfaction than attacking his father. Valya fell to the floor and he kicked her and she didn't scream.

With bruises on her face and hands and ribcage, she couldn't go to university. Valya spent a week in bed, taking deep breaths and thinking. Pedagogy, histology and clinical embryology would be tough exams, but she'd manage. Marxism-Leninism and party history were rather trickier.

And the modern language—what modern language?—the course where they pretended to be taught English, the hour a week when they pretended that the Iron Curtain had opened a chink, but in fact only sketched a door on it in chalk and ran into it—Valya wasn't sure she'd pass the English exam. She felt her gorge rise and her eyes mist over.

Then she went back to thinking. Chemistry, no problem. Anatomy, Latin, psychology, no problem.

I see her lying on the chequered quilt in jeans and a roll-neck jumper and socks darned at the toes, her hands on her domed belly. Behind her head, the big brown wardrobe forms a kind of wall; then comes the piano with the window above it, the drawn curtains resting on the closed lid. To the right of the piano is the desk with a stack of Valya's medical tomes and two faded turquoise exercise books, and next to that is the bed again, where Valya lies, breathing shallowly and staring at the ceiling, eight feet above her and clamped shut like the lid of a preserving jar. Perhaps I felt her shallow breathing back then, but there's no way of knowing now. I string my perhapses together, one by one, rough glass beads—not enough to make a presentable necklace. Apart from Valya's exam plans, nothing of what she thought or smelt or felt in those moments will ever penetrate to me.

I too am lying somewhere on that bed, but I can't see myself; I have no memories. I have an umbilical cord leading to nothingness, and beside me, in the same nothingness, another living being touches me, gentle as a balloon. I hear scraps of what Valya says and combine her words with images from sources I can't vouch for. Scenes from a film I fell asleep over late one night mingle with snatches of a song in my mother tongue that seemed to contain the essence of a life I once knew. But I can't tell them apart; everything eludes me. I know I was told all this—but it was somehow different.

THE BEGINNING

Anton had written a postcard. Well, 'written' was going a bit far. A postcard had come to the house, a black-and-white photograph of a narrow street lined with dilapidated buildings that leant crookedly against one another—and printed on the photo in red and white letters, the word: *Istanbul*.

His way of saying he's all right, thought Valya.

She was holding the card balanced on one corner when Ali came into the kitchen, steadying it with her index finger and flicking it back and forth with her thumb, her eyes fixed on the tiered cake stand. She'd heard her daughter come in. Ali had kept a key when she moved out nine years ago and made use of it every six months or so; this was the first time she'd dropped in since Anton had disappeared. The key jammed slightly and only the initiated knew that you had to lift the door and push against the frame to get the lock to budge. Ali shoved open the door, muttering something that Valya didn't catch, but was pretty sure wasn't a greeting. Valya heard the sound of shoes on the hall lino, and the smack of rubber as Ali kicked off her trainers. She crept into the flat and had soon disappeared, turning off into a room and leaving the place silent again.

Roditel'skii dom nachalo nachal, ty v zhizni moei nadezhnyi prichal, crooned the black-and-white image of Leshchenko in Ali's head. *You're a safe haven to me, my parents' house, beginning of all beginnings.* The legendary Russian musician sang with bloated face and twisted mouth, his eyebrows leaping into his forehead, his arms waving about, urging the audience to join in. And join in they did; the entire Soviet Union sang along. It was a mystery, though, what he was doing in Ali's head.

She'd forced herself to tread firmly before entering the flat where she'd kind of grown up, or at least spent an important part of her childhood. She remembered the corner where she'd been made to stand in disgrace after biting Anton's thigh—there on the left when you came into the living room. She used to hide her toy car in here so her brother wouldn't find it, and over there by the window, the plastic fir tree they had at New Year, not at Christmas, had wobbled when the pair of them pulled at it.

Ali's eyes were drawn to the spot on the floor where she and Anton had singed the carpet trying to fetch the big red star down from the top of the plastic fir. They'd buried each other in tinsel, pulling it off the tree like spiders' webs, pouring it over each other's heads, crushing the coloured foil between their fingers, nibbling at it with their teeth. The burnt place was now covered by a new leather sofa. Ali pushed it aside and squatted down to examine the tiny brown hairs around the hole. Then she remembered the burn hole in her parents' flat in Moscow and wondered if it looked the same as this one. It had been the same game they'd played—the same chewing around on the tinsel, the same attempt to topple the red star, the same drunk father who'd wept and then taken himself off to bed.

The pale brown of the new sofa made her eyes itch. The chipboard TV table was still there, the imitation oak scuffed now from all the dusting and the constant shunting back and forth of the TV magazines. No one read books here anymore.

The finely woven cotton curtains were also new, and too long; they trailed on the floor, stirring slightly when you passed. Ali reached out a hand and rubbed a corner of the cloth between finger and thumb. The wallpaper was polystyrene white with an embossed pattern of roses. Anton had traced over the roses behind the door, and Ali had told on him. The glass-fronted cabinets were filled with the busts of strangers and unframed photos leaning against cheap cut-glass vases—photos of Shura, Etya, Danya, Emma, Valya and Valya again, photographs of the children. All the photos of Ali showed her with hair down to her waist; nothing here told you she'd had her head circumcised. Beside her, Anton smiled broadly, *his* hair combed in a way that was unfamiliar to Ali, but then she'd never been able to resist mussing it up. She'd wanted hair like that too, but cutting hers was out of the question; hair was *a woman's honour—and you wouldn't throw your honour on the rubbish heap, would you?*

'What if I'm not a woman?'

'What are you then, an elephant?'

Everyone laughed, especially the visiting aunts with their spoonfuls of jam and their glasses of black tea and lemon. They shook their heads; one day the little thing would understand—*it's her age...head stuffed full of nonsense...not good for her to play out on the street... running around with the boys all the time...refusing to wear a bra.*

Ali stood in the doorway, leaning against the improvised growth chart that was marked on the wall in blue biro. The habit of measuring the children at the living-room door was one they'd brought with them from Moscow: the year alongside the height and then ever upwards, always measuring, always remarking on how time flies—*one metre twenty, one metre forty-seven, one metre sixty—goodness me, slow down a bit, won't you!* But Ali and Anton were less interested in the passing of time and their own growth than in the pretty pattern these made on the doorframe. They tried to join up the lines; Anton in particular was always trying to extend them into loops and curves, and getting cuffed on the head for it. 'How often do I have to tell you not to draw on the walls?' Kostya would shout, tearing the pen out of his hand.

'Why can't I draw? You do!'

The growth chart Ali was leaning against began at *1996—141 cm*. Running her fingernail over the lines Anton had drawn, connecting her height and his into constellations, she glanced over at her mother in the kitchen. There was nothing new here and Ali shrank once again to the child at the growth chart and smelt the old smell of naphthalene clinging to her hair. It seemed to linger no matter how short she cut it, as if her scalp began to exude the stuff as soon as she entered the flat. A trickle ran down her face; nothing had changed. All right, so her hair was gone, but nobody here noticed. To her mother, this woman sitting at the window staring at a biscuit on the cake stand in front of her, she was a transfer picture of a memory with long hair and a different smell—maybe her glands produced naphthalene so that her mother recognised her.

Maybe I'll get a face job, Ali thought. I'll have my nose enlarged and see if she notices. Valya didn't move. She was looking neither at her daughter nor at the biscuits, but at the cake stand itself, gold-edged black china painted with red cherries. She wondered why she hadn't chucked the tawdry thing ages ago. How long had it been there? Maybe fifteen years—definitely ten. It was old, that was for sure. So was the tablecloth. I should chuck the lot, she thought.

The skin on her cheeks was taut with dryness; she'd forgotten to moisturise after her shower. She'd stood under the water crying for a long time, then she'd dried herself and come and sat at the kitchen table—and here she was now, wondering, as she waited for Ali, whether she shouldn't do something about her face, inject a bit of poison into her cheeks, have the corners of her eyes lifted, or just some permanent make-up to be going on with. Then she felt panic—what if the doctors made a mistake? What if she ended up looking so different that her own daughter no longer recognised her?

When Ali had cut her curls off, Valya had felt every snip as if someone had been chopping away at *her*. She'd wanted to gather up the hair and keep it for better times when Alissa would finally change her mind and stop running about like a boy—even more of a boy than Anton. Is that what it was about—being more of a boy than her brother? What was she trying to prove? If she was a dyke, she could be one with long hair, couldn't she? There were no rules against looking nice.

'They the biscuits I brought you last time?' Ali asked. The question tumbled out of her and came to rest on the lino.

Valya smiled. She wanted to reach out her hand to Ali and ask her to sit down and talk about herself; instead, she pressed her fingers into the postcard on the table.

'Yes, it's possible, I don't know.'

Alissa edged along the wall, cupboard by cupboard, looking at the crooked hands on the clock that had stopped years ago, counting her steps. When she'd made it to the benchtop, she clutched the kettle in both hands and flicked up the switch. Splashes of red and brown had dried on the kettle's white plastic belly: red splashes of pomegranate juice (there were still a few squashed seeds on the marble surface);

brown splashes of tea. The hiss of water coming to the boil was a damp jet in front of Ali's face; she inhaled deeply and began to press the air slowly through her closed mouth, making her lips vibrate, bubbling along with the kettle, trying to keep pace. Then she opened the cupboard above the sink and took out a mug. It was navy blue with a cartoonlike sketch of a map of the Black Sea.

'Look, Crimea's on here.' Ali turned to her mother, holding the mug in the air.

'Course it is. Where else would it be?'

Ali turned back round again and pulled open the drawer where the tea was kept. There was a strong whiff of bergamot.

'Uncle Misha painted that; it's old,' Valya said to Ali's back.

'Who was Uncle Misha again?' Ali rummaged in the drawer, feeling her mother's gaze on her body. She was wearing a men's grey jumper over a baggy white shirt, both tucked into men's black trousers. Her body vanished beneath the layers. Ali saw Valya close her eyes and then open them. She poured water over the teabag and sat down opposite her. Valya folded her hands and pursed her lips slightly.

'Shall we go and get you some new clothes?'

Ali pulled down the sleeves of her jumper, burying her fingers in the wool. She clasped the handle of the mug. 'Do I know Uncle Misha?'

'He drew all the children's cartoons you used to watch. Why do you dress like that?'

'Can I have this mug?'

Valya stared long into her face.

'You can have anything. Take what you like.'

Ali pondered what she'd take from this flat—her grandmother's earrings that she'd never wear? The photos that would lie yellowing in removal boxes just like at her mother's if she took them home? All the toys had been sold or given away years ago; the pictures on the walls were poor-quality reproductions. Maybe her father's shirts, but she couldn't suggest that to Valya. She looked through the open door into the hall and her eyes fell on the door frame with the growth chart. That was what she wanted—to carry the door jamb with the growth chart out of here on her shoulder and lean it against the wall in her own flat. Ali opened her mouth and said:

'It's dark there now.'

'Where?'

'In Crimea. Pitch dark. They've cut the power lines. The trolley buses aren't running. Wonder what they're doing there now, in the dark.'

Ali glanced across the table; the other side seemed miles away.

'You can have the mug.'

Ali pushed her fingers into her curls and looked out of the window onto the street of this dried-up West German town where the neighbours knew whether or not you watered the flowers in your front garden and who'd stabbed next-door's cat. She'd learnt to ride a bike on this street. Her father had given her a push and shouted after her to look straight ahead and not back at him. She fell off a lot and was always grazing her knees, while Anton rode around her in circles, laughing.

'You do know, if the idea behind your clothes is to stop people looking at you, they have the opposite effect.'

Ali stared out of the window.

'You look like a scarecrow. Did you get the things from the Red Cross?'

'Yes, Mum.'

'Can you explain it to me?'

'I'm not in the mood for this discussion.'

'I'm sorry. What would you like to talk about?'

About the gravel path down there—my knees still remember.

About mugs painted by people I don't know, but who mean something to you. About the way you're waiting for me to fling my arms round your neck as a faint compensation for everything you couldn't have in life because you had me instead. About our need for intimacy and what we should do with it. About teeth discoloured by cigarettes and black tea. About why you still haven't moved out of this museum here—do you need this fug? Why not just burn everything, rather than buy new furniture to cover up old burn holes? Why not give away your clothes—donate them to the Red Cross for all I care—move to another town, move in with me, no, not in with me, please, but not too far away either, come and look for your son with me—but don't let's talk about it; let's just pretend we're going on holiday together. About this sense of lack I can't stop feeling. And nor can you, it flashed into Ali's mind. She said nothing.

She saw Valya bite her lower lip and breathe out through her nose.

It wasn't all the same old stuff here in this flat that Ali had run away from at the age of sixteen—first run away and then come back to pick up her things—and Valentina wasn't the same either, or perhaps she was gradually reverting to some old self Ali knew nothing of. Ali had no idea that the boys on the Arbat had once twisted their necks to look at her mother; she couldn't imagine them begging to be allowed to paint her. Ali had once found oil portraits of Valya in a cardboard box, but she hadn't made the connection with the swollen face that nagged her to school every day and wasn't there when she got home. She hadn't stopped to wonder who the young woman was with the broad cheekbones, the boyish smile, the pointy chin, the piercing eyes. For Ali, these pictures of her mother were as fictional as postcards at a kiosk. The face she knew was like a ball of cottonwool that had soaked up the lousy food of asylum-home canteens, the musty smell of dorms, the lack of sleep and decent cosmetics. It had shrivelled up on her short neck and looked as if it were digesting itself. Since her divorce from Konstantin, though, there was movement in the ball of cottonwool; the cheekbones were visible again, the eyes were once more deeper in their sockets; Valentina was a step closer to the beautiful young woman who had strolled along the Arbat, that small pedestrian precinct that Europeans talked about as if it were a big cosmopolitan street, though in fact it was narrow and lined with buskers and street artists and women selling woollen scarves. Her mother had liked the Arbat; she'd bought books there and got herself in trouble with her in-laws for wasting money, because if she had time to read books, she could just as well do the dusting instead—and Valentina had to lock herself in the loo to read. Now everything was possible—everything; she could read and go for walks and do whatever she liked. It was too much. All that Valentina had once been was squeezing itself slowly back into her face, through the moles and broken veins on her cheeks—but how was Ali to know all that? She'd never even been to the Arbat.

'Anton's written.'

Valentina held out the postcard her hands had been resting on. Ali grabbed it with as much control as she could muster.

'When did it come?'

'Yesterday.'

No writing. No greeting. The address was written in a nine-year-old's scrawl. Not so much as an *I'm well. Anton* or a *Hope you all rot in hell. I don't give a fuck how you are.*

Ali looked up from the blank card into her mother's face.

'Maybe he's touring the world.' Ali clicked her tongue.

Valentina nodded. She looked as if she hadn't slept; the bags under her eyes were stained blue. She might even have been crying, but that was hard for Ali to imagine. She'd never seen her mother cry.

An image flashed into Ali's head of Valya's face the day she'd rung round the relatives in Moscow to ask whether Anton had turned up at theirs. That was after the police had been called in and said that if he'd had the time and leisure to pack his bags properly, things couldn't be so bad; he'd turn up somewhere, sometime—though he hadn't. Ali couldn't hear what the relatives were saying; she couldn't even hear what Valya was saying, only saw her face, switched to mute, and realised that of all the situations her mother had ever been in, this was the most humiliating. Ali stopped hearing altogether that day. At first she'd only felt pressure in her left ear, then it had spread, opening out like a flower behind her forehead and bursting. The doctors diagnosed acute hearing loss; they couldn't say how long it would last. Ali wasn't afraid it would stay; she was afraid it might one day go away. That happened three weeks later.

'Tell me, when did you last eat?' asked Ali, laying the postcard aside.

Valya nodded.

'Have you eaten?'

'Drink your tea, it'll go cold.'

Ali got up and went to the breadbin that was hand-carved by her grandfather and said khleb on the lid in curly writing. *Bread.* Even that had come to Germany as a souvenir of the dacha on the Volga, though it was empty now, just a surface to put things on. Ali went to the fridge and rummaged for white bread. Everything edible in the flat was kept in the fridge: butter, tomatoes, gherkins, plums, an empty Emmental packet that she chucked out, a net of Gala apples, an open pot of cottage cheese, a tin of sprats, a dead-looking lettuce— that, too, she dispatched to the bin—a pear, jam, honey, even a loaf of Borodinsky, the black bread with coriander seeds on top.

The white bread was at the back, frozen fast; Ali had to prise it off. She cut two doorsteps, sliced butter as thick as her finger, laid it on the bread without spreading it, found the sugar basin where it always was, and strewed the butter with sugar until you could hardly see the bread on the small plate beneath the white crystals. She put the plate down in front of Valya.

'Eat.'

Valentina nodded, looked up from the plate, nodded again and smiled.

'You must eat. I can tell you haven't eaten for days.'

Valya smiled again, a proper smile this time.

'It's bad for your head.' Ali sat down opposite Valya again. 'Low blood sugar.'

'So now you're trying to kill me with a sugar shock?'

Ali watched her mother reluctantly move her hand towards the plate. Valentina looked out of the window, then at Ali, then at the glinting sugar crystals. Her eyes grew more alert. She reached for the bread with her right hand and her teacup with her left hand. For a moment she froze, arms outstretched, and Ali clearly saw Anton's face smile in Valya's.

Anton had taught Ali to read. Not that he could read when he was three, but he'd explained the letters to her as if he'd invented them himself. He ran his finger over the pile of the red-and-green Turkish carpet in the living room and made sounds, and Ali repeated them, staring at his lips, watching them forming objects—an apple, a crescent moon hanging points down, a wide-open window sticking out its tongue. She grabbed his face as he traced the imaginary letters on the carpet; she ran her fingers over his lips and crawled her fingertips into his mouth. Like sticking your fingers in blancmange, she thought. Anton drew alphabet patterns on her legs. Like drawing on blancmange, he thought. Gran came and pulled them apart, scolding loudly about something the three-year-olds didn't understand.

The twins slept on the fold-out sofa; their grandmother often sat beside them, stroking Anton's head, and Ali would lie there, her eyes half-closed, watching the sinewy hand with the veins sticking out of the skin like bones. She too would thrust her hand into Anton's hair and rub it between her fingers, until Gran's big grey hand knocked her little one away and hissed: 'Go to sleep now!' But eventually the hand disappeared along with the hiss, and Ali sank eight of her ten fingers into Anton's curls and fell asleep with the feeling of fine wool tickling her palms.

Because they had hardly any toys, they played with one another, moving each other's arms at the shoulders and elbows, turning each other's heads like balls, grabbing hold of each other's ribs, comparing each other's movements, freezing and mirroring one another. It wasn't that nobody bought them toys, but the toys they were given always went straight to the top of their grandparents' wardrobe, whose smooth walnut surface was too slippery to climb. They weren't supposed to play with toys; they were supposed to do homework and then they were supposed to do the extra work that Valya set them—reading books, improving themselves. 'Only stupid children with time to waste play with toys,' said Valya, but they didn't know what their mother meant; they were only five when they started preschool.

Valya was driven by the fear of not having enough time to cram her children with all the knowledge they needed if they were to get out; you had to move so fast—quick, quick, out of here! Read, learn, or you're lost! She was convinced that the only thing really worth instilling in children was a dogged ambition oblivious to health and self-respect, to make sure they didn't end up where she'd ended, in Chertanovo.

She'd say to Anton: 'You must be the best in school, much better than the Russians. If you can be three times as good as them, you might end up half as good, then you can be a good Russian doctor. If not, you'll be a poor put-upon Jew for the rest of your life.' In Germany, she said the same, replacing the Russians with Germans.

Anton didn't understand, so he made nodding movements with his head, because even a child knows that's the thing to do when a mother gets that look of panic in her eyes. He nodded and thought of her breasts, comparing them with the breasts of the woman upstairs, which were even bigger.

Alissa was told: 'You don't want to be the most beautiful; you want to be the cleverest. Beauty does you no good and doesn't last. But if you're the cleverest you can always convince everyone that you're the most beautiful, and you'll get a husband who'll buy you whatever you want, even good looks.'

This made no sense to Ali; she couldn't follow her mother's logic and, unlike Anton, she didn't nod. Valya had little confidence that her children were adaptable enough to get the better of the Soviet Union with its unjust natural laws. They were too quiet for that, too wrapped up in themselves; they cleaved to each other and tumbled over one another, as if there were no outside world. Kostya wasn't much help either, but she was determined not to leave her children's future—or lack of future—to chance. She didn't want her son in the army with the highest suicide rate and her daughter playing whore to some banker. She wanted them to make something of themselves, so she got them out, with an application for settlement, twelve suitcases crammed into a train compartment, and even more boxes. The toys stayed behind on top of the walnut wardrobe, but the children were allowed to pack as many books as they liked.

The Chepanov family's first room in a German asylum home was at the top of a converted hotel, on the sixth floor. At first Grandfather had one of the bunks, then he was moved down to the second floor to share with an elderly man who told himself work-camp stories in his sleep, waking Grandfather who would go and sit on the man's bed and put his hand over his trembling mouth. Valentina and Konstantin attended language classes and did their homework in the communal kitchen, along with twenty-five other emigrant couples, enveloped in the greasy smell of broth. The smell made Ali feel sick. She roamed the corridors, going in other families' rooms, opening ceramic jars filled with jewellery, peeping in bags of terry bed linen, sniffing at the bottles of Red Moscow perfume she sometimes found in the bathrooms, and filching cigarettes whenever she found an open packet lying around. Anton didn't accompany her on these prowls; he was too busy pursuing his own passion for balancing on narrow metal rails.

He'd climb onto the banisters and stand there, bobbing up and down, white-trainered feet at an angle, knees bent. He stretched out his arms like a skateboarder and looked straight ahead, his eyes fixed on the wall opposite as if he were challenging it. The first time his mother saw him on the banister rail, she froze. Suppressing the instinct to cry out in fear and risk startling her child, she crept up to him, wrapped her arms round his tummy and pulled him down. From then on she followed Anton on tiptoe wherever he went, arms extended, fingers like claws, and when she sat in the language class, trying to conjugate verbs, she'd see her son plummeting down the stairwell.

Every week she went to the home manager and asked to be moved to the ground floor or into the basement, next to the kitchen. It might stink of broth, but at least there were no banister rails down there. She explained the situation to the manager—the two small children she couldn't control: one of them was always trying to jump off things, while the other smoked under the covers in their room. She only had one pair of hands and there was the language class to practise for too. She begged him, but the moustached bloke with the grease stains on his collar only said: 'You must learn to take better care of your children, Mamasha; moving into the basement won't change that.'

•

This moustached bloke in a stained shirt cropped up in every asylum home. The family of grandfather, mother, father, child, child was sent from one home to another so often, they didn't know whether they were coming or going. Before each move Daniil would ask the name of the next dump the Germans were sending them to and say that it was a good thing his wife didn't have to go through this, but would soon be able to take the plane and plenty of money and come straight to a well-feathered nest. Valya was sick of packing suitcases. Kostya would go out for a smoke and come back in a good mood, rubbing his hands and saying 'Let's go' like Gagarin.

Ali took her bearings by Anton. When he began to pack, she began to pack; when he began to shout around, she set up a yell too. In every home, Anton played football in the yard with the other kids. Ali thought football boring, but joined in anyway, blasting the half-pumped-up plastic balls into the walls of the home as hard as she could. She filched one for herself and stowed it in her bag for the next home.

'I don't understand football,' Valya would say, shaking her head. 'I don't understand why millions of poor people would want to watch a small group of millionaires running after a ball.' Konstantin waved this aside. 'Because you don't understand anything about life.'

Valya looked at him. 'Yes, you may be right.'

Anton came running up, nestled to his mother's belly, put his head between her breasts. 'Football's great because you don't have to think of anything when you're playing,' he said, looking at his mother's double chin.

'Rubbish,' said Ali, who was sitting cross-legged on the bed, stuffing comics into the bag alongside the plastic ball. 'The whole time I'm playing, I'm thinking about how I can thrash you.'

It was always noisy in the homes—in the rooms, on the corridors. People flung open windows and shouted into the yard; the rattle of crockery in the kitchen echoed up the stairs; the alarm tones of Soviet wristwatches pierced the ceilings. When you argued, everyone knew about it—when you made love, they knew about that too. The walls melted away. You got used to a permanent clatter.

In school, though, it was quiet. Only the sound of the bell cut through the vacuum surrounding Ali and Anton. They understood nothing of what was going on around them. The others were a distant roar; nobody spoke to the twins and the twins didn't want to speak to them. The teachers wrote letters on the board, different from the ones they knew, and ignored Ali and Anton. They played alone, twisting themselves in knots like a pair of tussling cats, rolling over the schoolyard, pulling each other's hair, biting each other's shoulderblades, trying to leave marks on one another—and they shouted at each other, so as not to forget the sound of their own voices. They needed nothing and nobody. The other children were afraid of the twins, afraid of the determination with which they set on one another. They didn't like their clothes either; they pointed at the jeans Valya had bought with vouchers and laughed. 'Where d'you get them? In the dustbin?'

A few weeks after school had started, little groups formed on the yard. The twins weren't in any of these groups and paid no attention to the others—until the stones began to fly. Four or five boys closed in on them, shouting something. Anton went up to them and asked in Russian if they were looking for trouble. They replied in German:

'Russki, Russki, fucky fucky.'

Anton didn't understand the words, but he took note of them. That evening he went to Valya, who was poring over her exercise books like a schoolgirl, and asked why the others teased him for being Russian when she'd taught him to be proud that he was Jewish.

Valya put down her pen and looked at her son—his pink nose, his matted curls. She stroked the curls and said: 'We'll talk about it later.'

'When's later?'

'When you're grown-up.'

Anton got on Valya's lap and looked at her books.

'Can you read that?'

'Yes.'

'I can't.'

'You will.'

'When?'

'Anton, what is it?'

He looked into his mother's eyes. He could feel the blood pounding in his head and pressed himself to her breast.

'Come on, down you get, I've got to do my homework. Don't you have homework to do?'

He climbed down from her lap, clenched his teeth and ambled to the door.

'You mustn't tell anyone here,' Valya called after him. 'That you're Jewish. You mustn't mention it. Please.'

Anton pushed open the door with both hands and ran down the corridor to the stairs. He took them several steps at a time. On the third floor he jumped onto the banister rail and stood there with dangling arms, staring at the wall, thinking.

When more stones flew a few days later, Anton went up to the four or five boys and said: 'Stones okay. But I'm not Russian.'

The boys gawped, craning their necks.

'I'm Jewish.'

He didn't say it quite clearly. He'd tried to memorise the phrases; he'd collected a few words in the home, and Auntie Zoya, of all people, with that big fat cross round her neck, had helped him to put them in some kind of order. But now his tongue failed him, looping the loop in his mouth; he got everything muddled up and the rubberneckers laughed. They looked at each other and laughed, pointed at his clothes, grabbed him by the hair, dragged him across the yard, pushed him into the boys' toilets and played dodge ball with his body. When Ali finally found Anton and he explained why he looked so mangled, her face flushed crimson. She wanted to go straight to the teacher, but Anton gripped her by the arm. 'No way!'

She went anyway, shouted and cried and pointed at her brother. Ali's teacher understood little of her Russian yammering. She shrugged, said words Ali didn't recognise and vanished into the staffroom. Something must have got through to her, though, because when the four or five boys ambushed the twins on the way home, they looked as if they'd been in big trouble.

This time they didn't throw stones, but grabbed the two of them— Anton by the shoulders and Ali by the hips—and dragged them into the bushes where they punched their eyes deeper into their sockets, pulled their tongues and kicked them in the ribs. When they were done, the twins had melted into one body. It happened very quietly. They didn't scream or curse; the boys' fists and feet beat down on soft flesh; you heard only their panting breath as they drove the kicks home. When they ran away, the silence was complete. Ali and Anton lay in the bushes, listening to each other breathe. They lay in each other's arms, looking up at the sky—no clouds, no cracks. Dribble ran out of Ali's mouth onto Anton's forehead; he wiped it away with his shirtsleeve, pushed himself level with her and pressed the tip of his nose against hers. Their eyelashes meshed, their mouths were open, they were breathing into one another. It was only when Anton kissed Ali that she began to cry.

Valya wanted to go to the headmaster to report the attack on her children, but her German wasn't good enough. A woman she knew called Tanya was visiting when it happened. She was already out of the home because she'd entered into a sham marriage with a German who had no idea it was a sham marriage and seemed happy; Tanya was in the middle of telling everyone all about it when the twins appeared in the communal kitchen. Tanya screamed first; she was the first to see the children. Then Valya screamed, and soon the entire kitchen was shrieking as if a siren had gone off. The home was transformed into a coop of startled chickens. People said things like 'Nazis'; they kept saying 'Nazis' and 'They've got it in for our children'. The fathers banged the tables, so did the mothers. Nobody felt equal to talking to the head, but everyone was willing to give it a go. Since Tanya's German had recently come on in leaps and bounds thanks to her happy sham marriage, she was the one who marched out of the home with Valya and Kostya, and raised a ruckus in the primary-school staffroom. A few furious neighbours followed, letting out wails of lament as if it were a shiva.

The four or five boys were found; their parents were called in. Kostya had to be pulled off one of the fathers because he almost strangled him in his wrath, and when the tussle was over, everyone was sent home and nothing happened. Anton and Ali continued to go to school with the rubberneckers, first primary school then secondary school, and nothing changed, except that the group surrounding the rubberneckers grew larger—but then so did the group surrounding Ali and Anton.

In this, their last home, the Chepanov family were to spend a year, surrounded by people with big fat crosses on their chests.

'What are all these Christians doing here?' hissed Kostya.

'Well, you know,' said his neighbour Valera, 'strictly speaking my wife's Christian, but she's sucked so much blood out of me that she must be at least half Jewish by now.'

They'd all come with papers bearing the words *quota refugee*, which meant they'd searched their family trees for Jewish branches, and if they hadn't found any, they'd invented some—the precise number depended on the content of their wallets. People would do anything to leave the beloved Soviet land—they were even prepared to become Jewish.

In this last home, the refugees were given five deutschmarks per head per week for 'personal expenses'. Food was delivered; 'clothes and sundries' were distributed in the form of vouchers. For all additional desires, you had to apply to the immigration office, and Valya sent Kostya along, knowing he wouldn't be able to make himself understood and hoping to shame him into doing his own German homework.

Kostya stood outside the immigration office and smoked a cigarette. He smoked two cigarettes. After he'd had a few, he went in and sat down. The fluorescent lights whined like mosquitoes. He sat there rubbing his eyes for about an hour, then the man next to him tapped him on the shoulder with his index finger and pointed to the machine with numbered tickets assigning you a place in the queue. Kostya turned to the man and they fell to talking. The man spoke Turkish and Kostya Russian; they got on like a house on fire. The man told Kostya that he'd been a regular at the immigration office for seven years and the woman dealing with his case still pronounced his name as if it were a contagious disease. Kostya suggested going outside for a smoke and he never saw the inside of the building again.

Food was topic number one in the home, even hotter than the who's-with-whom stories. A lot of people couldn't eat the stuff delivered to the canteen—this was before it occurred to anyone that the mishpochas that had come to the country giving 'Jewish' as their reason for emigration, ought maybe to be offered kosher food. But the rejection of canteen food had nothing to do with religious beliefs; the truth was that people were scared of the fat pieces of Camembert melting on the table in front of them. They thought they'd been given rancid cheese from the morgue refrigerators, and saw only one way of dealing with such unfamiliar delicacies: everything must be re-fried or re-boiled. That kept them busy half the day. Some said: 'I don't like the food here.' The others replied: 'That's because your wife can't cook.'

Valya spent her first months in Germany at the stove in the communal kitchen, swapping recipes and listening to the women with crosses in their cleavages agreeing with each other that the Jews lived like pigs—anyone could see that—and that the family responsible for distributing the food in the home hogged the best for themselves. Jews—what could you expect? They also agreed that the Germans weren't the problem. True, they didn't understand the first thing about life—*the men can't fuck, the women are useless, useless, useless*—but the real problem was their own people who would do for you if you weren't careful—*your own kind hate you more than the Germans ever could.*

Valya felt as if she were in a postwar communal apartment and knew that wasn't what she'd come to Germany for; it was time to go flat-hunting—flat-hunting with no German, no language, but with her friend Tanya and the shamorous husband she called 'Schatz', stretching the shrill 'a' as if it were a cat having its tail pulled, and then adding under her breath in Russian that he should go to hell.

So Tanya and Valya began to hunt for a flat for the four of them, and perhaps Valya's father too if he could somehow be fitted in. Valya's mother still hadn't joined them; she rang from time to time and told them of the troubles she was having trying to sell the flat, and how lonely it made her to hear her spoon clink against the glass when she stirred her tea in the evenings. She said *her* parents didn't want to pack, but would get down to it in the end; she'd just have to stay a little longer and talk them round—she couldn't leave without them. And of course Valya had to find a flat for her first; she wasn't going in a home, so why should she bother packing when Valya herself was still in a communal apartment?

Tanya tried all the tricks in the book to find a place for the family in the small town, but people waved her away as soon as they heard the surname. Eventually she started to say: 'They're all doctors. With good employment prospects—this lady here's already got work.' And she'd push Valya into the room like a chess piece.

At the seventeenth flat, the undertaker, who owned not only the business on the ground floor, but also the entire brown-brick house, inspected Valya from head to toe and asked her what the hell she was doing in Germany.

'We're Jewish,' said Valya.

'Doesn't matter,' said the undertaker.

So they moved in.

The shift to the attic flat shrank the space in which the family moved, as if someone had pulled tight the drawstring on a sack. There were no longer eavesdroppers on the other side of the walls—or none who could understand what they were saying. There were no clothing vouchers, no warders in greasy shirts, no one to watch them—not even Grandfather had moved in with them—and so they dredged up old resentments and threw themselves into arguing. The built-up tension of the last years flung Konstantin and Valentina from one room to the next, in desperate search of something—deliverance, something promised, dreams they'd kept secret from one another because they knew that dreams only come true if you don't tell them to anyone.

The backdrop of sounds changed. Noise was no longer made up of individual sounds; it was a shockwave travelling through the flat. When the twins were together they didn't hear their parents; they played as if under a soundproof bell jar. When the bell jar failed them, they got into bed, undressed and looked at each other, looked at where Ali was getting breasts and Anton wasn't, and at the slight curve of their bellies. They interlocked their toes, pressed their pelvises together and smeared spit on each other's faces. By then, at the latest, it was quiet around them.

The first time Ali saw Anton kissing a girl on the schoolyard, she felt dizzy. The taste of chicken rose in her throat; something jabbed her between the eyes. The girl, Larissa, was older than Anton and Ali, old enough to buy cigarettes and ride a scooter; she wore skirts and had straight hair down to her shoulders, which were now turned towards Ali, while her pointy little nose was glued to Anton's face. Anton noticed his sister watching him and without letting go of Larissa, he looked Ali in the eyes and put his hand under Larissa's blouse. Ali ran to the girls' toilets and banged her head against the wall. She didn't tell anyone how she'd got the bump.

Then Anton began to stay out in the evenings. Valya and Kostya's screams pierced Ali's body, clung to her neck, and she went and pounded at her parents' bedroom door. Once, the room smelt strange and her mother sent her away laughing and told her everything was all right—but only once. Usually, Ali would fling open the door and go between her parents, lashing out at them herself, tearing their bodies apart.

Anton didn't want to hear about any of this and certainly didn't want to raise a hand against his own father—until he got back from Larissa's one evening, slightly drunk and very happy, and found his mother standing wide-eyed and motionless in the middle of the kitchen. He followed her gaze to the wall and saw Ali gasping for breath, Konstantin's hands squeezing her throat.

Ali had stepped between her parents again, and Kostya had swatted her against the wall like a fly. Her arms hung limp, her eyes were white, and Anton hit his father as hard as he could in the face.

Kostya let go of Ali. She cowered on the floor. Valya threw herself at Ali and they all froze and stayed frozen for days.

Words drained from the rooms, screams too, and arguments—everything drained away. Mother, father, child, child passed each other, their eyes fixed on the floor, the ceiling, the walls. If they happened to brush against one another, they mumbled something that nobody understood—and nobody stopped to ask. Kostya measured his walks in packets of cigarettes, puffing endlessly. The smoke stung his eyes and he thought how awful the weather was in this country—every bloody day too—and he thought about his parents and that he must fetch them over soon, not because he believed they'd be any better off here, but because it would mean that at last he wouldn't be quite so alone in the world. He thought of Ali's blue face that was Anton's face and Valya's too, in a way, and it occurred to him that none of them had a single red curl.

He walked to the filling station to buy himself another packet of cigarettes and watched a family in a VW Golf at the petrol pump. The children were unpacking sandwiches; their parents were rummaging in their bags. He went into the shop and found the magazine stand, pulled out the local listings magazine, and leafed through it for so long that the woman at the till shouted at him: 'If you get the pages damp or dog-eared, you'll have to buy it!'

He looked at her and smiled. He hadn't understood a word she'd said, but he had a plan. He went home and told his family—his wife and his daughter and his son—that he'd like to take them to the theatre, or rather, 'To see a dance. You don't have to understand the language and it's pretty.' Valya looked at the children and flung her arms round Kostya's neck. Anton looked at his parents. Ali stared at the floor.

Valya spent an entire week wondering what to wear. She rummaged around in her wardrobe for hours and eventually strutted out of the bedroom in a dress of rough, hessian-like material, with a leather waistcoat buckled over the top.

'What's that supposed to be?' asked Kostya, who was sitting on the sofa in black suit trousers and a blue shirt, legs crossed, hands folded over his belly which bulged further and further towards his chin.

'It's a peasant dress. It's what they wear here,' said Valya, beaming.

Ali and Anton had been allowed to choose what they wore, so they were both dressed in jeans, T-shirts and denim jackets. Valya took one look at them, shook her head and sent them off to get changed. Ali put on Anton's white shirt; Anton slipped on Ali's low-cut silver top over his bare torso.

'Look, I think I'm getting hairs on my chest,' he said, pressing his chin into his collarbone.

'You don't have any more than I do,' said Ali bad-temperedly.

They presented themselves to their parents and Valya grabbed them by their ears and dragged them back to their room again.

In the theatre foyer, the children had pretzels, and Valya and Kostya drank sparkling wine and called it champagne. As they clinked glasses, Valya said: 'Next I'd like to go to Paris.'

'What? Now you want to see the Mona Lisa?' Kostya said, helping himself to a piece of Anton's pretzel.

'I've looked into it. There are cheap bus tickets. Takes less than a day.'

'And café olé olé for breakfast?' asked Kostya, giggling.

Valya slapped him on the shoulder and began to laugh herself.

A male body crawled across the stage with a chair strapped to its back. It twisted and turned, stretching now one leg, now the other into the air, trying to sit on the chair behind it. Kostya closed his eyes and listened to the music. Was it Debussy? It could have been anything, so he decided it was Debussy, and smiled. Valya sat there with a dry mouth and moist eyes. She squeezed Alissa's hand and Alissa pulled her hand away and slid under the seat. Anton clambered over to take her place and laid his head on Valya's belly.

When a female dancer began to stomp across the stage, lugging stones half the size of her body and sighing as if she were singing, Kostya got up and went outside for a smoke.

He stared across the theatre forecourt. It was fucking freezing; even Debussy couldn't change that. He patted his jacket for a lighter, rummaged in his trouser pockets. Cursing, he decided to start saving for a piano right away, whether or not there was room for one in the flat. Once the piano was there, everything would sort itself out; he'd never be angry with Valya again—never be angry with anyone. He'd play to the children or, better still, he'd teach them to play themselves and they'd become musicians, playing duets and performing all over the country. One day, they'd go on tour. They'd travel to Russia and perform in the concert hall of the Gnessin Academy where he'd never been allowed to set foot, and his parents would come and watch, and finally realise where they'd gone wrong.

A child's hand was holding a lighter up to his face. Ali was standing beside him. 'Did you pinch my lighter?' he asked.

'It fell under your seat,' she said, staring across the theatre forecourt like him. It was milky and blurred. She was shivering.

'Do you smoke?' Kostya looked down at the child with the long brown curls, a tight, silver blouse over her no longer flat body. When had that happened? he wondered, taking off his jacket and laying it over her shoulders. She vanished beneath it. He passed her the cigarette and she took a few drags.

'Thanks,' she said.

'Ali—' Kostya began, but she interrupted him with a violent shake of her head, her curls flying so that he couldn't see her face. After that he was quiet.

Two years later Ali had moved out and had her hair cut. All Valya could say was: 'Get yourself a wig next time I see you!'—but it was better than directly calling her a dyke. Something inside Valya snapped like matzo when Ali left home; her throat felt dry and dusty. She decided not to touch her daughter's cold close-cropped head.

Ali had joined the Black Tomcat Group, Tom for short, a commune that was somewhere between socialist, communist and anarchist—they didn't want to pin themselves down. The name provoked various debates about sexism, which gave them plenty to discuss and a lot of reasons to get angry with each other and then have angry sex—or get drunk and smoke whole packs of cheap fags at a time. *Why's everything so fucked up, man?*

In the squat Ali had moved into, she had internet connection for the first time and discovered that you really could find instructions on how to make Molotov cocktails with a click of the mouse. She practised assiduously, experimenting first on building facades, then on rooftops. Once the Molotov flew into an empty pram, and although she could see from the roof that it was empty, she chewed up her lip in shock and only threw stones after that.

The first time she was arrested was on a demonstration. She threw stones at a policeman and when she was nicked she called the officer who was twisting her arms behind her back a fascist pig. He pulled the plastic handcuffs tighter, she thrashed about, and the deeper the plastic cut into her skin, the angrier she became and the more Russian the abuse she flung out. This surprised her; she found herself using words she hadn't even realised she knew. Although things had often got loud between her parents, these expressions must have sprung from deep childhood memories, maybe from the kitchen in Chertanovo. One thing was sure—she hadn't got them from the Russian eighties films she sometimes watched. No swearing there; only silence and weeping.

'Khui, blyad', pizda anal, yobanyi v rot ty menya żaebal, gvozd'
v podpizdok, chtob ty svernuvshegosya ezha ebal, blyadin syn, mat'
tvoyu poperek zhopy ebat'!'*

Valya fetched her daughter from the police station and they sat at
the kitchen table, the black-and-gold cake stand between them. They
hadn't spoken all the way home. For the first time in her life Valya
understood why people smoked; she felt the urge to puff thick clouds
out of her lungs, but she didn't smoke, so the thick clouds stayed inside.

'Do you think it's funny?' she asked at length. 'Do you think it's
all right to act like that? Is that how people behave in this country?'

By then Ali had got up and gone to the door; she didn't feel like
staring in silence into her mother's puffy cottonwool face; she felt like
going back to the commune, creeping under the covers to Nana and
smelling her armpits.

'*This country*. You brought me here. What do you expect?'

'Sorry I brought you here. Sorry your life's so tough. Would you
like to go back to socialism?'

'I don't want to go back; I want it here!'

'And then?'

'I'm not like you. I'm not content to crop my little patch of grass
and take things as they come. I'm not interested in a life where everything's available but nobody wants anything. I'm not interested in
all that tat that makes people like you feel fulfilled because you've
nothing else you can believe in.'

Valya stared at the contorted, angry face of the person before her.
Tat.

Her dilated pupils, her thin lips.

Tat. So that was it.

---

* String of obscenities along the lines of 'Go and fuck a rolled-up hedgehog!'

Valya wasn't in the mood for crying; she wasn't in the mood for anything. Her thoughts spiralled down to her gut. Her shoulders pulled towards the floor. She suddenly felt as if she were made of concrete—concrete that softens and melts and grows rigid again. Maybe it's heartburn, she thought, trying to withstand the gaze of her daughter, who'd sat back down at the other end of the kitchen table. It seemed impossibly long. Every time Ali sat down at this table, it grew longer.

KATO

Kato spread out the injecting gear on the table. He pulled a minute ampoule out of a wadge of cottonwool, held it up to his face, flicked down the liquid testosterone and snapped off the tip. The gel ran over his nails and he cursed; he didn't have many left. It wasn't that they were hard to get hold of; he got them on street corners from people who called him 'my friend'—but these friends charged more than the chemists, so not a drop must be wasted. He rubbed the liquid into the tips of his fingers and looked about him. Outside the floor-to-ceiling windows, the water of the Bosporus glistened, pricking his eyes. Big terracotta pots of withered plants stood on the balcony. One of the skeletons must once have been an oleander, and he thought he also recognised a lemon tree and a bougainvillea among the dead; they'd dried up in the sun and now stood stooped over the cracked grey earth. The flat was big—too big for Ali by herself. 'Belongs to my uncle,' she'd mumbled, disappearing into the kitchen to put on the samovar. There were three rooms, all with fully glazed outside walls; it was very bright. When the sun shone, you couldn't breathe. You were floating over the city, looking out far into Sultanahmet. There was a big worn sofa covered with books and magazines and cushions, and everything was red, even the pictures on the walls and the lampshades. A faded rug lay on the tiles, trodden so thin that the flowers on it were no more than streaks. The air conditioner above Kato's head coughed cold air into the room. Kato felt Ali's eyes on him and loosened his belt; his jeans fell to his knees. Then he pulled his underpants down below his buttocks and braced his arms against the table top.

'You coming?'

He stood leaning forwards slightly, trying to relax the muscles in his right buttock, ready for the injection.

'Don't you ever do it yourself?' asked Ali, without taking her eyes off the curve of his silhouette. She stood with her head against the doorframe looking at Kato's long legs that would soon be overgrown with black hair. Long feet flowed into calves, and calves into thighs that arched forwards. His bum, with the right buttock sticking out, was the only blip in the line; his back and neck and almost naked head formed a single sweeping arc; his forehead pulled downwards. A letter 'C' held up to the light. He turned his head to her; she couldn't make out his expression.

'I hate injecting myself.'

'Then how do you do it?'

'I find people.'

'I've never done this kind of thing.'

'Don't you want to?'

'What if I get it wrong?'

'Then I'll die.'

Ali went over to the table and looked at the filled syringe, the needle, the disinfectant spray, the cottonwool. She took the small plastic tube in her fingers and held it up to the light. Frowning, she thought: *My mother could do this.* And then: *She'd kill me if she knew what I was doing. She'd ram this thing into my neck.* Then: *Maybe she wouldn't.* And thinking to herself: *My mother was right; I should have been a doctor,* she took the syringe, sprayed sour-smelling disinfectant on Kato's buttock, somewhere between his hipbone and his dark brown mole—and, without warning, drove the thick needle into the flesh that she was grasping in her other hand.

She waited for an 'ow', but none came. She pushed the vanilla-coloured liquid slowly into the tissue; it was hard work. She forced her thumb down on the plunger. The more afraid she was that the needle would break, the more quickly she tried to inject. The liquid seemed to stick in the syringe like oil, refusing to budge. She knelt down behind Kato and looked up into his expressionless face.

'Is this right?'

'Just get on with it. But let me know before you pull the needle out.'

Kato's bare bum pushed slightly against Ali's shoulder. As she squatted down to see if all the liquid was out of the syringe, the tip of her nose brushed Kato's right hipbone and the tattoo of a bird in descending flight looked out at her—a greenfinch the size of her palm, wings back, claws out. Ali blinked.

These last five days, since Kato had been staying with her, she'd inter-twined her feet with his and fallen asleep in his smell, dreaming of red-headed mermaids with accordions. When she woke, she'd fling open the bedroom window and greedily breathe the cold air, then pull off the sweat-drenched jumper she slept in and stick her head into the flock of gulls outside. The gulls screeched, flew in loops and pecked her curls. Kato pulled Ali back in again and clutched her as if she were a pillow, his stubble scratching her skin.

Ali lay there sweating, her eyes wide open, thinking that she'd like to tell Kato about Anton, or Anton about Kato—and both of them about Uncle Cemal. She wasn't sure which stories she'd told whom, and she was no longer sure of her own story—what was she doing here in this city out of time? Was she really looking for her brother or did she just want to get away? She shivered and Kato pulled the jumper back over her body, swaddled her in blankets and told her about the wild-bird hunters and their symbol, the greenfinch.

She lay there all bundled up, only her eyes peeping out, unblinking, and Kato told her about old men who threw nets over their shoulders—rust-coloured nets that looked like tutus for overweight ballerinas—and set off through the city, sure-footed and noiseless, as if invisible. What they did was forbidden; you could go to jail for it—but they knew their moves and walked the streets as if nothing were up, rolled cigarette in one hand, cloth-covered cage in the other, careful not to let anyone see that beneath all those layers of cloth there were rare songbirds sleeping. They took them to places known only to a small circle of initiates, fixed the cages to the wall hooks in tea gardens and waited for the singing to begin. They didn't rouse the birds or shake their cages; they waited patiently for them to wake, and then they listened—and everyone in the tea garden listened with them, as if there were some conspiracy.

The cloths were never pulled off the cages; nobody but the owners ever got to see the birds—which weren't all greenfinches; there were goldfinches too. Brightness was harmful to them; they never sang their songs in the harsh light of day. The birdmen combed the city looking for them, searching in places where nobody else went—under bridges that led to Europe, on hills dotted with Byzantine ruins, in districts full of empty houses that were slowly reverting to nature. They threw their nets over the birds, caught hold of them and pressed them to their chests; they petted them and cared for them, shut them in cages and put a lot of thought into choosing the cloth for their covers. They took photos of the birds, which they propped on their chests of drawers, and they had pictures of them tattooed on their arms and legs.

Kato had read about the bird hunters in a travel magazine. Lying on the mattress at Pavlik's in Odessa, he'd devoured reports from all over the world, projecting himself into the landscapes described, no matter what the country or continent. One photo in particular had stuck in his mind because he couldn't work it out. It showed a night landscape on fire. Branches glowed orange, green grass fled into black shadows; it looked like an abstract painting, but the caption said it was the wild-bird hunters of Istanbul. On the next page was a man sitting cross-legged on a prayer mat, tugging at a tangle of rust-coloured net. Here too, it was night. There was a photo of a hook screwed to rotten wooden boarding in the middle of nowhere, everything grey. There was someone's retreating back, a road streaked with red-earthed skid marks, a square object covered in blue-and-white cloth hanging in a tree, a man's parting zigzagging through the back of his black, greasy head over a yellow collar.

When Kato reached Istanbul, he'd roamed the city in vain—walked from Kömürköy to Sanayi, trying to read the old men's faces, staring at their dry hands. A lot of them carried square bags, but none of the bags looked like cages. Kato followed likely-looking suspects and examined tea-house walls for hooks. He interrogated cafe owners, but most of them didn't know what he was talking about. He'd started walking as soon as he arrived, setting off on foot from the pier where the Odessa ferry docked—without a map, because he'd read that no map of Istanbul was accurate.

Time stretched in the heat, sticking his eyes together. His dwindling cash reserves told him time was passing; his savings were getting thin; his arms too. He was picked up by men who didn't pay him, but bought him food. One of them gave him a silver chain to wear round his waist; kneeling behind Kato, he fastened it for him, clinging tight to it and whispering in Kato's ear with a grunt that he wanted to keep him forever. Kato ran away, sold the chain and used the money to have a greenfinch tattooed on his thigh. He'd had enough of looking for the wild-bird hunters; let them come and find him. The pricking didn't hurt; over the sweaty head of the man painting his leg, Kato looked out at the hot street and saw veiled women passing. When the tattooist was done, he offered Kato a glass of tea and asked what he wanted to do in life. Kato said: 'Dance.' They drank in silence. Kato looked about him, then the tattooist breathed out noisily and said there were bars in Lâleli—might be something for him—you could dance there.

Dancing was Kato's dream. He'd always wanted to get out of Odessa, and his plan had been to study dance in Moscow after reading economics in Kiev—but then he'd got to ruminating and it hadn't happened. It was at about this time that his friends started to talk about their first paid work. They didn't all mean the same thing by 'paid work', but the situation was clear enough to them—any job that helped make ends meet was a respectable one. And everyone with a womb was getting pregnant and the rest were growing beards, and since Kato wasn't in a position to do either and didn't know how to explain this to his friends (who were starting to make jokes) or his mother (who was waiting for him to sort his life out), he thought maybe he'd go somewhere where nobody knew him—not any old place; it did have to be warm, and he wouldn't mind learning a new language either. The kind of things you think when you're desperate to get away.

His brothers and sisters were shouting in the next room as usual; his mother was laying into his drunken father. Kato ran out of the door—first the door to the flat, then the in-between door, padded with green foam, then the door to the building. He ran out onto the yard, to the others who couldn't stand being at home, but they were already stoned and speaking very slowly. He kept running. He passed his old playground, dived through bushes, panted past spitting old women, arrived breathless at Pavlik's door, rang the bell, dashed up the stairs, threw himself on the floor and clasped Pavlik's knees. Pavlik was playing the guitar and his kiss tasted of aspic. He unbuttoned his trousers. Afterwards Kato lay on the mattress. The light coming through the window was too harsh; he screwed up his eyes and felt a twinge between his eyebrows; every little hair stood on end. He turned onto his belly and there on the floor was this magazine with travel reports from all over the world.

'Pavlik, shall we get out of here?'

'What did you say, babe?'

'Shall we go somewhere?'

'Where?'

'Dunno. Istanbul?'

'Why?'

Then Kato knew that Pavlik would never go with him and never understand. He projected himself into the photos in the magazine. He saw himself as a greenfinch in the burning bushes, saw himself being saved, caught, covered up and cared for—only then would he let out his song.

When at last Pavlik fell asleep, Kato sneaked his wallet from his trousers on the floor, took out the contents, pocketed the travel magazine and went straight to the harbour.

His search for the bird hunters ended in Lâleli where there were agencies for people like him, or rather, agencies for women; Kato hadn't told anyone there he was a man. No one had asked; they'd examined him—his legs, his breasts—and everything had been in order; he was even pretty acrobatic. The men spoke his mother tongue and the women didn't have to speak at all; they sang their songs. One of them, Aglaja, really did sing like a bird, shrill and frenetic, her short red curls quivering to her voice box, as if they were charged with electricity. She was more than twice Kato's age, but didn't have a line on her face. Her skin was taut and when she smiled, her mouth jerked open as if someone had pulled a string. They became lovers, then friends. Aglaja would stroke Kato's hair when he clasped her knees, and when he told her he didn't want to be called Katarina anymore, she shaved his head for him. She asked around to find out how to get hold of testosterone and then practised injecting. She was terrible at it, but anything was better than doing it yourself.

The first weeks after starting with the injections, Kato felt either sick and dizzy or else hyper-aware, more aware of things than he'd ever been before. He could feel his bones growing and hear his own voice break. He opened his mouth and heard his vocal cords trying to get a purchase and failing. He cried a lot too—that was the testosterone, he told himself. Sometimes Aglaja laughed at him when he cried, but usually she let him climb on her lap without asking for explanation. They'd stopped sleeping together, but there was barely a night when they were apart. Until Gezi Park went up in smoke.

Kato was staggering along İstiklal Caddesi when the call came. It was one of those nights when the lights on the European continent's biggest shopping street irked him like lice. He turned off onto Mis Sokak and headed for the Bigudi Club, where women's bodies wanting to watch women's bodies dance could be sure they wouldn't get a man's cock pressed against their pelvises. He passed Kırmızı Bar filled with people whose sex varied depending on the time of day. In Bigudi, women in black jeans and baggy jumpers sat pressed up against three of the four walls like chickens on a roost, all of them, without exception, staring at their phones, as if they were playing games with each other online, or chatting, or fucking—there was certainly no action on the dance floor; it was empty. Only one woman glanced up from her phone when Kato entered the harshly lit room. She had dyed blond hair and was wearing green glittery eye shadow that glinted like broken glass when she blinked. Kato went to the bar, got himself a whisky and knocked it back in a few gulps. The blond with the glitter around her eyes had returned to her phone. Kato went and stood on the dance floor. He closed his eyes and raised his arms, his hips vibrating slightly. He imagined a hand slipping round his waist and holding him tight; he touched his own neck, ran a hand through his short hair, opened his eyes again. There didn't seem to be anyone there; the chickens up against the wall were as two-dimensional as wallpaper. He let his arms drop and went out.

It was warm, almost summer, and outside Kırmızı all the tables were full. An old man with a barrow full of vegetables stopped in front of them and swiftly peeled a cucumber for the streetwalkers teetering on their at least four-inch heels. He slashed a cross in the soft green flesh, down to his fingertips, and the cucumber in his hand opened out like a flower. He strewed it generously with salt. The women paid and strutted off to Tarlabaşı. Rakı glugged out of bottles. Giggling girls singed black stubble on their thighs, massaged each other's calves and read each other's coffee grounds. Kato elbowed his way to the bar, past strange-smelling bodies, cinnamony and earthy. In the men's toilets, at the urinal, a woman in a long pale blue glittery dress, its train flowing over the floor tiles, held her cock in her hand and looked enquiringly at Kato. He went into the cubicle and locked the door behind him, sat down on the toilet lid and propped his head in his hands.

His phone rang. It was Aglaja. He heard singing or shouting in the background; he couldn't quite understand what was going on. One thing he did understand, though: 'Come straight to Gezi.'

Aglaja was wearing the black hat she always wore when she wasn't working, a crumpled white shirt with a broad collar, and a pair of sharply creased suit trousers far too large for her slim body, held up only by wide braces. Even her shoes were too big—the general effect was of a clown in a black-and-white photograph. All about her, people were dancing in colour. Someone was banging a darbuka; the others were holding hands, moving in a circle, cautiously throwing up their legs as if in slow motion. The rainbow flag was rammed into the ground next to a tractor; further back, Kato saw a swarm of demolition vehicles, dozing silent and black as sleeping cockroaches.

Aglaja came charging up to Kato and pulled him into the circle of dancers. He shook his sweaty palms and lay down on the ground. Although it was evening, it was still light; it would be some time before the stars came out. Aglaja leant over him, her red curls covering his face.

'Will you sleep here with me tonight?' Her mouth was a huge black caterpillar.

'Don't you have to go to work? I thought you were working today.'

She sat down beside him, her face floating above his. 'No, I'm not. Maybe I'll never go back to work again.'

'And your accordion?'

'I'll just have to play on you.'

She pulled Kato up, clasped his body from behind, pressed her belly against his back, laid her head on his shoulder and played something very fast on his ribs.

He was woken by an acrid smell and opened his eyes. Aglaja's sharp nose was touching his cheek; he looked into her wide-open eyes through a milky film. Her lashes were long and very straight. The two of them were lying on the grass next to the tents, Aglaja's leg over his hip. At first he thought the tear gas was dew, then he began to cough and noticed that his face was smarting. Aglaja coughed too; soon everyone was coughing, then the coughing turned to crying and suddenly they were all on their feet. Masks appeared on people's faces, their red eyes gleaming over the top. The gas seeped through the thin cellulose above their mouths; the first coughers fell to their knees.

Kato spun round frantically, trying to find Aglaja, screaming her name. Panic coated his throat like a layer of flour. Then he saw a flash of red curls in the cloud of gas and ran towards it. Aglaja stood there mumbling: 'My hat, I've found my hat.' She picked herself up, smiled at Kato and keeled over.

The gas cartridge had got her on the right temple. Kato hadn't heard anything—or seen the cartridge hit her. He saw Aglaja fall down at his feet and not move again. Then he saw the orange can of gas beside her outstretched body. Blood was trickling out of her ears; her left arm had fallen on her chest as if she were clutching flowers. Her head was bent back; her whole body seemed to be made of rubber. It dropped quiet. A cloud spread in Kato's head and broke through his skull. The gas, he thought. He felt tingly and dizzy, then he was knocked down by a crowd that scattered like a school of fleeing fish. Some of the faces wore goggles; their mouths flew open and shut.

He groped his way along, running his hands over the ground, his head pulling towards the earth. He got back to his feet. The gas was no more than a fine haze now. He saw a man carrying off red curls; he'd thrown Aglaja over his shoulder; her head was wobbling as if it had become unmoored from her body.

'Hey!' Kato shouted, running after the man. 'Hey!' He tried to catch up with him, tripping over legs; all over the park, police were swarming like black flies. By the time he reached the man who was carrying Aglaja, he was almost out of the park and heading for the Divan Hotel. Kato tugged his arm so hard that the man almost dropped her and began to curse in Russian. Without thinking, Kato replied in Ukrainian, then switched to Russian. They shouted at each other until eventually Kato took Aglaja's shoulders and the man took her legs and they carried her into the hotel lobby.

The place was filled with screaming, weeping people, lying about or sitting, pouring water and milk and lemon juice over each other's heads. An elderly woman emptied a plastic bottle over Aglaja's face and Kato stared at the white liquid running into her mouth. Her lips didn't move; he was sure she was dead.

Paramedics appeared and bundled Aglaja's body onto a stretcher. Kato couldn't say whether minutes or hours had passed. He followed the gurney out, but wasn't allowed in the ambulance. He asked where they were taking her and ran along behind. He didn't have the money for a taxi on him, but a young man leaning against a yellow car recognised him from the club and offered to give him a lift. In the car they argued about what was going on in the city. The young man said sabotage; Kato said: 'Bullshit.' The young man said: 'These agitators want to destroy the republic.' Kato said: 'Let me out here, please.'

He somehow found his way to the right ward and sat at Aglaja's bedside, not moving, only going out for a piss or a cigarette. His eyes flitted back and forth from Aglaja's hands on the sheet to the screen of his phone. A wobbly camera showed burning barricades cut through by a jet from a water cannon. The picture kept cutting out. On TV there were penguins running across the screen. The next day, the doctors said Kato had to leave; they had new patients coming in and it was no good his sitting there like death; he wasn't helping anyone. He refused. A nurse promised to give him a call when Aglaja woke up. 'Will she wake up?' he asked, his fingers clawing his phone.

'Bakalım yani,' said the nurse.

He went straight from the hospital to the park and sat down to wait for another gas cartridge, but there weren't any. Or rather, there were masses, but none of them hit him, although he was sitting there in the middle of the park, unprotected and powerless. He watched a dervish spinning like a compass needle, the pipe of his gas mask lashing the air.

Kato held out until the chain of mothers broke his will. The authorities had appealed to demonstrators' parents on television, calling on them to fetch their children from the park—there could be no guarantees now; public order had to be restored; from now on serious action would be taken and anyone staying on in the park would get what they were asking for. And the mothers came out in force, but not to fetch their children; they came to form a human chain around the park, shoulder to shoulder, arm in arm, their eyes full of fear. The army might step in at any moment.

Kato sat there surrounded by mothers who weren't his, and burst into tears. Even without gas. He got to his feet, went home and dialled his mother's number. His father picked up. Kato considered hanging up, but thought better of it. First they both shouted, then his father cried, then he shouted again, then he said Kato must come home right away, pack his bag this second, his mother was sick with worry, his brothers and sisters too—what kind of a daughter was he?

'I'm not a daughter. I'm your son.'

His father went on ranting as if he hadn't heard. Kato repeated the words until it dropped quiet at the other end of the line.

'Dad, I'm your son, do you understand?'

When there was no reply, he said: 'It doesn't matter if you don't.'

And realising that his father was going to remain silent, he said: 'I know you love me. I know you'd never say so. You once told me we're animals, that love's an instinct—that's enough for me, Dad. I understand. And I'm happy here. You haven't asked, so I'm telling you: I think I'm getting on pretty well.'

There was static down the line.

'Dad, one more thing. Everyone knows you're taking Gran's jewellery into the yard a bit at a time and coming back with little bags of white powder. The bottom drawer in the kitchen isn't a good place to hide it. Maybe you could keep Sina away from the stuff, stop her from sniffing it. Is she well? Are the others well?'

He heard rapid pips.

'Dad, I'm staying put for the time being. I'll be in touch. Give my love to the others. Oh, and Dad...I got myself a tattoo.'

Ali turned her eyes from the greenfinch on Kato's thigh to the syringe in her hand. The testosterone had completely vanished into Kato.

'I'm pulling it out now.'

'Okay.'

Kato pressed a piece of cottonwool to the red pinprick and rubbed it.

Ali was still crouched in front of him. She looked up at him sceptically.

'Who usually does it for you?'

'Anyone in Lâleli will do it. There are experienced people on every corner.'

'And you just go to the corner and ask?'

Kato turned to face Ali, his pubes level with her head. Ali could see clearly into his sharply outlined pupils; there was a glimmer of green around them, then yellow. He opened his lips as if to reply, but instead put his hands in Ali's curls and massaged the back of her head. She pressed her forehead into the black fuzz above his mons and took a deep breath. When she breathed out, she pushed her tongue inside him.

Afterwards they lay naked on the streaky floral pattern of the rug and Ali looked at Kato's profile. He had two red spots close together on his jaw and another two further down on his neck—soon they'd start to swell and itch. Fucking bed bugs. Ali wondered if Kato looked more like his mum or his dad—and whether you always had to look like someone. Hadn't she had the feeling she knew his face that first time he'd spoken to her in the club? Quite possible that their great-grandparents had met on the Potemkin Stairs—that they'd bumped into one another on the overcrowded steps and shaken hands amid profuse beg pardons. Very likely even; Odessa wasn't a big city. And then? They'd gone on their ways.

And now their children's children's children lay side by side, hips touching, on a faded rug in Istanbul, mentally flicking through stacks of black-and-white photographs, imagining faces they didn't know, seeing familiar faces in strangers. They wished they could say more about themselves than the names of the places they'd left behind. They wished for ancestors like them: uncles who'd shaved their legs and squeezed their bellies into corsages and dresses at night, aunts with shingled hair and black lipstick, strolling through the streets in suits. None of these stories had ever found its way into the annals of family history, but they must have existed, so what was wrong with inventing them?

Ali rolled onto her side and ran her eyes over the shadow on Kato's upper lip that for once he hadn't shaved. Soon the shadow would be a square beard, framing half his face. It suited him.

'Let's go out,' whispered Kato.

The streets were full of emaciated cats and squashed plastic bottles. The air smelt of cabbage, and of lentil soup with red pepper, and now and then Ali thought she caught Kato's smell permeating the street too. They bought two simit and kaymak at Hassan Bey's and when they came to the water, they stared past each other for a long time.

'Sorry,' Kato said after a while, his mouth full of creamy butter.

'It's always happening to me.'

Hassan Bey hadn't looked at Ali; his eyes had fixed on Kato, piercing him from head to toe. Then he'd spat on the floor, stared at his calculator and said the price.

'That was nothing to do with you.' Ali brushed sesame crumbs off her knee. 'The old man's pissed off with me because he thinks I promised him a date. But I didn't promise him anything—definitely not a date. All I did was scribble my number on a piece of paper when he asked me to.'

'Well, that's pretty much the same thing.'

Ali didn't herself know why she'd done it. She'd come down the street drunk early one morning, glad to have found the alleyway where she lived. The taste of vodka still in her mouth, she'd trembled like a balloon on the water; you could have popped her with a pin. She'd laughed. She had a craving for sugar and went into Hassan's shop, and as she was piling her arms with squishy white bread and marmalade, he asked for her number and for some reason she wrote it on a scrap of paper, the right numbers in the right order, although afterwards she couldn't find her own front door and sat down at a crossroads to eat, tearing the end off the loaf and dunking it in the jar of marmalade. Since then, Hassan Bey had rung every morning and every evening— sometimes even in his lunch break—and she didn't know how to tell him that he was giving himself false hopes.

Ali thought of Hassan's sandpaper skin and of his smile when he'd first seen her and offered her fresh plums—then of the pram his wife had been pushing when she'd bumped into the two of them at the Sunday market. They'd pretended not to know each other. Ali would have liked to peep in the pram, but didn't dare. Instead she turned to look at the boys next to her who were standing in front of two cardboard boxes full of fluffy chicks you could buy by the bag. The chicks cheeped and wobbled about as if they ran on batteries, pecking each other and tumbling over one another. The boys stood cheek to cheek, drool running out of their mouths. Ali wondered if they were hungry—or hypnotised at seeing themselves in those cardboard boxes, at twelve lira a bag. Probably not. It was more likely that their dilated bloodshot eyes came from glue sniffing.

She thought of the market criers who sang arias to their vegetables like muezzins, 'domates, domates', of the little girls in long colourful skirts who juggled with stolen pomegranates, of the woolly socks she'd bought but couldn't wear because they smelt so strongly of washing powder that she'd decided to use them as pesticide for the bed bugs.

She imagined what it would be like to walk round the market with Anton, buy him grapes, pull him between the fruit barrows into the narrow doorways that led like tunnels into the nowhere of Tarlabaşı. What it would be like to push green grapes into his mouth, press her hand to his lips and her mouth to her hand.

Ali's memories piled up like transparencies and slipped. They complemented and contradicted one another, making new images, but she couldn't read them; even shaking her head was no use.

She followed the straight lines in Kato's face, soothed by them. She looked at his different-sized eyes, his high cheekbones, the curved shadow above his lip. Maybe she'd just stay here, she thought. Maybe she'd stay with him and they'd spend the rest of their days trying to make babies. The ring on Kato's finger gleamed in the sun. Beneath his hand on the steps was red graffiti that looked as if it were melting. It must have been years old. Faded red lines with fuzzy edges showed a woman with a flock of birds shooting out of her head. Ali could have sworn she knew the woman, but from where? Another image she couldn't place.

'Kato, that accordion player in the club—'

'Why do you think your brother left?'

Kato's voice broke mid-sentence; he cleared his throat.

Ali suddenly remembered the cold of the parquet floor beneath her shoulderblades. Under the sheet, Anton's body and hers hadn't touched. They'd stared at the ceiling. The room was smoky; a white layer of haze hung above them like over a swamp. Only the tips of their noses stuck out, and their curls. Anton had come to tell her something, but they hadn't talked. They'd passed the joint back and forth.

'I've no idea. I'm looking for him so I can ask him.'

'And then bring him back?'

Ali chewed her lower lip; it tasted sour.

'I'm not his wife. Or his mother.'

'And why do you think he left?'

Ali was missing so many memories; her brain looked like the toothless jaws of that old hag who used to beg at Chertanovskaya metro station. She was always there, hunchbacked and swathed in colourful shawls, a headscarf knotted under her chin; she held out her arm, stammering something, her hand shaped into a little dish. Whenever Ali and Anton passed the beggar woman with their gran, Ali clung to the woman's legs and couldn't be torn away. Anton would stand and watch the spectacle: a grannie tugging at the feet of her granddaughter who was clinging for dear life to the legs of a beggar woman, all three of them screaming. A self-destructing Russian doll— that's how it looked in her memory.

The transparencies shifted again. For a second she thought she knew what Anton had been going to tell her, but she didn't dare speak the words. Instead she said: 'Because he thinks we don't need him.'

'What about him? Does *he* need *you*?'

Ali clicked her tongue and made one of those gestures that could mean anything, from 'how should I know?' to 'hold me in your arms'.

She'd have liked to swim across the Golden Horn and lose herself between the narrow houses on the other side, lean against the wall of a house, take on its colour and be sucked into the facade, rib by rib, bone by bone.

Alongside a hut on the dock, four small ferries lay moored; at one of them a man with a voice bigger than himself was urging passers-by to get on board. Ali and Kato sat on the broad steps of the quay in the sun, watching the families board the flimsy little vessel. Daughters helped mothers in long robes, so that they wouldn't trip and fall in the water. There was no railing; the women clung to their children's skinny arms. Men in worn checked suits put their pipes in their breast pockets, went below deck to find themselves corner seats and looked gloomily out at the water.

'Odessa's just a hop across the Black Sea,' said Kato, pointing at the Bosporus Bridge. 'Practically round the corner.'

Ali looked out across the Golden Horn, at the rickety boat full of people going to the bazaar to drink coffee at Mehmet Efendi's, where the ground beans were wrapped in fine greaseproof paper by children, none of them older than fifteen. Their fingers twisted the bags so quickly, it looked as if they'd been fast-forwarded.

'What's it like there?' asked Ali. 'In Odessa.'

'Pretty much like here. Except that people have these ugly mugs.'

'What kind of ugly?'

'Droopy, you know what I mean. Like dough spilling out of a bowl.'

Kato shifted closer to Ali and laid his shorn head in her lap. Ali continued to stare out at the Bosporus, digging in her trouser pockets for cigarettes under Kato's head.

'With evil, flashing eyes that look through you rather than at you.'

'I know the type.' Ali lit a Player's with her left hand, propping herself up on the step with her right hand. Gravel dug into her flesh.

'Always look at the ground, never look you in the face.'

'Yes.'

'And the tea—the tea's much better here. If you don't know anything else, you think the piss you drink is tea, but since coming here, I know they can't make tea over there; it tastes of soap.'

Kato stretched out his legs. He put one arm under his head and wrapped the other around Ali.

'There are crows screeching all over the place.'

Ali looked down at Kato, then back at the boat that now, from a distance, seemed to be laden with mountains of black cloth. Several pairs of eyes stared out from the mountain, and right on top stood a little boy like a lightning conductor.

'And it smells sour. Like puke and cherry vareniki.'

'Stop it.'

'What?'

'Just stop.'

Kato looked up.

Ali blew smoke rings.

'I'd like to go to Odessa sometime.'

'Why?'

I couldn't answer that question. Why? I didn't feel I had to know, not just then. I watched myself half-lying on the quay with a slim body stretched across my lap. I saw smoke come out of my mouth and get in my eyes. I knew that the heel of my hand was smarting from the sharp gravel, but I didn't pull it away. I heard myself say things, saw myself kiss, get up, walk. I saw myself doing things that I hadn't decided to do, but that carried me along—and I'd be lying if I said I didn't care where. I had a goal, but I wanted it to come and stumble on me.

I don't know how or when I began to see things differently—why I decided to put the transparencies and images in my head in some kind of order, why I began to think and speak and even write about myself as me—but I know *when* it happened. It was when my great-grandfather pulled a thin folder out of his bureau two years before he died, and put it on the table in front of me. No, that's wrong—it was when I began to read what was in that folder. By then Shura was dead and I was back in Istanbul.

ETYA AND SHURA

Natan and Valentina were highly educated or practically illiterate; family opinion was divided. If the stories could be believed (and they were told with great feeling), the couple was either part of Odessa's intellectual elite or else destitute—or something in between, or everything at once. Valentina, of course, was stunningly beautiful, so aristocratic-looking and clever with her hands that she was known to those who loved her as Catherine the Great. The clothes she sewed were better than what you got in the shops; her cooking was (you guessed it) better than in a restaurant, and she was deputy head of all the kindergartens in town. But before any of that, she was married to Natan and moved with him from Balta to the wealthy city of Odessa, the Paris of eastern Europe, a thriving harbour town where the living, as Natan said, was good.

Between her domestic duties and her responsibilities as deputy head of all those kindergartens, Valentina won a beauty competition (and no wonder, with those black curls and blue eyes of hers) and edited a cookery book about healthy Ukrainian food—a loose collection of her favourite recipes which she pasted together herself and passed round her friends, so that it wasn't long before the whole of Odessa was cooking à la Valentina. It was rumoured that a publishing house was interested in the book, but if the venture ever came to anything, the masterpiece must have got lost in the war.

Valentina bore Etina, Etya, Etinka, and everyone agreed that she was the most beautiful child on earth. Etina's fine fuzz of hair shone around her forehead like a halo and her fate was sealed at an early age; this girl was to become what would later, in the world of cartoons, be known as a superhero. Natan and Valentina didn't have such words, but they invested all their love, all their energy and, most important, all their money in this little brat who never slept and is said to have been able to speak at birth.

All children born between the first two Russian revolutions of the twentieth century were burdened with having to be in some way special, not just a piece of flesh in a nappy; they were to shake up the world, make it better. That was the idea in my family anyway and Alexander was no exception. Also known as Shura and Shurik, and sometimes as Sasha, he was born sometime during those fraught years of the previous century and would later marry Etina. Later still, after the Great Patriotic War, Etina and Shura would adjust their years of birth in their papers to make things look respectable—Shura adding a few years and Etina making herself slightly younger. I suspect it was really the other way round and that the highly promising Etina was born first, but the calendar was at sixes and sevens after the war, like everything else, so to hell with it—they wrote what they wanted. They could have changed anything in those papers; they could even have changed their surnames. But they didn't.

Shura, Sasha, little Alexander the Great—whatever name he went by, he too was, of course, extremely good-looking. However inconsistent the facts of family history, and whatever the setting—Odessa, Chernivtsi, Grozny, Volgograd, Moscow, Germany, Germany, Germany—and Istanbul, where Kato lay on my lap down by the harbour and told me about Odessa—there was one constant: everyone in the family was very good-looking and very intelligent. That was the tradition, anyway. But Shura really was good-looking. There are several paintings and portraits of his proud, socialist-realist face to prove it; they hang to this day in museums of Soviet history and on the wall in Valya's bedroom—the Valya in Lower Saxony, Germany, that is, not Valentina, aka Catherine the Great, who lived in a hovel in Odessa at the beginning of the twentieth century; the Valya who was named after an astronaut, and perhaps also a little after the Valentina in Odessa, because however keenly the family believed in manned space travel and the technological progress of mankind in general, they believed more keenly still in old Jewish customs—that children, for instance, should be named after the dead so that their ancestors can protect them. As if.

The portraits in my mother's bedroom in Lower Saxony show a man with a broad forehead and a large, purposeful nose, bushy eyebrows and very soft full lips which seem, in spite of Soviet realism, to smile a Mona Lisa smile. Shura's eyes were purple. You couldn't see that, either in the black-and-white photographs, or in Soviet realism where they were painted blue or grey or green, and sometimes brown, but purple they were. And yet despite his eyes, Shura would have trouble winning Etina's heart when, at the age of seventeen—or there-abouts—the two of them found themselves at the faculty of medicine, on the list of exceptionally high achievers—doska pochyota.

This list hung in the corridor between the lecture theatre and the secretary's office and charted who had received what marks and achieved what great things for the good of the university, science and socialism. Etinka was number one, Shura number two. They had demonstrated exemplary commitment in holding voluntary lectures, had only the best marks in every possible subject and Etina's accomplishments in party history were outstanding.

The day the ranking list went up, Shura made it his business to find out who was to blame for his inferior position; it was plain to him that he should be first on the honour roll. But when he saw Etinka's proud face as she strolled past him down the corridor, textbooks pressed to her belly, without deigning to look at him—when he saw Etinka's hips and the back of her neck, he decided to wage a campaign of a rather different nature.

At first she ignored him with such ease that he began to doubt his own existence, as he stood there in her path, cigarette in one hand, the other hand in his hair. He wasn't used to brush-offs; with his purple eyes and soft voice, Shura had the girls queuing up for him. But either Etinka scented trouble, or else she had something or some*one* quite different on her mind. At any rate she didn't mention Alexander Farbarjevich to anyone. It wasn't that she was secretly crazy about him; she saw him only as the perpetual Number Two who didn't have a hope in hell of ousting her from the throne—and things stayed that way almost until they graduated. Sometimes, in the anatomy lecture, she'd glance across the crowded rows of students, and once, in the second semester, their eyes met for an instant. But there wasn't time for Shura to put any feeling or meaning into his gaze; his eyes had merely wandered, seeking distraction, and by the time he realised what had happened, Etinka had turned back to her notes, which I suspect were rather clearer and more intelligent than his.

Shura felt desperate, though that wasn't something people said back then either; the word wouldn't come into fashion until years later. In those days, people spoke of 'soul ache', *dusha bolit*, and 'torments',

123

muki, but it's maybe worth pointing out that Russians see everything rather more drastically because they express things more drastically. They don't say: *I like these apples*; they say: *I love these apples*. They don't say: *I'm married*; they say: *I'm bewived* or: *I-stand-by-my-husband*. They don't say: *mother-in-law*; they say: *my-own-blood*. Russian speakers don't just *not like* rain; they *hate* it, and by the same logic they speak of *heart torture* if they feel a slight twinge in their chests. That is precisely where Shura was heading. He couldn't sleep, wouldn't eat, and was smoking three times as much as usual. When his mother saw the rings under his eyes, she shook her head.

'What's the matter with you? Are you sick?'

'No, it's the exams. It's all too much.'

'You'll manage. You're the best—aren't you?'

For a long time Shura told himself that's what he was. He was the best, and if he couldn't sleep at night, it was because somebody else (a woman!) was preventing him from being number one—and the girl wasn't even flirting with her professors or cribbing. Free from unsocialist flaws, big-eyed Etina with her pinned-up hair and her hips twice as broad as her shoulders seemed quite capable of existing without him. His thoughts were confused; they ran on injured pride and envy, and got caught up on Etina's hips. In the end, he decided to give her a present.

The day the new ranking list appeared with the names of the crème de la crème of the medical faculty—and there were no surprises; further down the list there was fluctuation, but the top four names remained constant—early on the big day, Shura positioned himself between the lecture theatre and the secretary's office, and stood leaning against the wall with a cardboard box tied with a red bow, waiting for Number One to come along and see her name on the list.

Etinka was wearing a matching skirt and jacket with brown shoes which, despite their medium-high heels, didn't make a sound. Her face was soft and expressionless, as if she were crossing a deserted room, as if nothing existed except her—not the pungent smell of formalin, not Sasha, not even the damned list of students. She was carrying a stack of books pressed to her belly, and walked down the corridor as if on a finishing straight. Level with the honour roll, she stopped and turned first her head, then her entire body to face the notice. Shura stood beside her, staring openly because she seemed unaware of his presence.

When she made to move on, he said: 'Mazel tov.'

'I beg your pardon?' Etinka's head spun round with a violence that, in spite of her pinned-up hair and her firm stride, he hadn't expected.

'You're number one again. Mazel tov.'

He held out the flat packet in his hand.

'I don't understand.'

Etinka really didn't understand. Not *mazel tov*—she understood that all right; her family spoke plenty of Yiddish and she could easily have talked Yiddish with Shura, not fluently, perhaps, but well enough. It was just that she wasn't used to hearing the language outside the four walls of her home, let alone at university. And she didn't understand why this lout who was clearly after her, forever making clumsy efforts to waylay her in the corridor, his mouth open as if he were going to say something, though he never did—a boy who went out with older girls and made them laugh and goodness knows what else (she'd decided very early on that she wasn't *that* kind of girl)—she didn't understand why this perpetual Number Two was holding out a packet with a red bow to her.

'This is for you. A token of my respect.'

Shura swallowed, careful not to let his chin drop to his chest. He raised his head; his purple eyes shone into Etina's green ones.

'Thank you, but I can't accept it,' said Etinka, or something like that, and whatever she said, it was a brush-off. Her arms clung tight to the books at her belly.

'No, you must.'

Shura held out the parcel and opened his eyes wide as if he were trying to hypnotise her. For a second he wished she wouldn't ever look away again, but she did, quite effortlessly. She looked into his face, then at the gift, then at the floor, then at the clock on the wall, and then, with another glance at her name at the top of the list, she breathed out, and again she said something like: 'No, thank you, it's very nice of you, but I have to go now.' Something like that.

'Ikh bet dikh. Nimm.' *Please, take it.*

The Yiddish words made her look at him again; her eyes narrowed and flashed in annoyance. She was annoyed at herself because she realised that such a thing had never occurred to her—not that Comrade Farbarjevich was Jewish; the name spoke for itself. No, she was surprised that he dared speak Yiddish, speak it loud and clear, in a university corridor, to *her*. And her eyes lingered a little too long on his face, long enough to notice how purple, how very purple, his irises were—and she found herself biting the hook, reaching out an arm, taking the gift. She balanced it on the stack of books in front of her belly and looked expectantly into Shura's face.

'A shayner dank. Du bist zeyer khaverish.' *Thank you. You're very generous.*

Shura felt giddy. And sick. Sick and giddy from the scent of this woman, faintly sweet and cool as mint. Here she was, right in front of him; she couldn't ignore him now. So this was what her face looked like when she wasn't rushing past him. At last he was getting to see more than just her profile; here were her eyes; here was the smile in her eyes.

'Vos iz es?' she asked, cocking her head slightly. *What is it?*

'It's—'

Later he'd tell this story as a *khokhme*, making it sound as if he'd planned everything meticulously, casting himself as a lady-killer who knew how to impress the women and throw them off their guard. He'd decided to have his bit of fun; he knew exactly what he was doing.

At the time, though, Shura had no idea why he said what he did. He said it in Russian; such a delicate word had no place in his Yiddish vocabulary.

'Trusiki.'

Underwear. Pants. Knickers. The word popped out of him. Wham, bang, out it came and hung there between the two best students of the medical faculty of Odessa, whose names and portraits would one day grace the walls of the very corridor where they were standing facing one another. But that was later; now they both held their breath.

In those days you couldn't study medicine straight from school. Socialist citizens went to a workshop or factory first to learn a practical skill. Before Shura was admitted to the university, he'd learnt carpentry, a skill he never regretted possessing. Later, in the fifties, when the war was long past and victory seemed there to stay and he was living in his dacha on the Volga, he passed his time carving woodland spirits and household gnomes while his wife Etina and their daughter Emma and *her* daughter (who would one day show up with twins and set them turn and turn about on the swing) tended the tomato patch, cucumbers and vines. His wooden figures were skilfully hewn; he gave them to his friends as presents, and carved a breadbin with elaborate petals along the edges and the word *khleb* cut into the lid.

Between his carpenter's apprenticeship and the beginning of his studies at the faculty of medicine, he got into acting. That was the idea, at least. He wanted to write plays and direct them and carpenter the set singlehandedly. He went secretly to auditions at the acting school in Odessa. For weeks before, he rehearsed lines in his parents' garden and when his mother asked him what he was gabbling away to himself, he didn't say Shakespeare; he said: party history. He didn't get cold feet until he found himself in the acting-school waiting room surrounded by a lot of young men in suits and ties and a lot of young women in dresses and lipstick. Looking down at himself he saw what he would later describe in his memoirs as: 'nekazistyi paren' s Odesskoi Moldavanki'—a common little whippersnapper from Moldavanka (a district of Odessa known for its poverty and criminality and one day for Isaak Emmanuilovich Babel).

Shura had turned up at the auditions in a sheepskin waistcoat and a cloth cap. He stared at the other auditioners' ties and knew that his rabbi father would never teach him to knot a tie like that. He stared at the woman opposite, who'd crossed her legs, revealing an inch of thigh beneath her skirt. The sweat on Shura's palms seeped into the manuscript he was clutching. The woman's lips moved noiselessly; she seemed to be practising her lines. Her lipstick was as red as a Pioneer's neckerchief. Shura wondered how he was going to make it out of the room without anyone noticing his erection. He could go neither backwards nor forwards, so he sat on his chair, shrunk into himself like a leech until his name was called. Then, aroused though he was, he stood with tears rolling down his face and declaimed a wild mix of Shakespeare and party history before the entire admissions committee. The next thing he knew, it was off the street and onto the stage with him; a glittering future beckoned. That, at least, is the legend.

Blissfully happy and drenched in sweat, Shura ran home to report on his forthcoming career as a star of the theatre, but his father soon pulled the curtains on *that* plan: 'I'll have no balagula in this family,' he said. And that was that.

Shura wasn't familiar with the word; his Yiddish was pretty rudimentary, only enough for the odd phrase here and there—and a bit of flirting. But he got the gist. When he looked the word up, things weren't as bad as he'd feared: *balagula*, from *ba'al-'agala*, was a cart driver who travelled back and forth between villages with messages and deliveries, singing songs about his horses on the market square. A drunken vagabond with neither home nor family, good for nothing but singing and drinking. A clown, a street artist. That wasn't what Shura wanted at all; he wanted Shakespeare. But his Yiddish wasn't good enough to persuade his father, so he enrolled to study medicine.

Etina had also learnt a trade. There's much speculation as to what that trade might have been, but something worthwhile, that's for sure, something that came in useful no matter what course life took—because that's the way things were in those days: the state, as Etina and Shura explained to me, let humans be human. And when I asked whether it had ever made a difference that they were Jewish—when apprenticeships were allocated, for instance, or later, at university—had it annoyed anyone that the list of outstanding students (or any other list in that state where they let humans be human) was headed by a couple of yids?—they always said: Not before the war.

They said Stalin wasn't anti-Semitic. The Russians and Ukrainians and Moldovans were, but not Stalin; he was from the Caucasus, and anti-Semitism wasn't allowed out of people's hearts and onto the streets until after the war, in '53, when the Soviet Union began to clamour that the Jews had killed Joseph Vissarionovich Stalin—Jewish doctors like Etina Natanovna Vodovozova and Alexander Isaakovich Farbarjevich.

But all that was yet to come when Etina and Shura stood facing each other in the medical faculty of the University of Odessa—between them a parcel tied with a red bow, which, according to one of them, contained underwear.

We're talking 1936 here; we're talking about the Soviet Union where the housing situation and a belief in things higher than carnal desire reduced romance to going for walks. Going for walks and perhaps occasionally taking a girl's hand. That was all Shura knew.

A gentle, softly spoken man, rather short, with broad shoulders, eyes the colour of bruised raspberries and a forehead you could see yourself in, Shura was no womaniser, though you could be forgiven for thinking so, considering the number of women, young and not so young, who sought his company. He did a great deal of reading and writing, especially writing, because he thought it was the true socialist duty of everyone on earth to be happy, and writing was what made him happiest. That was before he'd seen the back of Etya's neck, but much later, when he felt he'd seen his fill of Etya, there would come a time when writing would once again become an anchor for him.

Etya, who'd never even let herself be persuaded to go for a walk with a man, turned red as a star.

She caught her breath. For some reason she heard her mother shouting and recalled the morning when they'd passed Rabinovich's shop together and she'd shown Valentina the red shoes with the medium-high heels. She'd had her eye on them for a while and asked her mother shyly whether she thought she might one day be able to own a pair like that if she saved up. Valentina had lashed out at her, only just missing her face, and shouted that there wouldn't be any of that in her family, and Etina Natanovna had to walk down the street with her mother yelling all manner of things behind her, cursing her daughter for everything that hadn't worked out in her own life—even her migraines, which had recently become more frequent.

All this came back to Etinka as she stared at the parcel on top of her pile of textbooks, and tears rose to her eyes, but without brimming over. That lout, that uncouth ape, that farshtinkener was never going to see her cry, that was for sure—nobody was, for that matter, but him least of all. And calmly, almost too calmly, she took the parcel from the top of the pile, dropped it on the floor at his feet, turned heel in her medium-high brown shoes and strutted back down the corridor as if pulled along by a string, not too fast and not too slow. As if nothing had happened.

From then on, things went downhill with Shura. He buried himself in his books and wrote and wrote and wrote, strictly forbidding himself from attempting love poems and telling himself over and over that he wasn't a number two—wasn't he a komsomol'skii vozhak, head of the student komsomol, the Communist Youth League, the youth organisation of the CPSU? Hadn't he been sent to Kiev to represent the entire region of southern Ukraine? One day he'd be the stuff of legends—why should he waste his time on women? That was for men with no other goals in life.

He set up a drama group, wrote plays about Dzerzhinsky, called his comrades-in-arms enemies of the revolution if they turned up late to rehearsals or didn't put enough pathos into the lines he'd written, and decided to become Russia's most famous what-you-may-call-it. He wouldn't settle for anything less.

After the incident of the red-beribboned parcel, Etina could think of nothing but Shura and his (in her opinion) cynical smile. She told all her girlfriends what a rude unsocialist idiot that Farbarjevich was— someone to be avoided at all costs. Just the way he held himself told you he was sly and weak; he was clearly a bad loser and probably a misogynist too. She repeated all this so often that one day her friends asked if she was sure she didn't feel something for this Farbarjevich. At that, Etina grabbed her things and stormed out of the library cafe into the fresh air, along Dvoryanskaya, along Primorskaya, and on to the harbour. She ran down all hundred and ninety-two steps of the Potemkin Stairs, only stopping once to look at a boy and girl in Pioneers' uniforms sitting at the edge. They were swapping marbles, touching each other's kneecaps rather more than was necessary.

Months later, during a surgery lecture in which an operation was performed on a corpse to show the students how to close an abdominal wall, Shura noticed that Etina wasn't looking at the choreography of hands and threads, or at the heads in their cylindrical surgical caps, but at him. Her green eyes flashed across the lecture theatre to him, and she didn't look away even when he turned his head so as not to have to squint at her.

That night he lay awake. His pillow was drenched in sweat, his feet itched, his chest swelled, and he sat up and made a decision. He stumbled through the dark to his desk and ejaculated everything that had been pent up inside him onto sheet after sheet of white paper. He wrote all night.

In the morning he didn't go and wait in the corridor; he went looking for Etina. When he found her, he walked straight up to her and asked what she had against the poetry of the great Mayakovsky—what had the man done to deserve her disdain? Taken aback, Etina said nothing, and Shura quickly explained that the parcel with the red bow had contained precisely that: Mayakovsky's poems. And practically in the same breath Alexander Isaakovich asked Etina Natanovna if she'd marry him and she, almost as quickly, answered yes. She felt ashamed, but didn't lower her eyes, because she'd learnt never to lower her eyes—a socialist citizen didn't look down.

In 1939 they both graduated with honours, then came the war. *If Russia's knocked out, England's last hope will be dashed. Then Germany will be master of Europe and the Balkans.* We all know what happened next.

Shura and Etya didn't want to speak to me about the war years. Whenever I asked, they'd tell me about how they met, giving a different version each time—a *very* different version. Most of the things I know about the war, I know from the memoirs Shura wrote years later. By that time he was having trouble telling a spoon from a biro, but then he'd been on the go for more or less an entire century. No one could say exactly how long, because the birth certificates were tinkered around with so much, but I do know that we celebrated his hundredth birthday before he closed his eyes for the last time. Those eyes remained alert to the end, and to the end he was writing astonishingly lucid thoughts on the tablecloth with his spoon.

On 22 July 1941 Shura stood at the window of a friend's flat in Balta, Etina's parents' city, watching tanks make their way down the main thoroughfare. When he looked up, he saw reconnaissance aircraft. Not long after, the first bombs fell.

Balta was a very leafy city, and the trees were burning within minutes. Soon chunks of wall were raining down too, but the house where Shura was staying wasn't hit. He ran out and, climbing over writhing—and no longer writhing—bodies, he tried to reach the hospital where his doctor friend was on duty. Low overhead, a plane was shooting at anything that moved, including Shura. By the time he got to the hospital, it had been bombed, but the ambulance parked outside was still in one piece. Shura found the driver hiding in the bushes and shook him until he agreed to help gather up the injured people and take them to a hospital further out of town.

Once in the ambulance, the driver refused to get out, and Shura couldn't lift the injured people on his own. He saw a man pressed against the side of a crater and ran over to ask him for help. They drove around the city together, loading and unloading wounded bodies, and in the polyclinic on the city outskirts they shook hands and promised to see each other again.

That day's dispatch was: *The Germans are advancing. They are close to Balta.* Anyone who didn't want to be captured or trapped in the besieged city should evacuate Balta immediately, leaving all their possessions behind.

Shura made it to Odessa on the open tray of an AMO-F-15. The man next to him lay with his head burrowed in Shura's jacket for the entire journey. Shura walked to his flat without seeing the city; he couldn't have said whether he recognised it, whether it had been bombed or destroyed. All he knew was that he must get there, collect his pregnant wife and leave with her—take her away, to relatives in the east. When he arrived, the flat was empty. All the furniture, all the things were in their places, but there was no sign of Etina.

Shura went next door and dragged his neighbour out onto the corridor by his collar. The man's alcohol-soaked breath made his face smart and the man said he knew nothing, hadn't seen Etya for days, no idea where she was, but the whole town was running for their lives—it was hardly surprising if she'd cleared off too. Shura almost threw him over the banisters, but then threw him back into his flat instead and went out onto the street. He decided to call on all his friends, one by one. Etina could be anywhere—but perhaps it was no bad thing that she wasn't here; why should a heavily pregnant woman wait around by herself in a city-centre flat? He tried to run, but his legs were numb and with every step it seemed less clear to him what he was supposed to do with his feet. He walked more and more slowly. He'd had nothing to eat for more than forty-eight hours, and barely anything to drink; it wasn't hard to diagnose the reason for his dizziness. He knew that he urgently needed water; he only had to find a shop or a public lavatory, but it was hopeless because he couldn't see anything of his surroundings. Aiming for the furthest point he could focus, he dragged himself along a street that seemed to soften and fray as he walked. He felt wind around his head, but it didn't cool him, only ruffled his hair and made his ears smart. He wasn't sure whether the bombing had already started in Odessa or whether it was the sun beating down.

When the road began to curve downhill like an overstretched bow, Shura sat on the pavement and stared in front of him. Pressing two fingers to his throat to take his pulse, he tried to breathe steadily, and the sharp stench of piss stung his nose and throat. Then there was a scratching at his calf, and something tugged at him and moved in his trouser leg. He heard a rustle beneath his feet. *Rats*, was his first clear thought.

He looked down at himself. The ground was heaving with grey furry creatures, but they weren't rats; they were tiny inch-long cats, swarming round him, crawling up him, getting under his trousers and shirt. He leapt to his feet and began to shake himself; then he noticed a woman standing on the pavement watching him—a woman draped in so many shawls, he could see neither her face nor her body. She was smaller than Shura, but beneath the mountain of cloth she looked like a giant caterpillar in a cocoon, inching her way towards him. She reached out a matted arm to him and slapped him on the back, beating him like a dusty cushion. 'There, there, my boy,' she murmured—or something like that. Shura could hear only mumbling; even her mouth was swathed in cloth. When she'd knocked the last cat from his body, she grabbed his hand and said: 'Come with me.' Shura looked at her hand, rough as oak bark, a gnarled root growing around his wrist— then into her clear blue eyes beneath the colourful shawls. For a second he thought he was going to faint, then a cat bit his calf and with a cry he tore himself free and ran off.

Etina was at Khava and Roman's. She was sitting calmly at their kitchen table drinking black tea with quince jam when Shura came charging in. His hair was all over the place, his clothes looked as if the entire German army had had a go at them, there was blood on his trouser leg. He couldn't get a word out; only made noises, pointing his finger at the door, the window, Etina—then starting all over again, jabbing his finger around the room. It was a quiet, hot day. The sun stole through the window onto the kitchen table, the parquet floor, Etina's cheeks. She put down her tea glass and told her husband to sit down and have something to eat, all the time stroking her belly with her left hand. She'd made up her mind that nothing was going to stop her from looking forward to this baby—not the war, not her clearly crazed husband, and not the advancing Germans.

After the Wehrmacht's invasion of the Soviet Union, doctors were in demand. When Shura was appointed head of the evacuation hospital, he was only twenty-five and urgently needed to acquire an air of authority if he didn't want his patients to gun him down before he'd had a chance to stitch them up. He grew a beard and a big bushy moustache to make himself look older, and smoked as much as he could to make his voice rougher, more manly, coarser, harsher. It never worked.

The drugs he took didn't make him older or harsher or coarser either. He was soon supplementing his corrosive Caucasian tobacco with caffeine tablets, and he drank too, though not much, more as a kind of mouthwash. There weren't many ways of deadening your senses. Painkillers weren't available at the front—not for patients or doctors—but later, when Shura had access to pharmaceuticals of every description, he used them all. Still he remained a soft, rather slow fellow with a voice that was pleasant to listen to.

He spoke quietly, but very clearly, enunciating every syllable of every word like an actor, stressing the final vowels and respecting the melody of the sentences. He'd trained himself to look knowledgeable, and the patients trusted his close-knit eyebrows, his prominent nose, his earnest, focused eyes. They couldn't believe that a man who looked and spoke as if he were reciting a socialist poem would allow them to succumb to necrosis. Often he could only half fulfil their hopes, and sometimes not even that, but hope isn't meant to be fulfilled. If anything, hope fulfils us—for as long as it lasts.

As head of the evacuation hospital, Shura was in charge of a cohort of doctors and a whole army of nurses and volunteers who scurried about like ants, hard-working but afraid that they might at any moment be squashed underfoot. Not so Shura. Since he'd run away from the cat woman in her cocoon of shawls and found Etina at Khava and Roman's kitchen table, since Balta and everything around him had burnt, it felt as if a trapdoor had slammed shut inside him with a crash that rang in his ears. He'd heard the clang of a metal hatch somewhere behind his Adam's apple, and tasted the echo under his tongue, and ever since, he'd been missing one of humanity's most primitive instincts. Here, in the middle of the war, he realised he could no longer feel something that was paralysing everyone else around him: fear.

He felt no fear when he saw the injured dying under his hands. He felt no fear when his daughter Emma was born and declared clinically dead, and no fear of the after-effects when she was resuscitated. He felt no fear when his wife was fleeing from the advancing Germans with her father and the baby, and sent word that his father-in-law had been fatally wounded by a bullet when he'd thrown himself over the newborn to protect her.

Shura heard all about the war and the atrocities committed by the armies, and when he held the results in his hands and fixed them up, he radiated a calm that seemed almost dangerous. There was something unnerving and hypnotic about it; Shura's reactions were out of all proportion to the apparently disintegrating world around him. His pupils never dilated—or rather, they were always dilated; they rested on the people he spoke to, as if eating them up whole, and who can say whether it was the drugs in his system or a psychopathological dysfunction—a trauma, a shock, or maybe a kind of paralysis.

'It is perhaps important to note,' Shura wrote in his memoirs, 'that being free from fear is by no means the same as being courageous.'

He was only a short distance from the front. Trains of injured people arrived every day; on some days there were about twenty wagons full of screaming half corpses who had to be operated on then and there—with or without anaesthetic, depending on the rations situation. Afterwards, those with some hope of survival were sent further east in the same trains, into the hinterland—and anyone who made it that far became a war hero.

Etina and Shura are said to have worked miracles. They are said to have healed children who had played with grenades—patching them up and stroking their heads and releasing them into a glorious future. Armed with penicillin, though not with painkillers, they are said to have been present at all the crucial battles against the Germans, operating day and night, and narrowly saving the most important snipers from certain death. In this way they had a decisive effect on the battle of Stalingrad and the fate of the Soviet Union—and with it, the fate of the entire world. It is even said that Shura, for whatever reason, treated and healed a German officer.

There are photos of Shura with Afanasyev—not the collector and editor of Russian fairytales, but the Afanasyev from Pavlov's House, the building that was able to hold out against the German Sixth Army for two months, and whose bullet-pocked façade was left as a reminder and stands there to this day like a piece of rotten Swiss cheese. It's possible, then, that my great-grandparents were instrumental in holding the world together on the frontline while simultaneously guiding the hand of Afanasyev, the legendary sniper of Stalingrad. Possible. Another version of the story has it that Afanasyev didn't come to Shura for treatment until after the war, by which time he'd already been blind for twelve years. The operation was a success and

Afanasyev, with his newfound sight, leapt straight off the operating table into Shura's arms, shouting: 'Ya vizhu! Vizhu!' *I can see! I can see!*

Either way, they were friends. There are black-and-white photos to prove it, one of which I have on my mantelpiece. It shows them drawing on the ground with sticks, as if Afanasyev were demonstrating something very important to Shura, in the scant sand on the shore of the Volga. They are both wearing bowler hats and long coats, and stand stooping low over their sketch of the future. The photo is from the sixties and could be a scene from one of Shura's plays.

Other people say there were no miracles—not during the war at any rate. Afterwards, perhaps—but not in the Soviet Union. No one was saved and no painkillers could have helped ease what they saw and went through—no painkillers, no penicillin and no magical powers. A lot of people died—most people. The story of Shura and Etya's survival is made up of fragments of memories, mumbled into their black tea. They slurped their tea noisily and the air around us was heavy with bergamot.

After the war, Shura's company stayed in Sumy, not far from Kharkiv, but a very long way from Odessa. Here he was appointed to the ministry of health as consultant and senior doctor, and very soon followed the party's call to Chernivtsi.

The invitation went like this: Come to Chernivtsi and choose yourselves somewhere to live, anywhere; size is no object. You can have whatever you like, even one of the former generals' period apartments with five rooms and high windows—something Etinka had always dreamed of. The magnificent prewar houses on the edge of town are all standing empty too. Come and help yourselves.

So they went and of course when they got there, all the grand flats and magnificent houses had been taken by high-up party officials. Goodness knows how they got there so quickly, but they came crawling out of their holes and took over the little town of Chernivtsi, so that all that was left for Etya and Shura and their daughter Emma was a flat far from the River Prut with small windows and a view of a blank wall. Etya wasn't having any of that. She shook her head very firmly and kicked up a huge fuss. She'd had a clear vision of their new flat on the riverbank, and was determined never again to live in such inhumane circumstances as she'd known during the war, with no medicine for the baby, and often nowhere to sleep but flat, exposed fields that served as everything at once: dorm, vomit pit, shithouse, changing table.

She rattled off her list of expectations, not stopping until a flat was found in the centre of town, with double doors, and windows overlooking a park, and the Prut only a walk away. On the floor above them, the first secretary of the regional committee had a flat with exactly the same layout.

But if Etinka had organised a decent flat for the family, she didn't often get to see her husband there; he was busy at the hospital, fighting those two postwar classics, goitre and tuberculosis. Shura dreamed of the beautiful high-ceilinged rooms and the leafy view as he dozed off on the bunk in the doctors' mess. He used the word 'home' when he told Etinka about his dreams and she thought, well, maybe that was something.

At about the same time Shura was appointed chair of the regional ministry of health, an office he assumed with the passion and conviction of a zealot, barely losing enthusiasm even after 1953 when the entire party was convinced that he and his like were responsible for the death of Joseph Vissarionovich Stalin. His colleagues were jailed by the dozen, but Shura remained a staunch believer in socialism to the end. He wasn't blind; he saw what was going on around him and knew that, had it not been for a sign from the chairman of the KGB office in Moscow that he rated Shura's work highly—his work, his hypnotic smile, his entire manner (in spite or perhaps because of the patronymic Isaakovich and the surname Farbarjevich, Shura knew how to make himself liked)—had it not been for that sign, he too would have been sharing a cell with his Jewish colleagues, fifteen and sometimes twenty men to a room.

Shura used the word *komnata*, room, and he described these rooms to me in great detail. The detail had been provided by those colleagues of his who had seen those 'rooms' from the inside; he passed on what was passed on to him, and the retellings all resembled one and the same film that everyone would watch years later on Soviet television. I didn't distrust Shura; I knew he'd never deliberately whitewash a past that had ploughed so many furrows in his face. But I distrusted the flowery language he used because I have a fundamental distrust of my mother tongue, which is improbably better than the world it comes from—more florid and momentous than reality could ever be.

This sign from the party chairman—the sign that preserved Shura from the 'rooms'—was something he told me about at length, and the story went like this: Alexander Isaakovich, his wife and his little girl were on two occasions invited to the dacha of a superior party official to stir jam into black tea and nibble at sushki.

Some of you may find this picture a little too reminiscent of the pictures adorning your bargain-basement samovar, but that's exactly what it was like: a young family in the flower-filled gardens of Chernivtsi, painted in just the same colours, and just the same naive style as a cheap samovar. They dunked their sushki in the sweet black tea, squinted at the American-looking mid-range car that was parked in the vine-covered garage construction—a dark blue Pobeda, a 'Victory'—and held sophisticated conversations about Russian literature and the German-Soviet war. They did this twice. After the second occasion, they were given to understand that people like them couldn't expect to be received in such circles indefinitely—and by 'people like them' the powers that be meant *nishchie*, paupers. However well-read they might be, the young couple couldn't rely on their knowledge of Russian literature to pull themselves out of poverty. This was conveyed to them with great tact and politeness, but Etina and Shura had acquired a taste for the life and wanted more. They tried every path open to them and each one, without exception, took them by way of the party, in which they believed with pure-hearted faith.

Then came 1953, delo vrachei, the doctors' plot. It's hard to credit, but you had to give reasons for firing someone in the Soviet Union—even a Jew. In Shura's file the reason for dismissal was 'insufficiently qualified'. He left—was made to leave. Were his concerns about feeding his family really uppermost in his mind at that time? Who can say. We must remember that his wife wasn't fired, and that as head of the paediatric tuberculosis clinic, she was senior enough to provide for the entire family—and indeed half the children on her ward. Deep, ineradicable humiliation settled on Shura's slightly protuberant eyes like a greasy film. By then he'd seen a lot and heard a thing or two—there'd been some wrangling over the zhid* Farbarjevich during the war—but Shura had never been deserted by either the state or his party, his real reason, his *only* reason for believing in a future after the horrors of the war. What good was a future without the party? Where would they go if the party let them down? What good was it Lenin saying: 'You must take the path of justice, comrades!' if Shura was left sitting on the street watching the party stride ahead without him? Without Stalin and without him.

A doctor from a nearby hospital offered to share his wages with Shura if he'd relieve him of three-quarters of his work. Before long, the doctor had stopped going to work altogether and was letting the Jew

---

* A Russian term of abuse for Jews.

do the lot. This worked out rather well because all Shura wanted was to see patients and talk to people—anything to avoid sitting around at home, waiting for the knock on the door, waiting for someone to come and take him away—him and maybe his wife and maybe his daughter. He knew it could happen at any moment, and then they'd be gone and no one would say anything, because all those who might have said something were already gone. It wasn't that Shura felt fear, because he didn't, but he didn't want to abandon himself to his disgust at the silence on the streets and on the corridors and in the consulting rooms—his disgust at having to be an ant.

In his memoirs, Shura wrote: 'I always knew that everything that happened to me was ultimately for the best.' What can you say? A true socialist. And indeed he claims in that slim document that he'd never have made it out of Odessa's gangster district to become one of the biggest names in the USSR if it hadn't been for the summer of '53, when, as he puts it, 'I got off scot free because I'd been fired'.

The summer of '53 was a real Chernivtsi summer. The asphalt melted and people hardly ventured out—except of course to watch the local football team; some things were sacred. To survive the scorching heat, everyone in town ate ice creams on sticks. The ambulance stood ready for action at the stadium gates, snapping up the occasional sunstroke victim. But one ambulance wasn't enough to cope with what happened in the summer of '53. The ice creams, at eight kopeks a piece, were eaten by all 746 spectators, and most of them had two or three each. Contrary to regulations, these ice creams had been produced using ducks' eggs, and those ducks' eggs were long past their use-by date. And so the whole town fell to puking—or at least that's what it looked like, and it's what it smelt like too, for the whole of that long summer and on into the autumn.

Two people died of food poisoning—they were the ones who'd

gobbled three ice creams. About a hundred sustained permanent damage—they were probably the ones who'd eaten two. And somehow or other, the ducks' eggs contrived to leave about ten people crippled for the rest of their lives. Nobody in the city of Chernivtsi (with one exception) touched another ice cream until the next summer.

Among the afflicted was Shura and Etina's daughter, Emma. She was thirteen at the time and not remotely interested in football, but she liked going out and mingling with other young people; it was one way of escaping the claustrophobic atmosphere of her tiny room in the communal apartment where her family had been forced to move when her father was suspended. She sustained no permanent damage—just puked for twenty-four hours without stopping and complained of awful headaches for days afterwards—a habit she never lost.

Also among the afflicted was Dyadya Iosif, uncle to Emma's future husband Daniil, who was still in Belz at this time, schlepping sacks of potatoes on his young back to earn money for the family, and especially for his little sister Dora. Iosif soon got over the vomiting—and was the only person in town to go and buy himself another ice cream the very next day.

A culprit had to be found for the match-day hygiene disaster. The whole town had been poisoned; somebody's head had to roll. Well, all right, it wasn't the whole town and there were no guillotines in the Soviet Union, but as I said, Russian-speakers tend to hyperbole; they think in hyperbole. It's no exaggeration, though, to say that the Chernivtsians were looking for a culprit to stand against the wall—one last cigarette and then God help you. A procedural plan was drawn up, stipulating that this culprit had to be chair of the health ministry, a position that Shura had occupied only three months before. But he'd been fired; *his* head couldn't roll.

The office was now held by a woman, a certain Inna Vasiliyevna Timosheva who had the reputation of being a *zheleznaya*, an iron lady. This woman had somehow managed to wangle the job with no medical qualifications or indeed any qualifications at all. Nobody quite knew how she'd done it, but in the same way, she also managed to avoid being shot. She got to sit in one of the 'rooms' instead, or maybe she was sent into exile, but the rooms are more likely, though not necessarily the best option—not at this point in history and not afterwards either, but still. Shura, at any rate, narrowly escaped death. What a good thing Joseph Vissarionovich was obliging enough to kick the bucket when he did, so that Shura lost his job rather than his head, with those soft purple eyes of his that got darker and darker as time went by.

Shura kept working, calmly and illegally, doing the job of his Ukrainian colleague and looking neither left nor right, but straight ahead into the future promised him by Ulyanov.

Etinka didn't think much of Ulyanov; she didn't think much of the dead—whether or not they were embalmed and mummified and lying in state in open coffins. She believed only in the living, and was determined to belong to them. But her will to survive had covered her beautiful face in a shiny coat of wax, and her little patients and hospital colleagues and even sometimes people on the street would stop and salute when they passed her, like people passing Lenin's mausoleum.

Management of the paediatric tuberculosis sanatorium had been transferred to Etina after the war. Tuberculosis was the top killer in the USSR even before the war, so you can imagine the situation during and after. You could say people were dying like flies, except that they weren't: unlike flies, they died slowly, spitting blood, the children with big beseeching eyes that Etina tried not to look at. Every day, between five and fifty child patients were admitted, some of them still infants, and Etina cut the tuberculosis out of their bones and lungs herself, as she'd learnt in the war, and then nursed them herself. She had a reputation for doing everything in person; there is said not to have been a single child in the two-hundred-and-thirty-bed sanatorium who didn't pass through her hands. She even tackled the building work more or less single-handedly; she was always having extensions built—'There's not enough room, anyone can see that. What do you expect me to do with the children—stack them in piles?'

Etina's capable socialist hands were always clad in turquoise plastic gloves. One day, one of these gloves ripped in the middle of an oper-ation. It was late at night and she noticed the rip and even saw a drop of blood on the left glove, but she was so tired she could hardly stand. She went on operating for as long as she could, then collapsed onto the sofa in the corridor and went to sleep, still wearing her shoes—the red ones with the medium-high heels. (She'd chucked the turquoise surgeon's gloves.)

She was the first to notice the symptoms. First her voice grew hoarse in the afternoons. Her high, imperious voice, which sounded like a siren's song when she wanted something and like a cannon shot when she didn't, grew gradually fainter, like that of a sleepy child. Next, the lymph nodes in her groin and under her arms swelled—and by then she knew. Soon she had all the symptoms—night sweats and shivering fits and fever—and there was no pretending it was mere over-exhaustion.

She had the infected hand put in plaster, hospitalised herself and took charge of her own case, giving the young doctors hoarse, but firm instructions on how to treat her. At the same time, she continued to run the sanatorium from her sickbed.

Shura sat in Etina's sickroom, watching her talk to three nurses at the same time. One of them was administering drugs that were never approved for use in the West because of their high toxic content; the other two were being given orders to relay to the children's ward.

Etinka rated her survival chances at ten to one and prescribed herself streptomitsinizoniazidpara-aminosalitsilovaya kislota. You could compare it to going to Chernobyl for a dose of radiotherapy, but that would be jumping the gun—Chernobyl was still in the future; this was the late forties.

Shura sat in his wife's room and said nothing. When at last everyone had gone out, she said: 'What will you do when I'm dead?' She asked him straight out; she wasn't one to beat about the bush. She was very lucid, still electrified from talking to the nurses; when she put the question to him, her face twitched as if she were plugged into an electric socket.

'Keep going, of course, what else?' she said, answering her own question, because still Shura said nothing. 'Stop looking like that. It's no help to me at all.'

'What would be a help to you?' Shura was sitting over by the opposite wall; he wasn't allowed to get close to his wife.

'Take Emma to Khava's and get her hair cut.'

So Shura did. For the first time in his life he took his daughter by the hand and off they went to Khava's, Emma somewhat taken aback that her father was going anywhere with her at all, let alone to a hairdresser. Khava and her husband Roman had also come to live in Chernivtsi and she ran an improvised beauty salon in their living room. 'Fancy seeing you here, Professor Farbarjevich!' she said when she opened the door to the two uncertain faces. 'Have you come to have your eyebrows plucked?' Shura was embarrassed. Etina always cut his hair and he'd never let anyone near his eyebrows. He felt that a socialist had no business to be in a place like this; in the chink between the bathroom door and the shower curtain he'd even glimpsed a sliver of naked female leg. He was suddenly reminded of the woman with the Pioneer-red lips who'd sat opposite him in the acting school he'd been so keen to attend. He set his daughter on the barber's chair on the balcony (her hair really did look like a bird's nest) and vanished into the kitchen.

Shura looked at his close-cropped fingernails and his shiny shoes. He looked at the clock ticking away on the wall, its crooked hands scratching the dial, and he thought to himself that if Etina were to die, he wouldn't do anything at all, simply because it wasn't going to happen; it was quite impossible. He needn't bother his head over it; she wouldn't leave him on his own; she was a woman with a strong sense of duty.

He turned out to be right. Etinka refused to be broken either by the disease or by the toxic drugs. Her expression for it was *sebya nodnyala*—she'd pulled herself out, like Baron Munchausen pulling himself out of the swamp by his own pigtail. 'Anything else would have been ridiculous,' she'd say to me, laughing, and her husband would give her a shy sidelong glance. By then his eyes were as dark as blackberries and the chapped skin around his mouth was grey.

Etina was every bit his equal when it came to super-heroic exploits. How could it be otherwise? She'd survived the war and saved a daughter who was doomed to die from birth.

Etina and Shura's daughter Emma was seven when Etinka fell sick, and she didn't see her mother for almost a year. This didn't much bother her because they'd never had a lot to say to each other anyway. She had her father. He, it is true, was lost in the higher reaches of science, but he radiated a sense of calm that was as much as Emma needed. Self-sufficiency was what she was best at anyway. Emma was a delicate little thing, prone to dizzy spells. She liked reading, especially poetry—she had whole reams by heart—amused herself with a bit of piano and a bit of acting, and spent hours in front of the mirror running her fingers through her freshly cut ash-blond curls. It would never have occurred to anyone to call her ideological or socially aware, let alone politically minded, but when news came in '53 that the great leader Stalin had died, she surprised everyone—her nanny Alina, the cook Darya, and most of all her parents who were, for once, both present—by falling into a faint. She sensed that it was a momentous event and probably one that boded no good.

Years later, her parents would tell this story as if it were an episode in the life of a true Soviet child, devastated by the immense loss—a child who would, of course, have given her life for the great leader, except that it was too late for that now: the children of the Soviet Union were all irrevocably orphaned.

Etina's 1953 resembled that of all Jewish doctors: she got the sack. Or rather, she almost got the sack. The necessary papers were lying ready in the health minister's office and he signed them all without even glancing at her name. *Posnimali* was the term used back then—*taken down*. Every Jewish doctor in the great and mighty Union was to be taken down like an unwanted portrait, even right out at the edge of town and in the remotest villages. That was the idea, at least.

For Etina Natanovna Farbarjevich, things turned out differently; her case was championed by Raissa Filatova herself, the first secretary of the district committee. It is perhaps worth mentioning at this point that although Russian is a gendered language, it has no feminine form for doctors, teachers and other workers (first secretaries included), so that any Soviet woman practising these professions necessarily assumed a kind of masculine persona and with it a degree of toughness, which suited most of them very well. Where else but in the Soviet Union did you come across such emotionally degenerate multi-talents, hardened by hunger and air raids and veteran husbands—women with no interest in feminine endings, feminism or antidepressants? For them, life was too short to bother about such niceties; there was the war-torn nation to take care of, a crippled husband, and of course the children. Raissa Filatova was just that kind of woman, and when she heard that Comrade Farbarjevich had been dismissed with immediate effect, she banged her solid wood desk with her solid palms and shouted: 'No way will I let her go! Do you want to send hundreds of children to their deaths, or what? Do you want the entire Union to die? Do you want *me* to die, damn it? What's the idea?' The subject wasn't open to discussion. Someone should have kissed the woman's reddened hands and cheeks. If only there'd been more like her.

So Etina stayed and continued to run the sanatorium. She could have made a great career for herself: it is said that her doctoral thesis was better than Shura's; it is said that she too could have been an inventor—who knows what she might have achieved. But Etina, proud Etina with her pinned-up hair, chose the other path and decided to be the wife of an important figure rather than an important figure in her own right. She knew that being important would mean giving herself body and soul not only to science, but also to more than one scientist, and that wasn't something she was prepared to do—she couldn't muster the necessary energy. The inevitable was quite enough for her.

Alexander Isaakovich Farbarjevich meanwhile, working illegally at a job that wasn't his, threw himself into his scientist's career, and things went fast. When he needed a supervisor for his dissertation, he found a medic who was said to protect Jews, and the man must have seen something in Shura—or else he had a guilty conscience because nobody knew that his surname was really Perlman and that he'd traded it for a Russian one during the war in exchange for a few roubles. This protector of Jews took Shura under his wing and did all he could to help him. Farbarjevich's paper on prolonging the effect of penicillin in the eye was quite a sensation. Shura observed that any penicillin dropped in the eye was flushed out again by tear fluid half an hour later, so he developed a method of storing semi-impermeable capsules under the eyelid that allowed the precious penicillin to be released gradually and act for up to two days. The method spread like wildfire through the hospitals of the Soviet Union and set the standard for the treatment of eye diseases for decades to come. It is used all over the world to this day in the administration of ophthalmic drugs.

For the rights to his invention Professor Doctor Farbarjevich received forty roubles and a decoration. It goes without saying that there were no patent rights in the USSR, where individuals were duty bound to place themselves entirely at the service of the nation and the perfection of Communism. But as well as a bit of money and a medal of honour, Shura got his first taste of fame. People recognised him on the street and shook him by both hands. That was the great thing about the village mentality of the Soviet Union and its tendency to serfdom: a successful doctor was worshipped the way a film star was worshipped in the West. And in those days forty roubles wasn't as little as it sounds. A doctor earned sixty a month—plus additional thank-yous in the form of chocolates and alcohol, and you could live off that—if not well, then decently enough.

Shura's next invention involved the use of light separation to examine the retina. Shura loved the various spectral ranges; he loved interference filters and narrow-band filters; he felt soothed by red-free, red, crimson, blue, yellow and orange filter discs. But when he walked the streets, he resembled a madman, with his dilated eyes—and though he looked left and right, he often seemed not to listen to the people next to him. He also had trouble focusing on objects for any length of time. By this point he was a genuine junkie, not yet hooked on cocaine but well past caffeine tablets. He was constantly thinking up new ideas, inventing and elaborating; he never stopped. His heady ambition was combined with a belief that he could change the world with his inventions, make it a better place, save the nation—he felt like an astronaut flying into the cosmos. People were having more and more trouble getting through to him; he withdrew from everyday life, was often irritable and refused to show an interest in others. But Shura's second invention struck like a meteorite. He got a call from party headquarters asking him to please pay a visit to such-and-such an artist to have his portrait painted for the city museum—the prerogative of every deserving comrade.

That was Shura's first portrait; many more were to follow, not to mention larger-than-life bronze head sculptures and photos documenting the casting process. None of them really captured his face; they couldn't compete even with the photo of him and Afanasyev on my mantelpiece. None of them showed the tousle-headed boy in beige trousers and sheepskin waistcoat who later (older now) sat opposite me over tea-and-quince-jam in his little modern flat in Lower Saxony, smiling as only Shura could smile.

I asked him why he hadn't packed us all up and cleared out of Russia as soon as the graffiti started to appear: *Zhid Farbarzhevich, ubiraisya v Israil'!** He'd made a name for himself in America; he could easily have got us out of the country; there'd even been invitations from New York.

Shura shrugged and said: 'Because I thought they'd find the culprits. The police were called in, after all.'

Etya snorted. 'Nonsense. Our caretaker Petya was nearer the mark. I met him sweeping the street one day and he said: "The police are looking? Who are they looking for? Have they asked me? I could point them to the culprit, but no one asks me." You didn't want to leave because you knew you'd be a nobody over there—that we'd all be nothings. And don't tell me you believed in the country's future—here it is, that future, and where's it got you? How long am I going to have to listen to these stories?'

---

* Farbarjevich, you fucking Jew, fuck off to Israel!

Shura and I stared at the plastic tablecloth and said nothing. Etinka took a big gulp of tea without scalding herself.

'I had the graffiti painted over every time. I had the wall painted so often that the decorators—Gena and Lyolya, they were called; I remember their names—came to me and said: "Etina Natanovna, we're glad to do this for you—we kiss your hands—but wouldn't you rather move away? This isn't going to stop, you know, and soon there'll be so many coats of paint on your house it'll start to look like a growth."'

We said nothing for a while, then Etinka took my face between her hands and ran her thumb over the stubble on my chin and upper lip. She looked long into my eyes and I could see her trying to make sense of something. Then she combed her fingers through my hair, stroked my neck and got up. Watching her slow progress to the door, I could see her almost hundred years. I hadn't noticed earlier; sitting at table she'd been the old Comrade Farbarjevich—the paediatric hospital tucked under one arm; husband, daughter and Soviet Union under the other. Time only struck when she got up. When she'd gone, Shura went to his bureau. He was no quicker than his wife—in him too, the century showed. His waistband was gathered in folds under his belly button, held only by a wide black leather belt; he was getting thinner and thinner. He rummaged through the drawers, mumbling something; I couldn't hear what. It was a new habit of his to talk to himself or, as he put it, 'to a friend'. Then he pulled a ten-page manuscript out of a drawer and put it on my plate along with the biscuit crumbs—the memoirs which he'd begun to type on his granddaughter's computer. Only ten pages—I'm afraid that's all I have. And I do wish Etinka had written too.

But Etinka didn't believe in diaries or memoirs; she didn't believe that her view of things was of any worth. One legend, though, has survived without ever being written down: it is said that she dreamed of singing on stage. She never told me; I have it from her daughter Emma. Not that Etinka ever sang. She never had lessons, made no attempt to realise that dream of hers; her daughter, husband, friends never even knew her to hum. It's true that her eyes would mist over when she heard the music of Iosif Kobzon, but there was nothing unusual in that. And yet it's said that she would have given all her achievements to appear once on stage; her daughter was quite clear about that. I must admit, though, that when I heard the story I did wonder whether Emma wasn't talking about herself.

DANYA AND EMMA

In ripe old age—he was well over seventy—Daniil, or Danya, or
Danichka stood at my desk, turning the pages of a South American
novel he'd found at the top of a pile of books. From the strained way
he held himself, I could see he was intent on understanding what his
grandson got up to all day in this Berlin flat, where he'd come to visit
him for the first and last time. I stood in the hall, a blue Crimea mug
in one hand for him and in the other a white mug, cracked at the edge,
for me, and I looked at his broad stooped back. He was wearing his
usual pepper-and-salt jacket; in my memory he is never anything but
sprucely dressed. He opened the novel without taking it from the pile
and turned the pages with a moistened finger. A lot of passages were
underlined—every five, ten, thirty or fifty pages, some in black biro,
some in blue, though without any method. On page 1150, he paused at
half a sentence underlined in red—perhaps because he imagined that

I'd gone to the trouble of getting up from the desk or sofa to fetch the pen specially: '...she and Werner and all the young people born around 1930 or 1931 were fated to be unhappy.'

He seemed to be studying the squiggly underlining and I supposed he was trying to decipher the notes I'd made in the margin. I wondered whether he even knew my handwriting. We didn't write to each other much and if we did, we texted or messaged. I was aware that a lot must have changed for him: my handshake was different; maybe my kisses were different too, now that I had a beard growing on my face. But as he turned to me with the book in his hand, I realised I had no idea how much he knew about the person I'd been before. Did he know enough to compare that person with the person I'd become? Enough to feel any kind of difference? How much had I let him share in my life?

I handed him the cup of tea and we sat down. He asked me whether I knew I'd underlined a lie—that the words weren't true: unhappiness wasn't limited to those born in 1930 or 1931; there were no limits to it at all; it pricked and chafed like empty sunflower-seed shells poking through the hessian sack on your back and the cloth of your shirt. At all events, unhappiness extended as far as 1937, the year he'd been born.

He said he'd tell me about it sometime if I liked and show me photos, and maybe even the cine films of his wedding. But I'd have to go to him, if that was what I wanted; I'd have to ask.

My grandfather Daniil had, in a traditional-minded way, been called after *his* grandfather, who'd been a rabbi. That was as much as Daniil knew about him, and he knew little more about any of the Levites and Cohens from whom he was descended. The family's knowledge of the Torah had run dry with Daniil's father, Boris, who had decided that the only way to get through life was godlessly; he'd never have guessed that his own son Daniil would end up believing. But nor would he have guessed how much times would change—or that his newly believing son would spend his last years in the very country where he, Boris, had left his faith at the front.

Boris's childhood, like that of so many rabbis' children, was quiet and poor and strict. When he was thirteen, his father explained to him that it was harder for a woman to get a foothold in life than for a man, so he was going to put all his money into educating Boris's sister Astra. If Boris wanted to go to university, he'd have to see to it himself. In those days, that meant getting top marks at school and generally being a model pupil; then, and only then, would you have prospects of further education—free further education, that is.

Astra went to Berlin to read modern languages at the Humboldt, which admitted female students from the early twentieth century. Whole hordes of ambitious young Jewish women put their heads together in the building on Unter den Linden, and Astra—little Daniil's auntie and big Daniil's daughter—was one of them. Besides modern languages, Astra studied engineering, which was how she met her husband. She married him and his respectable German surname in 1932, gave birth to a son (calling him, believe it or not, Albert, after Einstein) and got out of the country just in time in the mid-thirties, settling with her family in Almaty, where German bridge builders were in demand. In the early forties Astra Daniilovna fetched her parents to Kazakhstan, to preserve them from you-know-what, and since there was no leaving Kazakhstan once all the bridges had been built, she turned to giving language lessons. So it would seem that this particular branch of the family led a happy life, far from the horrors of the Shoah. Believe it if you can; I know no other version of the story.

Boris paid his way to a technical university in Bucharest, and it was there he met Clava, the eldest of six daughters born to a devout miller and his two-decades-younger blind wife who spent her days wandering the streets of the city, rounding up beggars to go and work at her husband's mill—she recognised them by the smells and sounds they gave off. All Clava's sisters made it to Palestine before it was too late, and presumably they—or at least their offspring—live there to this day. They were all spared by the war—and the Party. Not so Clava.

Clava had to share her husband with the Party; Boris's eyes and heart burnt for the Communist cause. He had proudly joined the Communist Party at a time when it was still called social democrat; now they were all Bolshevik—and none more than Boris.

Organisational skills, not armed combat, were Boris's strong point, and the Party gave him the task of evacuating all territories at risk of German invasion. One of these was the place where his wife and little Daniil were living; Boris's colleagues came for them, heaved them onto a barrow and smuggled them over the Dnepr.

Daniil, who was four when they were forced to flee, remembered only isolated scenes, such as his feet swimming away from him in the icy water when the barrow could go no further—like fish, only that they swam down, not along. Then there was the noise of the bombs, like meteorites striking Earth. He remembered the human bodies at the wayside, lying in their vomit, like fruit trampled underfoot. And he remembered his pregnant mother, shielding her tummy with her hands, and shouting, 'Get on the ground!' as she threw a blanket over him. Once, the blanket went up in flames. Miraculously Daniil wasn't hurt, but he would never forget the smell of singed skin. He made a careful study of the nuances of his mother's facial expressions at that time, because although she always seemed to stare stonily ahead, he was sure there was something underneath that she was trying to tell him.

When they got to Almaty, Boris's sister Astra put them up in her cellar. Food was almost impossible to come by in the city; you had to eat what you could wangle, but because Daniil's father had rendered great services in the war, Daniil was given buckwheat porridge in kindergarten. This was a privilege not granted to all the children; when he took up his spoon, the others stared at him with hungry eyes, and most of the time he was so unnerved he couldn't eat a thing.

Daniil's sister Dora was born in the cellar in Almaty, and Daniil stared at the newborn day and night, refusing for days to get off the sheet where the screaming, hungry babe was lying. Then he began to roam the streets in search of things to eat. He always found something, generally stealing from families who were no better off than his own. Whatever he got hold of—radishes, potatoes, apples, berries—he brought home and laid at Dora's feet, which were tinier than anything he'd ever seen.

There was barely enough room to sleep in the cellar and Daniil would often lie awake between his screaming sister and his mother, who lay there, huddled and motionless, her eyes closed. One night Clava opened her eyes and Daniil wasn't there. Fear gripped her. She dashed through her sister-in-law's house, whispering her son's name, afraid to wake the others, then out into the garden where her breath left her mouth in a milky broth. She pulled her shawl tighter around her shoulders and looked out into the grey nothingness of the city.

If Daniil's run away, I'll only have one mouth left to feed, she thought—and then: Oh please come back. Please, please, please. She must have spoken the words out loud, she realised, seeing her breath white in front of her face. Then she began to shout; she shouted Daniil's name, and he replied. Whatever was she shouting for? he asked. She knew Auntie Astra was asleep and hated being disturbed.

Clava looked down. The voice was coming from the dog kennel where Bella was kept, the German shepherd Auntie Astra had brought to Almaty along with her German family. Daniil was lying next to Bella in the kennel, only his head peeping out.

'What on earth are you doing in there?'

'There's more room here than in the cellar, Mum,' said Daniil sleepily, 'and I like Bella. She likes me too.'

Clava knelt down and studied the two faces, Bella's and Daniil's, looking out at her appealingly, cheek to cheek—four big, round eyes gleaming out of the darkness of the kennel. From then on, Daniil was allowed to sleep next to Bella whenever he wanted.

It was cold in the cellar, colder than outside, and the cold was heavy with the smell of damp earth. If they heated at all, they heated with the sunflower-seed shells that were dumped behind the market square—a sea of dry shells, prickly as brushwood, there for the taking. And plenty took; Daniil darted between the lumbering men with a big sack whose coarse weave couldn't protect his back from the pointy shells when he lugged the fuel home. He left a load at Auntie Astra's and took the rest into the cellar, emptying it in front of the stove, then sitting down at the end of Dora's mattress and warming himself at her little feet.

The war invalid from the next building, who had only one leg—and only half of that—managed to get hold of sugar, which he burnt on sticks to make lollipops that were shaped something like cockerels. He liked Daniil and let him help sell the lollies. The child's bright eyes and rosy cheeks were good for sales; people preferred to buy sweets from a cheerful boy with black curly hair than from a foul-smelling cripple. Daniil earned four kopeks a piece—a lot of money for him. He put the coins in his socks and ran home as fast as he could, terrified of being robbed by the other boys, who envied him his status as lolly-seller.

Daniil's mother made money by selling homemade plum jam. Her jam was famous; people came from the other end of town to try it and Daniil acquired the nickname Don Jam in school because he seemed to eat nothing but jam sandwiches. When Daniil's mother wasn't boiling up fruit and sugar, she was busy tending rosebushes.

She had a reputation for ringing strangers' doorbells and asking if she could take care of their gardens for them—especially the roses, which she was particularly fond of. When the householders asked how much she wanted for the work, she said: 'Nothing.' Most people paid her anyway; they weren't to know that if she came to them for work it was because she only really felt at peace with herself when she was gardening.

She was a strange person, who did a lot of looking, but not much talking. If times had been better, she might have gone out into the mountains and lived off herbs and roots, and her hair would have grown long and green, and her skin transparent and luminous. But times weren't better and Clava couldn't find any real use for herself, so she took care of others. She took care of her children and her sister-in-law's children and her neighbours' children and the children from the next street—and years later, when she was old and sick and dying, she said not a word about her pain, though she must have been in agony; it was the year when there was nothing but Pyramidon, after a gang of local doctors had made off with the entire stock of more effective painkillers and drugs and gone east with them. Clava's son Daniil, by then an established geologist, came from the mountains of Tajikstan to visit her—he'd managed to take a month's leave, because he knew it would be the last month he'd spend with his mother—and she didn't talk about herself at all, but said to Daniil: 'Will you promise me something, my boy? I'm worried about your father. He always forgets to wear a scarf and it's cold out; he'll catch his death.'

When Daniil's father returned from the war—the family were back in Chernivtsi by then—he didn't have a tooth left in his head; there'd been nothing to eat but herring. 'They didn't even give us water,' said Boris and then set about raising his son who'd turned into a khuligan in his absence—a word that may sound like 'hooligan' but means something different, namely wild-little-rascal-who-smokes-like-a-grown-up. Rascals like Daniil found cigarettes in attics and sneaked them out of men's pockets on the market, selling them back to the same men at five kopeks a piece, or more. Thus Daniil rose from lolly-seller to tobacconist. He smoked about fifteen a day himself, depending on sales and the emptiness of his belly, and he continued that way for forty-four years, only stopping when he realised that I was stealing cigarettes from him. I was exactly the same age as he'd been when he started and he knew I wouldn't stop as long as he was effectively supplying me.

Until Boris returned from the war, Daniil had no adult authority, but he was an authority himself, the leader of a gang of boys who'd once robbed him regularly. He was renowned for his skills as a thief, for the cheeky way he had of twisting his lips into a smile and whistling, and for managing to lead friends and neighbours up the garden path without incurring their wrath. Word got about that he exchanged everything he stole for useful things for his sister and mother—or at least that's what he managed to make people believe.

'Don't be too harsh on that son of yours, Borya,' a neighbour said, trying to coax the horrified father into leniency. 'I know he's a thief, but it'll stand him in good stead.'

'He'll end in jail. Is that what I lost all my teeth for?'

'Now, look here. Your son wangled this collection of photos out of my two boys, quite valuable photos, you know the kind I mean—girls in stockings, bottomless and all that, quality work—filched it from them and sold it on. And who did he sell it to? To me! Then he takes the money to my wife—*my* money to *my* wife—and points at the blue woollen shawl round her shoulders. Bold as brass he stands there, legs apart, hands on hips, and says he wants the shawl. For his sister, he says. Because it's so cold and damp in that hole you live in and his sister's always coughing.'

'Did she give him the shawl?'

'Of course she did—and the money stayed in the family.'
'And where did your boys get hold of the porn pics?'
'Stole them from me, what else?'

At the age of eight, Daniil possessed a whole arsenal of grenades and firearms. They were all over the place, he said. You stumbled on them in the street; you could go gathering them like mushrooms. The boys shot at empty houses with them, and sometimes at each other, but what they liked best was to throw the ammunition on a fire and watch it explode, shooting out in all directions, sometimes hitting one of the boys, sometimes a passing stranger. Once, an old woman in a headscarf was caught, a bent old babushka, who fell flat on the ground when the shell went off.

The first thing Boris did was to destroy his son's weapon arsenal. Daniil looked on with tears in his eyes as his father threw his treasured collection into the slaughterhouse pit. There was a beastly stench of blood and shit as the gleaming blades and heavy pistols sank into the brown-red wormy gall at the bottom.

But that wasn't the real punishment. The real punishment was the talking. Boris told Daniil about the war; he told him stories of what he'd seen and done—stories that went on for hours and invariably ended with the question: 'Did I go and fight in the war so that my son could become a good-for-nothing?'

One of the stories that Daniil had to listen to over and over—the story of Musya Pinkenzon—was particularly painful to him, because the boy killed was his age. Musya was Daniil's second cousin and twelve years old when he was shot dead by an SS officer for playing the 'Internationale' after being ordered to take out his violin and entertain the regiment. Daniil couldn't bear to hear it anymore. The images had branded themselves on his mind; they haunted him—the shattered violin, the screaming mother, the crowd of people staring at the ground as if frozen. He begged his father not to tell it again, but Boris was unrelenting. He believed that was the only way to get his son to understand what had gone on around him: to give him nightmares.

Jews from Belz and its environs had received orders to assemble in the market square. Musya's parents had sent him to his music teacher in the hope that she'd hide him, but when Musya stood at her front door and looked into her shrunken eyes, he knew it was hopeless and ran back onto the street, too fast for her to catch him. He ran and ran, his violin dangling at his chest—he was never seen without it; the local papers had described the five-year-old Musya as a musical prodigy, a wonder child—and he found his parents in a tightly packed crowd of people that looked more like one person, blurred and faceless. He screamed 'Mum!' and at first his mother didn't want to identify herself, hoping her son would be taken for a neglected Moldovan child, but when Musya made a beeline for his parents, she let out a shout.

The SS officer emptied his entire magazine, half of it into the boy's body, the other half into the body of the violin. Boris had seen the boy look the SS officer in the eyes and heard him strike up the 'Internationale' without a word. From then on, he knew the meaning of the word 'hero'.

Daniil would rather have had a hiding from his father than have to listen to these stories anymore. He didn't believe them; he didn't believe any war stories except his own. As far as he was concerned, his father's stories were fairytales, a way of creating a world that made sense. But the world didn't make sense; Daniil had worked that out long ago. He'd also worked out that his father hadn't lost his teeth for him, but for the war—so Daniil owed him nothing; if anything his father should settle his score with the war. He told him as much, and then said, 'Now hit me, if you want,' but Boris never hit him. Boris, who'd had to look on as the two soldiers he shared a gun with raped an entire family, mother, father and son—Boris, who hadn't dared intervene or run away, and whose memories of the war and its heroes had mingled to a red-brown wormy gall where he drowned his own nightmares—never again raised a hand to anyone. He'd forgotten how, so he talked instead. He talked on and on.

In order to preserve his son from a life on the streets and sure imprisonment, he found him work with a chandler, and soon Daniil was familiar with the smell of beef tallow—a smell he was to remember all his life. In the summer heat of southern Ukraine, the boy dipped cotton wicks into the seventy-degree yellowish white goo, absolutely riveted by the stuff. The skin on his face soaked up the smell of grease and more than once he thought of plunging his head into the melting vat and vanishing forever, but then he remembered Dora and resumed his work, pulling out the cotton thread with its thin coat of tallow, letting it dry, dipping it in again.

Daniil attended school regularly again. He got better marks and sometimes even very good ones, completed tenth grade and left school without any certification because by then they'd stopped issuing certificates to people with surnames like Pinkenzon.

'They knocked two points off because they said I made a political spelling mistake,' Daniel explained to his father.

'What do you mean, a political spelling mistake?'

'Apparently I spelt "Communist" with an "a": "Cammunist". And apparently that's libel and I should be glad they don't summon me to the nearest party headquarters.'

'And did you?'

'Did I what?'

'Spell "Communist" with an "a"?'

'What do you think?'

It was made clear to Daniil that a Pinkenzon had no business studying at the universities of Lviv or Moscow, but in Grozny they didn't seem to care and took all comers. Boris summoned him with all the gravity and pathos he thought the situation merited and said: 'My son, I have enough money for you to go and take an entrance examination anywhere in the Union of the Socialist Soviet Republic—and I mean anywhere. But it will only buy you a one-way ticket. If you pass the entrance exam, you can stay on and study and work and let us know that's what you're doing. If you don't pass, you can stay on and work and let us know that too. If you want to come back, you work until you've earned the money for a return ticket.'

The rabbi's son had renounced God, but he hadn't abandoned his father's methods of upbringing.

Daniil nodded, looking his father in the eyes and pitying him his toothless mouth and the meaningless babble that came out if it. He knew he'd pass the entrance exams; he wasn't the least bit worried about them—nor was he worried about making money. But he'd never forget that he'd been cautioned in spite of his good marks—'be grateful that you were even allowed to finish school.' That *did* worry him. He stared doggedly at his father and took the money for the one-way ticket.

In Grozny, Daniil passed oral and written exams in Russian, mathematics, physics, chemistry and a modern language—in his case, German. The teacher who examined him in this last subject and would later become his mentor and guardian angel was called Frida Isaakovna Garber.

He'd enrolled for German without ulterior motives. He'd never thought of leaving the Soviet Union; he didn't even know you could. It wouldn't have crossed his mind that he might spend the last years of his life in provincial West Germany, sitting at the window drinking tea in his only decent jacket, communicating with his grandchildren on a mobile telephone—Russian with one and German with the other—and paying visits to doctors with his daughter, because by that time his German was beginning to fade from his memory. Most things, indeed, were beginning to fade from his memory, but the name of his German teacher, Frida Isaakovna Garber, shot out of his mouth like a bullet.

Daniil had to choose a sport and picked boxing—rather than endurance running or swimming, which required even more endurance. 'Am I an animal or something?' he asked bitterly. 'I'll take up boxing—it'll come in useful if anything happens.' A bit of *podrat'sya i razoitis'*, as it was called in those days: fighting and separating.

He imagined the training as a kind of kulachnyi boi, that traditional form of fist-fighting held in the villages on Christian feast days to celebrate the local pack of boys, who would get into a huddle and thump each other with their fists as the older people stood around, looking on. Daniil was only a flyweight, but his university boxing teacher, a former Russian champion, threw him on the mercy of a middleweight who knocked him about so badly that after their first encounter in the ring, Daniil spewed half a tooth and could have sworn he saw stars—at any rate, he saw sparks and flames flying out of the middleweight's ears. Whatever it was the man did, Daniil wanted to be able to do the same. He watched the middleweight spread his fat arms as if he were drawing a bow, bring his right glove in front of his face, and keep throwing with his left, while his feet bounced up and down around Daniil like rubber balls. It was like watching modern ballet. Daniil ended up seeing a lot of sparks and stars, and his nose often came off the worse for wear, but he never gave up.

Of course Daniil couldn't really compete with someone a head-and-a-half taller than him, but the two of them got into the habit of going out for a drink together after training, and for three years they told each other things they didn't tell anyone else, even confessing to one another that the older they got, the more they understood their fathers—a thought that freaked them out so much, they had to drink faster. They also admitted to missing their sisters terribly; this made them come over all weepy, but that didn't bother them. After graduating, they drifted out of touch—then, some time later in Volgograd, they happened to meet in Chekists' Square. They stared when they saw each other, couldn't stop staring, and then they embraced, and kept embracing, only to push each other away, hold each other at arm's length, stare some more and fall into each other's arms all over again. They threw up their fists and bounced up and down, circling and dodging each other. They laughed. They threw punches and took punches, and they laughed and laughed.

'You've forgotten everything, you bloody egghead,' the middleweight shouted.

'Let's go and have a drink,' Daniil replied, throwing a hook just past his chin.

Daniil liked his studies, he liked his friends, he liked Grozny. On one occasion, he even saw Muslim Magomayev and Iosif Kobzon when they came to the city to vie for the title of Merited Artist of the USSR. Daniil and his friends had no money for tickets, of course, but they knew which trees to climb for a good view—it was almost like having seats in the front row of a box. All in all, Daniil was happy in Grozny—lonely, but happy.

Twice a year he went home to visit his family—once in the summer and once in the winter. He would kiss Dora's cheeks until they were quite red and his mother said: 'That's enough of that!'

One of these visits coincided with the wedding of a distant relative who seemed to have the same lips as Daniil and the same big earlobes—another Pinkenzon. Somebody-or-other was marrying another somebody-or-other—what mattered was that things were, in the broadest sense, staying in the family; it was a proper Jewish wedding with seventy guests—fifty more than fitted in the Pinkenzon family's tiny abode. For that was where the celebrations were held—though it wasn't the half pretty, half starved daughters of the house who'd been claimed by matrimony. Oh no. Uncle Pavel, the master of the house, was marrying off his niece, an orphan so poor that even Pavel's daughters wrinkled up their noses at her.

Also resident in the flat was Auntie Polina, who wasn't at all pleased that the family wanted her to open up her room to the wedding guests. She was in her late fifties, but looked closer to a hundred, had a severe limp and was usually to be found lying on her two mattresses, creaking and groaning, as if to make up for the missing bedstead. The family decided not to bother arguing with the old thing and to make do with the one room, so they hung a rug on Auntie Polina's door—one of those good Ottoman rugs with a lavish floral pattern in the centre, and red and green flourishes around the edges—to keep out the noise of seventy men and women and quantities of alcohol. Even so, Auntie Polina spent all evening banging her galoshes against the wall.

At the wedding, Daniil sat *generalom*, which is to say at the head of the table. He didn't know why he was granted this honour and he didn't ask, but it made him feel like one of the grown-ups; his nostrils flared, making his face even broader than usual. The guests drank a lot—an awful lot—and they sang, and Daniil joined in; for the first time in his life he was singing in front of people he didn't know. Everyone smoked and stubbed out their cigarettes in the butter dish and threw the stubs in half-full vodka glasses, and Daniil was happy in a way that was new to him. He suddenly realised that he'd never been to a party like this. When everyone got up, he didn't dance, but he clapped loudly to the beat, slowly and ponderously, keeping time with his chin. That evening he had an inkling of a different kind of life, but it was barely noticeable, a mere tickle at the tip of his nose, so faint that he couldn't work out where it was coming from and had soon forgotten all about it.

The day after the wedding, Uncle Pavel rang to say he needed someone to take down the rug from Auntie Polina's door—couldn't Daniil come round? He'd do it himself, but it was more than he could manage these days; he was tired and done-in, and a war veteran, too, don't forget, with only an arm and a half. Daniil had known Polina Ismailovna when his grandparents were alive, and he was happy to see her—or rather, he thought it his duty; he made no distinction between the two sentiments. He liked the old crone with her misshapen head. Thick white hair covered her face and seemed to sprout out of every pore; only her crazy eyes penetrated the thick growth. He was glad to be able to help her.

Auntie Polina was lying on her mattresses, swathed in faded blankets of many colours and cursing like a trooper. At her snugly wrapped feet sat a creature that Daniil did not at first notice. It seemed so slight that he took it for a child to begin with—a child swaddled in layers of wool. The creature seemed to belong to the true working class, for she was dressed in their particular uniform, whose distinguishing feature was a cap with earflaps that came almost to the floor.

There are various opinions as to why Emma was wearing this uniform on the day in question. Some say her parents wanted to teach her to be modest and keep her head out of the clouds. Others say she was actually wearing a long skirt over woollen leggings and a thick khaki parka with a finely knitted wool scarf and rabbit-fur gloves and looked just the same as any other girl who spent her days sitting in unheated rooms. Either way, Daniil paid her no attention, but turned straight back to Auntie Polina after a polite 'How do you do'.

He devoted himself entirely to the old auntie who gave him, from beneath her thicket of hair, a full and detailed account of her ailments, embellishing them as only a woman like that knows how. Daniil's sense of duty began to wane; soon he was sick and tired of these seemingly never-ending stories that unspooled from the old auntie like an endless tapeworm. Besides, he was cold. So when Auntie Polina paused to swallow—her throat quite dry from the excitement of at last finding a new audience for the stories that had been so many lonely hours in the making—he took advantage of the pause to tell her to take life by the horns, to get up and live in spite of everything, in spite of diabetes and gangrene and whatever else.

'To hell with all that! Get up and go for a walk, Auntie Polina! It's fine weather—cold but bracing; the fresh air will blow away your cobwebs.'

At this, the small creature at the foot of the mattress exploded beneath its many layers of clothes, making a noise like a beehive that's been knocked to the ground: 'What do you mean, to hell with everything? Auntie's sick, very sick indeed. She needs peace and quiet and medicine, and you want to send her into the cold to a certain death! What gives you the right, you bully? Who do you think you are?' Emma still had the voice of a young girl, though it would one day be as powerful as her mother Etina's.

Daniil and Polina stared at the young thing. Her cap had slipped down over her face; they could see only her lips quivering, maybe with anger, maybe with cold.

Emma pushed her cap off her forehead with a rabbit-fur hand and glared at Daniil. He said nothing. Then he reached inside his jacket, took a rolled-up cigarette out of his pocket and put in in his mouth.

'Don't do that, I'm sick. No smoking in here,' said Auntie Polina, entering into the spirit of things.

Daniil put the cigarette away again, still silent, and the old auntie took the opportunity to resume her tales. Daniil was so mortified that he couldn't listen. He didn't know where to put himself, but he was too well brought-up to leave the room. It was all his father's doing.

After a while, the old auntie, who had been sitting up in bed and practically dancing on the mattresses, so invigorated had she been by her own stories, dropped back onto the pillows as if all her lifeblood had drained out of her. Softly, already half asleep, she murmured: 'It's late, take the girl home.'

Emma and Daniil trudged through the snow, not looking at one another. Emma didn't think she needed accompanying, but pressed her lips together and said nothing, and Daniil didn't think they needed to be silent, but had no idea what to say. They walked to Emma's front door without exchanging a word, and there they shook hands.

Others say it was no chance that they met at Auntie Polina's and that Emma was sitting at the foot of the bed in her long-eared cap, fluttering her eyes at Daniil. They say it was good old Jewish match-making—nothing unusual in those days—and that the family had examined young Pinkenzon very carefully, made enquiries and judged him acceptable. He was, after all, prettier than most, with his nice broad nose—not that Etina Natanovna approved of good looks. She said a man should be no more handsome than an ape; he'd only run away from you otherwise.

'You're a fine one to talk,' Emma retorted. 'You took the best-looking of them all!'

What could Etina say to that? Her daughter was right. Shura remained to his death a better version of Frank Sinatra.

In the end Etinka yielded. 'The important thing,' she said, 'is to marry someone you're not embarrassed to divorce when the time comes.'

Shura was more laidback about the whole thing—or else he simply didn't care. When Daniil at last summoned the courage to drop in to tea with his future father-in-law together with his friend Genediy, who'd come from Grozny to spend his holidays in Chernivtsi, Alexander Isaakovich voiced enthusiasm over the young men's decision to become geologists and asked what they thought of Fersman's latest book *Reminiscences about Stones*. The young men looked at each other and then at the floor. The Chernivtsi flat betrayed nothing of Shura's lowly origins in the gangster district of Moldavanka; now that his picture hung in the National Museum, he always wore a suit and a dark tie, even at home, even at teatime. Daniil too had donned a tie, but knew he couldn't deceive anyone with the shirt he'd ironed himself and his filthy shoes—he'd cleaned them before setting off, but just try going anywhere in the Soviet Union without getting dirty. In his head, his mother's voice was saying: 'You can always judge a man by his shoes!' He looked into Shura's dilated eyes, decided not to lie and confessed to not knowing the book—or indeed Fersman. Shura leant towards Daniil, placed a hand on his shirt which was sweaty from all the excitement, and said: 'I envy you young men. You have so much ahead of you.'

The verdict had been delivered. From then on, Daniil was always welcome, and each time he sweated a little less.

Orchestrated or not, the incident at Auntie Polina's marked the beginning of a tentative courtship. Daniil would meet Emma from university and they'd debate about the advantages of classical medicine over the homeopathy practised by the old village folk, about the films of Grigori Alexandrov, Emma's father's inventions, Emma's decision to become a doctor like her parents, and the future of Communism. But the only topic they were really able to agree on was, can you believe it, the poetry of Nikolai Alexeyevich Nekrasov, and eventually Daniil said something about Emma's eyes, and her face opened up like a butterfly and gleamed.

Later, when Emma was pregnant, Daniil confessed to her that

when he'd found out who her father was, he'd thought of running away and never coming back, but by then he was already lost to that gleam in her face, a gleam that she managed to preserve in spite of Volgograd's industrial smog, and all through perestroika—even after resettling in another country where she was changed forever more into a migrant woman in a pink beret and a yellow puffer jacket, unable to make herself understood in the supermarket.

During their student years they wrote each other letters. Daniil returned to Grozny full of the urge to write poems, something he'd previously thought of as a woman's thing. He sent Emma observations from his walks in the steppe and Emma devoured his letters, learning them all by heart and later recalling the lovely things in them—especially during arguments with her husband.

'Who wrote all those beautiful letters, you *monster*? Did you get your friends to do it for you—or one of your *females*?' She'd had a strict upbringing; coarser insults had no place in her vocabulary.

But Daniil had written every letter himself, for three whole years. During those three years he visited his future wife every winter and every summer—he couldn't afford to see her more often.

They married in the summer of the fourth year. Etina took care of the invitations, and hordes of relatives came and processed through the streets of Chernivtsi with them to the registry office. Even before the marriage ceremony, the restless crowd began to dance and shout 'Gor'ko! Gor'ko!' which means 'Bitter! Bitter!' and is what Ukrainian wedding guests chant to get the bride and groom to kiss. Two photographers—one of them Shura—went on ahead. Emma and Daniil posed in front of the brass sign of the registry office, pointing at it with their be-ringed fingers and laughing. Daniil couldn't stop kissing Emma's temples and she kept having to straighten her cream felt melusine that slipped down over her face every time. In the photos she showed me, she is on the right, holding a bouquet of petrol-blue delphiniums, and Daniil is on the left, holding her arm. In the next photos, they're on their honeymoon on the beach at Odessa. Emma, a Huck Finn hat on her head, is wearing a striped bathing suit cut low at the back and, in some pictures, a white cotton shirt over the top. She laughs into the camera, her face cupped in Daniil's hands. Shura took the photos; the in-laws had tagged along to Odessa to wallow in reminiscences. Shura photographed Etina too, mainly from behind—mainly the back of her neck. In the photos that Emma and Daniil kept, the four of them look like sixties film stars. Move over Grigori Alexandrov! They stretch their bodies in the sun more provocatively than film stars of the time were allowed, and smile more broadly than I ever saw any of them smile.

There, on the beach at Odessa, the four of them decided to move to Volgograd, because Daniil had been offered a post there when he graduated and Shura held out hopes for a better job and a more decent salary. Every child born in Volgograd before perestroika was issued with a medal saying: *Born in the City of Heroes.* The year the young couple moved there with the in-laws, the city had just been renamed: Stalingrad was now Volgograd. The war had left a crumbled memory of a once magnificent town. Because it had been named after the great leader, there had been a rush to build it up again, and the colossal statue, The Motherland Calls, had been rammed into a hill in the middle of town. Chest out, mouth open, sword aloft, the Motherland was almost as tall as the Statue of Liberty, and down below, spread out at her feet, were the graves of fallen soldiers, the eternal flame, eternal remembrance—a Soviet Disneyland in several tons of concrete.

Emma and Daniil were given a room on the edge of town in a hall of residence belonging to the medical university, and when they first moved in, there was nothing in that room but a single bed and a window the exact same size as the bed. There are no photos of this room; only the story of how Daniil found Emma lying on the floor, curled up in pain, two months before she was due to give birth. He called for a doctor, who drove them from hospital to hospital looking for a free bed, only managing to get Emma admitted at the third attempt, by which time she was unconscious. It was assumed there was some problem with the foetus; Emma had been warned not to risk pregnancy with her frail health. Daniil held her hand all through the long hours spent driving from one hospital to the next, and later claimed that Emma had only been saved because the gynaecologists in the third clinic knew who her father was and were afraid it wouldn't look too good if they allowed the daughter of the great Professor Farbarjevich to die on them on the operating table.

'They wouldn't even have examined her till the next day!' Daniil said, his eyes moist. 'I saw them—standing around on the corridor smoking, they were, touching each other under their doctors' coats. They wouldn't have lifted a finger if I hadn't kicked up a fuss! And then—'

He stopped and began to cough. Emma pushed a glass of water towards him and said: 'You never drink, you don't drink enough, why won't you drink?'

He shook his head, his hand in front of his mouth, laughing and giggling—it sounded like a dog panting. 'Let me get on with the story,' he said.

Emma looked out of the window, lost in thought, her broad-boned face as open as a butterfly's wings.

'Are you cold?' Daniil asked her.

'Yes, I am. Did you turn the heating down?'

'No. Did you?'

'No, but then why is it so cold in here?'

'I don't like you not eating, darling,' said Daniil, leaning across the table to me. 'Is there nothing in the flat you fancy? I could make you something. Let me have a look; there must be something in the fridge you'd like. How about some dried apricots?'

I swallowed. I saw my ten-year-old self sneaking dried apricots in the kitchen, balancing on a cardboard box to reach to the back of the cupboard where Emma hid them from me. 'Don't you go touching them. I bought them for Danya. They're good for his heart. If you want something sweet, you can help yourself to a caramel.'

I realised that Emma and Daniil must have known all along that I'd stolen them, cramming into my trouser pockets what I couldn't fit in my mouth.

'Will you let me make you coffee?' I asked Danya, looking up from the table that was strewn with photographs.

'I'll make it myself. Don't get up.' He shuffled into the kitchen. 'Tell me some more about this book you're reading,' he called through the door.

I watched my grandparents moving slowly around the room, twiddling the knob on the radiator, opening and shutting the curtains, putting their hands on each other's shoulders. Now that they'd opened up to me, arguing in front of me about the possible interpretations of their lives, muddling their way through the various phases and stages, I felt that I owed it to them to say something about myself—not sidetrack them again by talking about books. I wanted to tell them a bit about what I'd done in Istanbul, how I'd tried to find Anton. And about the stubble on my face. They knew nothing and I was to blame. For a long time, talking about myself had been as impossible as asking Daniil and Emma why socialism had failed—some things you don't talk about. But the situation was different now. These polite, reserved people I'd grown up with had revealed something of themselves; these people I'd seen cry over politics and social security payments had forged a path for me, and now, with their broad, open faces and piercing anxious eyes, they sat naked before me, making me feel I was hiding behind their beliefs about who I was. I'd returned from the Bosporus as a version of myself they didn't know and didn't question—or if they had, they hadn't ever let it show. They treated me like something familiar in a different guise. Did they think I'd followed a new trend and that the old me was still lurking somewhere underneath?

Or maybe I really was still the granddaughter they knew; maybe I looked no different to them. Close relatives always store a younger version of you in their memories, superimposing it on the aging, changing body that visits them once a month, once every six months. Perhaps they still saw me with shoulder-length hair, riding my bike in circles under their window, my left arm sticking out, my teeth gappy like in the photo in the cabinet behind them, the one next to the picture of their daughter that's also several years out of date, on the same shelf as the two plastic hydrangeas and the menorah.

Back then, I was still used to thinking about myself from outside myself, in the third person—a story belonging to somebody else. So I told them a story, hoping they wouldn't leave me there, at one remove, but pull me back in, hug me, or at least look at me—even that would mean a lot. I knew I couldn't expect them to understand the story, but they listened as I told them about Ali and how she became Anton.

T

Ali had lived with Elyas ever since coming to Berlin—far from her divorced parents, far from her grown brother who'd moved back in with their mum, far from a father who was always leaving confused, drunk messages on her answerphone, which she sometimes deleted without hearing them through to the end.

They'd met at a party, both clutching glasses of vodka, both in a bad mood, both wearing well-fitting shirts. The other guests were a mass of fluorescent polyester tops, pink singlets, black leather open-toed shoes, faded trucker caps over unkempt hair, yellow faces with red lips, orange lips, black lips, glittery lips. Ali and Elyas had both, independently of one another, felt turned off. People rushed past them, asking questions, rolling cigarettes, taking sips from glasses that weren't theirs and twisting their lips into grimaces learnt from the movies. They felt watched; they *were* watched; they stuttered and laughed. Ali and Elyas's eyes met across the room; their gazes brushed. Elyas's eyes were set close together, angled towards his nose like arrows. He was wearing square, horn-rimmed glasses and when he smiled, his ears shot up. Ali was sure he could waggle them.

The smoke from a bong got in her eyes, making her blink. She opened her lips, took a deep breath and coughed, looking across at the cloud of smoke around a mop top whose matted hair stuck up from his head like the legs of a fat spider. Then she turned back to Elyas; he was still looking at her. They headed towards one another, slowly, not purposefully—they had no purpose; they didn't know what they wanted of each other, but not the usual, that was for sure. They danced sideways along the wall, heel-and-toeing it, closer and closer—and just as Elyas was about to turn to face Ali, a woman dived between them and Ali found herself with the woman's bum in her hand, while the woman's bare navel fitted itself around Elyas's belt buckle. Ali's hand jerked back; she wiped it on her trouser leg with a curse, put her glass down and looked about for the hostess to say goodbye. She pushed her way through the fluorescent polyester tops; out in the hall, a boy with no eyebrows squinted at her, barely of age, his head a polished wooden ball leaning against the door frame. When Ali felt for the door handle, he put his hand in her hair and closed his fingers to a fist, saying something Ali couldn't make out. She raised an arm as well as she could in the crush, and slapped the boy in the face. He let out a yell and began to cry; someone shouted and took the lad into the bathroom, and someone else pushed Ali; she couldn't see much now, but she saw Elyas's eyes and felt his hand in hers, pulling her into an empty room. They lay down on the bed; they could hear people looking for Ali. Someone knocked on the bedroom door and without a word to each other, they rolled under the bed, pulling the sheets shut like curtains. Their eyes gleamed among the dust balls. Elyas's glasses were slipping down his nose and he took them off. A dust ball settled on Ali's face;

she caught it between her fingers. Elyas grabbed another and tried to blow it away.

'I like this stuff.'

'What? Dust?'

'Yes.' Ali rolled onto her back and looked up at the bed slats and the bulging flesh of the mattress.

'I'm allergic.'

'I don't do mouth-to-mouth.'

'That's okay.'

They lay there breathing, uncertain whether or not to kiss; their needs were so different, but they didn't really know what else to do. Kissing would definitely have been easier than not.

'When I was little, my dad often went to visit his parents in Russia, and the day he was due back from Moscow, my brother and I had to clean the entire flat till it shone. But he always found something. He went from room to room with his gloves still on, and we followed behind—my brother used to tremble like anything. And he ran his fucking finger down every groove—he even stood on tiptoe and felt all along the top of the doorframe.' Ali ran her nails down the cracks between the floorboards. 'Then he peered at his fingertips and held them up to our faces.'

She felt sharp grit and dried-up dust gathering under her nails. 'The top of the doorframe—no child can reach that high.' Her breathing was shallow, but the dust balls swirled all the same. 'No child would even think of it. Would they?'

Elyas put his hands under his cheek and listened.

'Don't think I've done any dusting since I left home. No intention of starting either.'

Ali felt the blood rush to her head. She didn't know why she was telling him this; she never talked about her father—not at parties, anyway, and certainly not under beds with strangers whose ears seemed to go on forever.

'Can I ask you something?'

Elyas lay there without moving, his knees pulled up to his chest.

'Can you waggle your ears?'

They parted early the next morning outside a photo booth where they'd pulled faces, muzzy with tiredness, and posed with a plastic pistol that Ali had grabbed on her way out of the flat to keep other people at bay. (Elyas had grabbed a pair of sunglasses.) There was room for only one person on the metal stool in the photo booth, so they sat on each other's laps and held each other tight, kept awake by the flash of the camera. Then they tumbled out into the cold of the morning and stood looking at each other's feet, their bodies bent forwards like blades of grass, their foreheads touching. They almost fell asleep like that, as the machine blow-dried their strip of photos. A week later Ali moved in with Elyas. Dust balls continued to be a topic.

Ali arrived with two bin bags full of clothes and comics. The flat was big and empty; you could shout into it and your voice would echo back at you. Elyas was sitting on the floor at the other end of the hall, tinkering with a door.

'I'm just mending your door handle.'

The 150-square-foot box that was to be Ali's room had a big window overlooking a kindergarten playground; the noise level was as high as if it opened out onto a motorway. Ali looked down at the little heads flitting across the grass, lit a cigarette, ashed out of the window, looked some more.

The room was empty except for a mattress, and she left it that way. She piled up cardboard boxes, crammed socks, shirts, underwear and trousers into their ripped-open bellies, hung a curtain in front—she didn't want everyone seeing that her wardrobe was entirely dark blue and black—and ashed on the floor. Elyas was always offering to help her look for furniture, but a wooden board over two small chests of drawers did her as a table and she didn't feel the need for more. On the table she put Elyas's housewarming present to her: a cut-glass ashtray with a silver-plated stubber. The walls of her room were bare of any sign that she read, any sign that she had friends. She kept the mattress that had been lying on the floor when she moved in and loved the dependable emptiness the room exuded. When she was away, she didn't miss the room; when she returned, they greeted each other politely, then fell into a passionate togetherness, like lovers meeting only for wordless sex. Ali threw herself onto the mattress, digging her shoulderblades almost through to the floor and grinding her back to and fro as if she were trying to bury herself in the room.

She had no objection to furniture on principle; she bought crockery for the flat, amassed a collection of chairs that had been put out for the dustmen and once pulled half a sofa through town on its castors and heaved it into the living room. She bought a kitchen table in a junkshop and even oiled the table top, though you could still see traces of their habits in the cracks—wax that had dripped down the empty whisky bottles that served them as candle sticks, crumbs of amaranth flakes and cigarette ash, and a black line that couldn't be scrubbed clean even with a scourer and always reminded Ali of what she and Michal had been doing on the table the time that Elyas had come home unexpectedly. He'd hinted to her as tactfully as possible that she might at least close the door, and she'd said: 'You have to mend the handle first.'

Elyas left for work early and came home late, and if Ali hadn't budged from her room by then, he'd throw his car keys onto her belly.

'Oh well, at least she's nice and brown.'

There was a packet of profiteroles on the table. Cemal and Elyas were sitting at the ivy-covered window, drinking çay—Cemal smoking, Elyas peering through the smoke at Ali, who'd walked all the way from Karaköy because the rush-hour traffic had been at a deadlock. She'd been in the antique shops, putting photos of herself in the boxes of picture postcards and old photographs in the hope that Anton would come by at some point and rifle through them, recognise her on the photos and lose his mind.

Her temples throbbed in the heat; sweat ran down her forehead into her eyes.

'What are you doing here?' she yelled at Elyas when he got up and walked towards her as if it were the most natural thing in the world.

'Isn't she wonderful? What did I tell you?' Elyas looked at Cemal.

'She's nicer to me, I must say,' said Cemal, smiling.

Elyas put his arms around Ali; she felt his hands on her back through her sweat-soaked shirt. He kissed her temples, and she wriggled free and blinked.

'I had a sudden craving for profiteroles and this is the best place for them. So I thought I'd drop in.' Elyas sat down and poured tea for Ali, his eyes telling her to sit down too. Ali looked at Cemal.

'Can I roll myself a cigarette?'

Cemal pushed his crumpled packet of tobacco across the table and dug in his pocket for the papers that were so thin that Ali was always ripping them—she made the sticky strip too soggy when she licked it. The wrapper was marked with Arabic characters. Ali drew her eyes together and tried to concentrate on rolling.

'It's my fault that Elyas is here. I told him to come and check on you.'

Cemal looked at Ali, eyebrows raised, mouth open, as if he'd just given her the best news in the world. And because Ali said nothing—just lit up and kept looking at him—he added: 'I told him you cry at night when you think everyone's asleep.'

Elyas pushed his spoon into the chocolate-covered profiterole on the dish in front of him.

'Uncle told on you. You can never trust family, you know,' he said, champing choux pastry.

'Cemal was only kidding. He can't know what I do at night. I never sleep here.' Ali spat tobacco on the floor and peeled the strip of wet paper from her tongue.

'Yes, you do, kuşum, what are you on about? You lie here on this sofa and mew like a cat having its tail pulled.'

'No, I don't. I never sleep here because you have bed bugs that bring me out in a rash and give me red spots and make me scratch myself raw. It's disgusting. This sofa's disgusting. I'd never dream of sleeping here.'

Cemal let out a soft wheeze, sucked in a throatful of air and got up. 'I'm going out,' he said, coughing. 'I'll go and let your mum know you've arrived safely. Shouldn't think you've got round to it yet, have you?'

Elyas looked up at his uncle, his cheeks puffed with cream. He shook his head and smiled, and Cemal smiled back. Ali jumped up and kissed Cemal on both cheeks, murmuring: 'Say hello to Sibel from me.'

Ali knew Elyas's mother from her visits to their shared flat, when she'd put cress sandwiches and stewed tea on the kitchen table for the children who weren't children anymore, and expect them to eat up: 'I don't mind what you do, but you must eat.' Apart from that, Sibel was the gentlest of mothers. She had clear bright eyes beneath papery lids and still held herself like a young girl. Ali had never been able to guess her age and had never asked. She'd been a real young girl when she'd come to West Germany to work in a factory, and being one of the first in the home to learn the foreign language, she was soon the official interpreter for all the other women on her floor. She went shopping with them and accompanied them to the local authorities and lawyers and doctors; she knew all their most intimate secrets and complaints—whether bowel movements or embarrassing rashes or husbands. Sibel and Ali often talked about this. Ali had done the same in her asylum-home years, taking the old people on her floor to the doctor and having to listen to all kinds of stories in the waiting room because they thought the little girl was too young to register the word 'vaginismus'.

Sibel told her that she'd learnt German by looking up indecent words in the dictionary to write love letters for the other women, and Ali told her that she'd sometimes accompanied the old ladies to the hairdresser and looked on in silence as they pointed at the bald patches on their heads and tried to explain: 'My hair says goodbye.'

Whenever Sibel was coming, Elyas scrubbed the flat and gave Ali a talking-to about the dust balls that were creeping out of her room. He'd bang the vacuum nozzle against Ali's door and ask her to turn her music down.

'When Sibel gets here I'll be the best-behaved child in the world—even better-behaved than you. But leave me in peace till she comes.'

'She loves you more than me anyway. Couldn't you at least do the washing-up?'

'If you'll lend me a clean shirt. Mine are all in the wash.'

When Sibel stood in the door with a box of éclairs in her hand, Elyas nudged Ali aside with his hip so he'd be the first to give his mum a hug. He wrapped his arms twice round her and picked her up off the floor, making her scream.

Ali and Elyas grew together, sharing mother and shirts and dust balls until they'd forgotten the existence of anything outside themselves—until they'd invented a language all their own and barely needed words.

'Is that my shirt you're wearing?' Elyas asked, when Cemal had left.

Ali looked down at the shirt, then at her forearms, which really were very brown, then out of the ivy-hung window.

They sat there for a long time. Ali could have sworn she heard a clock tick, but it was only her own breathing. Elyas slid over to her, cream still in the corners of his mouth; Ali put her head on one side, Elyas mirrored her and they leant against one another, heads touching. Then she buried her curls in the hollow of his collarbone, scraped her teeth against his stubble and closed them over his chin. He gave her a push, almost knocking her off her chair, and she climbed on his lap and moved her eyes around the ceiling, drawing patterns. Elyas put his hand over her eyes, making everything dark and cool, and she pulled him over her like a blanket. After a while he said: 'Let's go out.'

They sauntered along İstiklal and turned off into a courtyard crammed with wicker stools so low that the people sitting on them, drinking tea, seemed to be squatting on the ground. Waiters carrying silver trays full of tea glasses scurried through the crowd, calling out to ask who wanted more. Elyas and Ali sat down side by side. He followed her gaze as she watched the darting waiters like someone watching a game of pool. A red ball shot to the right, brushing a tourist clutching a plastic bag, who looked up in fright. Pocketed. A green ball rolled backwards to fetch a tray full of tea glasses, then ricocheted back to its initial position. Pocketed. A black ball stood motionless in the middle of the courtyard, gesticulating as if under water.

'Come on, say something?' Ali said, as if to herself.

'What do you want to hear?'

'I want to hear your voice.'

'Are you seeing someone?'

'That's your first question?'

Ali peeled the sugar lump out of its paper and threw it in her tea glass. She sipped the brown liquid cautiously and threw in another.

'Dunno. I could ask when you started taking sugar in your tea, if you'd rather.'

'Yes.'

'Yes, you're seeing someone, or yes, you'd rather talk about sugar?'

'Yes, I'm seeing someone.'

'A he or a she?'

'Since when has that mattered to you?'

Ali stared into Elyas's gaunt face that suddenly resembled an old man's. His cheeks were sunken and there was a shimmer of silver in his stubble and at his temples. She wondered if she had grey hairs too—and thought what a long time she must have been in Istanbul, if she hadn't realised that her best friend was going grey. His ears seemed bigger too.

Elyas noticed Ali staring at the white threads in his hair and pushed the loose strands behind his ears.

'Of course it matters.'

'But why?'

'Because I have to know whether to ask if *he* is so important to you that you don't want to come back. Or if *she* is so important to you.'

'A question of grammar?'

'Exactly.'

'Have you come to fetch me back?'

'Is that what you want?'

'Do I look like someone who wants fetching back?'

They stared at each other. Ali knew that Elyas saw Anton and Valentina's faces in hers like shadows. Valentina had probably rung and asked him to find her and bring her back—she'd already lost one child; she couldn't go losing the other as well. And Elyas had probably promised her. He knew what Istanbul did to you; once the city had you in its grip, it was worse than the desert.

'We could catch a plane today. I've mended all the door handles.'

'I don't believe you.' The corners of Ali's mouth turned up.

'Why not?'

'Because none of the doors in that dump fit anyway.'

'You know what I mean.'

'*You* know what *I* mean.'

'Isn't there anything you miss?' Elyas said, without looking at her.

'Can I ask you something?'

Ali took Elyas's hands in hers; they were rough, and bonier than she remembered. Sibel hasn't been round with éclairs for a long time, she thought, resting her face on his palms.

'A *he* or a *she*?'

'What?'

Ali felt the weight of her head in Elyas's hands. Her chin filled the crack between his little fingers; her cheeks smarted with heat; the skin under her eyes was tense.

'When you look at me, do you see a *he* or a *she*?'

'Ali, what is all this?'

Ali pushed Elyas's hands away with a laugh and cracked her fingers. She looked at the waiters again—all those men, far too many of them and far too young, who'd left their villages to look for work, any work, in the city, and were now hanging about, five to a broom handle, as people had said under socialism. One of the waiters had Marx's face tattooed on the back of his hand. They came and went far more than was necessary, with their enormous trays full of bulbous glasses of tea which they pressed on the squatting customers, tearing half-empty glasses from their hands: 'That one's gone cold, here's a new one for you, my friend.' Two waiters were bickering; one of them suddenly kicked up his leg and kneed the other in the ribs, sending him flying into the crowd of tea drinkers like a high jumper clearing the bar.

Ali leapt to her feet. Elyas said something like 'don't' or 'stay here' or maybe just 'Ali', but she didn't hear; she went and stood by the young man who'd been floored, to make sure he didn't wring the other man's neck. Other people had got to their feet too; a whole army of ants was tugging at the fighting men, but they were spurred on by the shouts and all the more determined to set on one another. Ali had hold of one of them; somebody else had hold of Ali. Elyas stayed put. An elderly man came slowly out of the teahouse, kneading a tesbih and gave the two young men a talking-to. Their heads were as red as squashed tomatoes, but they weren't listening; they continued to kick their legs in the air, and Ali got her man in a lever hold.

Elyas looked at Ali and thought of the time she'd chucked in her maths studies to box. 'It's one or the other,' she'd announced, as if he'd demanded an explanation. 'You can't do sparring five times a week *and* sit up all night studying calculus.' Once, she came home black and blue and told him she'd provoked her coach until he'd grabbed her by the collar and lifted her twenty centimetres off the floor. She'd told him—calmly and scornfully—to put her down, and he'd hurled her against the padded wall of the boxing studio. It wasn't the end of their friendship, though; far from it. After that, they fucked even less uninhibitedly than before, in the changing rooms, on the stairs, even in the men's showers, which Ali had no qualms about entering with nothing on but flip flops. It made no difference how often Elyas tried to convince Ali that getting yourself hurled against walls was maybe not the only way of winning someone's affection; he had the feeling that the more he went on at her, the more bruises she came home with.

The squashed-tomato faces seemed to have calmed down; the tussle was over. Ali came back to the table breathing heavily, a big smile on her face. Her curls were tousled; her shirt ripped on the left shoulder.

'I've no idea who you're trying to impress. Your mum's worried, I'm worried, Cemal's worried, but you don't give a fuck about any of us. You do what you like and ask stupid questions.' Elyas dug in his pocket for change. 'I don't know what it's all about.'

'Are you going?'

'Yes.' He tossed coins onto the table; a couple of them rolled to the ground.

Ali picked them up and put them on the saucer. She lunged at Elyas, pulling at his trouser leg, fingering the hollow of his knee.

'Don't.'

'You don't want me to go?'

'Don't be angry with me.'

'I'm not.'

'Please, don't be angry. Please.'

He could tell she was crying from her voice, but he didn't dare look at her. He sat back down on the stool and stared in front of him.

Ali dabbed at her face, trying to roll a cigarette at the same time.

'You know why I'm here.'

Elyas heard her dry lips stick together and smack open again.

'It's not your fault,' he said at length.

The back of his hand touched Ali's. She passed him her cigarette. He hated the taste of rat poison on his tongue, but he took a few fierce drags and stubbed out the cigarette in the gravel. The next morning he flew back to Berlin.

Gizli Bahçe was on Nevizade; you had to push your way through a sea of heads to get along the narrow passageway. His hand on Ali's shoulder, Kato propelled the two of them through the crowd, ignoring the tables in the middle of the street, jostling the drinkers and whispering in Ali's ear. They squeezed into a narrow doorway, past boys in bomber jackets who were playing war on their phones, and laughed their way up narrow stairs. Electronic music, people in tight jeans and baggy jumpers, fluorescent beanies and dark glasses, a horde of bobbing bodies; everyone seemed to be dragging on a cigarette, sucking on a straw. Like a window to Berlin, Ali thought, heading for the bar. Kato vanished behind the DJ's console; a friend of his was spinning. A kiss on the right, a kiss on the left, bum to bum, and they were dancing. Ali peered through the smoky air across the dance floor and suddenly felt a hand on her spine—a cold, slim hand down her low-backed top. The hand ran over her bare skin and pinched her waist.

'Hi,' said the woman whose hand it was. Long blond strands tumbled over orange lips. She was so thin—a sketch of a person, Ali thought.

'Hi,' she said.

'Are you on your own?'

'No, my boyfriend's on the dance floor.'

'Oh, your *boy*friend,' said the girl, dragging the word out like an insult. But she wasn't deterred. 'My girlfriend's not coming to Istanbul till next month, she's Belgian, I kind of really miss her. You look like her, by the way, are you Belgian?'

'No.'

'What are you?'

Ali wondered what would be quicker—to go to the toilet with the girl and get it over with, or to try to explain that she wasn't interested.

'Guess.'

'Spanish?'

'Yes, that's right.'

'Wow, that's pretty amazing. Can you say something in Spanish for me?'

'Idi na khui!'* said Ali, her voice sweet and low.

'That sounds so beautiful!' The young woman's eyes fixed a mole on Ali's throat. 'And your boyfriend, is he Spanish?'

---

* Fuck off!

192

'No, he's Tunisian.'

'Did you meet in Istanbul?'

'No, we met in Iraq.'

'Do you work for an NGO or something?'

'Exactly.'

The music came to Ali's rescue. She saw the orange mouth opening and shutting in front of her face, but all that came out was the beat. She turned to the barman and screamed for a vodka and tonic. Then she saw Anton in the mirror above the spirits.

Between the Talisker and the Lagavulin, she saw his face that was her face, moving in profile about the room. She saw him pass her; she saw herself push through the crowded bar towards the door. She spun round.

'Hey, what's wrong?' the orange mouth shouted. Ali pushed her away and burst out of the bar onto the empty stairs and from there onto the street. She swung her head round and set off at a run, knocking into the tables on Nevizade—waiters helped her up and gave her an earful, but she pulled free, her head buzzing, ran past the street-walkers with their glittery eye shadow, slipped on the fish market, colliding with a father carrying his daughter on his shoulders—he only just managed not to drop her—and almost fell onto a chestnut seller's griddle as she crossed İstiklal. She yelled 'Anton!' as loud as she could. People turned to stare; all İstiklal turned to stare. 'Anton!' She ran, talking to him as she went, in Russian: 'Podozhdi. Podozhdi. Podozhdi.' Wait. Wait. Wait.

Outside the patisserie in Cihangir she stopped to get her breath back. Everything was a blur in front of her eyes; she'd run into noth-ingness. Her throat was on fire; she tore the skin from her lips with her teeth; her head was spinning and the road stretched like a bow. Everything went black and she sat down on the kerb and stared at the mosque opposite. Somebody laughed.

'There's a grain of joke in every joke.'

An old woman swaddled in shawls from head to toe, a shimmering, many-coloured cocoon, had sat down next to Ali and was counting notes.

'I'm sorry?' said Ali.

'There's a grain of joke in every joke,' the woman cackled.

'I don't understand.'

'Don't you speak Turkish?'

'Yes. No. Sorry.'

'In Africa they say there's a grain of joke in every joke. And where is truth? That's right. In Africa.'

Ali didn't know whether she was having such trouble understanding the woman because of the shawls covering her mouth, or because she felt dizzy.

'In Africa they tell the story of a young man who wanted to marry a young girl.' The old woman stared into the crowd of people outside the mosque as if she were peering down a long tunnel. 'But the girl's father said to the fellow: "You're too young. You've seen nothing. Go out into the world and look for truth and when you've found it, bring it back to show me and you shall have my daughter." So the young man set out in search of truth. He looked and he looked, dogged and despairing, convinced that he'd find it somewhere. He crossed a hundred and four borders, and drank out of a hundred and forty rivers. He saw war and murder; he saw what happened to people when the earth shook or when fire broke out—how they fought each other, how they turned into wolves or gazelles, hunters or hunted. One day he sat down on the bank of the Angereb, tired and broken, and realised he couldn't recall his beloved's face or her hands or her smell, and that his only wish on earth was to regain those memories. And as he sat there, he saw an ugly old woman walking along the water, dressed in rags, her teeth rotten, clumps of hair sticking up out of her head like grey wool. She reeked of foul apples, sickly sweet and festering. She sat down next to the young man who didn't look young anymore, but old—lined and sombre—and he asked her who she was.

"'I am Truth,' said the old woman.

"'Truth!' The young man leapt to his feet, suddenly remembering the reason for his journey. "Then you must come with me! I've been looking for you and now I've found you! You don't know what I've had to go through to find you. You must come with me and I'll show you to the father of my bride."

"'I can't come with you, my boy. I'm sorry," said the old woman.

"'But you have to. Five times I've almost lost my life and many, many times I've seen others lose their lives. I'd die for you, do you understand? But I can't force you to come with me."

"'Too true,' said the old woman. "And what happens if you show me to the father of your bride?"

"'I can marry her at last.'

"'Do you still want to marry her?'

'The young man looked out at the Angereb lying before him in deathly silence. He said nothing.

"'I can't come with you, my boy, but you can tell him you've seen me.'

'The young man looked down at the old woman. She was shrivelled as a prune and when she spoke, her cloak moved as if her skin were creeping with worms. Saliva dribbled out of the corner of her mouth.

"'And what shall I tell him when I get back?'

"'Tell him I'm beautiful,' said the old woman. "Tell him I'm young and beautiful.'"

The cocoon at Ali's side fell silent. Ali looked at the body swathed in shawls, then at the hands that hadn't stopped counting green and brown notes all through the story.

'Oh yes. That's the story they tell in Africa.'

The woman looked at Ali, her eyes shining. She laughed again, throwing back her body, and Ali saw that she had a big white rabbit with her in a cage, and that the bottom of the cage was strewn with slips of brightly coloured paper. She was one of those fortune tellers who went from cafe to cafe offering her rabbit's services to the tourists. At a given sign, the animal would lollop over the papers, picking out lots for customers, who would find their future revealed on the coloured tickets. Ali had see it done. She'd followed these fortune tellers a couple of times in her first weeks in Istanbul, to see the tourists being ripped off by a rabbit—to see if there really were idiots out there who let themselves be conned. There were.

The fortune teller noticed Ali squinting at the bedraggled-looking creature.

'You want future?' she asked.

Ali dug in her jacket pocket and produced a note for the woman. The rabbit didn't budge.

The woman rose, picking up the cage.

'Come with me.'

Ali looked up at her.

'Come on.'

They walked down to the water and turned into a side street that could have been in a Russian village; Ali could have sworn it was the Volga stretching out before them—the Volga with a big bridge across it, to Asia, and the family dacha just around the corner. There was a smell of cat piss and raspberry canes; she heard Anton's laugh and turned to look behind her.

The fortune teller led her into another side street—more of an alley, really, with corrugated-iron fences. Ali heard a rustle and saw that the place was covered with inch-long cats. The ground was a heaving mass of grey fur; it seemed to be made of the creatures, and they flocked around Ali, climbing up her, getting in her trousers and under her shirt, and tumbling out again through the slits between the buttons. The fortune teller lifted her skirts and drew out a small knife. The blade didn't flash in the dark, but Ali heard a soft chink of metal. The fortune teller took Ali's right hand and slashed her palm. Ali wanted to scream but didn't know how. Blood dripped onto the ground and the old woman said something, but Ali could make no sense of the words.

Ali ran down Nevizade, afraid she wouldn't find her way back to Gizli Bahçe. Then the reactions of the men in the restaurants told her that she'd stumbled this way earlier; they clicked their tongues and waved their hands as if they were swatting flies. She had no idea how long she'd lain unconscious on the road in Cihangir, no idea of the time. She imagined Kato's furious face and was afraid it might not be waiting for her anymore. She found the doorway with the boys in bomber jackets and climbed the stairs. Her hands were bloody and smarting and she didn't know why—had she injured herself when she fell? Must get it disinfected, she thought, disinfected with vodka.

Music was coming from the bar. She was about to push open the door when she saw Kato sitting a few steps higher up, looking down at her like a bird. His eyes were red.

'I'm sorry, I—' Ali began.

Kato let out a cry, a high, trembling note that gave way to a shrill staccato. Then he opened his mouth wide and groaned, sweat pouring down his face.

'They, they...there were...in the toilets...I went to the toilet and they—' It was only now that Ali saw the purple bruise below his right eye. She ran to him and clung to him and he trembled and vomited, and she held his forehead. Yellow bile sprayed onto her shoes and he screamed.

Ali took Kato to Uncle Cemal.

'We must tell the police,' he said, pressing a wet towel to Kato's face.

'Careful, he'll suffocate.'

Kato laughed from under the towel—or maybe he cried, but Ali thought it was a laugh.

'I'll ring my friend at the police tomorrow.'

'Ah yes, your glorious friend.'

'What's that supposed to mean?'

'Nothing.'

'Are you here illegally?' Cemal looked at the huddled body on the sofa. Kato didn't reply.

'Let him sleep.'

They went into the kitchen which was so narrow that they could only stand side by side. Ali perched on the hob and lit a cigarette; Cemal took it from her mouth and dragged on it.

'I told you, this country's a den of wild animals.'

'It could have happened anywhere.'

'But it didn't; it happened here, to you.'

'I wasn't there.'

'Where were you?'

'Doesn't matter.'

'What do you mean, it doesn't matter? Where were you when your friend was being attacked?'

'Swimming.'

'What?'

'Cemal, please.'

They smoked. Cemal put a finger under Ali's chin and pulled her face close to his.

'Why didn't you introduce him to me earlier?'

'Because of *that*.'

'Don't you think I'd have understood?'

Ali pulled her face away and stared at the cigarette in Cemal's hand.

'Don't you agree he has a strange way of laughing? Like a woodpecker hammering away at your temple. Ratatata. Ratatata. Ratatata.' Ali drilled a finger into her head.

'Ali.'

'Yes?'

'What do you live off?'

'I'm—'

She almost said 'on the game', but thought better of it. She clasped her hands to her head, then spread her arms. Cemal grabbed her right hand and examined the fresh gash on her palm.

'And what the hell is this?'

'Tripped, fell on my hands, how should I know?' Ali climbed down off the cooker and walked slowly to the door. 'Can't remember.'

She turned and looked into Cemal's tanned face. Cemal, who never gave up hope and always knew what to do. Cemal, who could be relied on to understand everything in the world. Ali wished he'd pick her up the way he did at Atatürk Airport—pick her up and rock her in his arms.

'Cemal, be honest with me. Will your policeman friend find Anton?'

'No.'

'Then I'd like you to call me Anton from now on. Would you do that?'

Kato had agreed to go to the women's part of Galatasaray Hammam with Ali. There were small individual cubicles to change in, glass-fronted down to waist height and white painted wood below. Kato and Ali shared one. They got undressed, took the disposable pants out of their packets and knotted the checked cotton scarves over their breasts. The purple under Kato's eye was only a shadow now, but the bruises on his thigh had darkened. Ali had tried not to look when Kato pulled his jeans off, but he looked at her openly. When Ali tried to push past him to slip into her wooden sandals, he put his hand between her thighs. Her head shot up.

Eight candles hung in the middle of the room over a hot stone that was draped with wet bodies like discarded towels. Ali and Kato sat down next to the marble basin and poured hot water over each other's shoulders. People were restless in spite of the heat; they all seemed to be talking to each other or muttering to themselves; the place was buzzing like a beehive and the noise echoed under the high dome.

Ali scooped up cold water in the brass dish and emptied it over her face, running her hand over her neck and breasts. A stout old woman with blue bruises under her buttocks, her thighs spongy from decades in these damp rooms, was washing a young girl on the hot stone. With a gloved hand, she scrubbed the soles of the girl's feet, her legs, belly, face; then she turned her over and massaged her back and scalp, swung the foam bag to and fro until it billowed with damp air, and pressed a cloud of foam through the cloth onto the girl's body. The girl's eyes were black raisins in a mountain of soapsuds. She coughed, her mouth full of soapy water, and the old woman wiped her face with her broad hand and began to scrub her with the foam bag.

Ali glanced at Kato, who was rubbing the soles of his feet with a pumice stone, staring straight ahead into the steam. The curly black hairs on Kato's breasts were growing thicker and thicker— he'd stopped plucking them—and a faint black trail ran from his belly button into the disposable plastic pants. His calves were already covered in black hairs.

'Kato, could I take some of that stuff too?'

Ali had got up and went to stand in front of him, her mons level with his nose. He looked up at her, past her flat breasts and pointy chin; her eyes, dark hollows in the steam, were turned on him.

'What stuff?'

'I want to start on testosterone too. Where do I get it?'

Kato pulled her down by her thighs and put his hands on her shoulders. 'Everywhere,' he said. 'The question is, what do you want it for?'

I hadn't prepared an explanation. I didn't have a speech ready, or a confession—not even a vaguely worded wish. Something in me had spoken and I followed the words that flew out of me like birds, assuming they knew where they were going. Migratory birds have compasses in their beaks that take their bearings from the earth's magnetic field; they know things with their eyes shut; they know everything as long as nobody breaks their beaks. So I trusted them. I let them fly and followed them and decided it must be right, more right than anything I could have come up with if I'd sat down and racked my brain for words.

It may sound strange, but what I was afraid of—or what I most clearly remember being afraid of—wasn't the injections, or hearing my voice break, or going bald, or growing hair on my back. It wasn't the looks on the street or the looks inside myself. What I distinctly remember being afraid of—and continue to fear to this day—is that being a son would mean turning into my father. Sometimes I wake with this thought even today; I hear his voice in mine when I get loud, and see his face before me when I inspect my thinning hair and my thickening chin. He never taught me how to shave—of course he didn't—but today, when I stand at the bathroom mirror, I often see him beside me, telling me what to do. My razor has five blades, which he thinks ridiculous. He only had two blades when he was my age, he tells me, breathing out noisily as if to say there's no hope for me. Then we both laugh and lift our razors to our left cheeks. I don't dare take the aloe vera shaving foam *for sensitive men* when he's around; I don't want him thinking I'm a wimp, so it's a wet shave—the bare blades along the cheekbones—and afterwards, when we slap aftershave on our faces, we both close our eyes. When I open mine, he's gone. And of course I wish he could see me now, though I know it's impossible that he'd ever understand who I am. I expect the same goes for most fathers. Most people from other worlds. And I know too that it's just as impossible that I'll ever know who he was, or who exactly I was so afraid of. I can only imagine him—can only piece together words and pictures to try to get some idea of his last weeks. To work out who he was before he plummeted off Vika's balcony.

KOSTYA

Kostya dialled the number for the eighth time that day, and for the eighth time an electronic voice told him that the person he was calling didn't feel like going to the phone. He hadn't thought he'd left any room on his daughter's voicemail and was surprised that the same announcement was still asking him to leave a message. All he could think of was: 'God, you're such a cunt.' He recorded the words and flung his phone down on the table.

His foot was swollen, but didn't hurt half as much as his head. He should have given the booze a miss yesterday; he should give the booze a miss altogether. He wasn't a drinker. He didn't like the smell; he didn't like the taste; he didn't like what it did to him and the people around him—especially the women. *If she smokes, she'll drink; if she drinks, she'll yield*, went an old Russian proverb—he'd tried to din that into his daughter, who'd smoked at a very early age; she'd had fags in her mouth and filched his lighters even before she filled a bra. Over and over he'd said it to her: 'Esli kurit, znachit p'et, esli n'et znachit daet.' But the girl didn't understand; she must have been too young, and he was damned if he was going to explain it to her. She'd see soon enough what came of it—a flat chest for one thing.

He lit up and spat on the floor. He should quit smoking too—another thing he didn't actually like. He'd started because everyone else had—same as with almost everything he'd started, except for making music.

His fingers itched and he squeezed them into a fist and then flexed them, looking at the hairs on the backs of his hands, coppery and grey. Real man's hands they were now, with thick calloused fingers. His mother would have liked them, he thought. His mother who, all his childhood, had shouted at him for being so skinny. 'Bloody hell, boy, are you anorexic? Eat up your pudding! You can't even lift a chair with those noodles you've got hanging from your shoulders, and you want a bleeding accordion!'

Kostya didn't like the pudding his mother put in front of him—apple gratin with matzo and raisins, slippery as custard; it tasted of eggs and butter and sugar, and the raisins swam in it like melon pips—but he applied himself to it diligently because he loved his mother and because she was shouting at him.

Now he'd have given his fingers to eat that mush and hear his mother's voice.

He picked up his phone again and called Vova. There was always a party at Vova's; you could always call him when your sense of male pride flipped over into naked loneliness—and Vova had a keyboard that Kostya was allowed to play whenever he liked, or at least until Vova's wife, Galina, decided it was time for Russian pop songs and put on a CD. Kostya hated those songs. They all sounded the same, like a never-ending advertising jingle—not that the people flinging their arms and legs about on the music videos looked as if they were about to smile into the camera to advertise anti-aging moisturiser. The climax usually came at around midnight when Galina put on Verka Serduchka's 'Vsyo budet khorosho' and everyone sang along hysterically as if they believed it. *Everything will be fine*—that's what he sang, that guy in drag who sounded like he had his mouth full of Vaseline—that fat scarecrow, round as a fucking disco ball, in that silver-starred cap of his—that lying Ukrainian queen. *Everything will be fine.* In his music videos he knocked back shots with policemen and kissed men and women. Yeah sure, everything will be fine. Everything will be just great. First he'd been banned from entering Russia, then he'd been banned from singing, but still his paean to optimism blared out of the speakers at every Russian party.

'Vovchik, why do you put up with this gay music?' Kostya asked Vova as they lay in each other's arms, their clothes damp from the vodka and the muggy air. The ceiling was only a little way above them and seemed to be coming closer and closer.

'You can't talk, Kostya. I've seen you jumping up and down to this song.' Vova buried his sweaty forehead in Kostya's armpit and fell asleep with his arms around him. Vova was always there for Kostya.

He picked up straight away.

'How's your foot?' he asked cheerily.

'Stinky. How about yours?'

'I was looking at this men's magazine at the garage the other day and apparently—you're not going to believe this—women like it when men wear foot deodorant. It turns them on.'

'Was this a German magazine?'

'Think so.'

'That doesn't count.'

'What are you up to? Do you want to come round? I've got fresh vobla. Semön's just back from Moscow and he's brought heaps of the stuff; it took a whole newspaper to wrap all the fish.'

Kostya surprised himself by wincing at the word Moscow. Then he thought, no, that's not why I winced. The pain in his foot felt like fire.

'Yeah, okay, why not? I'll come round.'

There were no photos on the walls of Kostya's flat; he didn't even have one of his mother, who'd died the year before. She'd had diabetes for as long as he could remember, but it hadn't kept her from eating sugar from the bowl with her fingers; she'd carried on even when she started to go blind. Valya had begged her to stop: 'Please, I'll get you medicine, good medicine, but you must eat less sugar or it's no use.' Kostya's mother had squinted at the floor and crunched a sugar lump between her few remaining teeth.

Then came the gangrene on her feet. First her toes turned scaly, then green and furry like seaweed, then black as a root and eventually they rotted away altogether. She could hardly walk, and dragged herself around the flat, holding onto the furniture. When Kostya saw his mother's feet on one of his last visits to her and watched her inch her way along a chest of drawers, he began to shout at her: he'd had enough; he was going to take her to Germany to see some proper doctors who treated people like human beings. He knew there was no point in yelling and crying and pleading with her, but that only made him louder. His mother was rotting away in Flat 120 on the fourth floor of this block in Chertanovo—the very flat he'd grown up in— and he was powerless to help. His father spent most of the day lying in the bedroom on his two mattresses and staring at the ceiling. When he wasn't doing that, he was at the kitchen table with his abacus, his fingers darting over the clacking wooden beads as he mumbled to himself, staring at the table as if in delirium.

Kostya had sent money—money that Valya had earned and a little that he'd earned himself—and he went on sending money until he found it all in preserving jars under the sink—fine, green dollar bills, scrunched up into a kind of compote in tightly sealed jars, beneath the packet of washing powder and a box of chocolates that had been past their best-before date even before Kostya had brought them from Germany. From then on, he and Valya sent medicine, food and even clothes, knowing full well that they too would end up stashed away in cupboards. By the time Kostya's mother was hospitalised, her body had been eaten away right up to her hips. He wanted to ring Semön immediately to book flights, but didn't know how many tickets to buy. He rang his son who didn't pick up, but sent a text asking what he wanted. Kostya wrote back: 'Your grandmother's dying.' Anton called and they argued for half an hour, then Anton hung up, or rather, he threw his phone at the wall. That was one of the last times he spoke to his father.

Then Kostya rang his daughter. She didn't pick up or text him or call him back, although he left messages until her voicemail was full. He didn't even bother trying Valya.

It was fucking freezing at the funeral, a merciless Moscow autumn. There was no one at the cemetery but him, his father and his cousin Misha—and Misha had only come out of politeness. They stood there with red noses and their hands in their coat pockets at the side of a freshly dug hole that looked as if it might be empty; they couldn't really see anything in the biting wind, and shifted, shivering, from one leg to the other until eventually Kostya said: 'Nu ladno. Khvatit.' *All right then. That's enough.*

They piled into Misha's old Lada and drove home.

They drove at twenty kilometres an hour; the white mud-spattered jeep in front kept braking, as if it were sinking; behind, a Volvo with a dented roof tooted its horn. Kostya could see the driver's twisted face in the rear-view mirror. They were stuck for hours until eventually Kostya's anger erupted. He yelled all the expletives he knew, and when he ran out, he began to invent some more.

At home the air was stale; the central heating had been turned on for the winter. The men flung open all the windows and went into the kitchen. Sitting on the table were a handful of sushki and a forlorn-looking jar of jam. With Kostya's mother dead, the kitchen table felt like something of a challenge and none of the men knew what to do; they stared into the corners of the room or up at the ceiling. Nobody spoke. Then Kostya got up and went to the fridge. He took out white bread, sausage and butter, laid three knives and opened a tin of home-made salty dill gherkins from under the sink.

They drank, but not a lot. Kostya was the first to puke on the table; bits of gherkin flew all over the walls. He couldn't hold his drink; he knew he couldn't.

The flat that Kostya had moved into after the divorce had three rooms—more than he needed, more than he'd ever thought he'd have. There was a living room, a bedroom and another room, which he didn't know what to do with. At first he'd thought it could be a spare room, for when people came to stay. After all, he wouldn't be on his own all the time; the children or whoever would come and see him, wouldn't they? It was ages since he'd last set foot in there, except to fetch the ironing board or the drying rack—and they were right by the door; he didn't even have to turn the light on. He'd taken the flat furnished; his daughter had found it for him and filled out all the papers. She'd looked after him to begin with, even interpreting for him at the divorce proceedings.

Kostya hadn't organised an interpreter for himself. 'They should be glad if I turn up at all,' he'd said to Semön, who'd kept topping up his glass. Kostya felt that it was his children's duty to help him—why had he had children, if not to get him out of the shit when he was in it? He'd slogged himself half to death so they could learn this foreign language; now it was only fair that they did their bit, not some lousy German bureaucrat who knew nothing about life. Semön could understand that. Ali agreed right away to act as interpreter; she guessed what was coming. Kostya had no idea.

Outside the courthouse they shook hands. Kostya greeted Valya as if she were a stranger and offered round cigarettes. Valya didn't even look at him, but stared at her daughter's shaved-off eyebrows, and tried to make sense of it all. Kostya and Ali smoked in the drizzle. Valya and her lawyer stood pressed up against the door and looked at their watches.

The echo of footsteps hung in the corridors like stale air. The rubber soles of Ali's trainers squeaked. In the courtroom, they sat facing each other—the judge on Kostya's left; Ali on his right, and Valya opposite, next to her lawyer. Kostya understood nothing, or only very little, of what was said. He did notice that Ali, close to his ear, translated rather less than the judge seemed to be saying, but he was too confused to question it. Ali summed up the essentials, and after a while she whispered: 'You must say you agree.'

'But I don't,' Kostya said. He began to get loud. He was scared and agitated; he suddenly had no idea what was going on and what consequences it would have for him. It was as if he'd just woken up. He screamed like a child and began to utter words that Ali couldn't have translated even if she'd wanted to, because her fund of Russian expletives was limited at that time. She didn't tell him to stop; she just kept saying: 'Dad, you must speak more slowly. You're stammering. I can't understand what you're saying.' Across the room, she saw the colour drain from her mother's face as if someone had pulled the stopper from a pouch of blood. The judge asked what

Kostya wanted and Ali said: 'Nothing. He's just asking about the maintenance settlement.'

'Vsyo budet khorosho,' sings Verka Serduchka. *Everything will be all right.* Kostya, of course, had no idea that his own daughter was lying to him, translating things he hadn't said at all, for fear he might put the divorce off even longer than he already had. Valya, listening to Ali juggling words between the judge and her father, understood all too well and sat there motionless. It was as if she were frozen, like that time in the kitchen when Anton had come in and seen his sister struggling at the wall—except that this time, Valya's mouth wasn't as wide open.

Kostya left the courtroom a divorced man. Ali went with him to Vova's place where he'd been living since moving out. She drank three shots with him and said: 'Dad, I'm going to help you.'

And she had. She'd found him the flat, read through his applications and even helped him practise phrases for a job interview, which turned out to be a waste of time because after a polite 'Thank you for coming', the department manager at the VW factory had switched into Russian. Kostya had put on his best shirt. His eyes were swollen shut, it's true, but you had to give it to him, he had a charming smile and laughed like one of those cocky young men you might expect to see leaning against the wall in a Moscow bar, one leg bent, a fag in the corner of the mouth. Kostya had never been in those bars—his parents would never have let him—but he had the smile and it was wonderful.

He got the job. All his colleagues spoke his mother tongue, or near enough—Ukrainian, Circassian. They got on well, laughed together, smoked together, touched each other's shoulders when they passed in the corridors. Ali came to see Kostya regularly to begin with, and he told her what it had been like to leave his parents and find himself on his own—only his fucking work and the fucking weekends when nobody spoke to him and nobody cared about his backache. No one had thought to ask how he was, although they all knew he'd worn a back brace for years. Put his back out for good, he had, but nobody was there for him. Not even Ali, in the end.

Kostya got his first job in a factory just after the Chepanov family had moved out of the home; it was so gruelling that it was a struggle for him to get back to the flat at knocking-off time. He had to drag himself up to the attic by the banister rail and once inside, he crawled onto the sofa, too tired to talk. When the children squabbled or got up to God knows what else, he'd summon up the last of his strength to yell at them, but other than that he was quiet. He usually worked night shifts and came home when it was getting light and the flat was already empty. His wife would be out working—she was always working—and the children would be at school. He'd fall asleep immediately, his arm over his face, and be woken by the racket when the children came in. Nothing is as loud as children coming home from school. He'd heave himself up, drag himself into the kitchen and make chicken broth and buckwheat porridge which he'd mix together and then eat himself, the whole pot, because he knew his children wouldn't touch it, and his wife wouldn't be back till late. For Ali and Anton there were shrink-wrapped hamburgers in the fridge, a pack of two, stuck together along their cheesy edges. Kostya heated them up in the microwave and the twins stood in the kitchen, wide-eyed, watching the buns swell like balloons as they went round and round on the turntable.

But their eyes grew wider still when Kostya bundled them into the car and drove them to McDonald's. They fought over the passenger seat and then both had to sit in the back. They played with the seat-belts, cranked down the windows and stuck out their heads, squealing with delight, like kittens. Kostya told them to close the windows, but it was pointless—this was before he had a car with an automatic window lock—and he told them to strap themselves in, something he'd never done himself before having children. When the two of them were in the car with him, he lowered the rear-view mirror so he could keep an eye on them, and sometimes the sight of the pair of them biting each other's shoulders brought tears to his eyes.

He bought them everything they wanted, everything he could afford—extra hamburgers on top of their Happy Meals, crispy chicken wings that Anton had all to himself, Coke and Fanta—and when Ali cried because she was missing a figurine from the Happy Meal collection, Kostya went up to the spotty boy at the deep-fryer and talked a mishmash of all the languages that came into his head until the boy went off and came back with the missing toy. All this was restricted to Sundays, when Kostya had the day off—until he got wind of the fact that Jews were allowed to take Fridays and Saturdays off without being fired.

'Shabbes,' he said, laughing like mad. 'Shabbes! Can you believe it?' He slapped Valya on the back like an old friend. 'They really mean it—I can work less because Shabbat shalom!'

'The children want to go on Klassenfahrt,' said Valya who was filling out the application for leave.

'What's that?' Kostya stopped laughing and looked fierce at the sound of the German word.

'The whole class is taking a trip up north and staying three nights. It's all organised by the school.'

'Why?'

'What do I know? It's what they do here.'

'And I have to pay?'

'They'll never make friends otherwise. They go about dressed like schleps, never go out, eat all that crap you stuff into them. Soon they'll look like us—is that what you want?'

Kostya looked at his wife's face, which seemed to be pitted all over, even her forehead. Her skin and eyes were covered in an unhealthy sheen, and her legs and upper arms had puffed up like the white burger buns in the microwave.

Kostya ripped up the application for religious leave and put in extra shifts to scrape together the money for the school journey. Although Valya had work in the hospital at that point, she wasn't yet being paid. She'd been told she'd never get any kind of job, not even part-time, if she didn't do some sort of internship first—a bit of unpaid slave labour. But six months later she really did end up getting a job, and not long after that she had a grant too, and her boss did what he could to help, and so it went on until Valya was earning good money—unimaginably good for a doctor used to socialism, where no one had any idea that it was even possible to earn that much. Where Valya had trained, doctors were paid the same as builders—and less, if they didn't accept the envelopes that were slipped into the pockets of their white coats—but here Valya's salary would soar to heights that neither Valya nor Kostya could ever have imagined. They went up and down the supermarket aisles, pushing the world's biggest shopping trolley and chucking things in until jars of frankfurters were cascading down the sides of a mountain of groceries.

But that wasn't until later. For the moment, Kostya was putting in extra shifts in spite of Shabbat shalom, so that the children could go on a school trip to Lake Steinhude. Ali and Anton came back early with fever and diarrhoea and Valya made them chew black charcoal tablets that she'd brought from home.

'That's what comes of sending them away,' muttered Kostya, standing helplessly next to the twins' bed. He'd have liked to hug them and hold them tight to stop them crying, but Valya was lying half on top of them, stroking their cheeks.

Kostya took a cigarette, lit it, stubbed it out again, had a shower, shaved (with his two-blade razor), put on a clean shirt and picked up a bottle of Yeltsin vodka at the filling station.

He was the first to arrive. Vova took his jacket and the bottle.

'Come in! Come in!'

'Do you mind if I—?' Kostya asked, the second he was in the flat.

'Go ahead.'

Kostya sat down at the keyboard. He tested the pedals and the sound, then ran his fingers over the black plastic surface, peered at his fingertips and got up and went into the kitchen.

'Hello, Galina.'

'Hello, Kostya.'

Galina was standing at the stove in a brightly coloured apron, frying something sweet and sickly smelling. He walked past her and took a cloth from the sink, then returned to the keyboard and gave it a thorough wipe before sitting down and pressing Beethoven into the keys, his swollen foot pumping the damper pedal. Vova and Galina let him play undisturbed until the room was full of guests and they decided they'd had enough of 'that tinkling of yours' and put on a CD.

A mountain of vobla lay on a spread of newspaper. Vova nimbly scraped off the dry, silvery grey scales, pulled the salty flesh off the backbone, teased it into shreds and piled it onto a plate that the guests instantly fell upon; he could only just keep up. The dried fishes stared at Kostya with their red eyes; he stared back and then began to help Vova, grabbing a fish by its fins and pulling them off.

'So how's life?' asked Vova, helping himself to a big piece of fish and beginning to chew. Kostya did the same; the salty crust made his tongue tingle.

'Azohen vey. Makes me want to puke.'

'*That* good?' said Vova.

'Oh, you know, the usual, but if my foot isn't soon—'

'You're being paid not to work. What are you complaining about? Does it hurt?'

'No, it doesn't hurt—just gets me down. Can't help thinking of my mother.'

'How Jewish of you.'

Vova looked across the room at a cluster of women, smoking at the window.

'Who's the girl over there at the window?'

'My wife.'

'Ha ha. I can see that. I meant the one next to her, with the black hair.'

'That's Vika. She's Chechen.'

'No!'

'But one of ours.'

'How do you mean, *one of ours*? Jewish black widow or what?'

'Never heard of Jewish terrorists?'

'Chechen, eh? But she's got some arse on her, my God, and if she smokes, she'll drink—'

Kostya gulped down the vobla in his mouth like a boiled sweet, breathed into the hollow of his hand to smell his breath, wished he hadn't, chased the salt fish with a slug of Yeltsin, belched softly, hiked up his jeans, hobbled over to the Chechen woman and got Galina to introduce him.

'What's the matter with your foot?' Vika asked. 'Do you always walk like that?'

'Stupid business. Got my bones mashed up by a generator.'

'A generator. I see. What happened?' Vika dragged on her cigarette and Kostya noticed her long fingers and her long, raspberry-coloured nails.

'Maybe I took a running kick at it.'

Vika gave a loud laugh. He lit a cigarette for her and they talked about waiting for better weather and how it was better to wait for that than for nothing at all. They dragged on their cigarettes, inhaling and exhaling together, and two weeks later she moved in with him.

He was still on sick leave, so they had time to drive to the 'dacha', as they called the allotment shed that had once belonged to Vika's husband. He wasn't around anymore; he'd gone back—back to the mountains, back to the steppe, back to another woman, whatever.

'Really gone?' asked Kostya, because he didn't want the husband appearing at the door with an axe, while he was having it off with Vika on the bench in the shed.

'Really gone,' said Vika, pulling him towards the bench.

At first everything was all right. Then everything was the same as ever.

Kostya came home with a net of miniature cheeses in red wax shells, stuttering excitedly: 'Look what I've got.' Vika didn't understand what he was so thrilled about; she found Babybel revolting. She hadn't been there when Kostya had seen his first red-wax-coated Edam in the chilled-food section of a shop in Chertanovo and carried it home like a piece of expensive jewellery. Kostya remembered Valya's face as they cut the cheese; he remembered the sound of the wax rind as it cracked open. The little balls of cheese he'd bought this time had tiny wax tongues you could pull to make the cheese fall out of the rind all by itself. He ate the whole net alone at the kitchen table. Vika was somewhere else.

More and more often, he dreamed of his children—that he saw them in a crowd on the street, but they didn't recognise him or pretended not to—and once that he chucked a shoe at them. He sometimes called Vika 'Valya' in bed, and his belly grew bigger and bigger, until he wondered whether he couldn't just have it chopped off—cut away with an enormous saw. Then came the call from Misha, telling him that his father had died. That meant one thing: there was now a flat belonging to him in Moscow.

Moscow was one of the most expensive cities in the world. Kostya saw a gloopy mass of brown banknotes swimming before his eyes like honey. He pictured himself in a new Mercedes and Vika in new clothes and high-heeled shoes. He saw himself fucking her on the backseat of the car, parked right in front of the factory so that the boys inside would hear the screams. He told Vika about his father, but didn't mention the flat; she said she'd go to the funeral with him if he liked and he said: 'Whatever.' He lay awake for nights on end, dreaming about how much he'd get for the flat and all the things he could do with the money—like buy himself a trip to America— and then one night, it came to him in a flash. He woke with a jolt, twisted his face into a smile, opened his eyes wide. Suddenly everything was clear to him and he started to cry. Vika was lying beside him on her belly, her open lips pressed into the pillow and pushed towards him in a pout, like a fish's; she let out a deep breath through her mouth. Kostya looked at her, then past her, and got out of bed, still crying.

At work, he explained that his father had died. Then he bought himself a ticket, one way only. He wouldn't let Vika join him. 'I must do this alone,' he said.

Soon the funeral was out of the way and Kostya was sitting at Misha's kitchen table, while Misha doodled on loose sheets of paper.

'Still the old cartoons?'

'What else? It's the only thing that stops me.'

'Stops you what?'

'From smashing in my wife and children's heads.'

'I see.'

'What about yours?'

Kostya looked at Misha's doodles.

'Can you help me find a buyer for the flat?' he said.

'I'll ask around,' said Misha.

•

Kostya knew what he wanted. He didn't want a Mercedes, he didn't want Vika in high heels to fuck on the backseat, he didn't want his furnished flat and his shitty factory job—and what he really, really didn't want was to have to hear the German language ever again; it had given him nothing but grief. Kostya had made up his mind to go back.

He wasn't good at making plans. He didn't really know what it meant to move to another country; Valya had seen to everything when they'd left for Germany and it wouldn't have occurred to him to think of moving to Moscow as moving to another country; to him it was just going back—going home. He didn't realise there's no such thing.

His plan was to rent a little city-centre flat. They were expensive, of course, but he thought he'd be making money—and not just from the sale of his parents' flat. After all, the cupboards were full of Adidas tracksuits and gold watches and chains; it was quite possible that the place was so jam-packed with valuables that the contents were worth as much as the flat itself. He thought, too, of those preserving jars full of dollar bills under the sink.

Kostya began to sell off the valuables, then he bought more—he started to invest, to speculate, something he was particularly bad at; the money slipped through his fingers. Still, he was happy. He walked around the city, got stuck in traffic jams, lost his temper at the jeweller's, gave his father's suits away to visiting friends. One of the friends who'd helped carry his piano up to the fourth floor all those years ago promised Kostya to help move the same piano to his new city-centre flat as soon he'd found one. When he left, Kostya gave him a gold watch. He lay on his father's two mattresses, listening to the upstairs neighbours shouting at each other, and grinning to himself because he understood every word. When a buyer was found who was prepared to shell out half a million for the flat, Kostya laughed hysterically. He wanted to ring Valya right away to tell her, then he remembered that those days were over.

Documents were drawn up and certified, hands were shaken, a notary recorded everything and asked for cash in hand. When the money didn't appear and didn't appear in Kostya's account, he sat at Misha's kitchen table, smoking cigarette after cigarette, jiggling his feet up and down and stuttering to himself. 'It'll come,' Misha said. 'Don't worry.'

But when Kostya took a taxi to the notary's office, a journey of four hours in that part of town, spent, as usual, stuck between honking Volvos and jeeps (the fare almost bankrupted him, but he no longer had a car of his own), and when, on his arrival, he found the office shut up and no one around who could tell him where the supposed notary might be, there was no use pretending he didn't know what had happened.

He returned one last time to Krasnyi Mayak 13, Block 2, Flat 120. He went into the living room, flung open the window, hung out over the windowsill and shouted. He left the window open, walked through the almost empty rooms and knelt down by the burn holes his children had left in the carpet, then went into the hall, leant against the kitchen doorframe and stared at the plastic tablecloth with the pattern of blue flowers that his father had scored with a knife, at the little television set that was still sitting on top of the fridge even though it hadn't had any picture or sound for years, and at the cooker that was as spotless as if it had never been cooked on. Then Kostya's eyes fell on the improvised growth chart marked on the doorframe in blue biro. It stopped at 132 centimetres. Two almost straight lines were labelled vertically in his own handwriting, one marked *Anton*, the other *Alissa*, and beside the names were numbers:

1987—82 cm
1988—91 cm
1991—110 cm

1994—126 cm
1995—132 cm

Kostya ran first his eyes along the lines, then his fingers. He scraped them with his fingernail; he spat on them and tried to wipe them off with his thumb; he rubbed and rubbed with the flat of his hand, but the biro had gnawed its way into the white paint, so he yanked at the doorframe, took the door off its hinges, prised the growth chart off the wall, carried it into the bedroom, put it on the two mattresses and lay down beside it.

For three days he lay in his childhood flat and cried. He puked in the bathtub, smeared the windows with shit, pissed on the Turkish carpet, aiming for the burn holes, smashed all the light bulbs and made sure he left the place as he wished it to be found.

He didn't say goodbye to anyone. Misha drove him to the airport; they hardly spoke. Kostya boarded the plane with the taste of salty dill gherkins on his tongue. On the flight, he looked at brochures of Germany and leafed through glossy catalogues, and when he got back to Vika with her long raspberry-coloured nails and her long-fingered hands, he saw that those long fingers of hers were stained yellow from nicotine. He hadn't noticed before.

VALYA

'I met Kostya the day he brought home his engineering degree, and that's how he was presented to me: a qualified man with a certified degree—job guaranteed. All that was wanting was a wife, and not just any wife, but a proper Jewish one—and there I was at the door. You can imagine, can't you? They'd got their teeth in me; I still have the marks. On the fourth day, Kostya said: "You're my wife." Just like that. Didn't ask. Nobody asked. Nobody waited for an answer either. And all this time he was in love with another woman, a regular goy. The love of his life, she was. Shame he didn't have the balls to marry her.'

That was the moment I realised I had been deluding myself into thinking I'd want to hear what Valya had to tell me, no matter what it was.

Today she was wearing a discreetly checked green blouse that hugged her shoulders and flowed over her body—a body that looked imposing when she held herself straight. She wasn't looking at me, but right through me, reading a script off my face, like a newsreader following a teleprompter—except that in her case it was yesterday's news and had already left lines at the corners of her mouth. A slight protuberance pulled her upper lip down; I don't think she ever smiled much, but not because she wasn't a cheerful person—on the contrary, my mother was more given to laughing than anyone else in the family; it was just that there was no place for laughter in the time that had spawned her—no place for laughter in that land called Socialism; it wasn't part of normal social behaviour over there. Deep down inside, though, she laughed a lot; I could see it in her eyes.

She was speaking several languages at once, putting them together in different combinations to fit the colour and flavour of her memories, making sentences that told a story different from the sum of their words. When she spoke, it sounded like an amorphous medley of all the things she was—things that could never have been reduced to one version of a story, or told in only one language.

She said: 'I wouldn't have married him if I hadn't got pregnant. I'd have left after the first argument, the first wallop, the first time I saw his face all red and puffy. Don't get me wrong, I don't regret it— don't regret having you, I mean. But you have to have children quickly before you've had time to get to know each other and be disappointed. No one would ever have children otherwise; the human race would die out—would've done in the Soviet Union, anyway.

'We had no word for love, no notion of what it meant, no mental picture of it. We had nothing to...what's the word...to *compare* it to. And we didn't have time for broken hearts. We were too busy building up socialism.

'Of course, you did see girls with tear-stained faces in the university toilets. It was always a mystery to me—that they could go around like that with their make-up all smudged and feel no shame. I'd have given myself a good slap in the face. Then again, I suppose I'd have cried and beaten my breast if I'd had anything to cry for. Any*one*.'

I could feel soundwaves flinging my brain from one side of my head to the other and wasn't sure whether it was because Valya's voice had suddenly shot up, or whether I was just being sensitive. Something furry was creeping up my throat, my temples felt as if they might burst and, as my mother pieced herself together, a little bit of story at a time, she became more and more of a blur to me. This wasn't a good time for a migraine. We always put off breakdowns in our family—postpone them to the solitude of empty rooms. I knew, too, that Valya was only just getting going.

I'd come without expecting anything in particular, stepping into a flat I had more memories of than I'd thought. Only the dimensions were different from what I remembered—the height of the ceilings, the size of the rooms and furniture. And Valya wasn't sitting at the kitchen table, where I always imagined her, but at the desk in her bedroom, her back pressed against the glass tabletop behind her, her hands resting on the plastic arms of the swivel chair, and Shura above her, looking down at us from one of his oil paintings. I suddenly loved her so much that I felt an urge to slide off the edge of the bed and rest my head on her lap—but I stayed put because I didn't want to interrupt her.

'Really, I should have stayed firm and refused to leave Volgograd. I didn't want to go to Moscow. Everyone thought you had to marry your way to Moscow—not me. I was the only one, but I knew it was a stupid idea. Moscow's evil; it stinks. Did then and it does now, maybe worse than ever now—a snakepit of a city. You can't even buy milk there without the shop woman spitting in your face. I didn't want to move; I wanted to stay in Volgograd, but they talked me into it. My girlfriends all screamed at me: "What? Are you crazy? It'll mean you'll be registered in Moscow. I'd marry an unemployed alcoholic for that, if I had the chance, and yours actually has a job." One of them, Dasha, had gone there to be mistress to a man thirty years older than her—he was married, with children and all—and do you know, she was happy—she was just happy to be in Moscow. So I thought the place must have something going for it.'

I tried to imagine the picture those eighties women must have had of Moscow, but saw only swings buried deep in snow, their rusty frame sticking up into a sky criss-crossed with white streaks. What a shame, I thought, that I can't imagine more. I was having trouble thinking straight.

It was the light that alerted me to the onset of the migraine. It sliced through my eyeballs, although the room was relatively dark—Valya liked it dim and the curtains were drawn. Then everything seemed too loud. I tried to ignore it; I didn't want to have to leave Valya, but already the smells in the room were keener too; Valya's perfume stung my nose.

'When I got to Moscow, they put on this act for me—I still can't believe the trouble they went to. Or that I fell for it. Actually I thought Kostya was ugly—he was covered in freckles and had a big belly, even in those days, and skinny little arms and red hair—but then he sat down at the piano and began to play, looking into my eyes and pressing his lips together and flaring his nostrils, and his parents sang his praises and told me about the hidden qualities of this sensitive young man—how well read he was, how considerate towards his parents and neighbours, how much he liked the theatre and the opera.

'To begin with, Kostya took me out—museums during the day and the theatre in the evening. Can you imagine—Kostya in a museum? And do you know something funny? He was a big eater, even in those days, and every time we went to the theatre he'd stuff himself first, shovelling it all in, any old how, sour cream and beef with onions and whatever, and then he'd have wind all through the play—and I don't

224

just mean on one occasion; this was every time he took me out. The orchestra in his belly would start up just as the lights went down, and either he'd belch or he'd fart, and it pained me—I felt for him; I was sorry for him, you know? I thought how awkward it must be for him; the poor thing's trying to make advances to me and ends up making a public spectacle of himself. But looking back on it, I don't think he gave a damn. In fact, I'm *sure* he didn't.'

Hearing people talk of the world as if they could rely on it always makes me feel lonely and helpless. They speak of being sure about things; they tell you how something was or even how it's going to be, and it always makes me acutely aware of how little I know about what might happen next. I don't even know what I'll be addressed as when I go to buy cigarettes—a he or a she? Each morning I'm surprised by my own face in the mirror, and I'm sceptical about any attempts to predict the future. My temples ache a lot; it lays me low for days. But I didn't want to burden Valya with the ins and outs of my emotions, which were on a rollercoaster ride from the testosterone, like a permanent adolescence. I was here to listen.

'I remember my mother ringing while I was there—she was off somewhere again, Hungary or Czechoslovakia, and wanted to know whether Kostya had proposed yet. And I said: "Mum, I don't even know him. We've only just met." And she said: "Feelings come with time, daughter."'

I was afraid of suddenly turning deaf again, like the time I realised that Anton was gone. Something inside me had started to run—it was charging against the inner walls of my body, desperate to get out.

Valya said: 'I got pregnant quickly. Russian men don't do contraception. Abortion was the standard contraceptive, but after two abortions during my marriage to Ivan, I'd had enough and had a one-hundred-and-fifty-per-cent reliable Soviet-tested coil put in. I got pregnant with you almost immediately.'

Since seeing me with designer stubble, Valya had stopped asking when I was going to give her grandchildren, and for that I was grateful. Grandchildren had been topic number two, second only to my bad eating habits. My uninterested uterus. The western way of living only for yourself rather than bringing something into the world that had even worse chances than you. But now that my shoulders had grown broader and the muscles in my arms more prominent—now that I could pick my mother up and lift her in the air—she'd given up asking.

'I wasn't prepared for that. I couldn't cope; it was all too fast for me. I didn't know where I was or who these people were, and of course we had to get married even more quickly than planned. The idea had been to do everything on the Volga in the summer, but because I was already pregnant, the wedding had to be in the winter. In the filthy, slushy Moscow winter. My white tights were a complete mess by the time we got to the registry office. Do you know how hard it was to get white tights in those days? They were my first nylons. I went to the ladies and tried to scratch off the muck with my fingernails, speck by speck, splash by splash, without ripping them. Didn't do much good; I look like a Dalmatian on the wedding photos. Mother-in-law teased me about it for years. And then things went even faster—too fast. The next thing I knew, along came you two. You were early.'

I hadn't expected her to talk about that. And she didn't really— only in her own way, leaving out all the things I'd never have dared ask about. All she said was: 'It was Kostya's birthday. I'd wanted to go to Etinka's in Volgograd and give birth there, but it wasn't to be. Kostya had this party and—'

Valya was a blur—I sensed her rather than seeing her—and the air was dry; it was only now that I realised she must have the heating turned right up. Valya was always cold. Like me. And before anything could burst in my ears again, I did a bunk. I went out of my body. It stayed there, sitting stiffly in front of Valya, and I leapt out of myself. I was on the outside; I could listen with impunity now.

'He had this birthday party and...anyway...premature labour...no petrol in the car...Kostya still completely pissed...the ambulance took two hours to come—or was it three or four?...Then it was off to the maternity ward, where fifteen other cows were already lying mooing with their legs spread. And in I march, with bruises all over my body and it felt as if the head was already sticking out—yours, it was your head, I know that now.'

Valya looked at the wall behind me. She didn't notice that I'd dodged her again, absconded; she was talking through my body, on and on.

'There was no bed for me at first and I wanted someone to pick me up and carry me, because I was scared that if I kept walking, I'd crush the head that was coming out of me—and then I split open completely; you ripped me open. I thought either I'd crush you to a pulp or you'd rip me to shreds. Push, crush, rip. But here we are today. We made it. I wasn't so sure at the time.'

I wouldn't be so sure now, I thought, looking on from outside. I left my stiff body sitting there and rose in the air, not breathing out until I was floating above the glass desktop. My empty shell was careful to keep blinking at regular intervals, so as not to arouse suspicion.

'So there we were: Mr and Mrs Chepanov. Kostya was fed up with being called Berman; he said it had given him nothing but hassle at work, and I had no trouble believing him; I'd grown up a Pinkenzon, after all. Don't ask me where the name came from—bought or invented, I suppose; someone had married someone at some point; it was floating around somewhere in the family. Kostya's parents approved. The only one who didn't was his grandad; he kicked up a row and said we were selling our souls to the Christians. He'd lived under the Germans, you see, and nothing had been quite right with him ever since; giving your own name away was like being sent to the gas chambers, as far as he was concerned.

'He came to see us once a month from Podmoskovye, the part of the country they all came from. Kostya's mother gave him food to take home so he wouldn't go hungry, but she had a good look at the best-before dates first and only ever gave him things that had long outlived their shelf life.'

The self beneath me laughed mechanically. Valya looked at it, not yet used to the tinny sound of my breaking voice—and who could blame her? *She* didn't laugh.

'Chertanovo was the outer crust of the city; you only had to walk through one wood and you were in Podmoskovye. But try walking that as an old man. He'd arrive all out of puff, sit straight down at table and fall on the food.

'We lived in this filthy part of town—an out-of-bounds zone—even the taxi drivers only went there if they had to. I didn't know that when I first came to Moscow, of course—that there was a death or a rape in the block every other day. You think I'm exaggerating—it's a blessing you *can* think that. That's why I brought you here—so you wouldn't believe all these awful stories. So you think I'm exaggerating when I tell you that the sixteen-year-old girl next door was found raped and murdered on the stairs. Or that the cobbler who lived opposite, a vast man, two metres by two metres, got a bottle smashed over his head by muggers, just outside our block, and bled to death on the spot. He'd no money on him, of course. And there was a child who fell out of the seventh floor—if he wasn't thrown. There were so many stories like that.'

I hung cross-legged over our heads, enjoying the new perspective; I'd never been up here before, never seen the room like this. The surface of Valya's face was constantly changing: one moment it looked like a ball of cottonwool, the next like the face of a Pioneer girl flying into space. Seen from above, her haircut was a strange mushroom shape, and I asked myself when she'd started to dye her hair. I should have asked *her*—and I should have asked too how she'd lost so much weight so quickly and what she liked to eat—I could cook for us.

She said: 'I never understood my in-laws. I don't know what they made of themselves. He was short and puny, a bristly worm—and that impossible cloth cap, like a street urchin; he even kept it on for his afternoon nap. When he wasn't working, he'd lie on the bed for days on end, just staring at the ceiling. He might have a drink of water every now and then, but that was it. Didn't move, didn't speak; all he did was breathe. Mother-in-law was a doer, though—always knew exactly what she wanted. If I hadn't got pregnant, she'd have carried on working. She liked working; I don't think she wanted to be a housewife, but you didn't have a choice in those days; somebody had to stay at home with the children. You couldn't send them to kindergarten—might as well poison them yourself and get it over with; if they didn't come home sick, they came home dead. So Mother-in-law stayed with you and I went to work. She cleaned and cooked and looked after you and washed all your nappies by hand. A maid of all work.'

I looked at the corners of the walls and the stucco on the ceiling—or the marks where it had once been.

'I think I felt sorry for her.'

From somewhere down below, I heard Valya say: 'My in-laws only had one friend—a man who'd moved to Moscow from their village. He was the only visitor we ever had; he came round a lot, and if I hadn't known they had no truck with beggars, I'd have thought that's what he was. It's what he looked like, and it's what he smelt like too. A quiet man he was, almost gentle to the pair of them—I never heard anyone else speak to them like that, least of all their own son—and they were almost human towards him, this one friend of theirs. I've forgotten his name. It's possible, though, that he only came so often because his wife was always drinking urine.'

The self below laughed again. Valya ignored the strange, tinny noise.

'She did this urine therapy, for years, and he was always telling us about the smell and how unbearable it was, having to live with it. It wasn't that you peed and then drank the urine; it had to stand around a bit. Fresh urine's no good, apparently. The poor thing was always desperate to get away from home. You can imagine.

'Their only real friend. I liked him.'

She went on talking about her in-laws and their friends and their friends' friends, and I understood. If I was asked about myself, I always talked about other people too, pretending that the stories I told revealed something about me, and knowing at the same time how hopeless it is to try to cover your tracks.

I only caught snatches now of what Valya was saying. 'This friend moved to America. When he came and told them he was emigrating, the friendship was over. They started some argument—said he'd stolen from them, taken something from the flat...he kissed their feet, ate out of their hands...apparently he'd nicked a radio of theirs—as you do, when you're emigrating to the States—just what you need in America, a Soviet radio...at some point they said he'd made it over there and now he was dead...'

I glanced to the side. Shura looked me straight in the eye. That painting had always unnerved me because the oil made it look as if his pupils were throbbing. I looked back questioningly.

Valya said: 'We always had a lot to eat—so much that I put on thirty kilos in my first year in Moscow. They fed me up as if it was an embarrassment to them that the professor's granddaughter was so skinny. They were war children; they had to have heaps of fat and potatoes with everything.

'Mother-in-law rubbed butter on her hands to stop them getting chapped; I'll never forget the smell of Soviet butter on her skin. I once bought her some hand cream from my savings, rose-scented, but she never opened it—just hid it away at the back of the cupboard. I bet she waited till it was past its use-by date, then gave it to someone as a present.'

I tore my eyes away from Shura's face and looked down at Valya's hands, thinking how I'd love to rub cream on them—feel her fingers, and the skin between them, and her nails. Then I thought of the hands of my other self down there, growing gradually rougher. I was sometimes startled by my own calluses, usually when I was in bed, half asleep, and laid one curled hand in the other beside my head. But perhaps it was only the strange feeling of holding my own hand. Valya, I thought, would never notice how rough my skin was growing, because we never shook hands and only touched each other through our clothes when we hugged.

She said: 'Mother-in-law wouldn't let me take photos of you; she said the devil would take your souls. That's why there are so few baby photos of the two of you...only the ones I developed myself...I'd cover up the kitchen window and close the door to make it dark enough. Then Mother-in-law would come in and rummage around in the fridge, saying she really felt like a bit of ham...by the time she'd found what she wanted, the negatives were overexposed.'

On the first photo of me, you see my bare baby's body—almond-shaped eyes wide open, pointy chin—lying on a white sheet, arms and legs thrust out as I try to push myself from my tummy onto my back. It looks as if I'm flying.

On another photo that for a long time was on the chest of drawers at my grandparents' in Moscow, you see my almost fully grown, flat body in a floral waistcoat that hangs undone from my bare shoulders. I'm holding an apple in one hand; the other hand is empty and clenched to a fist. On my head is a white cap that comes down over my ears, and I'm looking into the camera as if I'd lost something. And

I don't know—maybe I'm imagining things, but I seem to recall a colour photo of my brother and me: me in leggings and a vest, my arms folded, and Anton next to me in a golden dress, dancing.

I forced myself to listen to Valya again. I felt I owed it to her and began to stitch the half-sentences back together. It didn't hurt to listen, up here.

Valya said: 'Did you know that the Russians say if you can't prevent a rape, you must learn to relax? That's something I never learnt. I practically lived in the hospital, hardly ever left if I could help it, did overtime, organised conferences, talked to patients into the small hours—anything I could think of to avoid having to go *back there*. Kostya always waited for me—parked outside the clinic and left the engine running. Sometimes I didn't even bother going out, and sometimes I'd go out and say I was busy and then go straight back in again.'

She said: 'I remember the first Edam cheese Kostya brought home for me, with its thick red wax rind. I remember the taste. I only knew two kinds of cheese until I was twenty-five—kolbasnyi and rossiyskiy—and this was something exotic. I was so delighted, I threw my arms round Kostya's neck. He called me his little monkey and often brought me cheese after that—though God knows where he got it.

'I think he was the first to come up with the idea of emigrating. He was the first to talk about it, anyway. There were tanks on Red Square; we were expecting civil war any day, or a coup or whatever—and we knew who'd be the first to take a battering. A whole wave of people left for Israel; there were countless invitations along the lines of: where you are, things are troubled and dangerous; where we are, there are mangoes on the trees. They took all comers, whether genuine Jews or Russians who'd bought themselves names ending in -berg or -man or -stein—whatever sounded Jewish and dreamed of the desert. I remember Mother-in-law saying: "It's all a trick! The Russians want to find out where the Jews are living! They'll take your details and haul you away! You don't really think they'll take them to Israel, do you? How stupid can you be? The gulags—that's where they'll send them."'

Valya laughed suddenly, surprising herself. She clapped her hand to her mouth, feeling for something on her desk with the other hand. The gurgling sound came from deep in her throat and mingled with something shriller.

'At the embassy we were told we needed our parents' signatures if we wanted to leave the country. They had to give their consent. Children were people's retirement provision—why else do you think they had so many? The state pension was only enough to keep you in bread and milk till the end of your life, so the old folks had to sign to say they were prepared to do without their children. Mine were willing, but Kostya's said: "No way."

'We could, of course, have faked the signatures. You only had to slip someone something and they'd issue you with whatever you wanted. But Kostya's parents knew that and threatened to report us— and that would have been it for us; the door to the west would have been shut forever.

'Kostya made several attempts to talk his father round, but the old man just came up with all these stories about his life in the village— what an awful time they'd had of it, how much they'd sacrificed for us, and that we must be off our heads to want to go to Germany where our blood—Soviet blood—was barely dry on the pavements. I tried too. I talked calmly to him and said if it didn't work out, we'd come back— we could always come back; it wasn't far; you could fly or take the train and we'd be there right away if anything happened. He interrupted me—I can see his face now. "I'm the one who decides things round here," he said. Then he picked up the knife.

'There was more to my father-in-law than you might think. He may have been so short and puny, you had the impression you could crush him in your armpit, but apparently he did stuff in the army—tortured the other soldiers, poured hot oil in their eyes. I couldn't help thinking of that when I saw him standing there with that knife. Kostya, of course, immediately picked up the table and...

'I screamed. Mother-in-law screamed. You and Anton were standing in the door; I remember, I saw your faces and stopped screaming straight away. Then Mother-in-law saw you, then Kostya, then his father: we all turned to look at you, standing there looking at us.'

A knife floated before my eyes. I saw my dad hurl a table across the kitchen; I saw the frozen faces I knew from photographs; I called up images that seemed to fit.

Valya said: 'I knew nothing about Germany, nothing about anything—I had no picture of the place, no idea what I wanted from it. You say you want your children to have a golden future—yes, all right, that's what you say, but it isn't what you think. You don't think anything at all. You feel like a rolling stone.'

I was floating above us, watching that other self of mine listen to my mother talking about the move. My other self was sitting up very straight and so was she. I couldn't quite catch what we were saying; our words were strangely staggered. I saw Shura's purple eyes again, level with my forehead. *Are you talking to me, old man? Talk to me. Say something. I miss you. I miss talking to you.* But Shura said nothing and his eyes weren't purple in the painting. I looked down once more at mother and child, sitting, mirroring one another, and again I saw clearly how similar we were, especially in the way we let our arms dangle at our sides, slightly bent at the elbows.

I saw Ali and, suddenly, sitting there opposite his mother, it could have been Alissa. It was the familiar surroundings that did it; he was hovering between times and bodies; he was empty. I heard Valya say that the walls were damp in the first flat in Germany; I heard her tell Ali about the time her mother-in-law came to visit from Moscow and she, Valya, had a stroke. Her father, Daniil, had pushed her around the little West German town we lived in at that time in a wheelchair, because she couldn't walk for weeks. The patches of sunlight in the small park he sometimes took her to were full of old people asleep in wheelchairs. Valya wasn't yet forty then. I heard her say that the right-hand corner of her mouth never quite recovered from the stroke, and saw Ali lean forwards slightly, discreetly examining the corner of his mother's mouth to see if he could see anything. But all he could make out were the hundreds of little wrinkles on her upper lip, like shredded paper.

Valya said she'd had to move to her parents' and that her husband had come and taken the children away. He didn't bring them back until she threatened to divorce him. From diagonally above, I looked down into Ali's motionless face with his big nose and pointy chin; between his chin and lower lip, a deep dimple sprouted black hairs. He looked at Valya in silence as she told him about her daughter, who'd been so disturbed after seeing her father drag her red-eyed mother out of the flat that she hadn't spoken for weeks. Ali blinked without understanding.

I hung in the air. Time slowed, then tumbled past my nose in a rush. Floating up there next to Shura's picture, I stretched out an arm, ran a hand over the frame around his face and peered at my fingertips. I saw fine grey streaks of dust and rubbed my fingers together; the dust formed tiny globules that I flicked away over the heads below me. Nothing made any sense. I heard Valya reproach Ali for coming to ask questions—but in her own way. She didn't say it was presumptuous of him, or that he'd never understand the world she came from; she didn't even say that it was more than she could manage to explain everything. She said something very Russian like: 'Memory's a parasite. It's best to leave well alone if you don't want to end up like me, unable to stop. I—'

'I' in Russian is 'Я', the last of thirty-three letters. People say: 'Я' is the last letter of the alphabet, so put yourself last, forget you exist, don't rate yourself too highly, melt into the background. It seemed to me that Valya had taken this adage to heart; it made sense to her that she should be last; it was logical. Valya believed that there was a logic to things; she believed in a chain of events, each following the other, ineluctably. When she told me her life—or the part of it that she wanted to pass on to me—she described a chain of causal relations that seemed to her entirely natural, but that somehow, in spite of the firmness of her voice, failed to convince me. My thoughts were playing hopscotch, trying not to land on the lines. I couldn't think a 'Я', I realised, as my mother drew her picture for me. I didn't know how to place it.

My name begins with the first letter of the alphabet and it's a scream, a faltering, a falling, a promise of a B and a C that can't exist in the absence of historical causality. It's a mistake to think that people who go through the same things will come out together on the other side. I know a lot of people whose lives have followed the same path as mine, but their faces are differently hewn; they wear different clothes, play musical instruments, eat pickled herrings at their parents' every Sunday and manage to sleep through the night afterwards; they have jobs, buy flats, holiday in the south and return at the end of the summer to a place they call home. I'm not like that; I feel unable to state anything with certainty, to adopt a point of view, develop a voice of my own, a voice that would speak for me. A clear-cut 'Я'.

For me, time is a turntable. Images blur before my eyes, and over and over I guess how things might have looked, guess the names of streets I've never set foot in, of city stairways and empty boats. I try not to mix up the people whose names repeat themselves down the centuries.

I make up new characters in the same way that I piece together old ones. I imagine my brother's life, imagine him doing all the things I can't do, see him setting off into the world because he has the courage I've always lacked. I miss him.

And what did I do when I thought he was calling me, when I got this sign? I misread all the signals. I hung back, pussy-footed around, did all I could to numb my tension and bury it inside me. I lay down on a sofa, willing it to eat me up. I hardly moved; I waited—for what is waiting if not hope?

TWO

'HOME'

I always get taken along; nobody ever asks me and I wouldn't say no if
they did. Of course I want to go back. Of course I want to go and stay
with Gran and Grandad, and see the boys again, Valera and Petya—
Kirill too. I've got such a lot to tell them. I wrap presents for them—all
stuff that Mum's bought. Much too much, Dad says—'don't want
them to think we're showing off.' Mum says, 'Shut up,' and crams even
more into the bag: plastic robots and cars and a Lego box with a pirate
ship. A few books too, for learning German. 'You never know.'

I try to lift the bag; it's far too heavy, but I don't say a word. I climb
inside, dig out the pirate ship and push it under my bed.

'The blouses are for Angela, Nadya and Kitsa. The cream must go
to Marina, do you hear?' Dad nods obediently without looking up, but
kisses Mum on his way past. His hands are sweating, which means he's
happy.

My sister's standing in the hall, looking at us all through jam jars, as if she had a thousand eyes, turning her head from one shoulder to the other. Mum loads her with even more jars and lays a loaf of bread on top so I can't see her at all—'something proper for you to eat on the journey. You can be in charge of the provisions.' My sister hugs everything tight like a teddy bear and doesn't put any of it in her bag; her knuckles turn white from gripping the jars.

Somehow we make it downstairs and out onto the pavement where we stop and look up. Mum waves a hand out of the window, then slams it shut, and Dad starts to sing a song from the film about the three musketeers. Something about good times.

Thirteen-Krasny-Mayak-Block-Two-Flat-One-Two-O. I know the address by heart—always will. It bubbles up from deep in my belly even when I'm asleep; you can shake me awake in the middle of the night and even before I've remembered my own name, I'll know where I'm to be taken if I get lost. If ever I'm in the Moscow metro and slip free of the grip on my hand to prevent my arm being ripped out of its socket in the crush, I'll know what to say when I find myself all alone in the station, and Marx and Lenin and Stalin look down at me from their columns and ask where I live: *Thirteen-Krasny-Mayak-Block-Two-Flat-One-Two-O*. That's where I go every year. I get taken along.

The first time they take me, I think everything's going to be all right now, forever and ever. Gran feeds me up as if it's her last duty on earth. Grandad already has a walking stick and shuffles around the flat in his oversized slippers, as if he's ice skating. He's got so thin, I'm sure he'd snap in two if he fell over. Dad sits all day at the kitchen table, drinking tea with Gran and Grandad and crying. They all sob loudly.

I give them a quick wave as I pass the kitchen, and head for the front door. It's upholstered. I'd forgotten how thick the dark red padding is;

you can run at it head-first and you won't hurt yourself, no bump, no gash. Everything else seems smaller, flimsier—the cupboards, the rugs on the walls. It occurs to me that I've never gone out through this upholstered door alone before; I wasn't allowed. Now, for whatever reason, I am. Dad's busy talking and crying; Gran and Grandad are listening to him; my sister's curled up with a comic in the corner of the sofa that Mum and Dad used to sleep on, and doesn't want to go anywhere. She's a great big fleecy towelling worm.

I take the lift. The light flickers; it always did and, like now, I was always scared the lift would get stuck. The emergency button has been ripped out—I can't remember ever having seen it—but they tell me it's more dangerous to take the stairs. I get to the bottom and kick open first one door, then another. The benches under the ground-floor windows look like huge toadstools with mouldering caps; nobody's sitting on them; nobody calls after me to be careful. The metal bars of the climbing frame on the playground were once blue—I remember that. I pull myself up in my usual three moves—right foot, pull, left foot, pull, right again—and sit at the top of the latticed cube, looking down over the yard. It looks as big as a football stadium and beyond it, the world comes to an end—you can see where it stops. On the left there are willows, a curtain to the nothingness on the other side. Otherwise there are just the same grey tower-block walls everywhere, dotted with dark eyes. The sky's the same colour as the walls. Through my jeans, at the backs of my knees, I feel the metal bars vibrate.

Valera and Petya are squinting up at me, kicking the climbing frame. I'm so pleased to see them, I almost fall off. 'Hey!' I shout. 'Hey!' I hang upside down and reach out my arms to them. 'Where's Kirill?'

'Kirill's moved away,' they say. 'You've been gone a long time—you're out of touch.'

I scuttle down the climbing frame like a spider. I'd like to hug them, but I know we don't do babyish things like that anymore, so I hold out my hand. They don't take it; they're looking at my shoes. Valera walks around me, clicking his tongue. Petya stands with his face close to mine and stares at me in silence. His lips are all chapped; so are the outer corners of his eyes. He's so pale I feel like taking a handful of snow and rubbing it into his cheeks. I tell them I have presents for them, upstairs in the flat; they can come and get them if they like—or call round later, if they'd rather stay outside for a bit.

Petya twists one side of his face into a grin. Valera comes to a halt behind me and runs his hand over the back of my head, as if he's shaving off my hair. I jump to the side and look at the pair of them; they're so similar that for a moment I can't tell them apart. They don't laugh or even breathe—just stand there shoulder to shoulder in their white puffer jackets, and stare. You'd think they were looking through me, but they're looking *at* me, I can feel it. Valera's the first to say the word: *zhid*.

It's a word I've often heard before, but without knowing it referred to me, and without knowing what it meant: *fucking Jew*. They explain this to me—that it's what I am, and why. We stand there, our arms dangling at our sides. The two of them have grown together into a single barking beast.

They explain to me that I'm a fucking Jew because, like all fucking Jews, I got to leave the country, while they had to stay here and see off Kirill when his father was transferred and see off Dima—he got run over, by the way, by a cretin with slitty eyes like mine. One after the other, they've all moved away—or else they're about to—like me and my filthy clan, and now I've come back to visit with my white Nikes, and can shove my western gifts up my dick, or something like that.

'You're probably a poofter now, and all,' they say. *Pederast.* 'Just have to look at your western jacket,' says Petya. 'What kind of a poofy poofter's jacket is that? What kind of poofy colours are they?'

244

'Is that what you poofters wear?' Valera asks in the same voice. And before I can say anything—I don't even have time to get out *Thirteen-Krasny-Mayak-Block-Two-Flat-One-Two-O*—they push me, both at once, and I fall and go careening into the climbing frame. Something clangs and echoes in my head. When I open my eyes again, the pair of them are gone, as if I'd imagined them. I lie on the ground, and above me the sky is criss-crossed with bars that were once blue.

I get up, a fucking Jew and a poofter, and stroll across the yard, the broken rhombus of the tower blocks looming in on me. I put a hand to the back of my head, but feel nothing, no bump, no gash. I try to remember where I broke my leg, all those years ago, somewhere here, in the middle of the empty plot of land that the boys—the ones I was always too young for—used as a football pitch. The sheds on either side served as goals. I walk across to the shed with the junction boxes; it's the one I remember best, a low, flat building that the neighbours suspected was squatted: 'There are ten, twenty, a hundred of them in there. There's no electricity; it stinks too much for that.'

Mum's friends came round and said: 'Just think, Valya, they're living in there like animals!'

The reason I remember this shed so well is that it was here on the wall that I saw and copied my first swastika. I didn't know what it meant, but I liked the look of the thing. Now, looking at the shed through my poofy western eyes I see: *Only the dead have seen the end of war.* There's chalk lying on the ground, as usual. I pick it up and write: *KHUI*. Prick.

Gran gives me a good brushing down; I'm covered in filthy snow and chalk dust after drawing on my corduroy trousers, then banging them to watch the white powder fly into my nose. Gran looks like a troll under her shock of hair and has almost no teeth left; I can't understand what she's mumbling. Dad and Grandad watch us from the kitchen without getting up—sit and stare like dolls, their steaming teacups so big they have to hold them in both hands. My sister's lying on the sofa, asleep inside a comic, Batman and Robin sticking to her cheek, dribble on her open lips. I lie down beside her, the tip of my nose touching hers. Batman and Robin rustle at my ear; the back of my head is throbbing.

We're taken to see the family we used to go and see before we left the country. Our dad liked drinking chacha with their dad and we kids liked the same games.

When Tato opens the door to us, I almost keel over. He's taller than me—almost a whole head taller—and he has a beard where I don't even have downy stubble. Spots, too—huge pimples like a real man. Since his father's liver exploded at the age of fifty because of all the chacha, an uncle's been taking care of the family. Uncle Giso was brother to the dad with the burst liver and has wife, children and liver of his own to provide for.

'Giso's no help,' says the mother, whose face has fallen in on itself like a sandcastle. She puts tea on the table and a gateau that's drowning in lemon cream. 'Tato's the man of the house now.'

She says it loud enough for Tato to hear and his nostrils flutter.

Sari's even prettier than she used to be. She's shot up too—overtaken me. Her arse is half an apple; it wobbles past my face as if I wasn't there. The other half apple is stuck on her front and has a little gold cross resting on it. I'd like to be that cross.

Sari's starting at the police next year. She's going to be a militiawoman, she says; she's already been to the uniform fitting. The interview wasn't hard at all; they just wanted to know if she could speak fluent Georgian, then got her to sign straight away.

'So you're going to be a traitor,' I say, hoping she'll come closer. She doesn't, and my dad clouts me one on the back of my head which was painful enough as it was. I try not to let it show.

'Tato takes care of us,' says his mother. 'He sells tracksuits on the market—and cigarettes and spirits.'

'Homemade spirits,' says Tato, beaming.

I look at him. It's not possible the boy makes his own chacha.

'Last week he fixed the car for me, and sometimes the fridge gives up on us and he mends that too.' There follows a list of Tato's qualities and his daily good deeds to save the world. Tato's fourteen and his voice has already broken, while I still sing higher than my sister. She's sitting at the table as if she wasn't there, staring through us all, reading comics in her head.

I try to imagine Tato at Prazhskaya metro station, on the market that my sister and I sometimes dashed through with Gran—she'd hold our hands firmly grasped in hers and warn us not to look left or right. I try to imagine him behind a pile of plastic-wrapped clothes, a fag in the corner of his mouth, crying out: 'Tracksuits, tracksuits, fresh Adidas tracksuits! Come on and have a look!' Every now and then, to keep himself warm, he takes a little gulp of homemade chacha from the small metal hipflask he carries inside his sheepskin waistcoat.

My eyes drift back to Sari. I stare at her as openly as I can and try to smile, waiting for her to glance up from her tea. She doesn't. All through the stories of Tato's acts of heroism, she watches the billowing, rainbow-coloured steam above her cup. It looks like soap-suds. She blows over the gilt edge of the cup without even moving her lips. I stare at the dark opening between the pale pillows of her lips and feel myself being sucked in. I'd like to jump right in, feet first.

There was never anything between us. The last time we saw each other, I wasn't even aware of all the things that would one day be possible between us, but at that point she wasn't yet two halves of an apple, connected by a long, silky black stalk. I try to work out whether I'm in with a chance with her and imagine all kinds of stuff—I see my hands vanish inside her, one into her soft mouth, the other between her soft thighs, and I think about where I'd kiss her when my hands met inside her, under that little gold cross.

'Tell us, what's it like over there?' the mother asks, and I'm startled out of the handshake I was giving myself in Sari's body. I look away from her walnut-coloured skin and gawp at the colourful tablecloth as I wait for my father to deliver his spiel. I saw him rehearsing it in the little mirror in our train compartment—he wasn't embarrassed to be caught. As the train swayed from side to side, he tried out different pitched voices—once he even burst out laughing and said: 'Oh, *that* question!' He drew his eyebrows together and pushed them apart again; he didn't get far with his speech, but he had one. Meanwhile, I looked at him in the mirror. Every now and then he'd look back and our eyes would meet, and I understood that he needed someone to tell it all to. When he tried his spiel out on Gran and Grandad, they just burst into tears whatever he said, and then he ended up crying too, because crying is contagious. So that didn't count. But now his moment had come. The question. '*That* question!'

I can see the words bouncing around in his throat like rubber balls, but nothing comes out. He falters at the first syllables, dragging them out haltingly and then falling silent. We all look at him.

Later, when his friends ask him, he'll reply without stuttering. He'll produce a whole pack of jokes and anecdotes—most of them invented—and like a true gambler, he'll let the tension mount with his pokerface smile before saying anything. But this is the first time. 'You want to know what it's like, over in Germania?' he says, and blushes. We blush too. He sputters. We listen.

'They have this word, *Langeweile*,' he says at length, as if he's been speaking for a very long time and has finally reached the punchline. 'We'd say "boredom", but they mean something different.'

The mother nods. We hear the hum of the fridge and move our eyes about the room, tracking the invisible flies that are circling above us. Sari crosses her legs under the table; I feel it and try to think of her thighs again and forget about my father, whose face is getting damper by the second.

'And do you know, the children say to your face, "I'm not doing anything today, I'm taking the day off, I have to relax, I've got this awful headache," or, "I'm so tired"—or they come with this *Langeweile*. They're always bored; they think everything's *really boring*. Fifteen-year-old brats say that to your face. I can't remember us ever being bored. Can you?'

I get up, reach across the table and help myself to another slice of lemon cream gateau, trying to brush Sari's shoulder or at least get a whiff of her hair. She shrinks back and glares at me, sparks flying from the corners of her eyes.

'And another thing,' my father says. 'I've heard that if parents forget themselves and lash out at their children, the kids can take them to court. They can do that over there. That kind of thing happens. Can you imagine? Their own children?' He bites into a slice of gateau, licking the cream from between thumb and finger with his greasy tongue. The mother looks at him and then out of the window. I look out of the window too: everything's white; it's snowing again. Sari puts her cup down and folds her arms. Tato shuffles his feet back and forth on the floor like a small child. His big teeth stick out a long way, even when he isn't smiling. We eat in silence until we can see that the plate under the gateau is black with a gold edge and a pattern of red cherries.

When it's time for us to go, Tato holds the door open for us and offers to walk us to the metro station. My father says no, but takes him to one side and talks to him with his hands on his shoulders, and I try to guess how much he's slipped him.

I say: 'See you!' and give everyone my hand. Sari doesn't even look. Nor do I.

We go out onto the street. It's cold—colder than it ever is anywhere else. The tip of my nose turns to ice and a white film coats my lips, making the skin tighten and crack. I feel my Nikes soaking up slush— the bottoms of my trousers too; the filth works its way up to my knees, and my eyes smart so much I can't close them. I twist my head; it rolls from one side to the other, but I can't see anything because of my big hood. I stare at the lining of my poofy western jacket, then pull off the hood, undo the zip and chuck the jacket into the snow. I see my father, trying to work out why I've let go of his hand. He looks at my jacket lying in the dirty snow.

As he chases me home through the streets, I grow warm; my cheeks are burning. I look back, fixing his puce face on my mind, and I know: from now on, he's always going to be running after me.

ANTON

I didn't have any real plan when I got off the train at Istanbul. I wanted someone in my compartment to say: 'Here's where you get out. Here's where it's going to happen. This is the place. Thus it is written.' But no one said anything like that. My compartment was full of sweaty mountains of flesh, all looking through me or staring at the floor—and when they did fix their eyes on me, I wished I was invisible. Eventually, though, I got off. I heard the word 'Istanbul', picked up my bag, jumped onto the platform and began to walk. I left the station, wandered around Sultanahmet, followed the tramlines alongside the bazaar to a mosque that looked like a mass of interlocking building blocks. A flock of pigeons flew towards me like a huge grey sheet, and I ducked. I crossed a bridge so tightly packed with fishermen that the tips of their rods touched; I went down streets where the shop walls were covered in knives and hoses, bike tyres and wetsuits. I walked through rubber-boot tunnels and the fumes of gloss paint, forcing myself to keep going. I walked down a street without a pavement, my hands in my pockets; the wing-mirror of a car brushed my elbow and the driver yelled something out of the window, but I couldn't work out if he was yelling at me or to himself. I walked and walked, until the streets were so steep I was afraid I'd start to slide backwards. I sat down on the ground, squinting. Better take a bit of a breather, I thought—and I could do with something to drink. I smelt cat piss; the stench made me feel sick. I looked at the ground and everything was a blur. I thought: *I'm sinking*, then a young guy pulled me up, grabbed hold of me and said: 'Come with me.'

Barış gave me water and showed me round. He'd found himself a place with a few other boys in a building on Çıkmazı Sokak. The flat below had been gutted by fire; you had to walk up blackened stairs to get to it, and you got the feeling that underneath, below the soot, was nothingness. The boys who lived with Barış knew how to tap electricity; they lay around on mattresses, and there was always somebody playing tavla and somebody else making a hash of playing the guitar—I ended up having to cut the strings to get him to stop. Apparently the house had been sold and the owner was in Austria—it sounded as if we could stay forever. After a few days, I started to steal things for the flat: pans for the hotplate in the passage and slippers for Barış. He laughed when he saw the slippers, but pulled them on and put his hand on the back of my neck.

Further down the road was a football stadium. We climbed the trees in front of our house and had a bird's-eye view of the matchstick men running around the pitch. Barış was the most obsessed; whenever his team lost, he'd cry and tell me stories about his dad. I'd take him along on my walks through the city and as he talked and cried, I'd watch the mussel sellers kicking empty plastic bottles back and forth, heads down, eyes on the ground.

Barış' dad was someone high-ranking in the Turkish military, and when I heard that, I wasn't too keen to hear any more. Barış had run away from home. He made several attempts to explain why, but our languages didn't always overlap, and anyway, I couldn't hear what he was saying; the city was louder than anywhere I'd ever been. I'd open my eyes and find myself in shops with alarm clocks from the Soviet Union, lipstick from Cuba, records from the forties and open-mouthed rubber sex dolls that stared down at us from the ceiling. Pictures of Che Guevara, Hitler and Lenin started at two hundred lira. The shopkeeper explained to Barış and me that business was good—not because he ever sold much of the junk, but because the tourists knocked over the china goods with their rucksacks as they pushed their way up and down the tightly-packed aisles, and he made them pay up. Barış hummed away next to me and I walked through the city, watching men in battered old suits smoking their cigarettes at the roadside. At dusk, the smoke in the air hardened like amber, and for a moment it felt as if even Barış was quiet.

Everyone spoke of the impending earthquake, but at the same time nobody really seemed to care. You could sometimes feel the tectonic plates rubbing up against one another if you took the ferry. I spent days travelling back and forth between Kadıkoy and Karaköy—Asia, Europe, Asia, Europe, sunrise, sunshine, sunshine, sunset, lights and lights and more lights—days drinking tea and watching people whose faces looked like wax in the glow of the neon and whose hands in their laps were a strange shade of green. The to-ing and fro-ing made me hungry—and shaky on my legs; my knees buckled. The boys at the hot-chestnut stall down by the synagogue soon knew me; they rolled cones of newspaper for me when they saw me coming, and since I'd never stolen from them and they liked me, they gave me the bursting, charred brown nuts for free.

It was food that guided me through Istanbul and got me through the year. Everything was a blur; only the fruit and veg told of the passing of time. There was what there was, and if there wasn't, it wasn't the season. When I arrived in the city, it was watermelon time, and every day I ate half a watermelon in the morning and half in the evening, crumbling white cheese over the flesh and mashing it to a pink pulp—and sometimes Barış would stuff a fish roll in my mouth as we crossed the bridge where the fishing rods touched. Then it was plum time and I boiled the fruit up to make jam. You don't need much—I'd already stolen the pans and you can always find sugar—and it wasn't long before the black mixture was sweet and bitter enough. I spread it on bread and gave some to the boys. Then it was kaki time. The kakis were soft and sweet; they melted between my fingers like honey and left stains on my trousers and T-shirts—washing was tricky without running water—but the fruits tasted as if someone had made jam out of them and then poured it back into their firm skins. I couldn't keep away from them. Then it was leek time and when I was in a good mood, I'd cook them up with a carrot or two and the stew would last Barış and me for a couple of days. Orange time wasn't so good because the oranges tasted of sour rubber; you had to cut the skin open with a knife to get at the flesh. Then came the grapefruits—the ground beneath the market stalls was littered with them; it made no sense not to take them. After that, it began to get cold.

When the first snow fell, it fell metres deep. In the streets of Tarlabaşı, boys knocked the white stuff into statues and carved faces in them with butterfly knives. When I asked if I could join in, they chucked a snowman's head at me and it was hard as stone.

The world turned white, making your eyes smart. The street-walkers' bright umbrellas on Balo Sokak were all you could see on the snowy streets, and the thick hairy flakes that fell on the city left it fuzzy and shapeless. I bumped into buildings, groped my way along the pavements a millimetre at a time, and when I tried to stick my hand in a street seller's cart to warm my fingers on a boiled cob of corn—the man was looking the other way, warbling like a bird—I found myself grasping something synthetic and realised that yılbaşı süsü was the Turkish for 'New Year's Eve decorations'. I hadn't realised until then that the last day of the year had any particular significance; I didn't even know when the year came to an end—why should it make any difference to me when one year ended and the next began? But the boys in Çıkmazı Sokak wanted a party. I teetered up the blackened stairs to our flat and found myself face-to-face with a fir tree. I asked them what was going on and they said they'd stolen it. I said they didn't have to schlep home every piece of rubbish they saw; they said I should shut up moaning and contribute something myself instead. I went back to Balo Sokak and sat down next to Deniz. Her face was long and narrow; her lower jaw veered to one side and she had the highest shoes of them all, platforms with blue-and-white-striped heels.

'What are you doing on New Year's Eve?' I asked. Deniz laughed. A blob of flesh hung down in the big gap between her front teeth. I almost kissed her.

'Aren't you cold, sitting in the snow in that short skirt?' I added, when she didn't reply.

She took my hand and slid it under her bum. Her skirt was like liquid plastic; I could feel her buttocks.

'It's funny,' I said, more to myself than to Deniz. 'You come to a place where fir trees aren't part of the culture, and then you get home and find a fucking scarecrow of a Christmas tree in your room.' I kept talking; I suddenly couldn't stop. I think I mentioned my family too; I think I mentioned burn holes in Turkish carpets. Deniz put her head on my shoulder and I heard her wig rustle at my ear.

I went back to the warbling street seller and bought some of his yılbaşı süsü. I took Deniz a thick gold garland and put it round her neck; for the boys I got confetti and tinsel. On New Year's Eve they danced in a circle, clapping their hands. Barış cried and talked about his mum for a change. I lay on my mattress, biting the back of my hand.

I got through my first Istanbul winter by eating bread and sugar every night before I went to sleep—white doorsteps spread with butter, and so thick with sugar crystals that you couldn't see the bread anymore. And by keeping warm at an electric heater that Barış got hold of somewhere and stood next to our mattresses. Now and then the other boys unplugged it when they wanted to cook—the tapped electricity didn't run to both—and forgot to plug it in again. I'd wake up, drenched in cold sweat, as if I'd jumped into the Bosporus with my clothes on. Then I'd sit with my back to the boarded-up window, nibbling sunflower seeds until the salt numbed my tastebuds.

Sometimes I went out and stood in the doorway and saw Ali wandering around on the street or scuttling past me like a hedgehog in the snow; sometimes I saw her sitting on the blackened stairs, cracking sunflower seeds like me and staring in front of her. Once she looked up at me and said, 'Where are you?' and I didn't know. I looked down at the back of my left hand and saw *Istanbul* scrawled in biro between thumb and forefinger. I held out my hand to her, spreading my fingers so she could read what it said, but she was already gone.

Everything went pear-shaped when my old man went sailing off the balcony in a state of inebriation—I mean, who does a thing like that these days? Of all my Red Army relatives (and that's including the ones with a Shoah or perestroika background), he was the only one to die a death that wasn't natural, only embarrassing.

When he died, they stopped the clock. I'm not talking about some higher powers; I'm talking about my mum and sister. They did it all by themselves; I saw them. Their faces suddenly froze, their lips dried up, their eyelashes were full of gunk. They acted as if Dad's death had left a gap in their lives, which seemed strange to me, because

I hadn't realised the old man had ever filled anything. I'd always felt it had been the other way round—that he used up all the oxygen in a room. But suddenly they were carrying on as if there was something to grieve, and part of their grief involved playing dead themselves. Guilt has its own way of deadening.

None of this happened immediately after the divorce—another reason I didn't understand why they thought we were all to blame for his death. But then Jews don't take painkillers, just in case the pain goes away by itself—there was no point trying to discuss or explain anything, and no escaping the guilt.

After the divorce, it was clear how the roles were going to be divided: Ali would look after Dad and I'd look after Mum. Then, when Dad flew off the balcony at that party and Ali was out of action for weeks—not eating and not talking, and when she did talk, I wished she hadn't bothered—I thought it best if Ali looked after herself and I looked after Mum. So I moved back in with her. It wasn't something I'd been planning; I didn't want to give up my room at Larissa's, but on the other hand, I didn't want to have to explain anything to her either; I could do without that blank, everything-will-be-fine face of hers. So I packed my bag and went to Mum's, and told her I was going to make it my personal duty to bring her black tea with jam in bed every morning and every night. She laughed, but she really didn't look great, with those craters all over her forehead, and mumbling all this stuff to herself—she shouldn't have brought me here, it was all her own fault, look how it had turned out. Then she said: 'Migration kills.' It sounded like a warning on a packet of cigarettes: 'Migration seriously harms you and others around you.' You can say that again. I crammed plenty of biscuits and jam into her mouth and turned up the electric blanket, hoping she'd get to sleep before she had time to do any more thinking.

Sometimes she talked about this young goy Dad had apparently been in love with. I asked if she meant the one he'd been with at the party—the party he'd left by the window—but she shook her head and said something about a girl with long blond hair Dad had loved before he met Mum—and how she, Mum, should never have intervened, because this goy was the love of Dad's life, and Mum had ruined his life—killed him. She'd never loved him—wasn't capable of love. She was an animal, a monster, and he, my dad, my old man, had always been so good to her—never whored around and always brought money home. I put an arm round her and she burst into tears, but not so that you saw it; in our family, we always cry on the inside—an inner shower that rinses our lungs. If you hold us tight, you might feel us tremble a bit, but maybe not even that.

I realised it was going to take some time for her to recover, so I unpacked my stuff and told Larissa I didn't know when I'd be back, and then there I was in the stranglehold of not just one woman, but two—my mother and her cook. My mother paid the cook to make sure I had everything I needed, while she was soon back at work, leaving in the dark every morning and coming home in the same dark every evening, kissing me on the forehead and settling down next to me on the sofa. Sitting there, holding my hand, she seemed to have everything she needed, and I forgot all about the tea and jam I'd promised. I could have cooked for myself, but why bother when I had someone bringing me kefir pancakes in bed? I sat with the remote-control in one hand and Mum in the other, and she snuggled up to me. Like that, though, I only ever saw her after dark, so I started taking her flowers at work and going out to eat with her in her lunch breaks. On Sundays, we walked round the market hand in hand. She wouldn't let me buy her anything—it would have been her money, anyway, though I told myself it was the thought that counted—but she treated me to something every time: roasted chestnuts or a new notebook, not that I ever used the notebooks much—didn't even come close to filling one of them; I was too busy lying in and reading and talking to the cook. Zofa came up to my waist and when she clattered around the flat with her broom, in her black housecoat, she reminded me of one of the Oprichniks in the book I was holding. Only the dog's head under her arm was missing. She talked without drawing breath—didn't stop even when she left the room where I was stretched out on the sofa, pretending to read Sorokin—just turned up the volume, and the Dolby Surround of her voice rang in my brain: 'Anton, Anton, don't you think it's time you got yourself some decent clothes? Your mum's ashamed to go out with you.'

'I'm not her husband!' I called back through four walls. Zofa laughed as loudly as if she were standing over me, and the imaginary dog's head laughed too.

I went into the bathroom and looked at my clothes. Then I undressed and twisted in front of the mirror. I'd only moved in a few weeks ago and already my belly was bulging over the elastic of my underpants. I saw my old man and tried to imagine him lying in a puddle of blood and piss, somewhere out in the sticks in southern Germany, surrounded by spruce trees, in the yard of the eight-storey building he'd just dropped out of onto his big fat belly—and I decided I had to stop this.

I didn't know what to do, but I knew I had to find Ali to make things right again. If I could just see her face, something would go click and everything would fall into place.

I looked for her in all the bars she hung out in back then; I even went to her boxing club. Her coach gave me a funny look—must have thought I was her for a moment—and when I asked if he knew where my sister was, he said he'd no idea, but when I found her I was to tell her he didn't ever want to see her again. I went to Ali's flat last of all. She was lying on a mattress, staring at the ceiling, digging her shoulderblades into the floorboards.

She turned to look at me and smiled. Her face was all matt, like blotting paper. I sat down cross-legged next to her and we stared at each other for a while; then she stretched out her arms and pulled me down to her, pushing her hand up the sleeves of my jumper and knotting her calves with mine. I lay there, pressed against her flat breast and didn't know if she was crying onto my forehead, or dribbling. We stared at the ceiling. She said something about stars and asked if I remembered the afternoons in Volgograd when Daniil had parked us in the planetarium and gone off God knows where. I remembered how I'd always cried at first because I thought he was going to abandon us, but then fell asleep in exhaustion every time. When I opened my eyes again, Ali would still be sitting there, gawping at the little lights on the dome above us. Back at home in the evenings, she'd annoy me by reciting the constellations: Orion's Belt, Monoceros, Canis Minor, Ursa Major, the whole zoo, she knew them all, and Daniil would stroke her head.

Ali's chin tickled my scalp; she said something about the Charioteer in the sky. I stared at the white ceiling looking for pictures. Daniil's face pushed its way out of the stucco, then I saw the others' faces too. I sniffed Ali's neck, pulled myself level with her and pressed the tip of my nose against hers. Her face blurred and melted.

'Do you remember, when we were little, we always used to wonder how you're supposed to kiss without your noses getting in the way?'

Her pupils were almost as big as her eyeballs—no idea what she was on. I kissed her.

Her lips tasted sour and cold; it was like kissing metal. She didn't move at first, but her eyes grew suddenly clear—purple circles around the black of her pupils. She blinked a few times and held her breath. I kissed her again and felt her fingers digging deeper into my forearms; it hurt. I shook her hands out of my sleeves and pulled my jumper over my head and hers over her head. Her breasts were bandaged as if she'd been boxing. She pressed her head into my belly, grabbed my curls and pulled my face over her belly button like a huge paintbrush. I could smell her. A faint milky smell came from her navel and I thought: *That belly button is mine.*

I pulled off her trousers. Her toenails were flecked with white. I pushed my tongue into the spaces between the toes, and she sat up, suddenly alert, and looked at me. She pushed me away with her foot, knocking me backwards onto the floorboards, sat on top of me and leant over me. I wanted to undo her bandages, but she pinned my wrists to the floor, ran her open lips over my nose, sucked my eyebrows, bit my right earlobe, tugged at it with her teeth, then bit her way down me. She let go of my wrists, sunk her fingernails into my hips and turned me on my belly. I breathed through my mouth into the cracks in the floorboards and she licked the backs of my knees. I felt her hand between my buttocks, her finger inside me, burying deeper and deeper, thrusting fast. I reached for her and pulled her up by her hair; her pelvis pushed her hand deeper inside me, and the cloth of the bandage chafed my shoulders. I wanted to say something, but she pushed my head down with her head, and held my nose, and I needed my mouth to breathe. I was panting and heard her above me, pressing air out through her teeth.

I turned to her, grabbed her thighs and pulled her over me—over my belly, over my shoulders, over my face. Gripping her tight, I ran the tip of my nose along her labia and pushed my tongue inside her. She threw back her head and tensed her thighs. I scratched her shoulders. She leaned backwards and felt for my cock, then rolled over on top of me and took it in her mouth. Her lips were still cold. I pushed a hand between her legs until she arched her neck and began to scream. She screamed and screamed and fell on my belly and thighs, banging her chin on the floor. It was as if she'd stopped breathing.

We lay on the floorboards—they were cold now—and she carved

constellations into my shoulders with her fingernail. She was still wearing the bandages; I was naked and felt with my foot for a sheet to cover us, then sat up and stared into the empty room that suddenly seemed to have no walls, no ceiling, no mattress, no window—nothing I could grasp hold of or open or shut. I turned to Ali and wanted to ask something, but didn't know what.

'Got any grass?'

We smoked up the room, two hedgehogs in the fog, snuggling down for the winter, and as I lay there, peering through the haze, I suddenly saw everything clear before me.

I packed my things and decided to go somewhere; I think I wanted to see how far I'd get. I hitchhiked to Maribor, Zagreb, Niš and Skopje, aiming for aimlessness and maybe, eventually, for New Zealand, where I had friends who grew vegetables and had kids, loads of kids—I could babysit for them, I thought; I loved kids, especially babies, and I'd stay there till my hair grew back into my head. I wanted to be in a place where everything was new and strange and I didn't know the language—and where the few friends who spoke my language would be quiet. The money lasted me as far as Istanbul.

Most of the time I survived by hanging out in the bars around Tarlabaşı Bulvarı, nestling up to the boys until all they could think of was my wet mouth at their ears, and then pulling their wallets out of their pockets, or their phones, or both. Incredible how close people will let you get for a bit of hot breath under their earlobes.

In Tarlabaşı, I always got a fair price for the phones; at one point I even had enough to take a room in the Büyük Londra for a bit, just for the hell of it. I wanted to see inside that colonial-era coffin and Barış' crying was getting on my nerves; I'd had enough of his sob stories about his dad. And anyway, I wanted a warm shower, with soap, so I sauntered in at the heavy glass door of the Grand Hotel de Londres and slammed my money down on the counter. The gold curlicues on the wallpaper made me grin. The porter looked at me as if I was taking the piss; I returned the look and we took it from there. The rooms weren't half as pricey as I'd expected—seventy lira a night for spooky corridors and dank ceilings. Seemed fair to me. Amazing what a difference hot water can make to your outlook on life.

After an hour sitting in the shower, splashing about like a toddler, I walked down the marble stairs into the lobby, my hair dripping onto the burgundy-coloured carpet. The sofas and armchairs reminded me of the three-piece suite at my grandparents', similarly misshapen, over-the-top and extremely comfortable. I'd only just sat down when, in the corner by the window, I saw something move in a cage that was as tall as me. I went over to it; a parrot's gnarled claws crawled towards me out of the darkness and I pressed my nose up against the bars of the cage. The bird cocked its beak at me; the cere was crusted over and the beak snapped open to reveal a small, wormlike tongue. I opened my mouth, summoning a sound from my throat in the hope that we might be able to communicate, but the parrot only looked at me, turned away and scrabbled up the flimsy ladder into the high dome of the cage.

I wandered about the lobby. I tried out the row of phones hanging on a brick wall, but there was no signal; they were purely decorative. Opposite them were a few computer tables. A little girl was sitting at one of them, engaged in a noisy, clanging battle with some enemy nation, cursing under her breath. I stopped in front of the jukebox. On the start button it said: Sie hören jetzt...*You are listening to*...I wanted to put on a record; you could choose between songs like 'Green, Green Grass of Home', 'Let's Twist Again', 'Ben Buyum' and 'Drei Matrosen aus Marseille'. I ran my fingers over the buttons, then realised that the porter must have been staring at me for some time, and moved on.

There was a tarantula on display in a glass case and I fancied it was looking at me. In the middle of the room were two motorbikes, one BMW and another I couldn't identify. A huge china pug dog was sitting in front of a mirror in a cowboy hat; something about it reminded me of Dad. There were red plastic flowers growing above it and the mirror took up an entire wall. I stood in front of it in my only white shirt, hands behind my back, and thought: *I've made it.*

In Russian you say: 'I want to feel like a white man.' *Kak belyi chelovek.* My mother used to say: 'What is this? Don't you want to sleep like a white man? Have another pillow,' or: 'What is this? Don't you want to dress like a white man? Here's a clean shirt.' And here I was. I'd escaped. I was far away, in the famous Grand Hotel de Londres, wearing a white shirt.

I spent the days asleep in the stuffy air of the Londra, and the nights on the terrace. I couldn't get enough of the view—the black Bosporus, the golden yellow of the Sultan Ahmed Mosque, the countless gecekondular. The light flowed into the Golden Horn like the juice of a bleeding pomegranate. Feit, the barman, told me he'd heard that the Japanese wanted to buy that sewer of a river, and clean it up, return it to its former glory, but then it would be theirs forever more, a Japanese Golden Horn. They couldn't have that, of course—better to leave the sewer a sewer. 'Don't go swimming in there—you'll be skinned alive.' I nodded. Then he told me the porter was rumoured to be a faggot; the idea seemed to revolt him. As he was telling me all this, I watched a couple of elderly gentlemen peering into their glasses with red eyes. Most of them were German; I'd already begun to feel that the hotel was a kind of Darby and Joan club home for the Berlin-weary. I psyched myself up to approach one of them; at first he thought I was Turkish and grabbed my arse, then he was glad I spoke his language, and put his hand on my breastbone. I leant down to him and talked about the beautiful sea of light in the mountains and about pomegranates and suchlike—then I switched into Russian. When I was sure he was on the point of coming, I put my hand on his belt and let it drift to the wallet in his pocket. Then I noticed Feit watching us. I pulled the wallet out anyway. Later I went to Feit, put the cash on the counter and suggested we go shares. He pocketed the entire wad of money without taking his eyes off me and said: 'Fuck off.'

So I moved out.

I went back to the flat in Çıkmazı Sokak and looked in on the boys. I saw the tinsel still hanging on the unrendered walls, I saw Barış' sunken cheeks, and I decided to find myself a job. If I saved up, I thought, I could rent a place of my own. I started off as a shoe-shiner. You'd think shoe-shiners spend their days sitting on a corner somewhere, on the lookout for dirty leather shoes, but it's not like that at all. You walk the whole city; you choose your customers and you have your fun with them, while they're still peering at the crumpled city maps in their sweaty hands, unsuspecting. The trick goes like this: you walk around with your basket or box or whatever you have for your customers to put their feet on—some professionals have those lovely brass boxes with gilt studs and a special footrest, to make the tourists feel 'like white men'. I wasn't a professional, though, never have been, not in anything; all I had was a wooden box. So you walk past someone, preferably someone in leather shoes, and as you're passing, you drop one of your brushes out of the shoe-shiner's box you're carrying tucked under your arm. Then you keep going, of course, as if you haven't noticed anything. Someone always stops. Someone always feels sorry for the poor shoe-shiner who's going on his way unawares, maybe unable to work anymore, unable to feed his family because of that lost brush. They pick up the brush and even run after you, calling out in all different languages: 'Por favor espere! Attendez, s'il vous plaît! Warten Sie!' And they hand you the brush and you, with your shiny forehead and your shiny eyes, offer to polish their shoes to say thank you. You insist—'Insisto! J'insiste! Ich bestehe drauf!'—no, really you must, for your honour and your father's honour; you must polish their shoes right now, polish them good and thorough—and as you work, you ply them with stories about your poor family in the village and your dying mother. I always wondered why people were prepared to buy these stories about my supposed family—from me, a Russian-Jewish guy from Germany. But at some point I realised that you can sell people any story. People want to hear stories. And then you get them to pay up. Family tragedies are particularly lucrative.

I thought about selling my passport—the only thing of value I possessed. The money wouldn't take me to New Zealand, but it might get me to Greece. What would I do in Greece, though? The same as in Turkey. Then I thought I could travel further east and join the guerrillas—there was war again in that part of the country. Then I thought I should find a rich woman and marry her. She'd take me in and I'd never have to worry about anything ever again. I'd have four hot showers a day and in between showers I'd massage her feet. A man of leisure.

I was toying with fantasies like these when İlay picked me up in a bar in Mis Sokak. There was just one thing he was keen to make clear: he was absolutely not gay. 'No worries,' I said. 'None of us are. Just lonely.'

His flat was in a factory building in Osmanbey. The floor below was full of sewing machines; an entire family—some twenty men and women—worked the pedals. The needles beat in time as I groaned into the sheet. İlay was always very quiet and had to hold my mouth shut because we usually fucked during the day; at night we were in the bars and hardly ever got home before morning. İlay didn't want any trouble; he pressed his hand over my mouth as he pushed into me again and again, and I said through his fingers: 'İlay, they'll think it's the seagulls screaming.'

Everything smelt damp: the building, the stairs, the front door that İlay pushed me against while he was trying to find his keys, İlay's clothes, his skin, the stubble on his chin, the hair around his cock that was already white. I probably smelt damp too, after those autumn and winter months when the cold had us all in its grip, but I couldn't smell it myself and by the time it was summer and we'd thawed again, I'd left İlay.

The evening we met, he ordered endless drinks. Feeling suddenly dizzy, I clutched hold of him and said: 'I need something to eat.' He dragged me into Bambi Café on the corner of İstiklal, and when I bit into my dürüm and saw the eyes he was making at me, I couldn't stop laughing. He looked like a fat tomcat with whiskers. When I woke up next to İlay the following morning, I couldn't work out what kind of a place we were in. It was bitterly cold. Surely the point of a flat was that you woke up in the warmth? Large paintings stood at the windows, the canvases turned to face the backyard; light shimmered in different colours through the layers of paint, and there was a smell of paraffin. The man asleep beside me had a hairy back. He was breathing heavily through his open mouth, making sounds through his nose like a door that needs oiling.

The flat wasn't a flat; it was İlay's studio. There was paint all over the place and carefully cut-out clippings from lifestyle magazines spread in huge piles on a trestle table. Open tubes of glue lay here and there, and messes of toothpaste mixed with oils. I knelt down to look at the collages on the floor and realised I was still very dizzy. I stepped quickly into İlay's slippers and glanced at his bookcase— almost nothing but Thomas Bernhard and Oğuz Atay. *Oh dear,* I thought, and looked around for the toilet, but there wasn't one—only a small broom cupboard with a showerhead over a toilet bowl; the idea seemed to be that you had a shower sitting on the loo. There was cigarette ash in the basin and, in the rusty mirror on the wall above, I saw that the sleeping tomcat had left me with a purplish blue love bite on my neck—I hadn't had one like that since I was fifteen.

I leant my throbbing rakı head against the mirror and listened to myself breathe—thought my lungs were whistling until I realised that the cooing noises were coming from the wall. I put my ear to the damp wall; it felt mouldy and something or someone was moving on the other side—something or someone small. Rats don't coo, I thought, as I pulled the chain. A few days later, İlay explained that there were pigeons nesting in the hollow space between the walls, and after that I worried if I didn't hear the cooing—knocked gingerly on the wall till I did, then cooed back and pulled the chain to say take care.

But that first morning, the flat seemed like fairyland to me. Nothing made any sense. I didn't know what would happen when I went from one room to the next—would the rooms shrink and the ceilings grow lower? Would they suddenly taper off into nothingness or melt into thin air? It wasn't just the rakı.

When I got back from the toilet, İlay had got up and switched on a patio heater, the kind they have outside cafes to warm the smokers, only his was in the middle of the room. I hadn't noticed it in all the chaos. I hurried under the glowing coils and my hair fizzed as if I'd stuck my fingers in an electric socket. It was hard to breathe under there, but I soon warmed up; I could feel it in my cheeks.

İlay appeared with a pot of çay and scrambled eggs with pepperoni and tomatoes in a tiny brass-coloured frying pan, and sat down opposite me in silence. I ate, hoovering the stuff up like a vacuum cleaner—I'd have liked to lick the pan—and İlay watched me, his legs crossed, a cigarette between his thick lips; I could have sworn he had whiskers growing out of the corners of his mouth. When I'd finished, he pushed me up against the bookcase, pulled down my trousers and set about devouring my cock with an almost frightening hunger. Thomas Bernhard looked on.

I spent hours lying on İlay's bed, looking at the houses opposite. Every morning and every day at lunchtime, women leant out of the windows and down over the backs of the houses, as if they were diving. They fussed over chewed-looking bathroom mats that were drying on the washing lines, and beat their rugs and blankets, sending white threads flying like the seeds of an enormous dandelion clock. One of the women threw a tied-up plastic bag onto the roof below every day, which burst as it landed, scattering dry bread onto the tiles. The seagulls came and pecked the roof clean.

Now and then a man climbed out onto the roof and shooed the birds away with a long pole. The gulls circled him, screeching, and he kept peering in at our window. Once I went to the window naked, lit a cigarette and stared back. İlay dragged me away and pushed a canvas in front of the window; his pictures were his curtains—screens to stop prying eyes. I saw an ant run down his ear when he grabbed hold of me. The flat was full of ants; they crawled out of the leaves of the date palms, over the books and into my clothes and hair. Sometimes I thought they might make nests under my skin, crawl around in there, lay their eggs and breed. Every morning I combed them out of my hair; they fell on the little heaps of ash that İlay left in the basin.

İlay was almost always smoking. He smoked in bed and on the toilet. He smoked when he was reading aloud to me and while I was trying to wash myself, and he ashed wherever he happened to be standing. He smoked when he was making me menemen, chopping onions with a fag in the corner of his mouth, and if he cried, it was because the smoke got in his eyes. He smoked when he cut my hair. He even tried to keep smoking when I kissed him.

I liked him; he liked me. When he wasn't reading, he was usually painting—lying on the floor, mixing paints with toothpaste and throwing scraps of paper at canvases. I asked if he wanted to paint me, but he said no. In the mornings he laid his head on my shoulder, stroked my chest and looked into my eyes. One day he asked if I felt like driving along the Aegean coast with him; it was warm up there, he said, much warmer and sunnier than in town, and he was fed up with sitting under his patio heater in Osmanbey, always staring at the same crumbling houses. 'You need a good long view,' he said. 'Anything else does your head in.'

He went to his gallerist to ask for an advance and spent it on a freezer bag full of grass and two tickets to Antalya, where we hired a car. Olympus, the mountain of the gods, was shut, and our car got stuck in the mud; the engine made sounds of distress, and we smoked joints until some hippie tourists came by and pulled us out.

It was already dark when we got to Kaş. We stood at the reception of a hotel that reminded me of my childhood; the woman at the desk looked like the greasy warder in the asylum home—same shirt, same moustache. She looked at us, rolling her eyes from İlay's face to mine, and shook her head. İlay began to argue with her, and I began to understand the Turkish swearwords. I pulled İlay away by his sleeve before the woman could call the police; he cursed and spat on the ground. I heard crows overhead and looked up at the mauve sky. We decided to spend the night in the car and fucked as if it was our last day. In the morning we washed ourselves between the rocks in the bay and İlay read aloud to me while I rolled joints.

In Fethiye he laid me down on the pebbles of Ölüdeniz. That means 'dead sea', but it was the opposite of dead; it charged at me as if it wanted to carry me away. The sun tickled my belly like a small scuttling animal and for a moment it was quiet. Then we heard the whip of rods as the fishermen walked along the shore in their yellow rubber boots. They squinted in our direction, flicking their fishing lines through the air.

In Gümüşlük the streets looked as if they'd been blown clean, and the beer on sale in the bakkal was warm in the fridges. Boarded-up chemists were flanked by flashing cash machines. Signs promising *We sell everything* hung skew-whiff. In Ephesus, İlay pushed me in front of the Temple of Artemis, or what was left of it, and said: 'Sing! Go on, sing something!' At first I only hummed, laughing and pushing little stones back and forth over the ground with my foot—then I began to sing, louder and louder, the only song I knew in Russian: 'Pora, pora poraduemsya na svoyom veku.' It is time, it is time to rejoice in this time.

In Ayvalı we drank freshly squeezed pomegranate juice from paper cups that said *Oktoberfest*, and I tried on a Spider-Man suit and fooled around in the changing room, waving my blue-and-red-clad arms about and trying to climb the walls. İlay laughed and would have bought me the suit if I hadn't dragged him out of the shop.

Later, we pulled over to the side of the road to look at flocks of sheep and have a piss. One of the parking bays was strewn with cuddly toys—donkeys and rabbits in plastic wrappers with bows on the side. I bent down to sniff them; the smell of detergent penetrated the plastic. I picked up a pink donkey and stared into its button eyes, but I wasn't allowed to take it home. 'Who knows what it all means,' İlay said.

In Çanakkale we stood in front of the wooden corpse of the Trojan horse, worn out from all the driving and talking and fucking. I felt wobbly; it was the same dizzy feeling as after the hours on the ferry. I glanced at İlay; he didn't look at me, but his whiskers quivered. He said: 'Anton. Stay. Okay?'

I said nothing. What could I say? I went back to staring at the horse.

We spent most of the rest of the journey back to Istanbul in silence. İlay made one attempt to start a conversation, but I wasn't in the mood and answered in monosyllables, and suddenly he began to shout—I couldn't treat him like this; he did everything for me—and I yelled back, telling him to let me out at the side of the road, right away. I opened the door although the car was still moving and he slammed on the brakes, his head a throbbing muscle.

And then it was summer and İlay told me there were people dancing in the park in Osmanbey. 'Let's go and have a look,' he said and I said, 'Yes, in a second,' and pulled him into bed. By the following morning there was tear gas in the flat, and noise out on the street. I poked my head out: people were banging pans and tin buckets and the roads were full of banners, so we went out and then straight back in again because we were coughing so much.

I knew the smell of tear gas from the home. A few boys and I had once got hold of some and thrown it in the ventilator. The whole building screamed and some granny on the third floor almost jumped out of the window.

I grabbed a scarf, wound it round my face and went back onto the street, followed by İlay. The pungent smell stung my nose. I never found out why people pressed half lemons to their temples or poured milk in their eyes. That was before everyone started running around in facemasks—not that they were any use either. Something exploded like a geyser; thick white air shot into the sky and people ran every which way, wild-eyed, a startled pack of animals. An entire battalion of masked police rolled through the crowd, hitting everything that moved. People screamed; the smell of fear and sweat hung in the air, more bitter than acetone—and when the police charged at us, İlay ran away.

I saw his eyes widen, and then I saw him make a dash for it, arms flailing, and I realised how disgusting I found him—his mouldy flat, the white hair around his cock, the heavy, stoned eyelids he could never properly open. I lay down on the ground and listened to the quake. I wouldn't go home; it was summer; I could sleep in the park.

And afterwards, I'd have to see, but I didn't really care where I slept. I wasn't even sure there'd be an afterwards, and didn't mind if there wasn't.

I saw İlay only once more after that. He asked me to meet him—cried until I said yes—so while the rest of the city was rehearsing revolution, he and I sat in a cafe full of shisha pipes and I told him I'd never forget the way he'd run off and left me in a crowd of people all trampling each other.

'I have asthma! I'd have died in the gas!' he shouted, and I realised how little I cared.

AGLAJA

You couldn't miss Aglaja. In her black hat and black, sharply creased men's suit trousers, which she wore with braces over a crumpled white shirt, she stood out in the crowd of short jeans, tight, garish T-shirts and long, flowing hair—a clown in a black-and-white photograph. Only her hair was red; she looked two-dimensional. When I saw her, I opened my mouth; there was so much I wanted to tell her. But before I could work out what, she'd dropped down dead. I didn't know then that she wasn't actually dead; she certainly looked it. There was blood running out of her ears; her head was tipped backwards; her mouth hung open, and her tongue stuck out, twisted like plasticine.

Later, when demonstrators sprayed Aglaja's portrait all along İstiklal, she was pictured as a black-and-white silhouette with red birds flying out of her temples, but that's not what she looked like here; she'd been hit on the head by a gas cartridge. This made her the symbol of the movement, but that wasn't much use to her in the weeks she spent in a coma. Some of the graffiti images were still around in the streets off Taksim months later; I once passed one with her. She stopped and looked at it for a long time, and I had the feeling she was laughing.

The clouds of gas around us were orange. Aglaja's hat had blown away, and her head, too, was further away than it should have been. I picked her up and set off out of the park, but a girl with a shorn head and eyes that spat fire started to tug at me like a wild thing and curse at me in Ukrainian. I answered in Russian—told her to get out of the way—and soon we were talking Turkish to the staff of a hotel where we laid Aglaja on a sofa, the shaven-headed girl at her head, me at her legs. The lobby was full of tear-stained faces and doctors—or at least people who were doctoring the tear-stained faces. They were pouring a white liquid over their heads; it looked as if they were washing them with milk. If I hadn't known that the people lying on the sofas and on the rugs and in the corridors had been beaten to the ground, I'd have thought they were making a music video. The skinhead was kneeling over Aglaja, talking to her—to her shattered marble face that was almost transparent. I saw the bluish threads trickling out of her ears and thought: *She's so beautiful*. Then I thought: *She's dead*. After that I didn't think anything else, and went back to the park.

I saw Aglaja's name in the papers. Not that I ever read the papers, but I recognised her in a photo when I was boning a fish on the newspaper it had come wrapped in. Her face was covered in gunk. I found the hospital and took her flowers and a tesbih made of a tourmaline-like stone that could change colour. I lied to the nurses—told them I was a relative. They asked if I was her son and I was a second too slow off the mark; the question caught me off guard. The woman in the white hospital uniform shook her head, but jerked it towards Aglaja's door at the same time.

I felt slightly ashamed to be bringing Aglaja a tesbih—didn't want her getting the wrong impression and thinking I was religious or anything. I'd been given it by this rich guy on the Büyük Londra terrace—he was allowed down my boxer shorts in exchange—and I thought it was a beautiful stone and just right for her, though I didn't know at that point if she'd ever wake up and see it. She was in a coma when we got to know each other. I put the flowers in a vase and the tesbih on the sheet next to her warm hand and watched to see if the stone changed colour. Then I pushed the worry beads under her hand and closed her fingers around them, but still nothing happened. I waited a bit, looking into her cracked-up face—her mouth was all swollen, as if an animal had forced its way out of it—and then I left. When I asked later, she knew nothing of a tesbih that changed colour; she'd woken up alone in the room, with nothing in her hands.

The city smelt sour and it was quiet, as though someone had slapped me round the ears. I drifted slowly down empty streets, as if underwater; noises sounded like their own echoes; I could feel them on my skin. I looked down at my feet, but couldn't see them. A man came towards me—impossible to say how old he was. His face was half-covered with a white material that had something scribbled on it. He walked past me very slowly; I saw him bend his arms and legs in slow motion. When he was level with me, he looked at me and I stared at his face mask; it had a letter A on it, circled with a wobbly line.

Then everything was suddenly very loud and fast, like a flock of attacking birds. An old woman's lips flew around me as she tugged at me; a pack of policemen charged down the road; bloody shirts beat their wings; dislocated joints fluttered through the air; green goggles whirred past, filled with tears. The swarm rushed right through me, almost pulling me over, then suddenly a girl with a blond ponytail and a camera in her hand was standing in front of me, asking me to take her photo outside a gutted Starbucks. I took the camera and the girl posed, one hand on her hip, the other thrust into the spider's web of splintered glass. I put the camera in focus, zoomed in on the shattered window and then out again, looked through the lens at the damaged façades around me, at the blackened shop doors and the banners in the windows calling the president names. I twiddled the lens in and out of focus, heard the girl with the ponytail shout something, angled the camera down alleyways—in one, a cat was sitting, staring straight into the lens. I threw the camera on the ground and ran off after the cat.

No idea if it was hunger or anger, but my stomach was spinning like a top. I wasn't thinking straight and couldn't get Ali out of my head—Ali, for God's sake. It's not that I'd never thought of her before—I'd never done anything but think of her—but just then, in those sour-smelling streets, I could really have done with something else in my head. She was suddenly there, in front of me, looking at me; it was like learning pain all over again.

I did something that always helped, and decided to run her out of my system. I ran and ran, all through the city—away from Gezi Park, away from İstiklal, away from the tourists and grannies and demonstrators. I ran down to the water. I thought about taking a ferry, but they weren't sailing. I ran over Galata Bridge and back again, past the fishermen who were still standing there as if nothing had happened; I stumbled over the jumble of fishing rods, took a running jump and leapt onto the railings of the bridge. The men started to shout, just like my mother when I was little; they didn't understand any more than she had and pulled me down. As they tugged at me, I realised that my face was wet. I screamed, pushed the men away and carried on running. I ran until the air in my lungs was coming out of my mouth in red lumps, then I climbed a tree by the football stadium. The pitch was empty and above it was the whole of Fatih with its mosques, scraps of cloud in the sky like dried sage.

I don't know how long I sat there. I saw Ali reach for me the way she did when we were little; I saw her lash out at me the way she did when we thought we weren't little anymore. I saw her run away when I kissed Larissa—saw her tears and wanted to go after her. I saw Ali next to me on the bare boards of her empty room, her breasts bound, her slim hips naked, her legs twisted, her pale, bluish skin melting on the floorboards.

Something flew into my shin—once, and then again. I looked down and there was this kid throwing stones at me. I shouted at him and he laughed and said something in Arabic. I pulled off a twig and threw it at him, but missed and the little prankster laughed again and waved. I was about to climb down and give him a good spanking, when all at once he scrambled up the trunk and came and sat next to me. I could hardly push him off, so we sat there side by side looking down at the empty football pitch, and he began to tell me some story I couldn't understand. Then suddenly the clouds were shot through with grapefruit red and the boy pinched my thigh and pointed at the sky, almost screaming. I suppose he must have said something like 'Look! Look! Look!' And I looked. The tip of the boy's nose was red, and under it was a dry, yellowish crust. I wanted him to lean up against me, but he didn't move and I was afraid to reach out to him; I didn't want to startle him into falling off. I sat huddled there on that branch, hugging my knees, and I thought to myself: I badly need someone to hold me tight.

Aglaja was the second child of a Romanian circus acrobat and a Hungarian clown; from the age of three she performed in circus rings all over the world—she talked of Germany, Switzerland, France, Spain, Portugal, Argentina and sometimes of New York, but most of her memories were of Argentina and Spain, where she'd been a child star and a big attraction; her little body had been plastered on posters at every street corner, in colours that looked as if they'd come faded off the press. The posters showed her sitting naked on a swing with yellow and red ropes, a triangular toupee between her legs; her mother and aunt had thought it best to protect the girl's nakedness with fake hair. The child on the swing was grinning, legs splayed, hands in the air.

Aglaja had been in Spain soon after Franco. She remembered the clubs where she'd performed and the men's heavy breathing. Whenever she felt afraid of them, she simply lowered her head and looked at the floor of the ring, and her hair turned into red seaweed and fell over her face and protected her. She spoke in childish metaphors, and believed in fairytales and ghosts of all kinds. Superstition was part of her body language; she could hardly open her mouth without touching wood or tugging at her earlobe or pretending to spit three times.

All she remembered about Germany was the cold. In Switzerland she once ran off with a boy who promised to teach her to climb rocks, and the pair of them got eight metres up without ropes before anyone discovered them. Aglaja didn't break a single one of her precious bones, but her incensed father did his best to make up for that by beating her into the corner of their caravan. She couldn't remember a thing about France, but she remembered living at the seaside in Portugal and watching her mother practise her stunts over and over. It was at about that time that Aglaja learnt to fear death. She learnt it too early.

Her mother's tour de force was to hang from the roof of the big top by her long hair, and juggle. Why her hair didn't come out by the roots, her scalp peel off her skull, and her face stretch at the jaws like chewing gum, remained her secret. Not even Aglaja knew how she did it, but she combed her mother's hair every morning, and chanted spells over it so it wouldn't rip during the evening performance.

In Porto, her mother had the idea of advertising the show by hovering over the harbour with a big poster in her hands saying 'Circus in Town'. She persuaded a ship's crane driver to suspend her over the water by her hair, showing him her breasts to get what she wanted—Aglaja saw this with her own eyes and her father was standing next to them. The hovering act was a success and gawping passers-by gathered at the pier. Aglaja stood at the harbour's edge, whispering spells to the crane. Her father walked through the crowd distributing flyers.

When the time came for Aglaja's mother to be hoisted back on deck, the crane gave out and she was left dangling helplessly over the water, screaming like mad. She spat out her tongue and her eyes turned red.

They did eventually manage to get her down before her head was ripped from her body in front of the cheering crowd, but from that day on, Aglaja refused to work for the circus. She took the scissors to her long hair, tied it up like a bunch of flowers and gave it to her mother, who put it in a vase.

'My mother did all these things with me in her belly,' she said. 'I walked the tightrope on my head for eight months before I was born. I lay inside my mother doing the splits on the high wire.'

Aglaja sometimes scratched her head till the hair stood on end. Her scalp seemed to smart; she'd rub it and tear at it with her nails, making her hair stick up like prickles. 'In Romania,' she'd say, 'all children are born old.'

That's how she talked—like an old child—and it's the way she looked too. She was older than me—twenty, twenty-five years older—but when we walked around the city together, we looked like brother and sister, and I felt like her big brother. She had stayed the little Aglaja of her memories, the child who was sat in front of an accordion so that she was at least good for something in the circus, if she wasn't prepared to flaunt her little body anymore. She pushed the buttons down with her fingers and toes and liked the sound, especially the breathiness of the bellows when she pulled the instrument out with her hands and feet. She'd soon learnt a few sea shanties and went up and down the rows in the big top, playing and singing. Men pushed money into the slits in her costume; once a man put his fingers in too far and she brought the accordion down on his head. Her parents decided to send her to an aunt in Zurich where, aged thirteen, she learnt to read and write at a boarding school. She was always running away from the boarding school, back to her aunt's, where she'd wait on the doormat until she let her in. Aglaja never saw her mother again.

She did see her father once more, but not until she was in her late twenties. He was touring southern Germany with Circus Roncalli and she recognised him on the posters. She went to the circus grounds before the show, found his caravan and knocked on the door. An old bad clown opened up to her; he was just the way she remembered him. The clown recognised his daughter at once and greeted her with a nursery rhyme:

'Era un rățoi posac, Toată ziua sta pe lac, Și trecând striga așa: Mac! Mac! Mac! Mac! Era singur, singurel, Nici o rață după el, Apa nu învolbura, Mac! Mac! Mac! Mac!'

He said he was glad to see her because he'd been wondering what to do with all his Super 8 films; there was no one else he could entrust with the precious things. When she was little, her father had made trashy horror movies starring all the family; in most of them, he rescued Aglaja and her sister and their mother from monsters played by dolls. Aglaja's role in these films was to scream: 'Help! Help!'

He thrust more than twenty Super 8 films into her hands; then he took his black hat from the hatstand and put it on her head. They hugged goodbye and her father promised to write and let her know if he was ever in the area. It wasn't clear where he was thinking of writing, so they both knew it wasn't really going to happen. But Aglaja was glad; she said the one meeting was enough for her. Just knowing she'd made peace with her father was enough to make her feel human again—though she put it slightly differently; she said: 'It makes me feel humanly again.'

I thought that was a silly way of speaking, but decided I'd better not say so and filled my mouth with cigarette smoke.

She didn't talk much about her mother and sister. Her aunt had been her family; she'd taught Aglaja everything she knew, from reading coffee grounds to dressmaking to managing money. The only thing neither of them liked was cooking; they were both happiest eating porridge with milk and a layer of sugar. When Aglaja was little, she didn't know what this diabetes thing was that had caused her aunt to have both feet off, but she was amused by the silicone prostheses she could feel in her aunt's shoes; sometimes she stole them and stomped around the flat with them. When her aunt died, Aglaja took the shoes, silicone feet and all, and ran away. Since then, she said, she'd been all over the place. And now she was here. She looked out over the rooftops of Bayrampaşa.

We were sitting on a sloping tiled roof, looking out over a ragged sea of coloured houses—yellow and orange and red and violet squares. I didn't often manage to persuade Aglaja to go for a walk in town or sit in a cafe—there was more sun higher up, she said, so why stay down there? She always found a way onto the roofs. Below us, a whole horde of hungry cats was scampering over a street dog. It was lying in the middle of the pavement, eyes and mouth open, tongue hanging out.

'They poison the dogs in this city instead of feeding them,' said Aglaja, stretching to get a better view. I too leant forwards and looked at the dog; it was lying on its side like a person, its paws under its nose.

'In Moscow there's a monument to a street dog. Malchik, the bastard's called. At Mendeleyevskaya metro station.'

'Why?'

'No idea. Maybe so they don't have to worry about the people. Who knows.'

'As if anyone ever worried about *them*,' said Aglaja after a silence. 'Istanbul is a whore, an old whore with long, filthy hair. A whore that gets fucked to pieces, then stitched together, then fucked to pieces again. People can't take any more.'

I looked at Aglaja's feet dangling over the street. Her toenails were painted a colour that some would call 'Chanel red' and others 'Pioneer red', depending. I let my eyes travel up her. She was wearing baggy men's trousers with broad black and grey stripes, and braces over a black shirt. Under the shirt, her arm muscles were tense; her whole body was braced against the air and she was swaying back and forth on her toes over the city, as if she were on a swing. I fought back my fear that she might lose her balance or simply let herself fall—or what if she had another epileptic seizure?—but I said nothing, lit a cigarette and looked down at Malchik, panting on the street below.

The first time I saw Aglaja having a seizure was on a date, soon after we'd got to know each other. I'm not sure that she'd have called it a date, but whatever it was, I was busy trying to work out how I could get round to kissing her at last—and then it started. I didn't understand what was going on at first. She just stared through me—for thirty seconds or so, she just stared, as if someone had stopped the clocks. I almost kissed her—now, I thought, now's the moment. Than I saw that her hands had tensed into claws and a second later her head jerked back, and white foam came out of her mouth—a lot of foam, as if she'd swallowed a cup of detergent. Her eyes were wide open and fixed in a stare. Maybe she's dead, I thought, looks as if she might be—but her body was thrashing from side to side, up and down, and when I put my arms round her, I realised she'd wet herself. I'd heard somewhere that you should put a stick or a piece of wood in their mouths, so they don't bite their tongues off, but I didn't have a stick; we were up on a roof at the time and there weren't even any of those gnawed bones lying around that cats sometimes drag onto roofs. I tried wedging my forearm between her jaws, but the skin at the corners of her mouth tore and I pulled my arm out quickly, afraid I might break her teeth. I held her arms tight and pushed my shin against her thighs, thinking, don't break her ribs, don't break her ribs; her lungs are in there—and at some point, without warning, it was over. She lay there on my knees, breathing peacefully, her eyes closed, her trousers full of pee, her chest flecked with foam.

I thought she might never speak again, after her body had been given such a thorough shake-up—or maybe she wouldn't be able to stand; I geared myself up to carry her somewhere. The muezzin began to sing and when he was done, Aglaja said: 'I have a scar in my brain that won't go away; it's there forever. I can remember your name today, but I can't promise I'll know it tomorrow.' She wasn't even looking at me, nor was she looking at the sky; she was looking further than I could ever have looked. 'I was clever once,' she said. 'Now I'm just stupid.' Then she knocked her red curls with a tight little fist and it made a noise like someone knocking on a door. 'But I have a metal plate in my head that makes a funny sound. Want to feel?'

She grabbed my hand and laid it on her sweaty curls. I didn't move. I didn't want to knock on her head, or even stroke it. I looked down at her and she said she needed sugar—tulumba tatlısı. 'Those things are so sweet! Nothing but sugar syrup and flour and butter and oil. When I first got to Istanbul, I lived off them—didn't eat anything else for weeks.'

She put my hand over her mouth and licked the palm with her huge tongue, like a dog. Then she reached up and ran her fingers through my hair. Beneath my hand, I could feel her smiling. I blinked as many times as I could, trying to take photos of her with my eyes.

'I don't miss the circus, but there's one thing I'd like to have done. I wasn't allowed. My sister was, but I wasn't. My father said it wasn't for

284

me; I should stick to undressing myself on that swing.'

We stayed there, lying on that roof, for a long time. She talked and talked, chattering away into her puke-soaked collar, and I wasn't sure if she was talking to me or to herself—telling herself her own story to reassure herself that she was still alive.

'My sister's taller than me, altogether bigger in all directions, and she used to make herself taller still by walking around in these heels, teetering on tippy toes and waggling her bum. In the shows she'd wear these see-through jumpsuits embroidered with rhinestones and when she stood in the ring with her back to a target, arms outstretched, legs splayed, she gleamed like a jellyfish, a big fat jellyfish. My father threw knives at her. Sometimes there were paint bombs on the wall behind her. When the knives hit the bombs, they burst and red paint spurted all over my sister's costume. The audience screamed, they wanted more—encore! encore!—and some people fainted. I liked it. I stood behind the curtain, looking into their panicked faces as they sat there, open-mouthed and quivering, as if they were all about to come at once. When one of those paint bombs burst, the big top always smelt of sperm. But I was never allowed to have knives thrown at me. My mother said: "What do you want that for? Do you want your father to hit you with a knife?" And I said, "He never hits my sister," and she said: "Yes, but he loves her, doesn't he?"

'My father loved my sister in many different ways. I wanted him to love me too. I thought, why her, why not me? Was I too thin, too stupid? Was my bum too small? I never really found out why I wasn't allowed to do the things my sister did and why my mother put up with all that. I never asked her.'

It was about then, up there on the roof, that I made up my mind to marry her. I bought a chain for her waist in the Balık Pasajı, and when I put it round her, she laughed as if I was tickling her.

'Are you proposing to me?' she asked.

'Why not?'

'Because I'm old enough to be your mother.'

And from then on, I considered us engaged.

I told Aglaja's pretty Ukrainian friend—the one from the club. I was never sure whether there was anything going on between them, but I was never asked to join them. Katarina she was called, or Katyusha. I teased her by singing that military song, 'Vykhodila na bereg Katyusha'—'Katyusha Went Down to the Riverbank'—and she wasn't amused. She danced in the club where Aglaja sometimes played. Aglaja didn't like performing there; she only did it because of the accordion. She liked playing and singing and being listened to; she had other ways of getting money, she said.

Katyusha did this hot-pants number in the club. I only saw it once—fell asleep on the red sofa. We'd been in Gezi Park together— carried Aglaja out between us. I thought I could talk to her, but when I said, 'Aglaja and I are engaged,' I was afraid she'd scratch my eyes out. She completely lost it if I hugged Aglaja; we didn't kiss in public, but an arm around Aglaja was enough to make Katyusha tense her buttocks—I could see it was. She's scared I'm going to run off with Aglaja and take her to Germany, I thought jokingly, and when it dawned on me that that was exactly what I wanted, I caught a plane and flew back alone.

I'd saved money for the first time in my life, because I wanted to buy Aglaja an accordion. That way, I thought, she'd never have to play to panting old men again; she could practise at home every day and would soon be good enough to give her own concerts. We'd go on tour together, and every night after the performances I'd massage her hands and feet. I badly wanted to buy her an instrument of her own and asked around in the shops by Galata Bridge, but the things were expensive and I had too much respect to steal one; it didn't seem right. So I began to save. And as it turned out, I was glad I'd saved that money for an accordion, even if I did end up buying a plane ticket instead.

Aglaja had a lot of men and I could handle that. I'd watch her leaning on the bar, pretending she didn't know that every man in the place was staring at her. Some of them went up to her and put their hands straight on her bare back, and when that happened, she smiled. Her childhood in the circus showed clearly in her body language; everything her sphinx-like face concealed came out in the way she moved. The muscles in her neck relaxed, her head fell forwards a little, her red curls flew into her face, and I knew she'd go off with whoever it was.

On those evenings, I walked around the city, stopping here and there to drink tea. I'd think about writing to my mother or Ali, but never get round to it. I'd sit outside the mosque in Cihangir and try to get rid of the images of Aglaja with other men by drawing her in one of those notebooks my mother had thrust on me. I drew Aglaja the way I imagined her: on top of the men, underneath the men, in front of the men, behind the men.

Suddenly a long beard was hanging over my sketches; I looked up. The guy attached to the beard invited me, in German, to a game of tavla and I joined him at a table. He talked; I scanned his beard for leftovers and stared at his monobrow. 'Like to get involved?' he asked suddenly. I hadn't been listening. He began to tell me about his money-making venture. He worked for this agency, organising women who made clothes for H&M—but not directly for H&M; the factory gets this order from, say, Germany—thirty thousand T-shirts in a certain size and a certain colour, printed with a certain logo—and it accepts the order, although the managers know that such a large quantity isn't feasible in the given time; they call a subsidiary company and pass on part of the order, say twenty thousand T-shirts, to them—and then the subsidiary company in turn outsources forty per cent of their order to another, even smaller company, and so it goes on. Right at the end of the chain are men like him who are all day on the phone, coordinating calls. 'Like to get involved?' he asked again.

'No. Thanks.'

'You work-shy?'

'I'm not here for that kind of thing,' I said.

'Ah, you're one of them.'

'One of what?'

'One of those Germans. If you said in Germany ten years ago, "I live in Istanbul," you got these looks. Germans immediately started to treat you better because they thought you came from the Third World and had nothing to eat, and electricity only at the weekend. Everyone was suddenly nice to you and offered you extra helpings of liver dumplings. Not everyone, of course; some screwed you straight off; they were at least honest. And now you guys come along and cosy up here in our city as if it was the Mecca of the good life. Of course—you're young and good-looking and rich and the city seems made for you. You don't go to the doctor here; you don't know what it's like to grow old in this place. You loll around on sofas, drinking your coffee in the international chains that you know from all over Europe, and you sun yourselves on the terraces with our girls until the end of November. And then you go back and rave about the food here.'

'Wow,' I said, getting up and giving him my hand. 'Great story, thanks, I must write that one down.' And I headed off to Fındıklı for a walk.

It was on one of those nights that I met Mervan. Mervan's German passport had been annulled by his father just before his eighteenth birthday; he'd been told they were flying over for a cousin's wedding—only had a few smart shirts in his suitcase, and then got to Atatürk Airport to discover he no longer had a German passport; he was

Turkish forever now, or, strictly speaking, Armenian—'long story,' he said as he pulled down my trousers. He couldn't go back, had to do military service and then found himself trapped here. He missed Germany; he missed the food and the language and most of all, he missed his little sister. I almost lost it and hit him when he said that. He'd like to write to her, he said—maybe I could take the letter with me and give it to her. He wasn't sure it would get to her if he posted it; he was worried his father might confiscate it. I said I didn't know when I was going back—I didn't even know if I was going at all. But if I did, he could give me the letter—and secretly I thought I'd confiscate it myself, open it and read it, to find out what you write in a letter like that.

I introduced him to Aglaja. They liked each other and spent a few days together. Then Mervan was gone and with him Aglaja's TV and the jewellery out of the socks in her cupboard.

'The jewellery wasn't worth much,' she said, 'but it's a bummer about the television.'

I was seething with anger. I spent an entire week walking the streets looking for him; I came close to praying that I'd run into him.

And that was pretty much how I met Nour, who was waiting for his mother to arrive from Syria. Nour had no hair although he was only in his early twenties, but he had eyes as big as plane leaves to make up for it. He spent his days stealing furniture for the flat he'd found for him and his mum, and I helped him. You wouldn't believe how much you can walk off with from a cafe without anyone saying anything. I even got hold of a samovar for him—a real Russian one, electric.

The flat was shabby; there was no hot water and the floor remained sticky even after Nour had scrubbed it five times—but the only thing that really bothered him was the lack of heating. 'We'll get you electric heaters,' I said, running my hand over his cold bald head.

The flat was on the top floor, under the roof, and the roof was made of tin; you could hear the seagulls walking around up there, like pattering rain. Nour liked the noise, because seagulls' feet overhead meant there was water nearby—you could even see a sliver of it, if you leant far enough out of the window, a tiny sliver of blue.

Nour nearly fell out. He waved me over.

'Can you see the Bosporus Bridge?' he asked me, twining out of the window like a climbing plant.

'Nour, you can't see the bridge from here.'

'Yes, you can, look over there at those flashing lights.'

I often dropped in on Nour, but never asked him back to our place. He got very shy when Aglaja was around—shook hands at arm's length and looked past her with his plane-leaf eyes.

They caught Nour for some petty offence and he fought them, presumably because it reminded him of things that had been done to him before he came to Istanbul. He couldn't cope with being manhandled by the police—went pretty ballistic, by the sound of things, tried to knock or kick something out of someone's hand, though you can never know afterwards what happened, who smashed in whose what. Certainly nobody seemed to know. All anyone could tell us was: he was gone—really gone, not carted off to one of those camps where they usually send people like him. They'd whisked him straight back to Syria.

When he didn't show up for some days, Aglaja and I went round to his flat. I'd guessed something was up when he didn't open his door and I couldn't find him anywhere. I was worried. I don't think I could string two words together without mentioning him, and eventually Aglaja said: 'Then let's go and break his door down.' As it turned out, we didn't have to; the door was open when we arrived, and sitting on the chair under the light bulb was an old woman with folded hands. She looked at us; she had the same enormous eyes as Nour. I glanced at Aglaja, who'd frozen and was staring fixedly in the direction of the woman. She wasn't looking at her; she was looking through her, and I knew: any second now there'll be foam at her mouth.

When Nour's mother and I had sorted Aglaja out and she was lying curled up on the bed, breathing peacefully, we made tea in the Russian samovar and sat down on the floor to drink it. Nour hadn't got round to stealing a second chair, I thought. But there was no need for that second chair now.

Since Nour's deportation I could no longer handle seeing Aglaja with other men. I could no longer handle anything. This wasn't clear to me until the day I saw some guy pinch her arse and found myself pouncing on him and knocking his teeth in. I thought: *I'm going to smash his face into the ground till you can stick it to the windscreen like a transfer image.* I hadn't planned it that way; it just came over me.

Then, some other guys pulled me off him and made a transfer image out of *my* face, and Aglaja jumped up and down hysterically, and at that moment I knew: I want children with this woman; I want to marry her right away and make babies and there's an end to it. I want these affairs to stop; I want things to slow down a bit. The men were dancing a ballet around me, I could hear a rattle in my lungs and I thought: *I want a family of my own; I want this woman to be my family.*

I imagined the whole 'Mum, this is Aglaja, Aglaja, this is Mum' spiel. Pictured the two women sizing one another up, was sure that Mum wouldn't be able to resist Aglaja and that all would be well, just as long as Ali didn't bite my head off. But if I liked Aglaja, maybe Ali would like her too. I couldn't imagine anyone not wanting to suck this woman's toes, I thought, as I spewed blood and half a tooth onto Aglaja's feet.

Aglaja was so angry with me, she said she'd never speak to me again. I loved the way she said that and I laid her on the sofa and tried to put my head between her legs, though it was all swollen and ached like hell. She pushed me away and said she meant it. I said, I meant it too; I wanted her. She asked what that was supposed to mean and I asked when we were going to get married at last.

'I don't want other men to be allowed to fuck you; I want to be your husband and make babies with you and make love to you and go back to Germany with you. Let's get married; we'll move to a little village somewhere in the south and grow our own vegetables and grass and get fat, and have children who'll run around the house naked and jump on our fat bellies in the mornings, and I'll be a good father—at least I think I will—I think I can. I know the whole point about fathers is that they're supposed to be arseholes, but maybe I'm an exception. I think so, I hope so.'

I was expecting her to laugh in my face—to push me away again, so that I'd have to go crawling back to her. I wasn't expecting her to say: 'But Anton, I have no idea who you are.'

So I sat next to her and told her. I told her all I knew—all about me and my family, my grandparents and great-grandparents, Russia and Germany, İlay and a whole lot of others. But mainly I told her about my old man, and that was a mistake. I could feel my head swelling and swelling as if it was going to burst; I had tears in my eyes and bile in my mouth; I was carried away by what I was saying—that had never happened to me before. But something was at stake here—a woman, *my* woman, my *wife*—so I made an effort not to miss anything out.

When I'd finished, she looked at me, completely still except for her little toes on the sofa. Then she said: 'My father had backs growing all over his body.'

I stared at her. Something ripped inside my head; I felt as if my guts were hanging out of my mouth, and drew my eyebrows together, hoping that would keep my head in one piece. Aglaja's face was a blank.

I usually found her expressions—the childish metaphors with which she spoke of her father and her family—sweet and forgivable, but just then, after spreading out all my life before her, I couldn't take it. She went on talking; I couldn't listen properly—only caught snatches of what she was saying: she'd always wanted to go back to her family, but the police hadn't let her; they were sharpening kings who had pencil-sharpening competitions and wrote down her parents' crimes in their notebooks just like me—always noting everything down, as if it itched. Her mother, she said, had promised to pick her up from her aunt's some time, but she'd never come; Aglaja was still waiting for her—still waiting for her to call.

I tried not to move. I wasn't sure what would happen if I did.

I had told her things I'd never previously confessed, even to myself, and it had made my jaw ache. I didn't like doing it—didn't do it because everything suddenly came pouring out of me. No, I did it because I thought I had to, if I wanted her to stay with me—and now she was telling me a story of her own: her father had said that her mother only married him to get to the west, and so she, Aglaja, was determined not to do the same.

She was disgusted by me. She'd got me all wrong, but it was too late. I clutched my head; she was looking at me the way I'd looked at İlay that day in the shisha cafe. And she was right. The stories really were disgusting. You shouldn't tell stories like that; you should tell some other stories—the truth doesn't matter; nothing's true anyway—nothing. How can people even begin to talk about themselves?

She looked at me with her sphinx's eyes and I'd like to have skinned myself alive, but instead I started throwing things. I hurled the new TV I'd bought her at the wall, tore her cushions to shreds, overturned the table. Something broke and I know I shouldn't have hit her, but all this talking-about-myself had done something to me—something bad. I felt as if I was pedalling in too low a gear, as if there was no ground beneath my feet, no windows, no walls—as if everything I might have clung to was gone. The things Aglaja had told me about her family were pounding in my ears—those stupid fucking stories, I hadn't believed a word of them, except that her father had screwed her sister and she still wanted to be his friend.

Staring into her blank face as she lay there on the floor, I had only one thought: *It makes me feel humanly again* must be the most stupid remark in the history of the world.

15 JULY

'What's happened to your voice?'

'What about it?'

'Sounds different.'

'Maybe it is.'

'Have you been crying?'

'My voice is breaking.'

'Very funny.'

'I mean it.'

Ali squeezed the green telephone receiver in his hand; the thick cord was stretched across the room. The plastic shell of the receiver was coming apart along the join; he pushed his fingers between the two halves, felt the blood gather in his trapped fingertips and waited for something to come out of the receiver—a question, the right question. Valya breathed at the other end; there was a soft crackle.

'Mum? Are you well?'

'Yes.'

'What are you up to?'

'Working. I'm not one of those people who get up to things. I work.'

Ali ran the thumb of his free hand over the scars on his palm.

'I love you.'

'Come back some time—that's all I ask. Were you thinking of coming back? Or are you going to stay forever? Is that it? You've emigrated without letting me know?'

Ali scratched his throat, his arms, the back of his neck. The dust in Cemal's flat ate its way into your pores.

'*You* come and see *me*. It's nice here, especially in the evening when the lights come on—we could sit on a roof terrace and look at the lights. There are sweetmeats here that are filled with mozzarella—you'd like them. They make them with chicken too. Just imagine, a piece of chicken, boiled in milk till it's sweet. But we don't have to eat those ones; we'll eat the ones with mozzarella. They fry them in butter and sprinkle them with chopped pistachios.'

Valya said nothing and Ali counted the ivy leaves at Cemal's window. The black branches grew along the frame and Ali was reflected in the green and brown leaves that stirred and quivered, fine as skin.

'It's not safe to fly anymore with all that shooting,' Valya said at last. 'And if they're not shooting each other, they're bombing each other—how's the plane supposed to land? Why do you ask me to come and see you when it isn't safe? Nowhere's safe round there. I don't understand, Alissa. Do you really think I don't care that you live in a country where there are bombs going off all the time and lunatics gunning down hundreds of people at the airport? What's the idea? That I just fly over and we go out for an ice cream?'

Ali saw two round, lashless eyes blink in the ivy. He stood there, watching himself.

'Alissa, you must go to the station and get a train. You'll be with me in less than two days. Safe and sound. You like trains.'

He could feel the bed bugs burrowing away beneath his skin. His calves itched; he rubbed them against each other.

'It'll be lovely. It's a lovely journey. Get yourself some fruit and some of those sweetmeats with mozzarella, only don't leave them in the sun wrapped in tinfoil or they'll go off. And bring one for me; I'd like to try them—just make sure you wrap them up properly.'

'Yes.'

Ali could hear Cemal in the kitchen. He heard his rubber soles drag on the tiles, his heavy tread. He wished he'd come and take the receiver out of his hand; he was afraid he might stand here like this forever otherwise, his throbbing fingers clawing the plastic.

'And just think of all the nice things you'll see out of the window! All those countries rolling past—and the train will sway and the guard will bring you black tea. Make sure you have some change on you; you'll need it. Do you have enough money? Would you like me to send you some? Would you like me to buy your ticket? I can do it from here.'

Cemal didn't come out of the kitchen. Nobody came. Instead, Ali felt a scrabbling chicken crawling up his throat, biting into his vocal cords, sweating grease. His mouth was full of it.

'Don't you want to know why my voice sounds like this, Mum?'

Ali tried to recall his mother's hands, the soft, almost round palms, the far-apart fingers. He imagined those hands clasping his face, stroking it with their thumbs, undeterred by the stubble on his upper lip, the pimples on his throat. He imagined his mother kissing his eyelids, pressing his head against her shoulder and murmuring something about cartoon films and their next holiday together. The image didn't hold; he tried to piece it back together again, but he didn't even get as far as the bit with his upper lip.

'Text me when you get on the train. I'll come and pick you up.'

Ali pressed the cradle down, but didn't move. He heard the leaves rustle as they rubbed against the glass; he heard Cemal shuffle into the room—heard him talk, ask a question, take the receiver out of his hand, try to hug him. Ali fought him off and shook himself. Cemal grabbed him under his arms like a toddler and laid him on the sofa.

'What are you doing tonight? You ought to do something. Why don't you go out?' he said. 'It isn't a good idea to sit around indoors in your state.'

'And in yours?' Ali hissed through his teeth.

'It's like being with a rabid animal since you started taking that stuff.'

'I've always been like that.'

'Yes, it's true.'

Cemal stroked Ali's belly in circling movements, patted his thighs, ran his fingers over the red, inflamed boils on his calves, pressed crosses into the heads with his fingernails and stroked them flat.

Ali sat on the red sofa in the far corner of the club and swore to himself that if they played Nena's 'Neunundneunzig Luftballons' again he'd never move back to Germany. What was the obsession with that song? Didn't people understand the words? Ali had once seen his mother dance to it; she'd crooked her arms and drummed her fists in the air, swinging her enormous bum—that was before she lost weight. He'd never seen anything so embarrassing.

Text me when you get on the train. I'll come and pick you up. Yes, well.

And what did she mean by *come back*? Back into the loving arms of a woman who probably wouldn't recognise him on the platform?

He thought of Valya's question—had he emigrated without noticing?

Kato was beginning to get on his nerves too. Every day it was the same: 'How long are you going to stay here? What are you doing to find your brother? Are you really trying? Maybe I can help you. I'm sure I can help you. Please let me help you. I just want to know how long you're going to stay, so that I know if—'

'If what?' Ali's eyes were smarting; he beat his eyelashes the way a fly beats its wings and stared at the huddled body on his sofa. Kato hardly ever went to the club now—only when he really needed money—and most of the time he didn't go anywhere at all, but holed himself up in Ali's flat and ordered gadgets for the kitchen; it was driving Ali up the wall. Kato must be on the verge of losing his job, but that's probably exactly what he was hoping for. It wasn't clear how he'd earn money after that—but then, so much was unclear.

'I was only wondering.' Kato shrugged and returned to his book. He made it sound as if he'd been wondering what Ali would like for lunch. Recently he'd started wearing Ali's clothes and asking whether he should grow his hair. Ali's T-shirt, once Anton's, hung skew-whiff on Kato's narrow shoulders, and Ali felt like telling him to take it off then and there and get out of the flat.

He looked into Kato's flat-boned face, flushed red over the cheekbones as if he had a temperature. He breathed out and in, out and in, and said: 'Okay, listen, I'm going to toss a coin. Heads, I go back to Germany tomorrow. Tails, I stay here forever. Tamam?'

Kato grabbed the cushion he'd been leaning on, lobbed it at Ali's head, got up from the sofa and stormed to the door. Before leaving, he snatched up the thousand-page book from the top of the chest of drawers and tried to hurl that at Ali, but it was too heavy and landed in the middle of the room; they both stared at it, as if it were leaking. They looked at the floor, then at each other. Ali found himself laughing and Kato went out, slamming the door. Ali stood up, put the book back on the chest of drawers, got into his rubber boots, grabbed the bent five-lira umbrella whose spokes stuck out through the white nylon, and went out.

When it rained in Istanbul, it got into your bones. The wind shredded the umbrella almost instantly and Ali threw it in a bush even before he was out of Aynalı Çeşme. He pulled his jacket collar tighter, closed his eyes and wandered around the houses until he found himself outside Hassan Bey's greengrocer's shop, soaked to the skin, his fingers tinged with blue. He felt the hairs on his upper lip and wondered whether Hassan would spit on the floor again like the time before. He approached the shop door. The awning above him was full of water. Hassan was at the back by the till, polishing fresh plums on his sleeve. They looked at each other and Ali wasn't sure whether he took him for somebody else—a new customer, a tourist who'd arrived over the weekend and taken a flat in the neighbourhood. He found it impossible to say how he looked to others—completely different or pretty much the same as ever? Hassan came towards him, holding out a plum; it was soft and warm. Ali bit into it and the juice spurted onto his chin; he wiped it away with the back of his hand. Hassan smiled. He took Ali's wet jacket and draped it over a stool. Hassan had grey eyes. Asking eyes. He turned them on Ali and they went into the backroom.

Ali sat in the club, deep in the red sofa, trying to shake the memory of Hassan's rough fingers on his hips. Then he threw back his head and looked at himself in the mirrored ceiling.

He had a dragging pain in his stomach and kaleidoscope sparks in his eyes. The music was like a swarm of bed bugs, like missing a layer of skin, like being on LSD. But he wasn't on LSD—just testosterone, once a week.

He still had about eight hundred lira, enough for maybe another two months in Istanbul, waiting to run into Anton—and perhaps that was more promising than hanging missing-person posters in police stations. Cemal, bless him, had continued to ring his policeman friend regularly, and never failed to round off his long talks about life and his tirades against the president by inquiring about Anton. The day his friend had said, 'It looks as if we might have your Russian. Why don't you come round?' he'd almost had a heart attack.

Cemal and Ali had pushed each other out of the door, jumped in a taxi and said with one voice: 'Sarıyer-police-station-please.' Ali almost bit the driver's head off when they drove into a traffic jam, but it wasn't his fault, was it—'Istanbul is Istanbul,' he said, chewing his tongue—and the problem with Istanbul wasn't the high level of poverty, the bomb blasts, the suicide bombings, the attacks; it wasn't that they were pulling down all the old buildings and closing down the newspapers. No, the problem was 'trafik'—anyone could tell you that. They were stuck for an hour, cigarette smoke curling out through the wound-down windows.

When they got to the police station, it was soon clear that the young man wasn't Anton. A Russian, yes, but not Anton. He didn't even have brown curls; he was a sandy St Petersburger with a nasal Petersburg accent and a certain gracefulness, and he sat on the plastic chair with his legs crossed, combing his hair out of his face with long, slender fingers and winking at Ali, while Cemal's friend explained that he'd almost slit a Turkish boy's throat. This other boy had said something about the Russian fighter jet that had been shot down—something along the lines of: we should have shot down more than just the one. Cemal pointed at Ali and said: 'We're looking for her twin. Do you think he looks like her?'

The Petersburger said to Ali in Russian: 'Get me out of here. I'll pay you back.'

And Ali saw Anton. Here at the police station, with all these phones ringing and voices shouting, and this sandy guy undressing him with his eyes, he saw his brother in the corner of the room, doubled up with laughter at Ali's futile hope—his hope of finding Anton, his fear of finding him. Ali watched Anton's image climb out of the window, then got up and went out himself without a word, past the loudly disputing men, past the Petersburger, past all the blue shirts, out of the police station and into the fresh air. Before him was a busy multi-lane road; he crossed it, without looking left or right, and sat down at the crash barrier. Cars hurtled past, honking and trailing black clouds of exhaust, children's eyes glued to the windows. Ali was seething with anger. He was angry at himself—angry that he'd ever convinced himself that Anton might be found. His cigarettes were all gone. He watched the cars recede, his hands in his pockets, and he knew he wasn't yet done with the city. It was still tugging at him, sucking him in; it wouldn't let him go—not yet. Then again, he'd run out of P&S.

Ali was waiting for Kato, worrying his tesbih and watching the clubbers, especially the men. He sized up their broad shoulders and speculated about the length of beards that were barely visible in the reddish light. He studied the way the men held themselves, the way they stood, the way they leant against the bar, and he took note of their habit of letting their arms hang at their sides. More than anything, Ali envied them their height; the testosterone was doing all kinds of things to his body, but he couldn't hope for a growth spurt.

His ability to concentrate had changed; he was sharper and more focused, but had a shorter attention span, and at the same time he often felt weepy or irritable—usually both at once. He was hungrier than usual, too—in fact he was always hungry; the muscles in his shoulders and arms and calves felt like worms that were getting plumper by the day, and his labia were growing longer; they now looked like a rose

302

with a tongue sticking out. He wanted to fuck. He wanted to fuck long and hard. His back was strewn with adolescent pimples—a few more every day. He had his breaking voice more or less under control and was waiting for the hairs on his legs to grow.

His fingers fidgeted with the tesbih; he jiggled first one leg and then the other, threw back his head and looked at his reflection on the ceiling, then returned his attention to the stage, where Kato was dancing a kind of can-can with three girls. Ali wondered what to do with him. As he saw it, there were two possibilities: either he left him or he married him.

That really would make my mother wild, he thought, but it occurred to him, too, that Kato might like a big wedding. What was to stop them? They'd invite all the mishpocha—Emma, Danya, Etya, Shura—gather everyone together and get thrown up in the air on chairs and then apply for German citizenship for Kato. Ali thought of the only wedding he'd ever been to, and of how happy Elyas's cousin had looked with her little chipmunk face framed by a white veil, like a comic-strip bride. He thought how lovely it must be if that kind of thing made you happy—being your own little wedding-cake figurine, having babies, having a house, having a dog, having a job, having a better job, visiting your parents every Sunday—just wanting to stay together in the first place.

Kato's wig fell off his shorn head and he skipped out of line and put it on again with a laugh. Ali felt his skin smarting as if he'd been dabbed all over with methylated spirits.

That evening in the Lâleli club, he sat on the red sofa in the far corner, willing fate to decide whether he should stay in Istanbul or go back to Germany or disappear altogether—perhaps move on somewhere else, anywhere. Why can't it work like that? Why can't there be signs telling us: go that way, get on here, get off there, stay with this person, and for goodness' sake don't hang around here? Even one sign would be something—one small sign telling us we haven't completely screwed up. What the fuck was fate invented for?

Ali decided that if Nena's 'Neunundneunzig Luftballons' came on, the matter was settled. It didn't come on. Aglaja came on. Freesia and bergamot, pineapple, oranges, cedar wood and vanilla filled Ali's nose, almost stifling him.

Aglaja swam through the milky air of the club as if through a lake, surfaced right in front of Ali's face and bared her teeth. He hadn't realised that eye teeth could be so pointy. She looked right through him without seeing him. She was wearing a short dress that clung to her flat body like a scaly red fish skin, and high-heeled shoes that made her look even more like a child than usual because she couldn't walk in them and tottered slightly. Or perhaps she was drunk. Ali stood up. He was exactly as tall—or as short—as she was; the coloured light of the plucked-parrot chandeliers lit up their silhouettes. They were both pale; the Istanbul sun hadn't managed to drive the sallow white from their faces, but Aglaja's skin had a glow to it, Ali thought; it was almost phosphorescent.

Freesia and bergamot, pineapple, oranges, cedar wood and vanilla. What next?

Ali's thoughts were coursing through his body; he was trembling all the way down to his knees. He tried to reach out a hand to Aglaja, but his hand wouldn't obey. Aglaja couldn't see him in the fog-filled bar. He tried to catch her eye, but she just stood there, staring; it looked as if she were suspended in the fog. Was he invisible or was she trying to work out who he was? He saw her red made-up lips, her open mouth, the pointy teeth peeping out, the red curls streaming up from her head, as if she were underwater.

Ali imagined everyone else leaving the room—imagined that there had never been anyone there but the two of them, but the room was full, and what would he say to her anyway?

And Ali remembered: the graffiti, the accordion, the tongue sticking out at the ceiling. She was the reason he'd stayed in the bar—the reason he'd stayed in the city. Aglaja was receding, moving soundlessly, her body more blurred with every step. Ali stretched out his arms to her and took a few steps; his body was obeying him now. Aglaja turned her head; it was nothing but an eye and it was the first thing to burst. Like a bubble. Then her phosphorescent arms burst too, her shoulders, belly, hips—she dissolved like a sherbet tablet. Fizzled and was gone.

Kato knocked both knees against the bottom of the table, spilling his çay. He cursed. Ali, a cigarette in one hand, his arms folded, and the fingers of his other hand digging into his ribs, watched indifferently as the brown liquid ran over the table towards him. He pushed his chair away from the table and looked on as Kato fetched napkins and mopped up; he watched the grey paper soaking up the tea and Kato trying to rub the splashes off his white trousers. Kato looked down at himself helplessly; then he looked at Ali, sat down, and reached for the half-empty glass.

'You can't go,' he said, knocking back what was left of his tea. Black triangles of tea-leaf clung to his lower lip.

'Oh yes, I can. Just watch me.'

'No, you can't.'

'If you give me back my passport, I can.'

From the Molla Aşkı Teras you could look out over almost the whole of the European side of the city. Ali stared at the Bosporus Bridge, twinkling like a string of coloured fairy lights. In the distance he could hear a helicopter, circling the city, and the ground was trembling from the muezzin's call, which sounded closer than usual. 'All for nothing? The whole trip?'

'Looks like it.'

'And us? Was that all for nothing too?'

'Can I have my passport back, please? Or have you already sold it?'

'You don't care about us?'

'Not anymore.'

'You're lying.'

'My passport—'

'You could still find Anton.'

'Now *you're* lying. Nobody ever really believed that—least of all you.'

There was movement in the cafe. Chairs were pushed back; people gathered around the television, talking, their lighters clicking in sync. It was growing louder by the minute. The weekend buzz, Ali thought.

'And what if you've actually been looking for something else all this time?'

'What, like you?'

'If it wasn't for me, you wouldn't know who you are.'

'You think I know who I am? You think *you* know?'

'Don't you know?'

'I'd have to look in my passport, but you won't let me have it.'

Phones rang, just the odd one at first, then a whole orchestra. People picked up, yelled into their handsets, spat on the floor, waved their arms around. A man cried out; Ali glanced at him.

'And the T? The injections?' Kato drew his attention back to the table.

'An experiment.'

'Everything's a game for you.'

'What do you want to hear? That I suddenly know who I am and what it's all about, now that I inject myself with the meaning of life in the form of testosterone?'

'If you leave, I'll kill myself.'

306

Ali lit another cigarette and watched the crowd; it was heaving, like an anthill. Something was going on, but he couldn't work out what.

'I don't believe you. I don't believe you don't care about me anymore.'

Juddering backs and flailing arms blocked the television from view. He couldn't see the screen—didn't know what everyone was so keyed up about.

'I'm going. Keep the passport; I'll get out of here somehow.' Ali stood up and headed for the television.

'God, you're such a cunt,' Kato said, and began to cry.

Ali looked down at his twisted face, surprised by his sharp tone of voice. He sat down again, moved close to Kato and whispered: 'Is there some kind of conspiracy, or is that just a standard phrase you all trot out? Someone once left those exact same words on my answerphone.'

'What are you talking about?'

'I'm already responsible for the suicide of one arsehole who left my answerphone full of messages saying he'd kill himself if I didn't spend the rest of my life holding his hand. I don't need another arsehole threatening me, okay? If you're seriously planning to top yourself, do me a favour and don't call me beforehand, please. That would be nice of you. I don't think I could hack it a second time.'

Kato's eyes were glassy; he wiped his tears away with the back of his hand and stared into space. Ali tried to keep his voice as low as possible; the pressure on his lungs was making him stutter.

'He fucked up my entire life, and before that he fucked up my mother's life and the result was me and my brother, who then got to take the rap for the fact that they'd fucked each other up. But that wasn't enough for him; he was determined to put the blame for his death on me before he did himself in, to make sure I'd never have the chance of a life of any kind. So spare me your suicide threats. What was it you said? You put it so nicely. *Everything that could happen to me already has.* Leave me alone now. I have to go.'

People had begun to leave the cafe in a rush; some of them knocked over plastic chairs on their way out and didn't stop to pick them up. When Ali reached the television, only an old man was left standing there, smoking; he held a tesbih in his hand and was pressing it between finger and thumb, bead by bead. Ali stared at the screen and tried to make sense of things. The presenter was reading a text, her face white as a sheet. Ali's Turkish wasn't good enough to understand the words, but it was good enough to understand that the woman was being forced to read them. Uniformed men stood in the background. Ali glanced at the old man next to him. His lips were moving soundlessly. Then he looked at Ali and said, 'Darbe,' his eyes resting on the stubble above Ali's upper lip.

The silence roared in his ears. A phone started to ring. It was only then that Ali realised there was no one else in the cafe; even Kato was gone. It was another moment before he realised that the phone was his own. He took the call.

'Where are you?' Elyas yelled.

'In Balat,' said Ali. 'Where are you?'

'In Berlin.'

Ali's mind was awhirl. He didn't ask why Elyas was calling from Berlin. He knew he ought to say, 'I'm fine, don't worry,' so he spoke the words mechanically and waited for Elyas to explain why he'd had to say them—what was going on. Elyas asked: 'Are you by yourself?'

And when Ali didn't reply, he said calmly: 'I'll walk you through town.'

People were pouring out of the houses, pushing their way down the streets, avoiding eye contact, muttering, hurrying to get to the shops and greengrocers, jostling and snapping at each other. In a crowd of people outside a baker's shop, a young couple were arguing. The woman was saying it was embarrassing, stocking up in the shops at two in the morning; the man shouted: 'If the old folks are doing it, they'll have their reasons.'

Ali pushed his way through the crowd, getting caught on people's bags. His phone slipped out of his hand and he crawled about among sandals and slippers on his hands and knees, feeling for it under old women's skirts. When he found it, Elyas was still there.

'You mustn't do that. If you drop me like that, I don't know what's going on with you.'

'I don't know either.'

A muezzin set up a wail, then the next began; they interrupted one another, yelling.

'I can't understand what they're singing, but it isn't God is great.'

'I can't hear. It's too early for morning prayers.'

'They sing when they feel like it, anyway. They did away with time long ago. Do you know, there's a muezzin in Tarlabaşı I always imagine as a kind of Elvis. An Elvis lookalike with glittery silver sunglasses. A bit like you on that picture from the photo booth. Do you remember—those photos of us after that party, where you got me out of a fight? I still have mine. Do you still have yours?'

Elyas said nothing. He was probably staring at the news; Ali could hear the hum of the television and Elyas breathing fast.

'Have I ever said thank you to you, by the way? Do you realise that I've known you for longer than anyone else in the world? You're the only person I've known this long. Except Anton. And Valya.' Ali felt a sudden urge to laugh. 'I've just thought of that time you pulled my dad off me—do you remember? His friend had grassed on me—told him he'd seen me carrying on with a girl on the street, and he burst in and went straight for me and you pushed him out of the flat. You've always protected me. You're always there, aren't you? You're always there for me and I don't notice. I don't go with you when you come to pick me up, don't listen to you when you're worried about me, but you always get me out of these situations I land myself in. That's right, isn't it?'

Elyas said nothing. Ali could hear voices coming from the TV in the living room—the room Elyas had offered Ali, the room he'd got ready for Ali, mending the door handle and vacuuming the floor, so that he'd feel happy, instead of lying on the mattress every night, catching dust balls, and then running off and getting lost in a country with no solid ground.

'Where are you now?' Elyas clearly hadn't been listening.

'I'm walking along the promenade in Fatih; there's almost no one here. Something's on fire over on the Asian side.'

'The army's cordoned off the bridges, but it doesn't matter; you can take one of the little ones over the Golden Horn and then go up the side streets to Cihangir. You must get to Cemal's. Do you know the way?'

A helicopter was circling the water. The rotor blades felt like an axe in Ali's head and the connection kept cutting out; he caught only snatches. *Cihangir*, he heard, and *Cemal's*. Howls echoed through the streets like the cry of a pack of dogs.

'I'm scared,' Ali said into his dead phone. Elyas was gone; there was nothing at the other end of the line. Now he could say what he liked.

'If I survive this, I'll go and see Mum; I want to talk to her. She knows nothing about me—and I know nothing about her. And I'll go and see Emma and Danya and Shura and Etya—everyone who's still alive. I have such a lot to ask them. They're more or less strangers to me.'

Elyas's voice cut in; he'd been talking all the time, translating the news for Ali: 'Turkish armed forces have. The whole government. Of the state to. The constitutional. Order. Human rights and liberty. The state which. And public security. That have been damaged.'

Elyas translated slowly, dragging out the words, his voice distorted. The static between the choppy phrases was getting louder and louder, insinuating itself into Ali's ear.

'What does it all mean?' Ali yelled. 'What's going on?'

Then his brain signalled: 'Run!' He didn't know whether Elyas had said the word or whether he'd only imagined it.

The static grew even louder; it sounded as if someone were scrunching up tinfoil in Ali's ear. Elyas really was gone now.

The muddy green water of the Golden Horn seemed to be electrically charged; the boats were sparkling. He looked up at the metro bridge and saw people walking along the tracks. He kept out of their way; he didn't know what the red T-shirts with the three white crescent moons signified—danger or rescue. He suddenly knew nothing. But the outlines of things were growing clearer and sharper, cutting into his skin—he could feel the city closing in like a tunnel. He took the underpass to the little park and came to Galata Bridge. The fishermen had got into a kind of scrum and were holding someone trapped in their midst. A knife flashed—or at least Ali thought that's what he saw, but perhaps it was only the fishing lines. He ran past, without stopping to look.

The double doors of the hotel stood open; people were clustered around the television in the foyer. Ali ran down İstiklal, through a group of girls in shorts and red T-shirts; the polyester cloth of their flags hit Ali in the face. He passed cash machines, crowded as flypaper. Banknotes were flying through the air; the muezzins set up another wail.

A soldier with a rifle charged out of a side street into Ali, almost knocking his arm off; he was followed by two, four, seven men, armed with nothing but their hands. Ali stopped and watched them push the soldier up against the wall of a restaurant and set on him; he couldn't have been older than eighteen—maybe only sixteen; he looked twelve. Then more people appeared, more and more, from all sides. Ali heard dogs barking. He had the feeling he was bleeding all over his body, but when he looked down at himself he seemed to be in one piece—just covered in dust, with a sore arm. *Cihangir*, he thought, and carried on running.

In the narrow doorway between Cemal's and the empty butcher's shop, an old woman was standing, staring fixedly in front of her. Ali hurried past her, then stopped to catch his breath, and when he went back and looked into the woman's face, he recognised the fortune teller who'd told him the African tale about truth. He looked around for the rabbit in the cage, but it wasn't there. The woman reached out a hand to Ali, but he turned and ran up the stairs as fast as he could.

Cemal opened the door and smiled. He let Ali in, moving so gently that Ali almost asked him did he knew what was going on out there and why was he so calm, but the television was on, beaming images of charging crowds and keyed-up, pale faces speaking silently into microphones. Uncle Cemal seemed unperturbed. On a stool in the corner, Mustafa Bey was sitting in a crumpled suit, his head in his hands. He looked up when Ali came in and his eyes were red from crying. Ali said nothing. He looked uncomprehendingly at Mustafa with his chewed-up lips, and then into Cemal's soft, still face. He sat down at the table and Cemal brought him a glass of rakı without a word. It was warm and smelt of aniseed. Cemal handed Mustafa a glass too. Mustafa gave a loud sob, took the rakı and went back to staring at the floor. He put the glass down without drinking from it and buried his face in his hands. Ali sipped his own rakı and glanced across at him. The helicopter blades were still beating against the inside of his forehead, but although he could hear them, he could no longer feel them as intensely. Something popped in his ears.

'Why's he crying?'

Cemal breathed out loudly through his nose; his eyes narrowed; and for the first time since Ali had stormed into his flat, he pulled a face, bunching up his features so that his eyebrows pressed down on his eyelids, his lashes melted to black bars and his lower lip pushed up his upper lip. He looked at Mustafa, huddled on the stool with his head in his hands, and then at Ali.

'The actual coup's been underway for a long time,' he said, going to the television and turning on the sound.

Ali pulled her stool up to Cemal's. Tanks were rolling over Atatürk airfield. He didn't hear the news, though it was no longer on mute; he heard Cemal breathing through his open mouth. He thought he heard a clock ticking, but there was no clock in the room. He kept thinking something was walking over his feet. He squinted across at Cemal, at his curvaceous silhouette and the ash dropping from his cigarette to the floor. In the light from the television, the wrinkles in Cemal's face looked like cracks.

Ali stared at him for a long time, feeling the urge to tell him everything he'd seen on the way to his flat—the crushed face of the twelve-year-old soldier, the flying banknotes, the flags. He wanted to ask Cemal the meaning of the three crescent moons and the queues outside the shops. Then he wondered whether he'd have to go back now—but he no longer had a passport. That was another thing he wanted to tell Cemal—that his passport had been stolen, that Kato— and he suddenly realised that his passport was no more use to him anyway. They'd had enough trouble recognising him when he arrived in the country; now it would be impossible, even if he got shaved. His face was changed. Ali wondered if Cemal would go with him if he left, but as soon as the question had formed in his mind, he knew the answer. Cemal would never be persuaded to leave; he didn't even go out of the flat if he could help it. He had family waiting for him in Germany, hoping he'd join them—forever, not just for a few weeks.

But when it came to the question of leaving your country, Cemal was uncharacteristically calm: once you have a country, he'd explain, you can't leave it; you drag it along with you wherever you go—so what was the point?

That made no sense to me at the time; I had no idea what it meant to 'have' a country. I had no idea what it meant to live through a coup either. Cemal did; this was his third. I sat there next to this uncle of mine who wasn't strictly speaking mine, my arms dangling at my sides, my head empty—no idea where I'd come from or where I was going. Nothing made any sense to me. Tanks were driving back and forth inside my head, then Leshchenko began to sing that song about tanks driving down to the riverbank—'Katyusha went down to the river-bank'—and I wondered where Kato was and whether he was all right.

I saw his face under the black wig and his gold-clad hipbones as he put his foot on my knee and swung himself up to the go-go pole. I saw him walk across the bar to me, as if he knew me. I saw him smoking on the pier with his head in my lap as we looked out over the Golden Horn at the boats full of people on their way to the bazaar to drink coffee at Mehmet Efendi's. Then time went hurtling past me and I saw Kato standing in the bazaar, outside the coffee shop, watching the boys twisting paper bags with their fingers, too fast for the eye to see. I saw him between the stalls, months after all this—after us, after the unrest, later in the year when the days were cooler, maybe in October—saw him strolling around Kitap Bazaar, crouching to look at the old books with their thin covers—books he found beautiful, though he couldn't read them. He'd trip over the tourists as they sat on the street, slurping their fruit juice, but he wouldn't care. He'd ask to look at tavla boards in a little booth in the bazaar so that Uncle Cemal could teach him how to play, and he'd choose the one that smelt least of nail-polish remover, imagining Cemal's happy face when he unwrapped it. He'd buy something sweet for Cemal, too, queue up at the kuruyemiş stall and ask for a hundred grams of sticky brown apricots—and it would be then, just as the fruit was being filled into a paper bag, that he'd see him: the man with a bird tattooed on his right forearm, a greenfinch with its wings stretched back. He'd be in front of him in the queue, carrying something suitcase-like in his left hand—small, almost square, and covered in a white cotton fabric. Kato would clutch the bag of apricots and catch his breath.

The man would pay and quickly make his way along the rows of stalls to the water, and Kato would hurry along behind him, afraid of losing him, hiding behind cars whenever the man stopped. He'd follow him down the streets full of chandeliers and lamps and light bulbs, tyres and tools and fishing gear—streets where the air smelt of burnt rubber or lentil soup with red pepper—down past the ferries, rocking on the water, to an improvised tea garden—a small shack of four walls and a tin roof with a few chairs in front.

The tattooed man would shake the hand of each customer in turn. He'd order çay and go over to the wall of the little tea shack to hang up his covered cage.

Kato would order too, put the bag of apricots on the table, jiggle his feet, toss the black tea down his gullet as if it were vodka, and stare at the water, pretending he wasn't there.

And then, a little while afterwards, it would begin.

At first it would sound like a baby crying, then the cries would give way to a shrill staccato that would stop abruptly and start up again. The bird's voice beneath the cloth would be deep and full. It would sound like a question—a question that would make Kato feel his head might burst.

He'd approach the cage to have a look, and the owner would jump to his feet and ask in a whisper what he wanted.

'Just a look,' Kato would say. 'Just this once.'

The man would look at Kato, sigh and dig his thumbs into the cover, revealing another layer of cloth, and behind that yet another. He would pull the cloth open with his fingers, as if it were something indecent, and in the slit behind, Kato would see the bars of the cage.

That's how I imagined it—or something like that—as I sat on the stool beside Cemal, waiting for I didn't know what and, not for the first time, confused about what was going on. I was scared to move, scared that Cemal would say something, scared that he'd tell me I had to go. I sat there, staring at the wall above the television, imagining Kato's life and how it would continue without me, just as I had pieced together Anton's life—just as I had put together all the lives I didn't know, all the lives I was entangled in, lives that went on without me.

It was dark in the room; in the light from the TV I could see Cemal's silhouette and the ash on the floor. Random images flickered across the screen. I felt dizzy. I felt like going to the sofa and lying down, but couldn't get up. The room was spinning—Cemal, the blue tiles, the ivy at the window, the man crying in the corner, the bottle of rakı on the table, the open newspapers, the glimmer of the television. Everything was a blur—then the light went out.

Night didn't change to day; I missed the dawn. I woke up and saw Cemal sitting beside me on the sofa, his forearms resting on his knees, his hands folded, the thick black hair on his fingers almost touching the tip of my nose. His face was hanging over mine and I remember recalling that soon after I'd arrived, when I'd been lying on that same sofa, being consumed by bed bugs, Cemal had said something about a disaster that was about to hit Turkey, and I hadn't listened. I'd let him distract me with stories of Yılmaz Güney and the woman he loved.

I thought about the word that Cemal had used back then: *disaster*. It was a word I'd heard the old people use a lot, but for me it was an empty shell, little more than a sound.

I stretched out my arms to Cemal, wrapped them round his neck and hung there. I felt numb. I pressed my forehead against his shoulder. My eyes were covered in a film of dust and I blinked to flush it away. I heard a clock ticking, helicopter blades, Cemal's pulse in his throat. I smiled and for a moment I thought I'd never go anywhere else again.

'Anton, I've put çay on to boil,' said Cemal. 'Let go of me and I'll bring us some.' And he got up and went into the kitchen.

ACKNOWLEDGMENTS

This book exists thanks to:

Karin Doris Nadja Were Tucké Necati Emre Kiri Emma
Danya Shura Etya Sivan Michou Orhan Maria Ebru
Veteranyi Díaz Bachmann Bolaño Baldwin Cortázar
Louis Brodsky Preciado Eugenides and Istanbul

Thanks too to Ludwig Metzger for his documentary film *Hier
Himmel*, which allowed me to hear the voice of Aglaja Veteranyi.